THE
JENSEN BRAND
TOO SOON
TO DIE

P9-CDY-534

*Look for these exciting Western series from
bestselling authors*
WILLIAM W. JOHNSTONE
and ## J. A. JOHNSTONE

The Mountain Man

Preacher: The First Mountain Man

Luke Jensen, Bounty Hunter

Those Jensen Boys!

The Jensen Brand

Matt Jensen

MacCallister

The Red Ryan Westerns

Perley Gates

Have Brides, Will Travel

The Hank Fallon Westerns

Will Tanner, Deputy U.S. Marshal

Shotgun Johnny

The Chuckwagon Trail

The Jackals

The Slash and Pecos Westerns

The Texas Moonshiners

AVAILABLE FROM PINNACLE BOOKS

THE JENSEN BRAND
TOO SOON TO DIE

WILLIAM W. JOHNSTONE
and J.A. JOHNSTONE

PINNACLE BOOKS
Kensington Publishing Corp.
www.kensingtonbooks.com

PINNACLE BOOKS are published by

Kensington Publishing Corp.
119 West 40th Street
New York, NY 10018

Copyright © 2019 J. A. Johnstone

All rights reserved. No part of this book may be reproduced in any form
or by any means without the prior written consent of the publisher, except-
ing brief quotes used in reviews.

To the extent that the image or images on the cover of this book depict a
person or persons, such person or persons are merely models, and are not
intended to portray any character or characters featured in the book.

PUBLISHER'S NOTE
Following the death of William W. Johnstone, the Johnstone family is
working with a carefully selected writer to organize and complete Mr.
Johnstone's outlines and many unfinished manuscripts to create additional
novels in all of his series like The Last Gunfighter, Mountain Man, and
Eagles, among others. This novel was inspired by Mr. Johnstone's superb
storytelling.

If you purchased this book without a cover, you should be aware that this
book is stolen property. It was reported as "unsold and destroyed" to the
publisher, and neither the author nor the publisher has received any pay-
ment for this "stripped book."

All Kensington titles, imprints, and distributed lines are available at special
quantity discounts for bulk purchases for sales promotions, premiums,
fund-raising, educational, or institutional use. Special book excerpts or
customized printings can also be created to fit specific needs. For details,
write or phone the office of the Kensington sales manager: Kensington
Publishing Corp., 119 West 40th Street, New York, NY 10018, attn: Sales
Department; phone 1-800-221-2647.

PINNACLE BOOKS, the Pinnacle logo, and the WWJ steer head logo are
Reg. U.S. Pat. & TM Off.

ISBN-13: 978-0-7860-4400-9
ISBN-10: 0-7860-4400-4

First printing: September 2019

10 9 8 7 6 5 4 3 2 1

Printed in the United States of America

Electronic edition:

ISBN-13: 978-0-7860-4401-6
ISBN-10: 0-7860-4401-2

THE JENSEN FAMILY
FIRST FAMILY OF THE AMERICAN FRONTIER

Smoke Jensen—*The Mountain Man*
The youngest of three children and orphaned as a young boy, Smoke Jensen is considered one of the fastest draws in the West. His quest to tame the lawless West has become the stuff of legend. Smoke owns the Sugarloaf Ranch in Colorado. Married to Sally Jensen, father to Denise ("Denny") and Louis.

Preacher—*The First Mountain Man*
Though not a blood relative, grizzled frontiersman Preacher became a father figure to the young Smoke Jensen, teaching him how to survive in the brutal, often deadly Rocky Mountains. Fought the battles that forged his destiny. Armed with a long gun, Preacher is as fierce as the land itself.

Matt Jensen—*The Last Mountain Man*
Orphaned but taken in by Smoke Jensen, Matt Jensen has become like a younger brother to Smoke and even took the Jensen name. And like Smoke, Matt has carved out his destiny on the American frontier. He lives by the gun and surrenders to no man.

Luke Jensen—*Bounty Hunter*
Mountain Man Smoke Jensen's long-lost brother
Luke Jensen is scarred by war and a dead shot—the
right qualities to be a bounty hunter. And he's cun-
ning, and fierce enough, to bring down the deadliest
outlaws of his day.

Ace Jensen and Chance Jensen—*Those Jensen Boys!*
Smoke Jensen's long-lost nephews, Ace and Chance,
are a pair of young-gun twins as reckless and wild as
the frontier itself . . . Their father is Luke Jensen,
thought killed in the Civil War. Their uncle Smoke
Jensen is one of the fiercest gunfighters the West has
ever known. It's no surprise that the inseparable Ace
and Chance Jensen have a knack for taking risks—
even if they have to blast their way out of them.

CHAPTER I

Sugarloaf Ranch, Colorado, 1902

The door slammed so hard it shivered in its frame. The echoes of its violent closing mingled with the sound of a loud, disgusted, very unladylike snort coming from the hallway just outside Smoke Jensen's study and office, followed by angry footsteps stomping away.

"Well"—Sally Jensen looked at her husband from the depths of a comfortable armchair across the room—"aren't you going to go after her?"

Smoke leaned back in his chair behind the desk and looked at his wife, still slim and beautiful more than a quarter of a century after he had first laid eyes on her. The faint lines around her eyes and mouth, the streaks of silver here and there in her thick dark hair, were invisible to him.

"And do what?" he asked. "Denny's a grown woman. I can't exactly put her over my knee and paddle her."

"I don't recall you ever doing that even when she was a child. But you could give her a stern talking-to."

Smoke cocked his head a little to the side and

frowned. "You know our daughter as well as I do. Do you really think that would do any good?"

"So you're just going to let her be headstrong and stubborn?"

"At this point, I don't reckon we have a whole heap of choice in the matter." Smoke shrugged. "But that *doesn't* mean she's going to ride in that race."

"How are you going to stop her?" Sally wanted to know.

"The Sugarloaf is still our ranch. I reckon we've got some say in what happens around here."

"I'd like to think so."

Smoke stood up. Like Sally, he looked a good ten or fifteen years younger than he really was, a powerful, broad-shouldered man apparently in the prime of life. In his study in his own house, he wasn't wearing a gun, but a walnut-butted Colt lay on the desk within easy reach and on a rack behind him rested several fully loaded Winchesters and shotguns. He was the fastest, deadliest man with a gun in the history of the West, and having shooting irons all around him was as natural as breathing, although these days he considered himself just a middle-aged, peace-loving rancher.

Sally stood up, too, and moved to put a hand on his arm. "I'm too protective of her, aren't I? She's proven more than once that she's her father's daughter."

"She's tough and capable when she needs to be," Smoke agreed. A wistful smile touched his face. "But she's still my little girl, too."

"She and Louis spent so much time away from here while they were growing up, it seems like we missed their childhood."

Smoke rested his hands on his wife's shoulders,

then drew her into an embrace. "We did what we had to because of Louis's health problems and to give him the best chance for a normal life. Look at him now, studying law, marrying a fine young woman, and getting a son of his own in the bargain. I'd say things turned out all right."

"But you're an optimist, Smoke. You always think things turn out all right . . . and if they don't, you *make* them turn out all right, at the point of a gun, if need be."

"Well, I always said that a gun's just a tool, so you'd better use it the right way." His voice hardened slightly as he added, "I've known plenty who tried to use one the wrong way, and we might run into hombres like that again."

"Oh," Sally said, "I don't think there's any doubt of that."

CHAPTER 2

Denise Nicole Jensen was headed for the corral behind the biggest of the Sugarloaf's barns when she realized she still was stomping her booted feet against the ground like a little kid throwing a tantrum. She halted for a moment and drew in a deep breath, willing herself to calm down. She wasn't sure why she was so upset. She had expected her mother to react in exactly the way she had.

It wasn't like being forbidden to do something had ever stopped Denny in the past.

Moving at a more deliberate pace, she approached the corral. In her early twenties, Denny was a very attractive young woman with curly blond hair she wore loose at the moment under her brown Stetson perched atop her head and tilted back slightly. She knew her mother thought she didn't like to wear dresses, but that wasn't strictly true. She just preferred to dress appropriately for whatever the situation in which she found herself. On the ranch, that meant jeans and boots, and currently, a man's red-checked shirt with the sleeves rolled up over her tanned forearms.

Three people stood outside the corral, leaning on

the fence watching as one of the Sugarloaf hands worked with a horse inside the enclosure. One of the spectators was Calvin Woods, the ranch's foreman who had gone to work for Smoke as a young man— little more than a boy, really—many years earlier. He had grown to be a top hand and a more than capable ramrod for the ranch's large crew.

Next to Cal stood Denny's twin brother, Louis Arthur Jensen. The resemblance between him and Denny was strong, although Louis's hair was a sandy shade of brown, darker than Denny's blond curls. He took more after his mother Sally and lacked the rugged features of many of the Jensen males, although his jaw had a hint of toughness and his eyes were keen, penetrating, and intelligent.

Plagued by ill health growing up—a bad heart and an assortment of other ailments—Louis had spent much of his childhood living with relatives in England while seeking medical treatments from a variety of doctors there and on the continent. Denny had lived with him on the country estate, and it was there she had learned to ride.

In the past year, since the two of them had returned to live on the Sugarloaf, Louis's health seemed to have benefitted from the sun and the fresh air and the generally more active life he led, although he still had to be careful not to overexert himself. A specialist in San Francisco had warned that his heart could still give more trouble any time. Louis tried not to let that hold him back too much. His stubborn streak might not be as wide as his sister's, but he was still a Jensen, after all.

Next to Louis stood a dark-haired, nine-year-old

boy. Wearing range clothes and a cowboy hat, Bradley Buckner leaned forward and grasped one of the corral rails as he watched what was going on. Inside the corral, the ranch hand had just finished saddling a young horse. The animal was dark brown, with white stockings on the left foreleg and right hind leg and a white blaze on its face.

"When can I ride him?" asked young Brad with excitement in his voice.

Cal chuckled. "Don't get in a big hurry. We don't know how he's going to take to this whole process. He's still pretty green, you know. But there's nobody better than Rafael at getting a horse ready to ride."

The ranch hand, Rafael De Santos, was a middle-aged Mexican in ranch clothes. A small, pointed beard adorned his chin and gave his leathery face a mark of distinction. He ran a hand along the horse's slightly quivering flank and murmured to the animal in a mixture of soft, liquid Spanish and English. Some men *broke* horses. Rafael preferred to take his time and *build* them into being good saddle mounts.

Denny leaned against the fence on Brad's other side and looked down at the boy. "How you doin', kid?"

Brad pointed and said, "That's going to be my horse."

"I heard. A top hand needs a good mount, more than just about anything else."

Brad turned his head to look up at her. "You think I'm gonna be a top hand?"

"Of course. Everybody who works on the Sugarloaf is." Denny grinned. "I think it must be something in the air."

"I hope so." Brad added solemnly, "I want to earn my keep."

"You'll do that just by being my son," Louis told him.

"That's because you're about to marry my mother. That's not anything that *I* did."

Denny chuckled. "I like that. Kid's got an independent streak."

"I wonder who else around here does," muttered Louis. The comment drew a smile from Cal.

Inside the corral, Rafael continued talking to the horse. He put his left foot in the stirrup and rested a little weight on it. The horse shied, but Rafael stayed with him, hands stroking just like his voice. The horse settled down. Rafael took hold of the saddle horn and swung up.

Instantly, the horse exploded into wild bucking. Sunfishing, switching ends, twisting and writhing, and doing everything in its power to dislodge the unexpected weight on its back. Rafael stayed right where he was, stuck tight as a burr, until the horse slowed its frenzied bucking. Then he slipped smoothly from the saddle and started stroking and talking to the horse again.

Brad's eyes were wide as he said, "He woulda *killed* me if he did that while I was trying to ride him."

"That's why it's going to take some time before he's ready," Cal explained. "Sorry it won't be in time for the wedding, but you can keep riding that mare you've been riding until Rafe's got this young fella used to the idea."

"That's all right." Brad paused, then added, "I wish I could ride in the race."

Still grinning, Denny gave him a friendly push on

the shoulder and said, "Even if you did, you wouldn't beat me."

Admiration shining in his eyes, Brad looked up at her. "You're going to ride in the race?"

"I sure am."

Louis gave her a dubious glance. "Mother and Father agreed to that?"

"I don't have to ask their permission," Denny replied with a trace of anger in her voice.

"So in other words, they *didn't* agree. Especially Mother."

"Don't you worry about that. You just wait and see what happens tomorrow."

A new voice spoke up from behind them. "I know what's going to happen tomorrow. Louis and I are getting married."

Denny looked around to see that Melanie Buckner had come up to the little group at the corral. She was a very pretty, brown-haired young woman, several years older than Louis. That gap in their ages wasn't enough to make any difference, and it certainly hadn't stopped them from falling in love during a perilous journey from San Francisco through the Sierra Nevada Mountains the previous December. Nor had the fact that Melanie was a widow and had a young son given Louis any pause when he decided to ask her to marry him.

Denny, for one, was glad that her brother had worked up the gumption to pop the question. She liked Melanie a great deal, and she was looking forward to having Brad as her nephew.

All that was left was the actual wedding, which would take place at the ranch the next day. Of course, the ceremony itself wasn't *all* that was going to happen. There was also an honest-to-goodness fandango to be held, the likes of which the Sugarloaf had never seen before. Since Smoke was the most famous resident of the area, scores of folks would come from the nearby town of Big Rock and from all over the valley to help celebrate the union of Smoke's son Louis to Melanie Buckner. All of Smoke and Sally's friends would be there to watch the ceremony and then participate in the huge feast and party to follow.

Before that, however, would be a horse race in which the riders would gallop a couple of miles up the valley from the ranch headquarters before making a big turn and heading back to the finish line as fast as possible. That was drawing a lot of interest, too, as well as plenty of wagers. Nothing cowboys liked better than betting on their favorite horses and their own skill as riders. Louis had worried a little that his and Melanie's wedding was being turned into a rodeo, but she had assured him that she didn't mind.

Denny happened to know that Melanie's late husband Tom had been a cowboy and had died as a result of a riding mishap, so she suspected that Melanie might be putting on a brave face, at least to a certain extent, because she didn't want to kick up a fuss.

Denny admired her for that, but Denny's main interest in the race was *winning* it. She knew she could do it if she rode the black stallion called Rocket.

Louis went to Melanie and put his arm around her shoulders. "You're right. The most important thing is our wedding." He gave Denny a warning glance. "So we don't want any big arguments spoiling everything."

"There won't be any argument," she said. "I've

thought about it, just now, and you're right, Louis. This is a special day for you and Melanie. I don't want anything taking away from it. There'll be other races I can ride in."

A surprised frown creased Louis's forehead. "Really?"

Brad said, "You're not going to ride after all?" He sounded disappointed.

"Not this time," Denny said.

"Well . . . thank you," Louis told her. "I know Mother will be relieved."

"I'm sure she will." Denny turned away before Louis could see the sly smile that tugged at the corners of her mouth. *He was always a mite gullible while we were growing up,* she thought. It was true that she didn't want to ruin their wedding day, and honestly, she didn't want to upset her mother, either.

But what none of them knew . . . until it was all over but the shouting . . . wouldn't hurt them, now would it?

CHAPTER 3

Brown Dirt Cowboy Saloon, Big Rock

The battered old hat was tipped far back on the man's rumpled thatch of rusty hair. All his clothes, from the old boots to the patched jeans to the faded blue shirt and brown vest, showed signs of long, hard wear. The gun belt strapped around his lean hips had been gouged and torn in places by thorny brush. The Colt .45 that rode in the attached holster was clean and well cared for, though.

Steve Markham picked up the glass from the bar in front of him and threw back the shot. The whiskey burned all the way down his gullet. The Brown Dirt Cowboy was popular with range riders in the area because the who-hit-John sold there was cheap and packed a punch, not because it was smooth as silk going down.

Steve stood there for a moment, letting the booze kindle a fire in his belly, before he followed it with a healthy swallow of foamy, bitter beer from the mug next to the empty shot glass.

One of the bartenders ambled over, nodded toward the glass, and asked, "Another?"

"I'm all right for now," replied Steve. Still holding the mug, he turned so his back was to the bar and leaned on it, hooking his elbows on the hardwood as he surveyed the smoky, noisy room.

The saloon was packed. Men stood two deep at the bar in places, and every table was full. Gals with painted faces and wearing short, spangled dresses carried trays and made their way through the crowd delivering drinks to the tables. They were pawed almost nonstop, but there was no way to avoid those groping hands.

And truth to tell, most of them looked like they didn't mind all that much. From time to time, a customer would pull one of them down to lean over a table, whisper something in her ear, and then the two of them would adjourn to an upstairs room to complete the transaction.

Steve smiled faintly as he observed one of the saloon girls leading a nervous-looking youngster up the stairs. It had been a while since he had enjoyed any female company himself, but he wasn't in the mood for a soiled dove. He had other things on his mind tonight.

Turning his head to look at the big, florid-faced man on his left, Steve said, "The whole town looked fit to bust when I was ridin' in. Is it always this crowded?"

"What? No." The man shook his head. He was no cowboy, might have been a blacksmith or a freight handler. "Naw, Big Rock's busy sometimes, but not like this. A lot of folks have come into town for the big shindig tomorrow."

"There's a celebration here in town? It's not the Fourth of July yet. Or is it? I haven't been payin' a lot of attention to the calendar, bein' on the drift like I have been."

"No, no, the shindig's not here in town. It's out at the Sugarloaf. You know, Smoke Jensen's spread."

Steve arched an eyebrow and said, "Smoke Jensen? The gunfighter and outlaw?"

The man glared at Steve. "Watch your mouth, mister. Smoke's no outlaw. Yeah, there might've been some reward dodgers out on him years ago, but those were fake, put out by some fellas who had a grudge against him. He's always been a law-abiding sort. Well, other than going ahead and killing a bunch of lowdown skunks who needed killin', without waiting for the law to do it."

"Nothing wrong with that," Steve said. "I didn't mean no offense. And I notice you didn't find any fault with me callin' him a gunfighter."

"Well, it'd be plumb foolish to argue about that. There's never been anybody slicker on the draw than Smoke Jensen."

Steve swallowed some more of the beer and asked, "Why's he throwin' a party?"

"Say, you *did* just ride in, didn't you? Smoke's son is getting married. There's gonna be a big feast and a *baile* afterward, and kickin' things off in the morning before the ceremony, they're gonna have a horse race."

Steve's interest visibly perked up. "Is that so? I've never been much for dancin', so I'm not sure I'd be welcome at any *baile*, but I've got a fast hoss."

The red-faced man laughed. "If you're thinkin'

about entering, friend, I'd advise against it. The fastest horses in the state will be in this race. I don't reckon some saddle tramp's nag would stand much of a chance."

Steve drew in a sharp breath. He didn't want to lose his temper, but it was hard not to in the face of a comment like that. Keeping a tight rein on his words, he told the man, "My horse ain't no nag—"

Before he could continue defending his mount, someone bumped heavily against his shoulder. The impact was enough to make Steve take a staggering step to his left. The mug in his hand tipped, and the beer that was still in it splashed over the feet of the big, red-faced man.

"What the hell!" he roared, but the noise level in the room was already so high, the shout was less deafening than it might have been. "What in blazes do you think you're doin', stranger?"

If the man wanted an apology, he wasn't going to get one. Steve jerked his head toward the man who'd bumped into him and said, "It's not my fault. It was this jasper who's to blame for bein' so damn clumsy."

The offender was tall and kind of skinny. Steve probably outweighed him, but the man had broad shoulders, long arms, and big, knobby-knuckled hands. "What're you talkin' about? I didn't do a damn thing."

"The hell you didn't. You bumped into me and made me spill beer on this hombre."

"I barely touched you," the tall man said. "If you can't hold your liquor and start stumblin' around, it ain't my fault."

The red-faced man took hold of Steve's left shoulder and half-turned him. "I didn't see anybody run into you. You just up and dumped beer on my feet, probably because I called your horse a nag!"

For a second, Steve wondered if these two were working together, trying to provoke a fight for some reason that was beyond him. When he glanced back and forth between them, however, he didn't see any sign of such a conspiracy in their faces. They both looked genuinely angry and upset.

"I'm the only one who lost out here," he snapped. "I lost part of a beer, but it's not worth fightin' over, so let's just forget it."

"The hell we will," said the red-faced man. "I'm gonna have to get these boots shined before I go out to the Sugarloaf in the morning. That ain't gonna be free, you know."

Steve set the empty mug on the bar and inclined his head toward the tall man again. "Talk to him. It was his fault, like I told you. I'm gonna go find some friendlier place to drink." He stepped away from the bar, toward the saloon's batwinged entrance.

Both men caught hold of him, a hand on each shoulder, and jerked him back.

The tall man said, "The hell you are," and the red-faced man declared, "You ain't goin' anywhere!"

CHAPTER 4

They shouldn't have done that, thought Steve. And then he didn't think anymore. Instinct took over.

He lashed out with his right arm, holding that hand stiff so that the fingers dug deep under the tall man's ribs and forced the air out of his lungs. As the man gasped, turned pale, and bent forward a little, his hand slipped off Steve's shoulder.

The red-faced man yanked hard on him. Steve made use of that and allowed the sharp tug to turn him. He lowered his head as he came around and then bulled forward, ramming his right shoulder against the man's barrel chest. Steve balled his fists and slammed a left and a right into the man's thick belly.

Unfortunately, the layer of fat soaked up most of the power from those punches. The man roared again and threw a punch of his own. Steve jerked aside so the blow missed his face, but he took it on his left shoulder and it landed with enough force to make that arm go numb for several seconds. The impact also knocked Steve backward, and his feet slipped on the sawdust-littered floor. He sat down hard as the crowd along the bar quickly scurried back to give the combatants room.

"Fight! Fight!" The inevitable shouts echoed from the high ceiling.

The red-faced man charged at Steve, evidently intending to stomp him into the floor. Steve recovered quickly and rolled aside, thrusting a leg between the red-faced man's calves and tripping him. With a startled yell, the man went down face-first and landed hard enough to stun him.

Steve didn't get any break, though. The tall man had recovered from having the breath knocked out of him and grabbed Steve's empty mug off the bar. He swung it at Steve's head.

Steve ducked under the sweeping blow and dived at the tall man's legs, tackling him around the knees. That should have knocked the man down, but the crowd still pressed in closely on that side, and several men caught him and shoved him back up.

Steve got one hand on the brass rail and reached up with the other to grab the front edge of the bar. He pulled himself to his feet just in time for the tall man to crash both clubbed hands down on his back. The brutal blow drove Steve's chest against the bar. The tall man raised his arms, intending to strike again from behind.

Steve pushed off the bar, lurched back, and rammed his right elbow into the man's midsection before the blow could fall. That knocked the tall man back a step. Steve whirled and hooked a right to the man's jaw. Steve was fairly tall himself and his punch landed cleanly, followed with a left to the body. He had his opponent backing up, giving ground, and was confident that he could continue boring in until he put the man on the floor.

He might have succeeded if the red-faced man hadn't recovered enough to reach out, grab Steve's ankle, and jerk his leg out from under him.

Steve windmilled his arms but couldn't keep his balance. As he toppled to the floor, the red-faced man clambered up onto his feet and the tall man stopped backpedaling. He shook out the cobwebs from the battering Steve had given him and clenched his fists again so the big knuckles stuck out prominently.

Steve was sprawled in the sawdust. He pushed himself into a sitting position and saw the two men stalking toward him from different directions. A snarl twisted his face and his hand started toward the holstered gun on his hip. The last thing he wanted to do was shoot his way out of there, but he was sick and tired of those hombres whaling away on him for something that wasn't even his fault.

His hand had not yet touched the Colt's grips when the batwings slammed open and a loud, commanding voice said, "Everybody step back! Step back, damn it, and clear a path!"

The Brown Dirt Cowboy's customers, who had been yelling encouragement to the battlers, fell silent and pushed back to give the newcomer room. Steve looked in that direction and saw a solidly built man in a white shirt with a string tie and black trousers and vest standing just inside the entrance cradling a double-barreled shotgun in obviously capable hands. His gray hair was still thick under the black Stetson he wore. His lined, weathered face showed his age, but clearly, the man was still a ways away from being ready for a rocking chair.

The star pinned to his vest proclaimed him to be a lawman. Steve would have known that even without the badge. He had seen plenty of star packers in his time.

The lawman walked toward Steve and the two men with whom he'd been trading punches. Steve moved his hand farther away from his gun butt and made sure to keep it there. He didn't want to give the newcomer any excuse to get antsy with that scattergun. The sheriff, marshal, whatever he was, still had plenty of bark on him, that was plain to see.

Addressing the stocky, red-faced man, he demanded, "Hiram, what the devil are you doing?"

Looking a little embarrassed, the man called Hiram cleared his throat and said, "Uh, sorry, Sheriff. This fella here"—a thick finger poked toward Steve—"spilled beer on me and then wouldn't even say he was sorry."

Steve said, "I didn't say I was sorry because it wasn't my fault. This long-stretched galoot bumped into me and caused the whole thing."

The sheriff looked at the tall man. "That true, Parry?"

"Well, uh . . . it's mighty crowded in here, Sheriff Carson. You know, on account of so many folks being in town for Smoke's boy's wedding. I might've jostled this fella a little, but I don't think it was enough to have caused all this ruckus."

Steve stood up and slapped sawdust off the seat of his pants. "You can see how it is, Sheriff. I got caught in the middle here, and then these two decided they'd both try to whip me."

"Looked like they were on their way to doing it," the lawman commented dryly.

"No, sir," Steve said with a shake of his head. "It might've looked that way, but that ain't how the hand would've played out."

"Well, the hand's over now," said Sheriff Carson. "Emmett Brown!"

A slick-haired gent in a tweed suit stepped out of the crowd. "Yes, Sheriff?"

"You've got men working for you who are supposed to keep the peace. They need to do a better job of it. I know the town's crowded and everybody's in high spirits because of the fandango at the Sugarloaf tomorrow, but that doesn't mean the lid's coming off tonight."

Emmett Brown, the proprietor of the Brown Dirt Cowboy Saloon, swallowed and nodded. "Yes, sir. There won't be any more trouble."

"Better not be," growled the lawman. He had lowered the shotgun's twin barrels to point at the floor. As he tucked the weapon under his left arm, he jerked his right thumb at Steve. "You be on your way."

"I told you, I didn't *do* anything," Steve insisted.

"And I believe you. But you staying here is like an ember in a fire. It's liable to flare up again after a while."

"You're not making them other two leave," Steve said sullenly.

"Yes, I am, as soon as you've had a few minutes to drift. Parry, you go back home to your wife. Hiram, you head for that boardinghouse where you live. No more ruckuses tonight, and for damn sure, none out at the Sugarloaf tomorrow." Sheriff Carson narrowed his eyes at Steve. "That is, if you're planning to go out there, which I wouldn't recommend."

Steve drew in a breath and calmed his raging emotions again. Quietly, he said, "Unless that's an order, Sheriff, I was sort of thinking about it. I heard there's gonna be a horse race."

"That's right."

"Can anybody enter?"

"As far as I know."

"Well, then, I think my horse might just have a chance."

"It's a free country," the sheriff said. "As long as you're not causing trouble . . . which I *really* wouldn't recommend if you're on the Sugarloaf."

"Why's that?"

Sheriff Carson smiled. "Because then you'd have Smoke Jensen to deal with, instead of me."

Steve shrugged and didn't say anything else as he allowed the lawman to usher him out of the saloon. But as Steve untied his horse from the hitch rack and led the buckskin away into the night, the thought came to him that meeting Smoke Jensen might be exactly what he needed to do.

CHAPTER 5

The Sugarloaf

The Pitchfork line camp got its name from a peculiar rock formation atop the ridge that loomed over the grassy bench where the camp was located. Three fingers of rock, all roughly the same height, thrust up and looked like the tines of a pitchfork, especially from a distance where it wasn't so obvious how gnarled they were. Neither Joe Bob Stanton nor Harley Briggs knew who had first called the camp by that name, and they didn't care. They were inside the shack, pleasantly full of stew and coffee, and were playing poker for matchsticks.

"Call," Stanton said as he pushed five more matchsticks into the pot.

"Two pair, jacks and sevens," Briggs announced as he laid his cards on the rough-hewn table between them.

Stanton laughed. "Three treys," he said as he revealed his hand. "Threes have always been lucky for me."

Briggs shook his head glumly. "If we was lucky, we'd be down at the main ranch so's we could enjoy all the big doin's tomorrow, instead of stuck up here in this high pasture mindin' the summer graze."

"It was our turn. That's only fair. If Smoke had given us a break, somebody else would've had to take our place, and then *they'd* be grousin' about missin' out."

"Yeah, I reckon." Briggs brightened a little as he added, "And Cal *did* promise me that when Andy Sawyer and Tex Bell come up next week with our supplies, Miss Sally's gonna send along a mess of bear sign."

Stanton grinned. "That ain't as good as gettin' to dance with all the pretty gals who are gonna be there for the party tomorrow, but it's somethin', anyway. Shuffle up those cards and deal 'em again."

The two men were like thousands of other cowboys scattered across the West—somewhere between twenty and forty, their real ages difficult to determine because the life they led had honed them down into strips of rawhide, tough as nails, accepting of an existence devoted to hard work for little reward because at least it left them free.

Briggs gathered up the cards and began shuffling them clumsily with callused fingers while Stanton stood up and headed toward the potbellied stove to see if any coffee was left in the pot. He hadn't gotten there yet when he stopped short and lifted his head.

After a moment, Briggs noticed and stopped shuffling the cards. "Somethin' wrong?"

"Hush. Thought I heard somethin' out by the corral. Horses seem a mite spooked."

Briggs dropped the cards, scraped his chair back,

and came to his feet. "Panther prowlin' around, maybe?"

"Don't know, but one of us best go see."

"You go ahead and get your coffee. I'll take a look."

Briggs went to the door of the one-room shack, picked up a Winchester leaning against the wall, and stepped outside. The line camp consisted of the log cabin and a corral with an attached shed the horses could get under if a thunderstorm rolled through. Each of the cowboys had brought three saddle mounts from the Sugarloaf's remuda, so six horses milled around in the corral.

Briggs couldn't see very well, his eyes not having adjusted to the starlight after being inside, but he heard the animals nickering and moving around. They were more skittish than usual. Stanton had been right about that.

He closed the door behind him and stood for a moment on the slab of stone that served as a step, getting used to the darkness and listened intently. He didn't hear a mountain lion's distinctive growling *chuff*, but that didn't rule out the possibility that one of the big cats was skulking around.

The Winchester was fully loaded and had a round already in the chamber. The cowboys left the rifles that way, because they never knew when they might need one in a hurry. Each carried a handgun for killing snakes while they were out riding the range during the day, but Briggs hadn't buckled on his gun belt before going outside.

When he could see where he was going, he stepped down off the rock and started toward the corral. The horses were still upset, and Briggs wanted to call out to them, assure them that everything was all right. He kept quiet for the moment, though, figuring it was better not to announce his presence just yet.

He came up to the fence made of peeled poles and looked inside the corral. In the dark, he couldn't make an accurate count of the horses. They were just a dark, shifting mass. He believed all six of them were in there, but he couldn't be sure.

"What the hell?" he muttered. "What's got these critters so spooked?"

As Briggs started to circle the corral toward the shed, movement caught his eye. A figure had just stepped out from behind the shed. Not a mountain lion, he realized. This was a two-legged varmint, not a four-legged one. A man, when there wasn't supposed to be anybody else around the line camp . . .

Briggs lifted the rifle toward his shoulder and opened his mouth to call out a challenge, when orange flame suddenly stabbed through the darkness at him. What felt like a sledgehammer slammed into him, high on his left chest. He went over backward, dropping the Winchester as he fell. He didn't feel anything, even when his head bounced off the ground. The shock of being shot had made him go numb all over.

The small part of his brain that still worked realized a bullet had crashed into him and knocked him down. He gasped, because he couldn't seem to get any air in him. His ears rang from the sound of the shot, but he thought he heard footsteps rushing past him.

A man's voice ordered harshly, "Get the one in the shack. I'll finish off this one."

A dark shape loomed over Briggs, blotting out some of the stars that shone brightly in the ebony sky. Starlight glinted on something as the man pointed it at him. Instinct made Briggs fumble around on the ground beside him as the man standing over him chuckled.

"Your luck's run out, cowpoke." The man sounded like he was enjoying it.

Not numb anymore, Briggs closed his hand around the Winchester's stock. Pain had begun flooding through him. He used that fiery agony to give him strength as he tipped the rifle's muzzle up, thumbed back the hammer, and pulled the trigger.

The Winchester cracked. In the instant that the muzzle flash ripped the darkness apart, no more than a shaved fraction of a second, he saw the man's ugly, beard-stubbled face. The slug from the rifle struck him somewhere and twisted him around but didn't drive him off his feet.

The man grunted, caught himself, and then yelled, "You son of a ——"

The blasts from the gun in the man's hand were like a never-ending volley of thunder from the worst storm that ever rolled through those mountains. That gun-thunder was the last thing Harley Briggs ever heard as slug after slug pounded into his chest. His last fleeting thought was the hope that his friend Joe Bob might somehow get away from the killers.

But he died knowing there was little hope of that.

CHAPTER 6

Denny took her time going down the stairs because she knew some of them creaked pretty loudly. She carried her boots and placed her sock-clad feet close to the wall to diminish the chances and put her weight on them carefully, backing off each time one of the steps started to make a racket.

Her father had the best hearing of anyone she had ever known. He wouldn't necessarily be upset if he knew she was leaving the house in the middle of the night, but it would simplify matters if she could keep the little jaunt to herself.

The hour had to be close to midnight. The big ranch house had been quiet and dark for several hours, and when Denny had looked out toward the bunkhouse from the window of her second-floor bedroom, she hadn't seen any light or movement out there, either. People worked hard on a ranch, which meant they slept hard, too. Satisfied that everyone had turned in for the night, she had slipped off her nightdress and pulled on socks, jeans, and a shirt, then started downstairs.

She didn't pause to put her boots on until she

reached the front porch after easing the door closed behind her. She sat on the steps and worked her feet into the boots. A moment of intent listening after that told her she hadn't roused anyone in the house, and she headed for the barn.

Even though the moon was just a tiny sliver and low in the sky, the stars provided enough light for Denny to see where she was going. She didn't need much. She might not know every square foot of the Sugarloaf the way her father did, but she knew the ranch headquarters well enough to get around just fine. She would have to light a lantern once she got into the barn, though. She had several matches in her pocket ready to do that. She had prepared for this.

Denny knew she could lift the heavy wooden bar resting in the brackets on the main barn's big double doors by herself—she had done it before—but she headed to the smaller door leading into the tack room.

She closed the tack room door behind her and felt around in the gloom until she found the lantern with its bail hanging on a nail in the wall. She snapped a match to life with her thumbnail—Smoke had taught her on one of her visits to the Sugarloaf when she was a little girl—and held the flame to the lantern's wick.

When she had the lantern burning good, she carried it above her head in her left hand and went into the barn's main area. She walked down the wide aisle between two rows of stalls and then turned left at the T-shape that stretched right and left in front of another dozen stalls in the rear part of the barn. The lantern's glow washed over the hard-packed ground at her feet and the bits of straw and hay that spilled out under the gate of each stall.

When she reached the final one, back in the corner, she turned and raised the lantern a little higher so that its light reached over the solid gate into the enclosure. The horse that looked back at her flared his nostrils and pawed at the ground with a hoof. The look in his eyes was challenging.

The animal's coat was a sleek, glossy black. He wasn't overly big, just a medium-sized horse, but everything about him was perfectly formed, from his head to the tail that switched back and forth in agitation.

"Take it easy, Rocket," Denny said quietly. "You're smart enough that you ought to know by now I'm not going to hurt you."

The horse blew out a breath.

Darn if that didn't sound disparaging, thought Denny.

Rocket was a mustang, having been brought in with a group of wild horses caught back in the spring. All the others had responded to Rafael De Santos's methods and had been turned into decent saddle mounts. Smoke had sold some of them and added the others to the Sugarloaf's riding stock.

Rocket, though, had been stubborn. Rafael had proclaimed him to be half-gentled but still needing a lot of work. Sometimes he cooperated, and when he did, he showed he had the makings of a fine horse. When he didn't, it took a skillful cowboy to stay on his back until he'd calmed down . . . and sometimes he never reached that point and kept bucking until the would-be rider gave up. Problem was, the cowboy never knew which Rocket he were going to get when he swung up into the saddle.

But one thing was absolutely certain. Rocket was *fast* . . . hence the name. When he settled down and just ran, no horse on the ranch was faster.

Denny was convinced that no horse in the whole valley was faster.

Rafael had allowed her to ride the young mustang a few times, when Rocket was in a good mood and not giving any trouble. Denny loved the way the horse responded to her. At its best, the relationship between horse and rider was such a bond that it almost seemed as if the two had become one. Denny had sensed something of that with Rocket.

"When you're finished with him, Rafael, I want him to be mine," she'd told the horse tamer.

Rafael had shaken his head. "I may never be finished with this one, Señorita Denny. He is stubborn like the mule. Perhaps the stubbornest horse I have ever seen." Rafael had paused, then added, "And your padre saw you riding him the other day. He was not happy, even though the horse behaved well. He says El Volador has the eyes of a killer."

"That's ridiculous. He's just a horse."

Rafael had just cocked his head to the side. "I only tell you what Señor Smoke says, señorita. He will not be happy if you try to ride this one again."

Denny tried to go along with her father's wishes . . . most of the time. *But he was wrong about that one,* she thought as she looked at Rocket in the lantern light. The connection was there between them. She was sure about that.

"What are you doing, Aunt Denise?"

The unexpected question made her jump. She almost dropped the lantern, but she tightened her grip on it in time. Swinging around, she saw Brad standing at the corner where the aisle made its T-shape. He wore a nightshirt, but his feet were in boots.

"Brad, you shouldn't be out here," she told him, ignoring the question he'd asked her. "It's the middle of the night."

"It's the middle of the night for you, too," he said. "You look like you're going riding."

"What? No. I'm not . . . I was just out here looking at the horses—"

"Why?"

"What do you mean? Why am I looking at the horses? Well, I like horses . . ."

"So do I," the boy said, "but I don't sneak out of the house in the middle of the night and come out here to look at them."

Denny frowned. "Are you *scolding* me?"

"Of course not, Aunt Denise. I wouldn't do that."

"Don't call me Aunt Denise. That makes me sound like I'm positively ancient, like I was forty years old or something."

"Miss Sally said I shouldn't call you Denny. She said it's disrespectful, since you're going to be my aunt once Louis marries my ma." He thought about it. "And that's only about twelve hours from now, isn't it?"

"Well, I don't mind being your aunt. I'm pretty happy about that, in fact, but I'll be da—I'll be darned if I like being addressed like I'm some old maiden aunt."

"What's a maiden aunt?"

"Never mind about that," Denny said. "You'd better scoot on back to bed."

If he left, she could still salvage her plan.

But in the morning, he might mention to his mother or Louis or someone else that he'd seen her out here with Rocket, and that might cause a problem, so it might be better to make an adjustment now . . .

"What are you gonna do?" Brad's question broke into her rapid thoughts. "I still say you look like you're going riding."

Denny shook her head. "I swear I'm not. Not yet. I was just . . . talking to Rocket."

"That wild killer mustang?"

"He's *not* a wild killer mustang! He just needs the right rider."

"Which is you, I reckon," Brad said.

Denny gritted her teeth and drew a deep breath between them. "If I'm going to be your aunt, that means I'm almost like a parent, and I can tell you what to do. So get on back in the house. You shouldn't have been spying on me and followed me out here in the first place."

"I wasn't spying on you. I just happened to be up because . . . well, I just happened to be up, and I saw you, and I was curious. There's nothing wrong with that, is there?"

"Didn't you ever hear about curiosity and the cat?"

"There are cats here in the barn, aren't there? Cal told me there were, to keep the mice down. Where are they?"

"Curled up somewhere asleep, I guess," said Denny, "where you ought to be, blast it. Are you going to do what I tell you?"

"I want to look at Rocket first."

Denny hesitated, then moved her head to indicate he should come on down the aisle. "All right, but as soon as you've done that, you're going back to the house."

"Sure, sure." Brad ran along the aisle to the last stall. "What about you? Will you walk back to the house with me? It's, uh, kind of dark out there."

That reminded Denny that he *was* just nine years old. Still a little kid. She sighed, nodded, and said, "Sure, I'll go with you."

Brad put a booted foot on one of the gate's crossbraces, grabbed the top edge, and pulled himself up so he could look over into the stall. Rocket watched him warily but didn't spook. Brad hooked his left arm over the top of the gate and held out his right hand. "Come here, Rocket," he urged. "I won't hurt you, boy."

Denny began, "He's not going to—", then stopped short as Rocket took a couple of steps forward and nosed Brad's hand.

The boy was beaming as he glanced over his shoulder. "Look! He likes me!"

"Yeah, it appears that he does," Denny murmured. She watched as Brad stroked Rocket's muzzle.

The mustang seemed to enjoy it.

Maybe she had been wrong about who was destined to be the perfect rider for Rocket, she told herself, then discarded that idea. He had allowed her to pet him, too, at times. After a few minutes, she said, "All right. We'd better go. We all need our sleep. Rocket, too."

Brad gave the mustang's nose a last scratch, then

dropped to the ground outside the stall gate. "I've heard that he's really fast," he said as Denny ushered him back along the aisle toward the front of the barn. "It's a shame he's not gonna run in the race tomorrow. Or rather, today, I reckon."

"Yeah, that's a real shame." She was smiling to herself as she blew out the lantern flame.

CHAPTER 7

Smoke arose well before dawn, but not early enough to be up before Sally. When he came into the kitchen, the air was already full of the smells of bread and pies baking, coffee, and fresh-cooked bacon. He came up behind her as she stood at a counter kneading more bread dough, rested his hands on her shoulders, and nuzzled her thick dark hair.

Sally sighed and leaned back against him. "Are you ready for today, Smoke?" she murmured.

"Sure. What's not to be ready for?"

"We're going to have a daughter-in-law. We're going to be *grandparents*. Step-grandparents, I suppose would be the proper thing to say, but considering how precious that little boy is . . ."

"He'll be the same as our own flesh and blood," Smoke said. "I know that. And it's fine with me. Louis and Melanie may well have some kids of their own, too. It's sort of the natural order of things."

"Not necessarily. Denise doesn't show any signs of settling down and having a family."

"Denny's still young."

"The same age as Louis. And I wasn't much older

than she is now when you and I were married and starting this ranch."

"Well, times change." Smoke kissed the back of Sally's head, then moved over to the stove to pour himself a cup of coffee. "Folks don't get married quite as young now. And don't forget about that young Rogers fella. One of these days Denny might get serious about him."

Sally looked around at him. "You mean Brice? He's a nice young man, but half the time Denny acts like she can't stand him."

Smoke sipped the coffee and then said, "And the other half of the time she's making cow eyes at him. Just let things take their own course. If it doesn't work out with Brice Rogers, some other young man will come along."

"I don't know what to hope for," Sally said with a shake of her head. "He's a deputy U.S. marshal, after all. That's a dangerous job." She glanced at Smoke. "I know all about falling in love with a man who tends to ride *into* danger rather than away from it. I'm not sure I recommend it for my daughter."

"Well, lucky for us Denny's headstrong enough she won't give a damn what we think!" He could tell that Sally tried not to laugh, but she couldn't hold it in.

"You have an odd idea of being lucky, Smoke Jensen!"

"I don't know about that. I'd say I was mighty lucky to ride into a town up in Idaho that had hired a gal from back east named Sally Reynolds to teach school." He took his coffee and went outside to stand on the front porch for a few minutes and watch the day being born.

At that elevation, the air was cool early in the morning no matter what the time of year. Smoke enjoyed the crispness of it as he sipped his coffee. The sun wasn't up yet, but the eastern sky had lightened with its approach and displayed a faint golden arch. The sky was clear except for a few long, fluffy streamers of cloud that also caught the sun's rays and stood out brightly. It was going to be a beautiful day, he thought.

The ranch had already started coming to life. Even on such a special day there were chores to be done. Lights glowed in the dairy barn where a couple of the younger hands would be milking the cows. Out in the bunkhouse, Cal would be rousting out the men who would ride the range instead of taking part in the celebration. They had drawn lots to determine who those unfortunate souls would be. Somebody had to check on the cattle in the lower pastures. Smoke would try to make it up to them with some extra free time later.

Men were also stationed at the line camps up in the higher ranges, but those fellows were in the middle of their assigned jobs and wouldn't return until the end of the month, when other members of the crew would take their place.

Smoke spotted a bow-legged figure coming toward him and raised a hand in greeting. As the man reached the bottom of the steps, Smoke said, "Morning, Pearlie."

"Mornin', Smoke." Wes "Pearlie" Fontaine had been the Sugarloaf's foreman for many years, as well as

Calvin Woods's best friend and mentor. A former hired gun and outlaw, he and Smoke had been on opposite sides of a fight when they first met, but Pearlie had decided pretty quicklike that he wanted to throw in with Smoke. They had been friends ever since, and Smoke had never had a more staunch ally.

Pearlie was retired from the foreman's job—Sally had dubbed him *Foreman Emeritus*—but he would always have a place on the Sugarloaf. He spent his days advising Cal and helping out any way Smoke needed him to.

He thumbed his hat back on his grizzled head and went on, "I was just out in the barn lookin' over the horses, and I noticed somethin' odd."

"Why were you looking at the horses?"

"I *like* bein' around the critters. Had plenty of good friends of the equine persuasion—ain't that a plumb fancy way of sayin' *horses?*—over the years. I don't sleep as well as I used to, neither, and I got a mite restless." Pearlie sounded a little defensive. "Anyway, I like visitin' ol' Max. He's been put out to pasture, too, sort of like me."

Max was the horse Pearlie had ridden most of the time for many years, but he was too old for regular ranch work. Smoke suspected that being retired bothered Pearlie a little more than it did Max, though.

"What did you notice that was odd?" he asked to change the subject, and because he was curious, too.

"That Rocket hoss ain't in his stall."

That news made Smoke frown. He looked toward the corral where Rafael worked with the green horses, but it was empty. Rafael wouldn't have had any of his charges out there at this time of the morning, anyway.

"You don't mean he busted down the gate and got out, do you?"

Pearlie shook his head. "Nope. Didn't see any signs of that. And his bridle was gone. Looked for all the world like somebody opened up that stall and led him outta there."

"I can't think of any reason for anybody to do that."

"You reckon we got a hoss thief on our hands, Smoke?" Pearlie almost sounded a little eager for that to be the case, as if he would welcome the chance to hunt down such an interloper.

"Anybody who stole that devil of a mustang would probably regret it," said Smoke, "but I don't think that's what's going on here." He rubbed his chin, his fingertips rasping a little on the beard stubble he hadn't yet shaved off this morning. "I've got a hunch it's something else entirely."

"What do you reckon?"

Smoke hesitated, then answered, "I'd rather not say just yet. Not until I'm sure."

"Dadgummit, Smoke, you know if you want me to keep somethin' under my hat, I can dang sure do it—"

"I know," Smoke broke in. "It's not that. It's just that if my hunch is right, I'm not quite sure how to handle it."

Pearlie frowned. "Huh. Smoke Jensen not sure what to do about a problem. I ain't sure I've ever seen that before. Generally, whenever somethin' rears up to cause you trouble, you just punch it or shoot it, and that takes care o' the problem."

"I can't do that this time," Smoke said. "Why don't you go hunt up Rafael and make sure he doesn't know anything about Rocket being missing, and I'll go check on something else."

Pearlie nodded and headed off toward the barn again. Smoke could tell he still wanted to know what was going on.

Preferring to be certain first, Smoke drank the rest of his coffee and went inside, set the empty cup on a small table in the foyer, and headed upstairs, moving with his usual quiet, easy grace that didn't cause much noise on the steps. He went along a hallway on the second floor and paused in front of one of the bedroom doors.

He rapped a knuckle on the panel lightly and listened for a response from inside. Hearing nothing, he knocked again, a little louder but not loud enough to disturb anyone who was still sleeping in the other rooms.

When there was still no response, Smoke reached down, closed his hand around the knob, and turned it slowly. It wasn't locked, which came as no surprise since for the most part nobody locked any doors in the house.

Smoke eased the door open a few inches, leaned closer to the gap, and said, "Denny? You in there?"

When his daughter didn't answer, he called her name again, then opened the door wider. Outside, the dawn light had grown stronger, and enough of it spilled through the gap in the curtains over the window to show him that Denny's bed was empty. The bedclothes were rumpled enough that he could tell it had been slept in—or at least tossed and turned in—but Denny wasn't there.

Neither were her boots, Smoke noted as he

glanced at the empty spot beside the bed where they usually sat. He grunted and backed out of the room, then eased the door closed.

With a look on his rugged face that was half worried, half amused, Smoke shook his head. "Denny, what the hell?"

CHAPTER 8

People began showing up early for all the festivities that were scheduled to happen. Cowboys rode in on horseback, people who lived in Big Rock rolled up in buggies, families from outlying farms and ranches arrived in buckboards, spring wagons, and even a few old-fashioned Conestogas. For today and part of the next day—because a lot of folks would spend the night—the Sugarloaf would have as big a population as a lot of small towns.

Smoke and Sally spent a lot of the morning on the porch greeting visitors. Sally looked lovely in an elegant, dark blue gown, while Smoke still wore jeans and boots but had consented to honor the dignity of the occasion by donning a white shirt with pearl snaps and a string tie. That was about as dressed-up as he ever got.

It would have been nice if his brothers Luke and Matt could have been there, as well as his nephews Ace and Chance, but all of them were off elsewhere in the West and had their hands full with their own doings. As for Preacher, Smoke's oldest friend and surrogate father, he had gone off to the mountains a number of years earlier and never returned. Smoke didn't even know if Preacher was still alive . . . although it seemed unlikely because he would be more than a hundred years old.

Still, where Preacher was concerned, Smoke had learned never to rule out anything.

He put those thoughts out of his head and concentrated on saying hello to the people who *were* there, making them feel welcome. All of his friends from Big Rock were showing up, most prominent among them Louis Longmont, the gambler and gunman who had sided Smoke in many battles, and Sheriff Monte Carson, who like Pearlie was a onetime enemy turned perennial friend and ally. Phil Clinton, who still edited and published the *Big Rock Journal*, was covering the wedding for his newspaper, of course, but would have been there anyway as a friend. Smoke was glad to see all of them, shaking their hands enthusiastically, and they all got hugs from Sally, too.

Even though the dance wouldn't take place until the evening, it was impossible for that many Western folks to get together without the fiddles and guitars coming out. Lively strains of music soon filled the air, blending pleasantly with the talk and laughter of old friends seeing each other again for the first time in months, in some cases. Spread out as the farm and ranch families were, special occasions were always welcomed as an excuse to socialize.

Women trooped in and out of the house carrying bowls and platters of food they had brought for the feast. Sally had done a lot of cooking to get ready, as had Inez Sandoval, the Sugarloaf's regular cook and housekeeper. Inez had recruited several assistants to help them, too. Smoke and the hands had several sides of beef smoking over pits of coals, but there would be plenty of other dishes as well. The food would be brought out later, but a table with pitchers of lemonade and glasses had been set up so people could quench their thirst.

While Smoke was standing on the porch, a hand fell on his shoulder and he looked around to see his son standing there with a big grin on his face.

"Today's the day, eh?" Louis said.

"Appears to be," Smoke responded dryly. "Are you doing all right? Did you sleep last night?"

"Hardly a wink. I was too full of anticipation. It's not every day that a man gets married, you know."

Smoke nodded. "I know." He had tied the knot twice in his life, the first time to a beautiful girl named Nicole who had given birth to Smoke's other son, Arthur. Both of them had died young and tragically, although their memories lived on in the names of his twin offspring. He didn't want to dwell on such painful recollections, so he put those thoughts aside, knowing that Nicole and Arthur would understand and not hold it against him.

He went on, "You're not feeling under the weather? I mean, your heart—"

"It's fine," Louis assured him. "Nary a twinge in weeks now."

"I'm mighty glad to hear that. And Melanie? How's she doing this morning?"

"I wouldn't know," Louis replied.

Smoke frowned in confusion, but Sally laughed and said, "Of course he wouldn't know, Smoke, because he hasn't seen her today. On the wedding day, it's bad luck for the groom to see the bride until the ceremony."

"Oh, yeah, I reckon I have heard that," Smoke admitted.

"But speaking of Melanie," Louis went on, "I'd appreciate it if you'd go check on her, Mother. She's made a few friends around here and they're supposed to be helping her get ready, but since I haven't bothered her, I'm not sure that's the case. If she needs anything, someone needs to be there to see to it."

It was Sally's turn to frown. "What about Denise? I'm sure she'd be glad to lend a hand."

"I haven't seen Denny this morning," Louis replied with a shake of his head. "Maybe she *is* with Melanie, but I don't know that." He paused, then added, "Anyway, I'm not sure how much help she would be with . . . well, with bridal things."

"That attitude toward your sister doesn't help things," Sally said tartly. Her voice softened as she continued. "But I'll go up and see if Melanie needs anything. There's no rule that says a mother-in-law can't see her prospective daughter-in-law on the wedding day!" She put a hand on Smoke's arm. "You make sure that everyone who arrives is made to feel welcome."

"I will," Smoke told her.

Sally hurried into the house.

Smoke turned to his son and said casually, "You haven't seen Denny all morning, eh?"

"No, not that I recall. Should I have?"

"No, no reason that I can think of. She's around somewhere, I suppose."

Louis said, "There *is* something I want to talk to you about, though, Pa."

"Sure. Any advice I can give you—"

"Well, it's not actually *advice* I'm looking for. Remember when I said I wanted to study law and was thinking about going to Harvard?"

Smoke nodded. "I remember. Last year around Christmastime, wasn't it?"

"That's right. I've looked into it and talked it over with Melanie, and she agrees with me that if that's what I want to do, I should give it a try."

"That's the way I feel about any man's ambitions. But are you telling me that you're leaving the Sugarloaf, son?"

"That's right," Louis said. "I've applied to Harvard and been accepted and plan to start on my law degree in the fall."

Smoke slipped his hands into the hip pockets of his jeans and stood there for a long moment without saying anything. When he finally spoke, he said, "A man's got to follow his dreams. Preacher went west to the mountains, and so did I. If your dreams lie in the east, that's where you should go. But . . . have you told your mother about this?"

"Not yet." Louis shifted his feet nervously. "In fact, I've been dreading doing so."

Smoke grunted. "Likely with good reason. You and Denny haven't been back home all that long. Sally's not going to be happy if you start talking about leaving again."

Louis summoned up a smile. "That's why I was sort of hoping . . . maybe after the wedding is over, of course . . . that you could tell her . . ." His voice trailed off as Smoke shook his head.

"No, sir. You're going to have to do that yourself. It's your responsibility."

"I figured that's what you would say," Louis responded with a sigh. "But I didn't think it would hurt to ask." He nodded. "All right. I'll take care of it when Melanie and I get back from our wedding trip. But there's one more thing you should know, Pa. I'm not planning on leaving for good. Once I'm ready to start practicing law, I intend to come back and do it in Big Rock. That's where we're going to make our home."

Smoke grinned. "Well, I have to admit I'm glad to hear that. I thought you might decide to settle down in Boston or New York or Philadelphia or some such place where we'd hardly ever get to see you."

Louis shook his head and said, "No, sir. I've spent enough time out here to realize that this is home and always will be. I may not be cut out for running the ranch, but I don't want to be stuck in some giant city. I want to raise Brad—and any other children we may have—in a place where the air is clean and you can see the mountains."

Smoke clapped a hand on his son's shoulder. "I'm mighty glad to hear that. I've got a hunch your mother will be, too. And don't forget, there's a legal side to running a ranch, as well. We'll be turning to you for that."

"And you'll have Denny here to handle the day-to-day operations."

"Wait . . . you don't think your sister's ever going to get married and move away?"

"Well, I . . . I hadn't really given it much thought,"

Louis admitted. "She seems to fit in so well here. To be honest, after we'd been here a few months, I couldn't really imagine her anywhere else"—his eyes scanned the crowd—"which again brings up the question . . . where is she now?"

Smoke saw some cowboys leading horses toward the area where the race would begin in another half-hour or so. "I reckon we'll find out before too much longer."

CHAPTER 9

Denny stood in a grove of trees about two hundred yards from the ranch house, holding Rocket's reins. The growth was thick enough to hide her from a casual glance, although somebody might spot her if they looked hard enough, or knew exactly where to look. In jeans and a brown shirt and brown hat, she sort of blended in, she hoped. She had piled her blond curls on top of her head, pinned them down tightly, and then crammed the hat over them and drew the chin strap taut so it couldn't go anywhere. Rocket's dark hide would be difficult to spot, too.

She had been out there since before dawn, and she was getting pretty antsy. She had never been the patient sort. At least once the sun was up and people began to arrive, she had something to watch. She occupied her mind by trying to identify as many of the guests as she could. Plenty of them were familiar to her from the time she had spent on the Sugarloaf, especially the citizens of Big Rock, but some folks she didn't recognize. They probably came from the outlying spreads and she hadn't happened to ever see them in town.

From that spot, she could see her mother and father on the porch of the ranch house, too, and she wondered if they had missed her yet and realized she was gone. She hoped they weren't too worried about her. Her pa probably wasn't. If he had noticed her absence, there was a good chance he might have figured out what she was up to. The question was whether or not he would tell her mother. Denny hoped he wouldn't. She thought he might not.

It wasn't as if Smoke Jensen had made a habit of doing everything polite society demanded of him, after all.

Later in the morning, Louis appeared on the porch. Denny watched him talk to their parents for a few moments, then Sally went inside. Louis stayed where he was and appeared to be having some sort of earnest discussion with Smoke. Denny wasn't sure what that was about. She and her brother weren't as close as they had once been and didn't confide in each other about every little thing like they used to. That was natural enough, since they weren't kids anymore. Still, Denny sometimes missed that.

Whatever Louis and Smoke were talking about, the conversation was interrupted by Brad, who came out onto the porch dressed in a suit and a shirt with a stiff collar. He was going to take part in the wedding ceremony and walk his mother down the "aisle," although since they would all be outside it wasn't a real aisle like in a church. Brad tugged at his collar, which must have been uncomfortable, and said something that made Louis and Smoke laugh.

For a second, Denny wished she was down there taking part in the joyous occasion instead of hiding out in the trees like an owlhoot. But there would be time for celebrating later . . . after she had proven that Rocket was the fastest horse and she was the best rider in the valley.

The fifty-yard-wide open area between the barn and one of the corrals was where the race would get underway. Denny kept an eye on the area. When cowboys and young men from town began congregating there to get ready for the race, she would slip out of the trees and join them as unobtrusively as possible.

She would have to be careful not to be noticed, especially since some of the racers were members of the Sugarloaf crew and had seen her plenty of times around the ranch. The hat and shirt she wore were new, though, and if she kept her head down with the hat brim obscuring her face, she hoped there was a good chance she wouldn't be recognized. She would try to find a place in the line well away from her father's cowboys.

The race was supposed to start at noon, with the wedding ceremony to follow at one o'clock and then the feast and party, which would stretch throughout the afternoon until the dance that evening under the light of lamps hung from tree limbs. Denny slipped a turnip watch from the pocket of her shirt and checked the time, then decided the area around the starting line was getting crowded enough to give her sufficient cover.

She put the watch away, then patted Rocket on the shoulder. "You sure have been a mighty good boy to wait out here like this," she told him. He'd been cropping at the sparse grass under the trees from time to time, although she hadn't allowed him to graze enough to slow him down. "Are you ready to run a little?"

Rocket hadn't given her the least bit of trouble when she'd snuck him out of the barn early that morning, well before dawn. He hadn't shied or spooked when she'd saddled him, and although she hadn't put any weight on his back yet other than the saddle, he'd cooperated perfectly when she led him out to the trees. Maybe he finally had decided that it was best just to let the humans be the boss . . . that particular human, anyway.

Denny tightened her grip on the reins and muttered, "All right. Let's go." She walked out of the trees and headed for the starting area, moving at a brisk clip as she led the mustang. Rocket followed obediently.

She kept her head down but listened for any telltale exclamations of surprise when somebody recognized her. None came, at least that she heard. But there was such a hubbub of music and conversation and laughter in the air that she might have missed it. She risked lifting her gaze to the ranch house for a second and saw her father, Louis, and Brad still standing on the porch, talking and smiling and, in Brad's case, fidgeting.

Denny dropped her head again and turned Rocket

to bring the mustang around in the right direction. Rocket blew out a breath.

He wasn't too happy about being around all the other horses, thought Denny.

It was a mustang's instinct to fight, to seek dominance.

She pulled his head down a little, stroked his nose, and said quietly, "Settle down now, boy."

"Still a mite green, ain't he?"

Without thinking, Denny lifted her head to glance over at the man who had spoken to her. She realized too late that he might be someone who knew her.

Luckily, she had never seen the cowboy before. He was a year or two older than her, she supposed, rangy and rawboned with red hair under his battered old hat. Everything about him had a slightly down-at-heel look except his buckskin horse. If Denny was any judge of horseflesh—and she believed she was—the buckskin was a good saddle mount.

That didn't lessen her annoyance at his presumptuous comment. Keeping her voice low and rough to disguise the fact that she was a young woman, she said, "Hell no, he ain't. He's just fine."

"Sorry," the stranger said. "He seemed a mite skittish to me, like he might want to tear into some of these other horses."

"Don't you worry about that. Just tend to your own business."

"Sure, sure. Don't get a damn burr under your saddle. Hell, I was just tryin' to be friendly."

"I ain't lookin' for friends," Denny said.

"Yeah, I reckon that's mighty clear. That bein' the

case, I won't bother mentionin' that my name's Steve Markham."

Denny put her back to the man and didn't introduce herself. She would have had to come up with a fake name, anyway, so it wouldn't have been a real introduction.

"Fine, go ahead and sull up like an old possum," Markham went on. "It don't matter none to me."

He was one of those hombres in love with the sound of his own voice, Denny decided. She wondered if she could move away from him along the starting line without being too obvious about it. Probably not, because the rest of the riders seemed to be settling down where they wanted to be.

Besides, Smoke was striding in her direction, and Denny knew her father was getting ready to start the race.

"Hate to break it to you," Markham went on, still jabbering, "but I'm gonna win this here race and claim the prize. What is the prize, anyway? I don't reckon I've heard anybody say."

Denny couldn't stop herself from answering. Anything to shut the saddle tramp up. "There isn't any prize. It's just for bragging rights. But you'll get to take in the biggest and best feed anybody's thrown around here in a long time."

"Well, that's somethin', anyway," Markham replied with a grin. He rubbed his belly. "I'm still a growin' boy. Got myself quite an appetite. Who's that fella by the corral? Smoke Jensen, the old outlaw his own self?"

"He's not an outlaw," Denny said hotly. "He was never an outlaw."

Markham held up his hands, palms out defensively, as he continued grasping the buckskin's reins in his right hand. "Hold on, hold on. I didn't mean no harm. It's just that I've always heard about how Smoke Jensen was this gunfightin', hell-raisin' peckerwood. They tell me now he's settled down and become a rancher. This is his spread, ain't it?"

Denny wanted to punch Steve Markham for talking about her father like that, but she couldn't very well give in to the impulse without also giving away her real identity. So she muttered, "Yeah, this is his spread. But he's not an outlaw."

"Fine, whatever you say. All I care about is it looks like he's gettin' ready to start this race, and I'm about ready to show the rest of you my heels when me and my horse run off and leave you in the dust!"

CHAPTER 10

Smoke climbed halfway up the corral fence, standing on one of the rails and holding onto the top one with his left hand to steady himself. He took off his hat with his right hand and waved it in circles above his head to get everyone's attention. When the noise died down, he called out in his powerful voice, "Howdy, everyone, and welcome to the Sugarloaf!"

The crowd responded with cheers, applause, and whistles.

"Thank you for coming here today to help my family celebrate the marriage of my son Louis to Melanie Buckner. We're welcoming two fine folks to the Jensen family today, not only Melanie, but her son Brad!" Smoke held out his hat toward the porch, indicating where Louis and Brad still stood.

Brad waved as the guests yelled and clapped some more.

"Now, in a little while," Smoke went on, "things are going to settle down and we're going to hold the wedding ceremony with all the dignity and reverence it deserves. Marriage is a mighty fine thing, and I ought to know since I've been hitched to the most beautiful woman in the world for a lot of years now!"

"You'd better not start getting too specific about the number of years, Smoke," Louis Longmont called with a grin on his handsome face. "Sally might not appreciate that!"

The good-natured gibe drew plenty of laughter. Smoke waved his hat in acknowledgment of the response, then went on. "After the ceremony, we're all going to have a fine dinner and spend the afternoon visiting with friends. Then, this evening, get ready for plenty of music and dancing in an old-fashioned fandango!"

That brought whoops and applause.

"Before any of that, though, we have another treat for you to celebrate this day," continued Smoke. "Fellas from all over the valley have brought their finest, fastest horses here today to put on a thrilling display of speed and horsemanship! It's a race, folks, and let's hear it for the men and horses who are going to take part!"

Another sweep of his hat indicated the riders arrayed at the starting line. The men hadn't mounted yet, but a sense of anticipation was palpable among them, and among the horses, as well.

"The course is well marked with flags. It's two miles up the valley, then you turn around in front of Elephant Butte and ride two miles back here to where you started. First horse back gets to claim the title of fastest horse in the valley, and I reckon his rider can claim to be the best rider, but we all know it's the horse who does all the real work, right, folks?"

More laughter answered that.

"All right, boys, mount up!" Smoke called. "Keep your eyes on my hat, and when it comes down, that's your signal to take off!"

Denny was about three-fourths of the way along the line between Steve Markham on her left and another cowboy she didn't know on her right, although she thought maybe she had seen that man a time or two in Big Rock. This was the first real test of how Rocket was going to behave, she thought as she lifted her left foot to the stirrup and grasped the saddle horn with both hands. She took a deep breath, held it, and swung up onto Rocket's back.

The black mustang shifted but didn't start bucking. Denny was grateful for that. Under the brim of her hat, she glanced right and left, saw the other riders watching her father up on the corral fence and waiting for his signal to begin the race. She wanted to look, too, but she wasn't going to risk peering directly at him. If he spotted her and recognized her, would he stop the race before it ever started and demand that she drop out? She didn't believe he would make a scene like that on Louis's wedding day, but she didn't want to chance it.

When the others all took off, she would, too. Rocket was fast enough that a split-second delay wouldn't make any difference.

As she settled into the saddle, Markham said from beside her, "Good luck."

"Same to you," she growled, not wanting to be completely rude. She leaned forward as tension gripped her.

"Go!" Smoke shouted.

From the corner of her eye, Denny saw her father's hat sweep down swiftly. She dug her heels into Rocket's flanks, and he took off running straight ahead.

And she had been right, she saw immediately. The slight lag in his start didn't make any difference. Rocket's opening lunge more than made up for it.

He ran easily, cleanly, muscles working smoothly under the sleek black hide. It was as pure a stride as anyone in those parts had ever seen. Over the thunder of hooves, Denny heard the crowd yelling and imagined they were yelling for her and Rocket. Logically, she knew they were just cheering the start of the race, but it felt good, anyway.

As was to be expected, the horses started the race bunched up but quickly began to spread out as the speedier animals moved to the front. Of course, some of the horses back in the pack might be fast, too, and their riders were holding them back, conserving their strength for a stretch run. Denny knew that was the smart thing to do. She wanted to pull Rocket in a little, but he was running so effortlessly with such seeming joy, that she didn't have the heart to do so. Was he strong enough to maintain the pace for the entire length of the race? Denny doubted it and was about to force herself to haul back on the reins when Steve Markham's buckskin swept past her with Markham leaning forward in the saddle, whooping at the top of his lungs.

Denny gritted her teeth and started to urge Rocket to a faster pace instead. She suppressed the impulse at the last moment and followed through on her original plan, slowing the mustang. As Markham pulled away from her, he threw a cocky grin back over his shoulder at her.

Again, that almost ruined Denny's self-control, but she managed to keep a tight rein on her temper as well as on Rocket.

They were in the middle of the pack, with more than a dozen horses ahead of them. They had covered about half the distance to Elephant Butte. Denny could see the huge, hump-backed rock formation looming ahead of them. Bright red flags on stakes that marked the course flashed past them. Another few minutes and they would reach the big, sweeping turn that would take the horses back toward the ranch headquarters.

Denny had seen Cal and Pearlie laying out the course a couple of days earlier. That might have given her a bit of an unfair advantage, she thought, but she wasn't going to worry about it. It wasn't like there were any tricky twists or turns. The whole thing was pretty easy to follow.

She could tell that Rocket wanted to run harder and faster, but she continued holding him in. Once they had made the turn and covered about half of the distance back to the finish line would be the time for them to make their move, she told herself. If she could keep the mustang under control until then.

Up ahead, the frontrunners had reached the turn. They swept around it and headed back in the direction from which they had come. That leg of the course angled in and gradually followed the same route as had led out.

Denny saw Steve Markham ahead of her on the

buckskin. The horse had slowed, but not for the turn, because they hadn't gotten there yet. The buckskin wasn't exactly faltering, but Denny could tell that it was tired. Markham had pushed it too hard. Maybe he had overestimated how much stamina his mount actually had, or maybe he had just allowed his own enthusiasm and overconfidence to get the best of him. Either way, Denny and Rocket were overtaking them, and when Markham glanced back, the dismay on his face showed that he was aware of it.

Denny would have liked to tip her hat to him in a mocking salute as Rocket drew even with and gradually passed the buckskin. She couldn't do that, of course, since her pinned-up hair might come loose and tumble freely around her shoulders, and she didn't want that to happen until she had won the race and could reveal who she was without having to worry about her parents stopping her. She settled for looking over at Markham and touching a finger to her hat brim as she passed him.

Now who was leaving whom in the dust?

Elephant Butte was only a couple of hundred yards away. Denny could see the rock's rough surface rising ahead of her. Off to the right of the butte lay an area of deep, brush-choked gullies, not worth anything as graze, although cows sometimes insisted on getting stuck in them. Denny shifted her grip on the reins as she got ready to steer Rocket into the turn back to the left.

But Rocket didn't turn. Instead the mustang lunged straight on, lowering his head as if he intended to plow right into Elephant Butte. The sudden, unexpected jerk on the reins caused them to slip out of Denny's fingers.

"Rocket!" she cried as she fumbled for the reins but failed to grasp them. "Rocket, stop!"

Rocket didn't heed the order. He was running full-tilt as if nothing in the world could stop him.

And with the butte in front and the gullies to the right, if the mustang didn't stop, disaster was rushing straight toward Denny.

CHAPTER 11

Denny clung tightly to the saddle horn with her right hand while groping for the reins with her left. Finally, she got hold of them, but it didn't do any good. She sawed at the bit in Rocket's mouth, but he ignored the discomfort and continued his headlong plunge toward the butte. It was almost like he intended to punish her for daring to ride him by crashing both of them into the rock.

She knew it wasn't possible for the mustang to be thinking that way. Animals didn't have the capacity for such a spiteful attitude. But even if Rocket was just acting on some crazed instinct, that didn't make the runaway any less dangerous.

Denny had forgotten about the race. At that point, she was just trying to bring Rocket under control again and save both of their lives. The mustang ignored all her efforts and charged toward the butte at dizzying speed.

The rough gray rock, so like the hide of an elephant, loomed in front of them. Denny bit back the scream that tried to well up her throat. She couldn't stop herself from lifting her right arm in front of her face, as if that would offer any real protection.

At the last moment, with the nimbleness of a true mustang, Rocket changed direction, twisting and darting to the right. For a second, Denny's left stirrup brushed against the rock. Then Rocket lit out into the area with the gullies slashing through it.

"Rocket, no!" she cried, but he paid no more attention to that than he did to her efforts to haul back on the reins. The first of the gullies was just a few strides away. She felt Rocket gathering himself underneath her.

Then, with a powerful kick, Rocket leaped into the air and soared over the slash in the earth. Denny couldn't hold back the scream as she clamped her legs to the mustang's sides and held tight to the saddle horn.

Rocket cleared the gully easily and landed with nimble grace. Denny hoped he would stop, but he didn't. He pounded on at full speed toward the next gulch, wider than the first, clearly intending to jump over it, as well. Denny wasn't sure he could make it.

She jerked on the reins, trying futilely to get Rocket to stop. Curses that would have made her mother blanch and gasp in horror spilled out of her mouth. The gully was only about twenty yards away and the brink came closer with each racing stride of the mustang.

Suddenly, from the corner of her eye, Denny saw another rider moving up alongside her on the right. She looked over frantically. Steve Markham was there on his buckskin. Sweat foamed and streamed off the horse's hide as he was obviously running his heart out.

Markham leaned toward her and held his left arm out. "Come on!" he shouted over the thundering hoofbeats. "You gotta get off of there!"

Denny didn't want to. She didn't want to give up on bringing Rocket under her control again, and she didn't want her life being saved by Steve Markham. But that was what it was quickly coming down to—life or death—so she didn't really have any choice. She kicked her feet free of the stirrups and leaned toward him. His arm went around her and closed tightly on her torso. As the buckskin veered away, Markham lifted Denny off the saddle and held her against him.

He slowed the buckskin as he turned away from the gully. Denny writhed loose and dropped to the ground, stumbling when she landed. She tried to catch her balance but failed. She wound up sprawling on the ground. From where she lay, she saw Rocket come to an immediate skidding halt ten feet from the gully. He turned and gave her a disdainful look.

Denny scrambled up and charged at the mustang. She yanked her hat off and started swatting at him as she yelled, "You loco crazyman! Were you trying to kill both of us?"

Rocket shied away from the blows, snorted angrily, and reared up. His front hooves pawed at the air. An arm went around Denny again, this time from behind, and jerked her away from the rearing horse.

"Looks like you're the one who's tryin' to get killed," Markham said as he held on to her. "Quit swattin' that dang horse!" He had dismounted and run up behind her. His arm was clamped around her torso at

66   *William W. Johnstone*

the bottom of her breasts, and even though she had bound them before donning the shirt she wore, he could probably feel the sort of bulges he wouldn't expect to find on a cowboy's chest.

As if that wasn't bad enough, her hair had come loose when she yanked her hat off and was swirling around her shoulders as she struggled. Given all that, if he hadn't figured out that she was a girl, he had to be pretty damned stupid, she thought. She writhed and twisted and jerked free of his grip, stumbling again as she pulled away from him, but she didn't fall.

Rocket had settled down and stood a few yards away looking amused. He was sweaty from the hard run, too, although his sides weren't heaving the way Markham's buckskin was.

"Leave me alone!" Denny cried, not bothering to disguise her voice anymore.

"If I'd done that, you'd likely be dead now," Markham responded.

Denny waved a hand toward Rocket and said, "He wasn't going to try to make that jump."

"Maybe not, but if you'd still been on him when he stopped short like that, you'd have gone flyin' off and fallen into that gully, more than likely. That horse is a killer."

"No, he's not!" Denny cried. "He's just . . . high-spirited." That sounded ridiculous even to her.

Rocket might make a good horse someday, but as Rafael had said, that day wasn't there yet and might not ever come.

"Well, because of him, we've done lost the race, no doubt about that," said Markham. "And ol' Buck"—he turned toward his horse—"poor ol' Buck may not ever be the same. I hope I didn't run the heart plumb out of him."

"I'm sorry about that," Denny called after him as he started striding toward the buckskin. "I hope he's all right."

Markham rubbed the horse's nose and patted his shoulder as the buckskin continued breathing hard.

Denny followed him and asked, "Is there anything I can do?"

"Reckon you've done enough, ma'am," Markham replied without looking around at her.

"I'm not a ma'am," Denny said out of habit.

"Who are you, then?"

"Denise Nicole Jensen."

That was enough to make him look around. "Jensen," he repeated. "Any relation to Smoke Jensen?"

"He's my father," Denny said tautly.

Markham stared at her for a moment, then let out a bray of laughter and slapped his thigh. "And here I was, goin' on about how he was an outlaw! Reckon I'm lucky you didn't kick me in the shins."

"I felt more like punching you in the face."

"Then I really *am* lucky," he said as he turned back to the buckskin. "I think maybe ol' Buck here is gonna be all right."

"I hope so," Denny said. "I mean that."

Markham nodded. "I know you do."

Both of them looked around at the sound of approaching hoofbeats. A couple of riders were headed toward them. Denny recognized Cal and Pearlie. The Sugarloaf's foreman and former foreman reined in and stared at her.

"Dadgum, Miss Denny," exclaimed Pearlie, "when

some of the fellas in the race said a couple of riders looked like they was in trouble, I didn't figure one of 'em would be you!"

"Are you all right?" Cal asked.

"I'm fine," Denny assured them.

Pearlie's eyes narrowed as he looked at Rocket. "I'm guessin' that dang mustang had something to do with the trouble."

"He ran away with Miss Jensen," Markham said. "Luckily, I was able to lend a hand before they both piled up in one of these gullies."

"Who are you, mister?" Cal wanted to know.

"Name's Markham. Steve Markham. I was ridin' in the race." He gave a rueful laugh. "Reckon I can forget about winnin' it, though. By now most of the other fellas are probably back at the finish line."

"Yeah, the race is just about over. I'm glad you came along and saved the lady's life, though."

"Wait just a doggone minute," Denny objected. "I never said he saved my life. I would have gotten Rocket under control again."

Markham cocked his head to the side. "That ain't quite the way it looked to me."

"Well . . . well . . . you don't know what might have happened!"

"Neither do we," Cal said, "but you're alive and that's all that matters. What in the world were you doing riding in this race, though, Miss Denny? Do Smoke and Miss Sally know about this?"

Pearlie rested his hands on his saddle horn, leaned forward, and grinned as he said, "I'd bet a brand-new hat that they don't."

"That's not important," Denny said with a wave of

her hand. "I guess we'd better get back. People may be starting to worry."

"Yeah, I reckon," said Pearlie. "I'll catch that mustang and lead him back, Cal. Miss Denny can ride double with you."

"Or with me," Steve Markham suggested.

Denny just snorted at that idea and reached up to grasp the hand that Cal extended to her. He took his foot out of the stirrup and she used it to help her swing up behind him. They rode back toward the ranch headquarters with Markham coming along slowly behind them, leading the buckskin.

CHAPTER 12

After starting the race, Smoke went back to the ranch house's front porch where he found that Sally had come out of the house and joined Louis and Brad there.

"How's Melanie doing?" Smoke asked his wife.

"She's fine," Sally replied. "Very nervous and excited, of course."

"But she's not getting cold feet," Louis added. "I'm very happy about that."

Brad frowned, looked up at him, and asked, "Why would her feet get cold? The weather's warm, and she's wearing shoes, isn't she?"

Sally laughed and put a hand on his shoulder. "That's just a figure of speech, Brad. It means that someone who's about to get married decides not to."

"Well, she'd better not," declared the boy. "I know she's my ma and all, but she'd be a durned fool to back out now."

Smoke couldn't help but chuckle, which drew a faint look of disapproval from Sally. He patted Brad's other shoulder and said, "Don't worry. Your ma's a smart woman."

"I always thought so."

Sally turned to Smoke and went on. "There's one thing that has *me* a little worried, though. Denise isn't up in Melanie's room. Melanie said she hasn't seen her all day. Where could she be, Smoke?"

"I don't know, but I'm betting she'll turn up soon."

Smoke was telling the truth about that. He *didn't* know exactly where Denny was, right that minute, but he had a hunch she would be around again . . . when the horse race was over.

"I'm always a little concerned when someone's not where they're supposed to be. I mean, she could have been *kidnapped* or something. You know how many enemies you have, Smoke."

"I know, but I don't think any of them would be bold enough to try staging a kidnapping in the middle of this many people."

Louis said, "This crowd might actually be a good cover for some sort of nefarious activity—"

"You're not helping, son," Smoke said.

Before the discussion of Denny's whereabouts could continue, one of the guests shouted, "Here they come!"

Other enthusiastic cries went up as the leading riders in the race thundered back toward the starting line, which had become the finish line. Smoke, Sally, Louis, and Brad turned to watch. They would have a good view of the race's conclusion from the porch, and it was liable to be a thrilling one.

As the riders came into sight, Smoke noted that several in the lead were neck and neck, leaning forward in their saddles and straining to get that last little bit of speed out of their mounts, that extra push that would gain them the victory. Crowds of spectators lined both sides of the course as well as being gathered well beyond the finish line so the horses would have plenty of room to stop. Some of the Sugarloaf hands who weren't taking part in the race had been charged with keeping the course clear and guests out of harm's way.

The horses charged down the final stretch. A couple faltered, having reached the last of their strength. Three surged ahead, two chestnuts and a roan. At the very last second, the roan extended to a seemingly impossible length and beat the other two animals by a nose. A huge cheer went up as the victor and the other horses right behind swept across the finish line.

Smoke joined in the applause for the winner, but a slight frown creased his forehead. He had expected to see a black mustang among the leaders with a familiar figure in the saddle, but there was no sign of such a horse—or rider. He waited as more of the racers arrived at the finish line and joined the crowd milling around but still didn't see who he was expecting to see.

A faint worry began to nag at him. He had been convinced that Denny had slipped out of the house early, spirited Rocket out of the barn, and planned to ride the mustang in the race, probably disguising herself as a cowboy in order to do it without being discovered. He knew that was *exactly* the sort of thing his headstrong daughter would do.

Calvin Woods came to the bottom of the porch steps and lifted his voice above the hubbub to say, "I need to talk to you for a minute, Smoke."

"Trouble?" Smoke asked. He knew his foreman quite well and could see the concern in Cal's eyes.

Cal shook his head "Probably not. Just something that needs to be looked into."

Smoke went down the steps and gave Cal a nod. "Go ahead."

"Some of the fellas who were in the race are saying that a couple of horses went off the course out by Elephant Butte. Said that one of them looked like it might've been a runaway, and the fella on the other horse went after it trying to help."

"There's some rough country out there," Smoke said as his frown deepened.

"I know. A runaway could fall or even go sailing off into one of those gullies. I was thinking I could take Pearlie and go have a look, just in case somebody needs a hand."

"I'll come with you—" Smoke began.

"No need for you to do that," Cal said. "This is a big day, and you need to spend it here with your family. If there's a problem, Pearlie and I can take care of it."

Smoke knew that was true, but what Cal didn't know was that if Smoke's hunch was right, part of his family might be out there by Elephant Butte, maybe hurt or even worse.

Smoke drew in a breath. He wasn't going to allow himself to think that. Cal was right. Sally was liable to be upset if he stampeded off like he wanted to. He forced himself to nod and say, "All right, you and Pearlie go check it out. Just let me know what you find."

"Sure, Smoke."

Cal started to turn away, but Smoke stopped him.

"Those fellas who were talking about the runaway . . . did they describe the horse?"

"Not to me," Cal answered.

Smoke nodded again and waved him on.

"What was that about?" Sally asked when Smoke had gone back up the steps to the porch.

"Nothing to worry about," Smoke said, hoping he was right.

The minutes dragged by while Smoke waited for Cal and Pearlie to return with news.

He was a little distracted by everything else that was going on, including the moment when the young cowboy who had won the race was brought over and introduced to him.

"Name's Jim Gale, Mr. Jensen," the man said as he shook hands with Smoke. "It's a plumb pleasure to meet you."

"Same here, Jim," said Smoke as he managed to put his worry over Denny aside for a moment. "That roan of yours is mighty fast."

"Yes, sir, he sure is."

"If you happen to be looking for a riding job . . ."

"I'm obliged to you, sir," the young man said, "but I have a spread of my own up at the far end of the valley. Got some beeves but raise mostly horses."

Smoke clapped a hand on Gale's shoulder. "If that roan is an example of the sort of stock you raise, son, you're going to do just fine. In fact, next time you're ready to sell some off, come and see me first. I'll pay you a good price."

Gale grinned. "I'll sure do that, Mr. Jensen."

With his hand still on Gale's shoulder, Smoke

turned the cowboy to face the crowd and said, "Let's hear it for him, folks! The big winner!"

Whoops, whistles, and shouts filled the air.

"Everyone keep on enjoying your visit," Smoke went on. "We'll be having the wedding ceremony in a little while, and then all the food will be brought out and ready a short time after that."

As the crowd in front of the ranch house broke up somewhat, Sally came to Smoke's side "It's all going well, isn't it?"

"So far," Smoke agreed, even though he wasn't completely convinced of that. He kept glancing in the direction of Elephant Butte, even though he couldn't see the rock formation from where he was. After several more minutes, he stiffened as he caught sight of a familiar rider. He had no trouble recognizing how Cal sat the saddle.

Someone was riding double with Cal. As Smoke caught a glimpse of sunlight on thick blond hair over the foreman's shoulder, he felt relief wash through him, followed by a sense of vindication that his hunch had been right.

He looked past Cal and spotted Pearlie riding about fifty yards behind, also with a second rider. Pearlie was leading two horses, a nondescript buckskin— and the sleek black devil of a mustang called Rocket.

Sally's hand suddenly tightened on his arm. "Smoke, is that Denny riding with Cal?"

"It sure is," he replied, and now that he could tell Denny appeared to be all right, he was looking forward to hearing what she had to say for herself.

CHAPTER 13

Cal didn't say much on the way back to the ranch house, and Denny didn't go out of her way to make conversation. He probably didn't know what to say and wanted to stay out of whatever ruckus developed between Denny and her parents. Cal might have been impulsive when he was young, even reckless at times, but he had grown into a sensible man.

Hearing Pearlie and Steve Markham talking behind them, Denny looked over her shoulder and saw that Markham was riding double with the former foreman. He had offered to let her ride with him, but she wouldn't have done that even if his horse hadn't been exhausted. She was glad to see that he was leading the valiant animal instead of riding.

Pearlie also had hold of a lead rope tied to Rocket's reins. The mustang came along peacefully, as if he'd never wanted anything other than to be docile and cooperative. Damn devil was snickering at her, thought Denny. She wanted to take a two-by-four and wallop him between the eyes just to get his attention and let him know that what he'd done wasn't the least bit funny.

She wouldn't do that, of course. She loved animals and had never mistreated one.

A lot of cheering and applause came from the crowd gathered at the house. Cal said, "Smoke must be congratulating the winner of the race. I know he planned to do that." He turned his head a little toward Denny. "You figured that would be you, didn't you?"

"It would have been," she said through clenched teeth, "if that mustang hadn't gone loco."

"He didn't *go* loco. He always has been. Rafael told you that."

"I thought he liked me. I thought he'd be willing to cooperate with me."

"Horses have minds of their own. Every day's a new day for them, too."

She knew what he meant by that. The way a horse behaved one day might not be the way he acted the next day—at all.

"I'm just glad you weren't hurt," Cal went on. "It's a good thing that fella Markham was around."

"I'd have been fine without him," Denny snapped.

"Uh-huh."

Her jaw clenched angrily at that dry retort, but she didn't say anything. She had enough to worry about knowing that in a few minutes she'd be facing her parents.

The crowd had spread out some by the time Cal rode up to the porch. Smoke and Sally had seen them coming and were standing there with Louis and Brad. Denny could tell by her mother's expression that Sally was angry.

With Smoke, it was harder to tell. He wasn't happy,

Denny decided, but maybe he wasn't all that upset, either.

"Young lady, what were you thinking?" Sally demanded as Cal reined to a stop and Denny slid down to the ground.

Her chin jutted out defiantly as she replied, "That I'm just as good a rider—or better—than anybody else in that race, and I deserved a shot at winning it."

"By taking a chance on getting yourself killed?"

Smoke said, "What happened, Denny? Did Rocket run away with you?"

She hesitated but knew there was no point in lying. "That's right. He had run a really good race up to that point. He'd done everything I asked of him. Then all of a sudden he . . . he . . ."

"Did what *he* wanted to do," Smoke finished for her. "The mustang blood is strong in him. He may act like he's tamed sometimes, but he's not. He's just biding his time until he gets a chance to go wild again."

Denny frowned. "He had the chance today. After I was off of him, he could have run away. Nobody would have been able to stop him. He could have vanished into the hills and maybe we never would have seen him again. But he didn't. He stayed there close by, like he didn't want to leave me."

"There you go again," Louis said, "giving an animal human feelings. It doesn't work that way, Denny."

"I reckon I know more about animals than you do," she told her brother coldly. "I've spent a lot more time outdoors working with them than you have."

She saw the flash of hurt in Louis's eyes and instantly regretted the harsh words. But he hadn't been very careful of her feelings, either, so she told herself not to worry about it.

"Did that horse throw you?" asked Sally, concern overcoming her irritation. "Are you hurt?"

Denny shook her head. "No, I'm all right. I wasn't thrown."

"How'd you stop him after he bolted?" Smoke asked.

Denny hesitated. She didn't want to answer that question, but a glance over her shoulder told her that Pearlie was approaching with Steve Markham riding double with him. She couldn't see any way to avoid spilling the truth.

"One of the other riders helped me," she said. "He managed to catch up to me and lifted me out of the saddle before Rocket ran into one of those gullies. Then Rocket stopped as soon as I was off his back."

Smoke nodded toward Pearlie and Markham and said, "I'll bet you're talking about that hombre right there."

"That's right."

"Don't reckon I know him." Smoke let those words hang in the air meaningfully as Pearlie brought his horse to a stop in front of the porch.

Denny gritted her teeth again for a second, then took a deep breath and said, "Pa, this is Steve Markham."

"Mr. Markham," Smoke called. "I understand you gave my daughter a hand out there. Thank you."

With that annoying grin on his face, Markham jumped to the ground and took the buckskin's lead rope from Pearlie. "Why, it was a plumb pleasure, Mr. Jensen. I reckon you *are* Smoke Jensen?"

"That's right." Smoke went down the steps and

extended his hand to shake with the cowboy. "I'm glad to meet you." Inclining his head toward the porch, he went on. "That's Mrs. Jensen up there, our son Louis, and our soon-to-be grandson Brad."

Markham nodded. "Howdy, folks." He snatched his hat off his head and held it to his chest as he bowed a little to Sally. "Mrs. Jensen, you got a lovely home here and I purely do appreciate you openin' it up for folks to come and celebrate with you today."

"Well . . ." Sally's tense mood softened slightly at Markham's charming manner. "It's an occasion worth celebrating, don't you think?"

"I sure do. Congratulations there, Louis, if you don't mind me callin' you that. I ain't never been hitched my own self, but I hear that holy matrimony is a plumb blissful state."

Denny wanted to take her hat off and start whaling him over the head with it. Anything to shut up his silver-tongued blather. And her family was falling for it, too! Next thing you knew, her mother would be inviting Markham to sit at the same table as them once dinner was served.

"Mr. Markham," Smoke said, "thank you again for helping Denny." A thoughtful expression crossed his face. "You wouldn't happen to be looking for a riding job, would you?"

Denny wanted to yell *No!*

Markham scratched his chin and said, "Well, as a matter of fact, I ain't lined up any employment since I rode into this valley yesterday."

"That young fella there is Calvin Woods, my foreman. Talk to him later. Tomorrow, maybe, once things have settled down a mite."

"I'll sure do that," Markham replied with a nod.

Smoke fixed Denny with an intent look. "You and I are going to have a talk, too, but not now."

"And that includes me," added Sally. "Right now, though, Denise, I want you to go inside, wash the dust off your face, and get dressed for the wedding. For goodness' sake, you're supposed to be Melanie's maid of honor! How were you going to do that in . . . in boots and jeans?"

Denny didn't bother explaining that she'd always planned to clean up and change clothes after winning the race. There was time for that.

Of course, as the maid of honor, she should have been there to help Melanie this morning, she knew, and she felt a significant twinge of guilt because she hadn't been. Melanie had other friends, though, who would have shown up to assist her with her hair and dress and whatever else needed to be taken care of.

"I'm sorry," Denny muttered as she went up the steps. She glanced at her brother and added, "I'm sorry, Louis."

"Just go ahead and get ready," he told her. He summoned up a smile. "It's all right."

She returned the smile gratefully and went into the house as she heard her father telling Cal to take Rocket back to the stable.

"Put Markham's buckskin in there, too, and see that it's taken care of," Smoke added.

The screen door banged behind Denny, and rapid footsteps sounded as Brad hurried to catch up to her. "Are you in trouble?" he asked as he looked up at her.

"Not really," she told him. "At least, I don't think so."

"I knew what you were gonna do. As soon as I saw

you out in the barn with Rocket last night, I said to myself, 'I bet Denny's gonna sneak him out and ride him in the race today.'"

She paused and looked down at him. "You did, did you?"

"Yep."

"But you didn't say anything to anybody?"

His eyes widened and he exclaimed, "Gosh, I wouldn't do that. You can trust me, Denny."

"Good. And I'm glad you stopped calling me Aunt Denise!"

CHAPTER 14

A large shady area under some trees served as the site of the wedding ceremony. Chairs were set up for family and close friends, and the others in attendance stood in two large groups around the location, with a path in between for Melanie to walk, accompanied by Brad and followed by Denny as maid of honor. Louis waited under the trees with Smoke, his best man, and Walter Cordell, the minister from the Baptist church in Big Rock who would perform the ceremony.

As Louis shifted around a little, Smoke smiled and said quietly, "Are your feet getting a little chilly now, son?"

"No, not at all," Louis replied without hesitation. "Melanie is wonderful, and I'm convinced that marrying her is the best thing I've ever done. I just don't like waiting, you know? I'm ready to get on with it."

As if taking a cue from what he'd said, the Big Rock town band struck up the chords of the "Wedding March." Unlike some small-town bands, these musicians were actually pretty talented and well-rehearsed, and Smoke thought the song sounded good.

When the music started, everyone turned to look. Melanie had started from the house with Brad walking beside her, his arm linked with hers, and a bouquet of colorful flowers in her hands. She wore a cream-colored gown with no veil and looked absolutely lovely with a serene smile on her face.

Louis swallowed hard and stood up straighter as he watched his bride coming toward him.

Denny, looking unusually feminine in a sky-blue gown, followed Melanie. Nobody would have guessed that half an hour earlier she'd been dressed in range clothes and covered with trail dust from the race. The sort of transformations that ladies could make in such short periods of time never failed to astound Smoke. He glanced over at Sally, saw how she was beaming with happiness, and his heart warmed at the sight. Hardship and danger had played such large parts in their lives that it was good to witness moments of peace and happiness.

Then Louis stepped forward to position himself beside Melanie as she came to a stop and turned to hand the bouquet to Denny. The ceremony was underway.

For being such momentous occasions, weddings didn't really take very long. Louis and Melanie's concluded with the usual promptness, and it seemed to Smoke that barely any time had passed before Louis and Melanie had said "I do" and the preacher was telling Louis that he could kiss his bride. Cheers went up as he did exactly that.

As the band played again, the newly married couple went back down the aisle between the groups of applauding spectators.

Smoke put his arm around Sally's shoulders as she leaned against him. "Well, they did it."

"And it was a beautiful ceremony," she replied.

The whole thing had seemed pretty cut-and-dried to Smoke, but then, he wasn't a woman. And if he was being really honest, there had been a moment or two during the ceremony when he'd felt a little emotional tightness in his throat. Life had not been easy—all too often, in fact, it had been fraught with potential disaster—but his family had come through it all, was still together, and was even growing with the addition of two new members. With maybe more to come in the future . . .

That thought made him glance around and find Denny, who stood with her hands clasped in front of her as she smiled after Louis and Melanie. He couldn't help but think that maybe someday he would get to walk her down the aisle like that, to where some fine young man was waiting for her.

He frowned slightly as he realized that he hadn't seen Brice Rogers at all today. Everybody in the valley had been invited to the wedding and the accompanying festivities. Smoke wondered if Brice had chosen not to attend, or if his duties as a deputy U.S. marshal had him busy elsewhere. He would ask Monte Carson about that later, Smoke decided.

"I reckon we've got a feast to get started on now," he said.

Sally nodded. "That's right." She came up on her toes and kissed his cheek. "I need to get busy."

"Anything I can help you with?"

"Just make sure everyone's having a good time. I'll let them know when all the food is ready."

Smoke grinned. He knew what that meant. Sally would ring the iron triangle hanging on the porch, just like she was calling the ranch hands in for a meal.

She hurried off, leaving Smoke to amble back to the ranch house and climb the steps to the porch. Louis Longmont and Monte Carson joined him there. Louis offered them cigars, and even though Smoke wasn't much of one for using the things, he accepted on the special occasion.

When the three of them were puffing on the cheroots, Monte said, "That was a mighty fine ceremony, Smoke."

"Got the job done, anyway, I expect."

"Melanie is a beautiful young woman," said Louis. "The young man is very fortunate."

Smoke grinned. "He's always had an eye for a pretty girl . . . sort of like the fella he's named after."

"Speaking of pretty girls," Monte said, "Denny looks mighty nice today."

"You mean since she cleaned up after that horse race."

"I saw her when she rode in with Cal," Louis said. "What was that all about?"

Smoke explained about the near-debacle to his friends, which made both of them laugh.

"Miss Denny's got a mind of her own, I don't reckon anybody could argue with that," the sheriff said. "But sooner or later some fella will come along and figure out how to tame her down a mite, I'll wager."

Smoke wasn't sure he wanted that. Denny would be happier if she found somebody who could accept her as she was and not try to change her too much. Although it would be all right if she had a fella who'd rein in some of her more reckless impulses . . . He blew out a gray cloud from the cigar and said, "I was just thinking about Brice Rogers a little while ago. He and Denny sometimes seem like there's a spark there."

Monte grunted. "And sometimes it seems like they're at each other's throats."

Smoke shrugged in acceptance of that point, then went on. "I haven't seen him here today."

"He got a wire from the chief marshal in Denver a couple of days ago that sent him off on the trail of some federal fugitive," Monte explained. "He said he planned to be here for the wedding if he got back in time, but he didn't really expect to. I guess he didn't."

"He seems to be pretty devoted to his duty."

Monte nodded. "He's a good lawman. Better than what I expected when he was assigned to this area, him being as young as he is."

Louis smiled and asked, "Are you thinking about playing matchmaker, Smoke?"

"No, sir," Smoke answered without hesitation. "I'd rather face down a whole gang of owlhoots than get mixed up in Denny's love life." He put the cigar in his mouth, clenched his teeth on it so that it stuck out at a jaunty angle, and added, "I'll leave it up to her mother to do that!"

CHAPTER 15

Denny supposed her father had really meant it when he said they would talk about Rocket, the race, and everything else later. She sat with her family at dinner, and not a word was said about any of that . . . for which she was grateful, since this was Louis and Melanie's day, and she didn't want to ruin it for them. That had never been her intention.

There was enough food for an army, which was good because that was sort of what had shown up at the Sugarloaf. Big Rock had to be almost empty. The same was true for the rest of the valley. Everyone seemed to be having a wonderful time, and the level of noise in the air remained high as the guests ate, drank, and visited with one another.

After the meal, Sally, Denny, and a number of volunteers from among the guests cleaned up, but the tables and chairs the ranch hands had set up remained in place so people could sit and talk.

Denny was walking around when she saw Brad sitting by himself at one of the tables. "Hey, kid," she said as she took one of the empty chairs beside him.

"What are you doing? Why aren't you with your mother and Louis?"

"Everybody keeps coming up to them and shaking Louis's hand and telling them congratulations. It's boring."

"Yeah, I can see how you might get tired of that after a while."

His expression brightened as he suggested, "Why don't we go out to the stable and see how the horses are doing? I reckon Rocket's back in his stall by now."

"That da—darn mustang! I don't care how he's doing."

"I'll bet you don't mean that. He ran really fast out there in the race, didn't he?"

"He did," Denny admitted. "We would have won if he hadn't gone loco."

"Yeah, I'm sure you would have. So why don't we go see him?"

Denny gestured at the elegant, expensive gown she wore. "I'm not exactly dressed for clomping around in a barn." She lifted a foot shod in a lightweight slipper. "And if I stepped in anything with these on, my mother wouldn't be happy."

Brad sighed and shook his head. "All right. If you want to be a *girl* about it."

A new voice said, "I don't reckon Miss Denny can be anything else, son, and a mighty pretty girl, at that."

She looked up and around and stiffened as she saw Steve Markham standing there.

"Who are you?" Brad wanted to know.

"Name's Steve." The cowboy stuck out his hand. "And I know you. You're the young fella whose ma married Miss Denny's brother a while ago."

"That's right. I'm Brad Buckner." He shook hands with Markham like a grown-up. "Pleased to meet you, Steve."

"Likewise." Markham looked at Denny and commented, "The two of you seem to be hittin' it off pretty good."

"Brad and I are old friends," she explained coolly.

Without being invited to, Markham pulled out one of the chairs, reversed and straddled it. "I'm hopin' you and me will get to be friends, too, especially if I go to work here on the Sugarloaf. Your pa offered me a ridin' job, you know."

"Not exactly. He told you to talk to Cal about it. As far as I know, we haven't been hiring any new hands lately, so I wouldn't get my hopes up if I were you."

Markham chuckled. "Reckon I've always got my hopes up. It's just my nature. And speakin' of which . . . I hope that once the *baile* starts tonight, you'll do me the honor of sharin' one of the dances with me, even though I got to warn you I ain't what anybody would call nimble-footed."

Denny reached over and linked her arm with Brad's. "Sorry, but all my dances are promised to my new nephew here."

"What?" Brad exclaimed. He hurriedly extricated his arm. "I'm not gonna spend all evening dancin' with a *girl*."

"You'll feel different in a few years, pard," Markham told him. "I can promise you that." He turned his attention back to Denny. "I reckon that means your dance card is wide open . . ."

"Not hardly." She stood up. "Come on, Brad. Let's go out to the stable and look at the horses."

"But I thought you said—"

"Never mind what I said. Come on."

Brad looked at Markham and rolled his eyes, which made the grin on the cowboy's face get even wider. Denny saw that and tamped down the irritation she felt. She motioned for Brad to follow her and started toward the barn.

When he caught up to her, he said, "You don't like that fella, do you?"

"He just gets on my nerves."

"He's the one who saved you when Rocket ran away with you, isn't he?"

"He didn't . . . well, yeah, sort of . . . But that doesn't mean he and I are friends, and it sure as he— heck doesn't mean I want to dance with him."

"I didn't mean to hurt your feelings when I said I didn't want to dance with you, Denny. I really don't mind . . . I guess."

She put a hand on his shoulder and said, "Don't worry about it, kid. I don't need you to rescue me from Steve Markham. I can handle varmints like that myself."

"Pearlie says sometimes you have to shoot varmints."

Denny grunted. "Let's hope it doesn't come to that."

CHAPTER 16

Some of the guests headed back to their homes, either in Big Rock or on one of the other spreads in the valley, after the meal was over, but most stayed to enjoy the rest of the day and some would even spend the night.

Youngsters organized games or just chased each other around, squealing happily, while the grown-ups sat at the tables or stood in the shade under the trees as they caught up with their friends on everything that had happened since the last time they had seen each other. Births, deaths, other marriages, good roundups and bad, all were topics of great interest.

Clouds of pipe and cigar smoke filled the air above some of the groups as the men hashed out the country's problems and what the government ought to do about them. The weather was also a popular subject. It had been good lately, mighty good, but everybody figured that couldn't last. It was probably going to be a hot, dry summer.

By the middle of the afternoon, some of the kids had gotten sleepy and crawled into the backs of wagons to take naps. More than one adult stifled a yawn and wished that he or she could follow the example of those young'uns. A siesta sounded like a mighty good idea.

Smoke, Sally, Louis, and Melanie sat in cane-bottom chairs on the front porch. Later, Louis and Melanie would be leaving in a buggy bound for town, where they would spend their wedding night at the Big Rock Hotel before catching a train for Chicago the next morning. Their plans called for them to spend a couple of weeks on a wedding trip that would also include visits to Philadelphia and New York. Brad would remain on the Sugarloaf while they were gone.

In the late afternoon, ranch hands under Cal's direction began hanging lanterns from tree limbs and along the awning over the porch that ran around three sides of the main house. Fiddle players rosined up their bows, and guitar pickers tuned and tightened strings. The sleepy respite was ending, and the buzz of anticipation for the evening's festivities began rising. Louis and Melanie would have the first dance, of course, but then they would slip away and everyone else would join in.

Smoke left the others on the porch to go talk to Cal and Pearlie. He told them, "Keep your eyes open this evening. I imagine there'll be some cowboys passing around flasks, and I don't want things to get out of hand."

"You're right about that," said Pearlie. "Wouldn't surprise me none if some of the boys are a mite snockered already from sneakin' sips of that Who-hit-John."

"As long as they don't get carried away, that's fine," Smoke said. "I just don't want any brawls breaking out."

"We'll keep the lid on, Smoke, don't worry about that," Cal promised.

"Say, earlier I told that fella Markham to talk to you about a riding job."

"Do you want me to hire him?" asked Cal.

Smoke said, "That's up to you. Yeah, he helped Denny when she'd gotten herself in trouble, but that doesn't mean he'd make a good hand. I trust your judgment, Cal. If you think there's anything off about him, just tell him that we're not hiring anybody right now."

"Speakin' of that . . ." Pearlie began.

Smoke looked at his old friend. "What is it?"

"You know that young fella rode back in with me from Elephant Butte. After I caught that Rocket hoss, I started back in this direction and came across him trudgin' along and leadin' his horse. Figured it wouldn't hurt to let him ride double with me."

Smoke nodded, knowing that Pearlie had to proceed at his own rate in revealing whatever he was thinking.

"Well, we talked some, of course, and he seemed like a mighty friendly sort. Wanted me to tell him some about Miss Denny, but I sorta steered clear of that. Didn't want to talk out of turn, you know."

Cal didn't have the same sort of patience that Smoke did. "Are you getting to a point here, Pearlie? Was there something about Markham you didn't like?"

"Nope, not at all," Pearlie answered without hesitation. "Seems like a plumb friendly fella. It's just that somehow he looks familiar to me. I'm pretty darned sure we ain't ever met before, but when I look at him, it seems like he oughta be somebody I know. He ain't, though."

"He's not that distinctive," Smoke said with a shrug. "Just another young cowboy."

"Yeah, I reckon. It just struck me as sorta odd, and I ain't been able to shake the feelin'."

Cal nodded and said, "I'll keep that in mind when I talk to him tomorrow. Maybe ask him a few questions and see if I get straight answers."

Smoke clapped a hand on the foreman's shoulder. "That sounds like a good idea. Let me know what you decide about him, Cal."

As Smoke headed back toward the house, he saw the very man they'd been talking about. Steve Markham was walking toward the trees, and he looked like a man on a mission.

"I've come to claim that dance, Miss Denny."

She turned around, not the least bit surprised to see Steve Markham standing there. At least he'd been polite enough to take his hat off before he spoke to her, but he still had that cocky grin on his face.

Denny had been talking to a few girls from Big Rock with whom she was acquainted. They laughed at Markham's forthright proclamation, and one of them said, "We'll see you later, Denny."

"Wait!" she said. "You don't have to—"

It was too late. They were already walking away, laughing and talking among themselves.

Blowing out an exasperated breath, Denny turned

back to Markham and said, "The dancing hasn't even started yet. It won't until my brother and his wife have had their first dance together. And I don't recall promising you a dance at all, Mr. Markham."

"Call me Steve," he suggested. "And I reckon you'll find that I'm a persistent cuss, Miss Denny. As soon as I laid eyes on you . . . well, as soon as I figured out you was a gal, anyway, and not some cowhand . . . I said to myself that there was a gal I'd plumb admire to have a dance with, even though, like I've said, I ain't much of a dancer. Or more 'n one dance, even. I'd fill up your dance card if I could, but if I did that, your feet 'd probably be pretty sore from gettin' stepped on before the evenin' was over. I'm hopin' I can make these ol' clodhoppers of mine do like they're supposed to for one dance. I'll do my dead level best, I can promise you that."

Denny narrowed her eyes at him. "I was starting to wonder how long you could go on without taking a breath."

His grin took on a sheepish cast. "I do ramble a mite sometimes, don't I? I reckon that comes from ridin' by myself so much. If I didn't talk, I wouldn't have nobody to listen to."

Denny looked at him for a moment and then finally nodded. "One dance. Will that satisfy you?"

"Well, I don't know about satisfied"—he held up a hand quickly when her look started to turn to a glare—"but I reckon I can make do just fine, thanks. And I really do appreciate your kindness."

"The dancing should be starting soon. You can have the first one with me—"

"It's a plumb honor, that's what it is."

"And we can get this over with," Denny finished. When she saw the slightly crestfallen look on his face, she thought maybe she was being a little too harsh. But he was so sure of himself that he annoyed her, whether that was his intention or not.

Markham hung around, yammering about things that Denny barely paid attention to as the light in the sky faded and the warm yellow glow from the lanterns grew stronger. A quartet of cowboy musicians climbed onto the porch and warmed up for a while.

Smoke greeted them and said, "Len, Bob, Tim, Hugh, are you boys ready?"

"We sure are, Smoke," one of the young punchers answered. He looked at the others and grinned. "Hit it, boys."

The music welled up as Louis took Melanie's hand and led her down the steps. Taking her in his arms, they began sweeping gracefully around the open area in front of the house while everyone looked on in respectful silence. After a few minutes, they paused and Louis lifted an arm to wave the crowd forward as he called, "Friends, please, join us!"

Over under the trees, Markham said to Denny, "Dang, that's sweet. It's gettin' me all misty-eyed."

Denny took his big, rough hand and said, "Oh, come on. If you're determined to dance with me."

"I durned sure am," he said as he clapped his hat on with his other hand and they joined the crowd filling up the open ground.

Despite what Markham had said about being clumsy, he was actually a decent dancer, Denny found. He moved well, had no trouble leading, and after a few wary moments, she wasn't really worried about her toes getting stepped on.

"You're doing all right," she said grudgingly.

"That must be because I got the best dance partner there ever was."

"You don't have to keep flattering me, you know. I'm already dancing with you."

"It ain't flattery. I'm just tellin' it the way it seems to me. Between that good music them boys are playin', and havin' you in my arms to inspire me, Miss Denny, this is the best I ever danced, I promise you."

Surprised to hear the words come out of her mouth, she said, "You don't have to call me Miss Denny. You can just call me Denny."

The big grin lit up his face. "Does that mean you'll call me Steve?"

"I suppose so."

"Well, this is turnin' into an even better night than I expected!"

"Don't get carried away," she warned him. "It's one dance. And calling each other by our first names doesn't mean anything."

"It's a start," Steve Markham said.

Maybe he was right, thought Denny . . . and for some reason, that idea was vaguely troubling to her.

CHAPTER 17

Black Hawk, Colorado

Black Hawk was a town on the decline, thought Brice Rogers as he rode slowly past some empty cattle pens and then along its main street. A decade earlier, the settlement and nearby Central City had been boomtowns, crowded with men determined to wrest a fortune in gold from the steep, thickly timbered slopes surrounding the communities. The would-be mining magnates had brought with them all the things that followed a strike—honest businesses, sure, but also an abundance of saloons, gamblers, and soiled doves.

With the mines beginning to play out, the gold-seekers were drifting away, heading for new fields where the hoped-for riches might materialize. The brick buildings to Brice's right, with a slope rising close behind them, were starting to look seedy and run-down. Some were empty and abandoned. A mercantile with dirty windows was still open for business, but it had the look of an enterprise with few customers. The same was true of a blacksmith shop, a gunsmith, and a saddlemaker. Something about each of the places said that it, too, would be gone in a matter of months or even weeks.

Brice felt sorry for the people whose businesses were failing, but *his* business—chasing down men who had broken the law—was all too good, and that was what had brought him to Black Hawk, in the mountains west of Denver.

The deputy U.S. marshal was a young man in his mid-twenties, compactly built but stronger than his slim build would indicate. He already had laugh lines around his eyes, a testament to his normally good humor. The light brown hair under his high-crowned hat had a slight wave to it. His clothes weren't fancy; he was dressed like a drifting cowpuncher. The Colt .45 holstered on his right hip had plain walnut grips. Most people wouldn't look twice at him . . . which was a good quality for a lawman to have.

The last building in the block to his right was the Casa de Oro Saloon. Its batwinged entrance was on the corner, and judging by the number of horses tied at the hitch racks in front, it was just about the only place in Black Hawk still doing a brisk business. Brice reined in, swung down from the saddle, and found a place at the rack to tie the reins of his sorrel. He patted the horse's shoulder and then stepped up onto the boardwalk.

Before he could reach the batwings, several men pushed through them and out of the saloon. The one in the lead stumbled a little as he turned toward Brice. Brice tried to move aside to let them pass, but the unsteady gent knocked his left shoulder pretty heavily against Brice's right.

The man jerked back and exclaimed, "Watch where you're goin', you little pissant!"

"Take it easy, mister," Brice said in a calm, steady voice. "You're the one who ran into me, but there's no harm done."

"No harm? I'm the one who . . . who'll say whether there's any harm done, by God!"

All three men looked like miners. The fact that they'd been in the Casa de Oro drinking in the middle of the day told Brice that they were probably out of work and spending what few coins they had left on booze.

He was there to do a job and didn't want any trouble, so he just muttered, "Sorry," and tried to step around them.

One of the other men said, "You gonna let him get away with that, Clegg?" His slightly gleeful tone indicated that he was egging on his drunken friend, hoping to see some excitement.

It worked. The miner called Clegg put a big hand in the middle of Brice's chest and stopped him short. "Where the h-hell do you think you're g-goin'?"

Brice shook his head slowly and, with his voice still level, said, "You don't want to do this, friend."

"I ain't your friend, you little—" The obscenities that spilled out of Clegg's mouth then, accompanied by raw whiskey fumes almost strong enough to get a bystander drunk, would have had most men reaching for a gun.

Not wanting to draw attention to himself, Brice put up with it for a long moment, hoping Clegg would either run out of steam or pass out from the booze and fall down.

He did neither of those things, continuing to cuss as he shoved Brice up against the wall of the building. Although a couple of inches taller and at least forty pounds heavier than Brice, Clegg couldn't have had any idea what was going to happen next.

When Brice finally lost his temper, it was like a bundle of dynamite exploded on Clegg's jaw. The punch knocked him across the boardwalk. His back hit the railing along the edge, and he flipped up and over it, landing on his face in the street with his arms and legs spraddled out. He didn't move and clearly was out cold.

The other two miners gaped at Brice for a second, then one of them snarled, reached under his coat, and pulled out a heavy-bladed knife. "You can't—"

"Reckon I can," drawled Brice. The Colt had appeared in his hand as if by magic. He held it rock-steady, its barrel pointed at the knife-wielder's belly. At that range, Brice couldn't miss, and the slug would tear a fatal hole in the miner's guts.

"Hold on," the third man said hastily. The things that had happened in the past few seconds seemed to have chased the drunkenness out of him. He sounded relatively sober as he hurried on. "There's no need for any shootin'. Jeff, put that knife away."

Jeff looked like he wanted to argue, but at the same time, he couldn't take his eyes away from the dark muzzle of Brice's revolver. After a few heartbeats, he growled, "Who the hell are you?"

"A fella who doesn't like being pushed around," Brice answered. "But one who's not looking for trouble, either. Wouldn't have been any if you hadn't goaded your friend into it."

"Yeah, yeah," Jeff muttered. He sighed and slipped the knife back into the hidden sheath under his coat. "Didn't mean nothin' by it."

"You just thought watching your pard bust me up would be some cheap entertainment, didn't you?"

Jeff didn't say anything, but the answer to that question was obvious.

The third man said, "That was one hell of a punch, mister. I never saw anybody knock Clegg out like that. Would've bet that it wasn't even possible!"

"'There are more things in heaven and earth, Horatio . . .'" Brice let the quote trail off and jerked his head toward the man sprawled in the street. "You'd best pick him up and take him back wherever you three came from. You two had your fun whether he enjoyed it or not."

The third man chuckled "Yeah, I guess you could look at it that way. Come on, Jeff."

The two of them stepped down from the boardwalk, got on either side of Clegg, who was starting to groan and move around, and helped him to his feet. They weaved away, half-supporting, half-dragging Clegg, who kept shaking his head groggily.

Brice slipped his Colt back into its holster and turned toward the saloon's entrance again, only to stop as he saw a man leaning against the wall next to the batwings with an insolent smile on his face.

The hombre patted his hands together in mock applause. "That was impressive, even if Clegg *was* drunk as a skunk. It takes a pretty good punch just to move that much bulk."

"Well, I got lucky," Brice said.

"That didn't look like luck to me," the stranger insisted. "Come on in. I'll buy you a drink."

"And I'll be obliged," Brice said.

"By the way," the man added over his shoulder, "my name's Harding. Al Harding."

That comment he'd made about being lucky was true enough, thought Brice.

Al Harding was exactly the man he had come to Black Hawk to find.

CHAPTER 18

Brice followed Al Harding into the Casa de Oro. The saloon was busy, with a good number of men at the bar and most of the tables. More than half the customers were miners, Brice estimated, but there were quite a few cowboys on hand, too, from the ranches in the valleys between the mountains. Because of that, Brice sensed an uneasy truce in the air. Miners and cowhands often didn't get along, but at the moment they were more interested in drinking than fighting.

Despite the number of men in the saloon, only one bartender was behind the hardwood. A couple of tired-looking doves delivered drinks to the tables. A single frock-coated gambler dealt cards in a poker game, and a woman spun a roulette wheel. The Casa de Oro might be the most successful business still in Black Hawk, but obviously the saloon wasn't making money hand over fist or more employees would have been working.

Harding led Brice to the bar and crooked a finger at the apron. When the bartender came over, Harding looked at Brice and asked, "What are you drinking?"

"Beer's fine."

"Make it two, Dewey," Harding told the bartender.

Brice hadn't offered his name, and being a Westerner, Harding hadn't asked. But Brice volunteered it now—sort of. "I'm called Smith," he said.

Harding smiled. "A time-honored name."

"As it happens, that's my real handle."

"I don't doubt it."

The bartender placed mugs on the bar in front of them.

Harding picked his up and went on. "Here's to you, Mister Smith. That was a hell of a punch . . . and a mighty slick draw, too."

"Thanks," Brice muttered. He lifted his mug and acknowledged Harding's words, then took a drink. The beer was weak but reasonably cool, which helped.

"I don't remember seeing you around Black Hawk before."

"Just rode in." Brice smiled. "I think I got here too late."

"Yeah, the town's dying, I'm afraid. But there's still money to be made in these parts if a man knows what he's doing."

Harding didn't elaborate, and Brice didn't press him for details about what he meant. Brice didn't want to push the luck he'd already had.

Harding was lean, a couple of inches shorter than Brice, with a slightly lantern-jawed face and a shock of dark hair under his thumbed-back hat. He was from the hills of Kentucky and his voice still held a faint twang. He had started his outlaw career by holding up stagecoaches and had moved on to robbing trains and banks. Stealing mail sacks from trains had brought him to the attention of federal authorities. As far as Brice knew, Harding had killed an express messenger, a bank guard, two deputies, and three innocent bystanders who'd had the misfortune to get in his way. What Harding had never done was work by himself. He'd always had a gang with him or at least a partner.

Knowing that gave Brice an idea.

"What brings you here?" Harding asked after a few minutes.

"A wandering nature," Brice replied, which brought a chuckle from Harding. "Actually, I've been down in New Mexico Territory lately, and the climate got a mite hot for me."

"Well, it *is* summer."

Brice nodded and said, "Yeah, it's definitely summer down there. At least it's a little cooler up here in Colorado, even if the pickings do look to be a mite on the slim side."

"Not as slim as you might think." Harding sipped his beer. "One of the mines in these parts is still producing pretty good. Called the Fountain Mine. The writing's on the wall, though. From what I hear, the vein's not going to last much longer and so the owners are trying to strip out every last bit of color they can. For now, that means a decent shipment over to the railroad in Golden every week or two."

Brice grunted. "Glad to hear that somebody's still doing all right."

"Somebody else could share in that . . . with the right help."

Brice wasn't completely surprised that Harding

would approach him so quickly, right after meeting him. The chief marshal had said that all of Harding's former partners were either dead or behind bars, which meant the outlaw had either been lying low or working by himself, which he was known to dislike. Harding probably needed money, and more than likely he deemed himself a good judge of character. After witnessing the run-in with Clegg and the other miners outside, Harding had pegged Brice as a hardcase, and Brice hadn't said or done anything to make him think otherwise.

"Maybe you'd better talk a little plainer."

"All right." Harding pushed the empty mug back across the bar. "I happen to know that a shipment of gold from the Fountain is headed to the railroad at Golden pretty soon. The road goes through a perfect spot to jump the wagon, but the mine owners will have four guards on it, two outriders and two men on the wagon with the driver. One man can't do the job alone, but two could . . . if they were fast on the shoot and didn't mind spilling some blood." Harding smiled. "I'm just talkin', though. Don't mean anything by it, if you're not interested."

"I never said that," Brice replied. "Where's this perfect spot you mentioned?"

"Place called Fiddler's Notch. Want to take a look at it?"

Brice drained the last of his beer and nodded. "I wouldn't mind."

"Let's go, then. Not much time to waste if we don't want that gold wagon to get through there ahead of us."

They left the saloon. Brice untied his sorrel and Harding swung up on a big bay. Harding led the way out of Black Hawk, heading north. Over his shoulder, he said, "We'll hit the trail from the mine a few miles up thisaway."

It didn't matter where the trail was, thought Brice. He just wanted to get Harding out of town before he made his move . . . and Harding had cooperated with that right along the line.

Harding turned and followed a faint path up the slope with Brice behind him. The climb was steep enough that the horses had to labor some. If Brice had been alone, he would have dismounted and led the sorrel, but Harding didn't get down from the saddle so Brice didn't, either. When they reached the top, Harding rode through a gap that ran for about a mile. Pine trees grew close on both sides of the trail.

Brice was about to slip his gun from its holster and call on Harding to throw down his weapons and surrender, when Harding reined in sharply and wheeled his mount around so he was facing Brice. The trail was barely wide enough for him to do that.

Harding's gun was already in his hand. Instinctively, Brice started to draw, but Harding wagged the barrel back and forth and said, "Don't do that, *Smith*."

"What the hell is this?" Brice demanded, trying to sound indignant.

"Don't waste your breath and my time, boy. You jumped at this whole thing way too quick, and that means I can't trust you. You're either plannin' on double-crossing me and taking all the gold for yourself after you shoot me in the back . . . or else you're a law dog." Harding chuckled. "With that fresh-faced, innocent look of yours, I'm betting it's that last. You packin' a badge, son?"

"Don't be a damned fool," Brice said coldly. "You're the one who said there was no time to waste. I figured I'd better make up my mind quick. You also said one man couldn't do the job."

"Yeah, but two can, and then one of 'em can gun the other one."

"So why didn't *you* wait and double-cross me once we've got the gold?"

"Because like I said, I think you're a lawman and you never would've gone through with it. I'm a fair-minded man, though. Convince me otherwise, and I might not kill you."

"If you kill me, you sure won't get that gold today."

"I never said the shipment was going through *today*. I said pretty soon. Fact of the matter is, it's due tomorrow. So if you want to change my mind, you've got time to do it." Harding shook his head. "I warn you, though, I don't think it's gonna happen. I think I'm gonna shoot you and leave you here in the woods for the wolves."

Brice had noticed that Harding's bay didn't seem to like standing on the narrow trail. The horse was the skittish sort, big and strong but nervous. Easy to spook. That would be running a long chance, and as he pondered the idea, the thought of Denny Jensen suddenly went through Brice's mind.

"What's the date today?" he abruptly asked.

Harding frowned in surprise. "The date? What the

hell?" He told Brice the date and then said, "What does that matter?"

"I was invited to a wedding today. There was somebody there I would have liked to have seen."

"Well, it's too late for that, ain't it?"

"Yeah, it is." Brice jammed his boot heels into the sorrel's flanks and sent the horse lunging forward, spooking the bay. At the same time he bent low over the sorrel's neck.

The bay tried to twist out of the way as Harding pulled the trigger, and the bullet screamed past Brice, missing by several feet.

Brice's Colt was in his hand as he leaned to the side to get a clear shot at Harding and fired. He aimed at Harding's right shoulder, but the bay was still dancing around some and the slug caught Harding at the base of the throat instead. He rocked far back in the saddle and threw both arms up and out. The gun flew from his fingers, he swayed forward again, and blood gushed from the wound in his throat and from his mouth. His hands pawed at the saddle horn as if he were trying to hold himself on the horse, but his fingers slipped off and he sagged even more forward.

Seeing the life fading in Harding's eyes, Brice said, "You were right. I'm a deputy U.S. marshal."

Air bubbled from Harding's ruined throat. He twisted out of the saddle and thudded to the ground with his right foot still hung in the stirrup. Brice moved the sorrel forward quickly and made a grab for the bay's reins because he didn't want the horse to bolt and drag Harding's body along the trail. Taking the outlaw's carcass in was going to be a grisly enough job without it being battered and busted all to hell.

Brice got the reins, tied them to a tree branch, and then dismounted to begin the grim chore of rolling Harding's body in a blanket and tying it over the saddle. The smell of blood was going to make the bay even more skittish, he thought.

It would have been nice if he'd been able to make it to the Sugarloaf today for Louis Jensen's wedding, he thought. A lot nicer than the ride he had facing him. He wondered what Denny was wearing to the wedding. He would have been willing to bet that she looked mighty nice.

CHAPTER 19

The Sugarloaf

"All right. You've got to keep the loop shaken out wide," Smoke told Brad. "Swing it around over your head a few times."

"How do you keep the loop shaken out if you're swinging it around your head?" the boy asked.

"Practice. You'll get to where you can do it."

"Like drawing and shooting a gun?" Brad said eagerly.

"Right now just worry about roping," Smoke told him. "It's a lot more important for a cowboy to know how to do that."

They were standing out by the corral where Brad had been trying to rope a fence post. The loop kept collapsing on him, but he stuck the tip of his tongue out the corner of his mouth, frowned in concentration, and continued trying to get it right. Smoke stood watching with his hands tucked into his hip pockets.

Brad did well enough with the rope to attempt another throw, but it fell short. As he gathered up the rope again, he said, "My pa was a cowboy. My real pa."

"I know," Smoke said. "I've heard your ma talk about him a few times. Sounded like he was a fine man."

"Yeah, I reckon so. I don't really remember that much. But Louis is a fine man, too." Brad looked around at Smoke. "Do you think I should start calling Louis Pa?"

"I don't figure he'd mind," Smoke said honestly. "But you should do whatever feels right to you. Man's got to learn how to follow his own instincts. Most of the time, they won't do wrong by him."

Brad nodded and went back to working with the rope. A few minutes later, one of his throws sailed out perfectly and settled over the fence post at which he was aiming. "Hey, look at that!" he called excitedly.

"I see," Smoke said. "But you didn't pull the loop tight. If that had been a calf, he might have run right out of it."

"Oh. Yeah." Brad jerked the rope tight around the post. "I'll remember next time."

"I'll bet you will," Smoke said.

From the corner of his eye, he saw three cowboys riding out, heading for the range to take care of some chore Cal had assigned to them. One of the riders was Steve Markham, Smoke noted.

Several days had passed since Louis and Melanie's wedding. Markham had spent that night sleeping in the hayloft in the main barn, along with some other cowhands who had stayed too late at the dance and hadn't wanted to start back to their home spreads in the middle of the night. They had all ridden out the next morning, but Markham had stayed to talk to Cal about that job.

Cal had come to see Smoke later that morning and said, "I hired that fella Markham. Made it clear, though, we were just taking him on for a month to see how he works out."

"Was he satisfied with that?"

Cal had chuckled. "I'm not sure I've ever seen anybody as happy to go along with what anybody else says as he is. Carefree is the word, I guess. He said that was just fine and promised we wouldn't be disappointed in his work."

"A saddle tramp like that usually doesn't get worried about too many things," Smoke had commented.

"No, I guess not."

"Did you say anything about Pearlie thinking he looked familiar?"

Cal had shaken his head and said, "No, I didn't think that would be a good idea, but I did ask him what other spreads he'd ridden for. To hear him tell it, he worked for every spread in the Texas and Oklahoma Panhandles, and quite a few in Kansas. Seemed like he was telling the truth, and I didn't have any reason to challenge what he was saying."

"All right," Smoke had replied with a nod. "I trust your judgment. You know that, Cal."

"I know . . . but I might be wrong one of these days, Smoke."

"If you ever are, we'll deal with it then."

So far, though, Steve Markham seemed to be working out well. Cal had been keeping an eye on him and deemed him to be a good hand, capable of every job he'd been given so far. Given his amiable nature, he also got along very well with the other members of the crew.

Brad noticed the riders and said, "There's Mr. Markham. He's pretty funny sometimes. He sure did want to dance with Aunt Denny at the party the other night."

"Yeah, I saw them dancing," Smoke said.

"I think he likes her."

"I wouldn't be surprised."

Denny had brought up the subject of whether Markham was going to be working on the ranch, and when Smoke told her that he was, he hadn't been able to tell for sure how she felt about that. She'd seemed a little annoyed, but at the same time, *she* was the one who'd asked about him.

In the year that Denny had been home, Smoke had grown accustomed to cowboys falling in love with his daughter. It was almost impossible for young men to be around a girl as pretty as Denny without falling for her. So far, she had seemed impervious to their attentions.

Smoke Jensen was no snob. A lot of forty-a-month-and-found cowpokes had the makings of something much better, and if Denny fell in love with some ambitious young man and they wanted to make it on their own, Smoke was just fine with that. He didn't worry about her getting involved with some shiftless chuck line rider because that just didn't seem like something Denny would do. Hombres like that might be fine fellows in most ways, but they were better off without wives.

To all appearances, Steve Markham fell into that

category . . . and yet Denny was thinking about him, even though at the same time she seemed to be avoiding him. Smoke hadn't seen them together at all since Markham had signed on. He wondered if that was going to last . . .

The sight of some dust boiling up into the air in the distance broke into Smoke's thoughts. Markham and the other two cowboys had seen it, too, and reined in. Smoke frowned as a wagon being pulled by a team of four horses came into view, barreling toward the ranch headquarters on the trail that led up to the higher reaches of the ranch, where much of the Sugarloaf's stock had been moved to summer pasture.

Earlier that morning, the supply wagon being manned by Andy Sawyer and Tex Bell had set out to deliver provisions to several line camps, Smoke recalled. Even though he couldn't see the two men on the seat well enough yet to identify them, he was pretty sure that was the supply wagon coming toward ranch headquarters. Andy and Tex shouldn't have been back until sometime that afternoon, he thought as alarm bells began to clamor in his head. Something had to be mighty wrong to make them race back to headquarters.

"Brad, give me the rope and go on back in the house," Smoke said without taking his eyes off the approaching wagon.

"What's wrong?"

"Didn't say anything was wrong, I just think you need to go in the house."

"But I can tell—" Brad stopped short at the stern

glance Smoke gave him. He handed over the lasso, which he'd been coiling up before trying another throw. "Do I need to tell Miss Sally that something's going on?"

"No," Smoke responded firmly. "Don't say anything to Sally or Denny just yet." No point in upsetting the women if this turned out to be nothing—even though Smoke didn't believe that was the case.

"All right. But if you need me—"

"I'll know where to find you." Smoke dropped the coiled rope over the fence post and walked a few feet to pick up the Winchester that leaned against the corral gate. He didn't wear a handgun around the ranch.

It was the twentieth century, after all, and the wild old days were over . . . or at least most people thought so. There was usually a loaded rifle or shotgun within easy reach, though. Smoke just didn't feel comfortable otherwise.

He strode forward, toward Markham and the other two cowboys who still sat their saddles, waiting for the wagon to get there.

Markham said, "Them fellas are comin' like bats outta hell, Mr. Jensen. That ain't normal, is it?"

"No, it's not," Smoke agreed. He looked at the other two men, who were veteran members of the Sugarloaf crew. "That's Andy and Tex, isn't it, boys?"

"I believe so, Smoke," one of the punchers replied. "They weren't supposed to be back from the line camp supply run until this afternoon."

"Yeah, the same thought occurred to me." Smoke had cradled the rifle under his arm, but he shifted his grip on it so he would be ready to use it if he needed to.

Smoke could see the two men on the wagon seat better. Chunky, curly-haired Andy Sawyer was handling the reins with Tex Bell perched tensely beside him. Andy hauled back on the reins to slow the team. The cloud of dust kicked up by the horses' hooves and the wagon wheels billowed forward and obscured the vehicle for a moment, as well as making Smoke's eyes and nose sting. The saddle mounts on which Markham and the other two cowboys sat shifted nervously.

"Smoke!" Andy called in his gravelly voice. "Smoke, we got trouble!"

The air around them cleared as a breeze carried the dust away.

Smoke strode forward and asked, "What is it?"

Andy swallowed hard, tried to find his voice again and couldn't.

Tex poked a thumb at the wagon bed and said in his laconic fashion, "Back there."

Smoke walked alongside the wagon and peered over the sideboards. Most of the supplies the men had started with that morning were still there, but they had been rearranged to make some room. Filling that space were two blanket-shrouded shapes. The sight of them made Smoke's heart sink, as did the all-too-familiar smell that filled his nose.

Andy found his voice again and said, "The Pitchfork line camp was our second stop, Smoke. We could tell somethin' was wrong soon as we got there, 'cause all the horses were in the corral and they acted spooked. We found Joe Bob and Harley inside the shack. They was dead. Shot all to hell!"

CHAPTER 20

The bodies of Joe Bob Stanton and Harley Briggs had been taken out of the wagon and placed in the barn, and a rider was dispatched to Big Rock to summon the undertaker and Sheriff Monte Carson. The two ranch hands had been dead for several days when Andy and Tex found them. Rats had been at the bodies, and the coffins would remain closed when the men were laid to rest in the Sugarloaf's private cemetery about half a mile from the ranch house. Both men had families elsewhere, but under the circumstances, shipping the bodies back to them wasn't an option.

Smoke had his gun belt strapped on as he stepped out of the house, gripping the Winchester in his left hand.

Sally came out of the house behind him and put a hand on his right arm as she said, "Smoke, there's no chance the men who did this are still anywhere around that line camp. Why don't you wait for Monte to get here?"

Smoke shook his head. "The trail's already too

cold. If we're going to catch up to those killers, we need to get after them as soon as possible."

"Do you really think you can catch them after this much time?"

"We sure can't catch them if we don't go after them," Smoke snapped. Realizing that he had spoken more sharply than he intended to, he softened his voice. "I'm sorry, Sally. We dealt with this sort of thing a lot in the old days . . . too much, in fact . . . but it seems like since the turn of the century, things should've settled down some." He shook his head. "I guess as long as men are greedy and don't want to work for their money, there'll always be rustlers and killers."

The screen door banged as Denny came through it. She was in boots, jeans, man's shirt, and Stetson, although her hair was loose under the hat. Like her father, she had a gun belt strapped around her hips, with a Colt riding in the attached holster.

Sally turned to face her daughter and shook her head. "Denise, you're not—"

"I happen to know that you put on trousers and picked up a gun and rode out with Pa to hunt down bad hombres more than once, Ma," Denny said, "so arguing with me isn't going to do you a lot of good."

"Yes, I did those things," admitted Sally, "but it was a different time then. The only law and order around here was what we imposed ourselves. The valley is civilized now—"

"Tell that to Joe Bob and Harley," Denny broke in.

Sally's face flushed with anger.

Smoke said to Denny, "Don't talk to your mother like that."

"Sorry," Denny muttered, but she didn't sound completely sincere.

"You should stay here," Smoke went on. "We don't know how long we'll be on the trail."

"I've camped out before, plenty of times."

"I know that, but I'll feel better knowing that you're here keeping an eye on things. I'm not expecting any trouble here at the ranch, but you never know."

Denny narrowed her eyes at him. "You're just saying that to get me to agree to stay behind."

"It's the truth," Smoke insisted. "Pearlie's staying here, too. He can't spend all day in the saddle like he used to. Between the two of you, I'm confident you can handle anything that might crop up."

For a long moment, Denny stood there looking argumentative, switching her gaze back and forth between her mother and father. Finally, she said, "All right. I'll stay. But I don't like it."

"Nobody said you had to," Smoke told her.

The door opened again and Brad rushed out onto the porch. "Can I come?"

"You know better than that," Sally said.

Brad pointed at Denny. "But she's goin'. Look, she's wearin' a gun!"

"Forget it, kid," Denny told him. "They're making me stay here, too." She summoned up a smile. "But I'm in charge of defending the ranch if there's any trouble"—Smoke let that claim go by—"and I'm making you my deputy."

Brad's eyes widened. "A deputy? Really?"

"That's right."

He frowned slightly and pointed out, "But you're not a sheriff or a marshal."

"Look, do you want to be my deputy or not?"

"Sure, whatever you say, Denny."

A group of cowboys rode toward the house from the barn, with Cal in the forefront leading a saddled horse for Smoke. Behind him came a dozen members of the Sugarloaf crew—all of them grim-faced and ready to avenge the murder of their friends. All except Steve Markham, who looked solemn enough but had never met Joe Bob Stanton or Harley Briggs. They all rode for the same brand, though, and that was what really counted with knights of the range. Each of the men wore a handgun and had a rifle sticking up from a saddle boot. They were packing considerable firepower.

"We're ready to ride, Smoke," Cal reported.

Smoke kissed Sally on the lips and Denny on the forehead and clapped a hand on Brad's shoulder for a second. Then he went down the steps, swung up into the saddle of the horse Cal was holding, and led the group out of the ranch yard toward the trail up to the high pastures. He didn't look back but knew his wife, daughter, and brand-new grandson were watching from the porch.

It was early afternoon before the group of riders approached the Pitchfork line camp. Smoke firmly believed the killers were long gone, but just in case he was wrong, he pulled the Winchester from its sheath and rode with it held across the saddle in front of him as he scanned the high ridges around them for any sign of an ambush.

Nothing happened as they rode up to the line shack. Smoke saw the dark patch of ground over by the corral that Andy and Tex had spoken of seeing. They had said it looked like a lot of blood had been spilled there. Smoke figured one of the cowboys had been killed there and then the murderers had tossed the body back in the shack.

Smoke reined in, studied the layout, and then said to Cal, "One of the boys was headed out to the corral when they gunned him. The other one probably heard the shots and they got him when he came out to see what was going on. Could've been at night."

"That would explain why they put the bodies back in the cabin," Cal said as he leaned forward to ease his muscles. "If they had left corpses out in the open, the buzzards would have started to circle as soon as the sun came up. That might have drawn attention from some of the other line camps, and what happened here would have been discovered sooner than they wanted. Same reason they didn't bother to burn the line shack. This way, they had several days to make their getaway."

"That's the way it looks to me," said Smoke. "There are so many tracks around, studying them probably won't do any good, but let's have a look anyway."

The two of them dismounted and spent a while intently surveying the ground around the shack and the corral. Smoke saw dozens of boot prints, but there was nothing special about any of them, nothing that would help him identify any of the wearers in the future.

He stepped into the shack and looked around there, too. Other than dark stains where blood had soaked into the puncheon floor, nothing seemed unusual. The killers—and it was obvious there had to have been more than one—had done their bloody work and then disappeared.

"Let's check on the stock," Smoke said, although he had a pretty good idea what they would find—or *wouldn't* find.

Sure enough, the pastures that normally would be monitored by the hands assigned to the line camp were empty.

"How many head should be here?" Smoke asked Cal.

"Close to a hundred and fifty," the foreman answered. "The bastards made a pretty good haul."

Smoke was bothered more by the two lives lost than he was by having that many cows stolen, but the rustling added insult to injury. Jaw tight with anger, he said, "Let's see if we can pick up their trail."

The rustlers couldn't have taken the stock lower down. Smoke and his companions would have run into signs of that if they had. That meant the stolen cattle had been pushed still higher. Prophet Pass was up above them, Smoke knew. A hard climb, especially pushing a hundred and fifty beeves, but if the thieves had been able to get over the pass, they could hit a trail on the other side that led to the southwest through rugged country and eventually came to some of the mining settlements west of Denver. Even though the boom of the previous decade was largely over, many of the mines were still being worked, and men who performed hard labor underground all day were hungry when they came back up into the light. A good market for beef still existed over there.

That seemed the most likely explanation to Smoke, and when he and the other men from the Sugarloaf began climbing toward Prophet Pass, it wasn't long before they spotted signs of cattle being driven in that direction.

"Danged if we ain't on their trail, boys," Steve Markham exclaimed.

Smoke looked back over his shoulder at the new hand. "You probably didn't figure on winding up in a jackpot like this so soon after signing on, did you, Markham?"

"I don't know as I'd say that, sir," the young cowboy replied with a grin. "As soon as I found out I'd be ridin' for Smoke Jensen, I figured hell 'd be a-poppin' sooner rather than later!"

CHAPTER 21

The trail through Prophet Pass was so rocky that it wouldn't take hoofprints, but Smoke saw some shiny places where horseshoes had nicked the stone recently. Along with fairly fresh droppings from cattle and horses, that was enough to tell him that several riders and a considerable amount of livestock had gone through there. He couldn't prove that it was the rustlers and the stolen herd that had left those signs in the pass, but he was confident they couldn't have gone anywhere else yet.

The tracks they found late that afternoon, heading southwest toward those mining settlements, confirmed his theory. They couldn't miss the signs that a group of cattle had gone through there several days earlier.

As they stopped to let their horses rest, Cal said, "They've probably sold those cows already, Smoke. We're not going to get them back."

"You're right," Smoke agreed. "The chances of that are pretty slim. But the bunch that stole them might still be hanging around somewhere down there, enjoying the money they got for them."

"And you want to catch up to them."

"They came onto Sugarloaf range," Smoke said, "killed two men who rode for me, and stole my beef. I don't much cotton to the idea of them getting away with any of that."

Mutters of agreement came from several of the other men, and Markham said fervently, "Damn right!"

They pushed on until it was too dark to see the trail, then stopped to rest the horses again, brew coffee, and eat some of the jerky and biscuits they had brought along. The men slept a while after that, until the moon rose and Smoke woke everyone. The wash of silvery light was enough to keep them from getting lost.

Smoke was pushing them hard and he knew it, but the need to settle the score for Joe Bob Stanton and Harley Briggs burned within all of them. The need to keep from ruining the horses was all that slowed them down the rest of that night, all the next day, and through the night after that.

Black Hawk

More than forty hours had passed since leaving the Sugarloaf when they rode into the settlement. It was early in the morning, not long after sunup, and the town really hadn't started coming to life yet, although thumping could be heard from the stamp mills at the mines up in the nearby mountains.

Smoke heard something else, too, that caused him to rein in and lift his hand in a signal for the others to stop. He said to Cal, "Listen."

"Good Lord!" the foreman exclaimed after a moment. "That sounds like a good-sized bunch of cattle."

The lowing was unmistakable, all right. Smoke nudged his horse into motion again and followed it to some large pens on the eastern edge of town. At least a hundred cows milled around inside the fences.

"That's them!" one of the Sugarloaf hands said excitedly. "I'd know that old brindle cow anywhere. She was in a bunch I hazed up to that pasture below Pitchfork Ridge."

Smoke hadn't expected to be able to recover any of the stolen stock, but at least two-thirds of the herd was still there. He hipped around in the saddle and told the others, "Half of you boys stay here and keep an eye on these cows. The rest of you, come with Cal and me. We're going to see if we can locate the men who drove them here."

Cal quickly called out half a dozen names, among them Steve Markham's, and gave them the job of guarding the rustled cattle. Then he and the other hands followed Smoke along the street toward the single business block, which was surrounded by a scattering of crude miners' cabins and a few more substantial dwellings.

A man in a canvas apron was sweeping the boardwalk in front of a general store. A sign on the building read TOOBIN'S EMPORIUM. As Smoke, Cal, and the other riders drew up in front of the business, the balding proprietor leaned on his broom and blinked at them through thick spectacles that kept sliding down his nose. He pushed them up and appeared rather alarmed to be confronted with such a group of beard-stubbled, well-armed, tough-looking hombres so early in the morning.

"You boys ain't here to loot the town, are you?" he asked. "You're liable to be a mite disappointed if you are."

"No, sir," Smoke told him. "We're from a ranch up in Eagle County called the Sugarloaf. We've been on the trail of some stolen stock, and I reckon we've found it."

The storekeeper raised bushy gray eyebrows. "The Sugarloaf," he repeated. "Seems like I've heard of that spread. Belongs to Smoke Jensen, don't it?"

"That's right. I'm Jensen."

The eyebrows climbed even higher. "Lordy! Smoke Jensen his own self, right here in Black Hawk. Here I thought the town was about to dry up and blow away, and now all sorts of excitement is goin' on."

"What do you mean by that?" asked Smoke as he rested his crossed hands on the saddle horn. "Are you talking about that herd of cattle being driven in?"

"Well, that ain't all that unusual. Enough of the mines are still goin' concerns that there's a market for beef here, sure enough. I was talkin' more about the fact that we had a deppity United States marshal come through here a few days back, leadin' a horse haulin' the carcass of an outlaw he'd tracked down and killed. *That* was the most excitement we'd had here in a while."

Smoke didn't really care about some lawman passing through the former boomtown, although he wondered briefly if it might have been Brice Rogers. Brice had missed Louis's wedding because he was off chasing some owlhoot, according to Monte Carson.

Smoke was more interested in the rustlers, so he said, "What about those cows? Are the men who brought them in still here in town?"

"Reckon so. From what I've heard, they were sorta disappointed that nobody would take the whole herd off their hands at once. They sold off some o' the stock to a few of the smaller mines. Jack Buell, the superintendent of the Fountain Mine, will be in town in a few days, though, and he'll likely take the rest of the cows." The garrulous old storekeeper frowned and blinked behind the spectacles. "No, wait, you said them cows was rustled. So Mr. Buell won't be buyin' 'em from the fellas who brought 'em in."

"No," Smoke said. "No, he won't." He straightened in the saddle. "Where can we find those men?"

The storekeeper started looking nervous again. He wiped the back of his hand across his mouth before he answered, "They're, uh, they're stayin' at the Casa de Oro, I believe. We had a hotel, but it done closed down a couple months ago. Not many other places to stay in Black Hawk right now."

Smoke inclined his head. "The Casa de Oro. That's the saloon down at the end of the block?"

"Yes, sir. I'm, uh . . . I'm gonna go back inside now and close the door."

"Not a bad idea," Cal commented as he turned his horse to follow Smoke toward the other end of the long block.

Nobody else was moving around on the street that early. The saddlemaker stepped out of his shop and started to stretch the night's kinks out of his back, then stopped as he caught sight of the group of riders moving along the street. He ducked back inside and hurriedly shut the door behind him.

As they approached the Casa de Oro, the saloon's double doors at the corner opened and a man stepped out. The pail of water he carried and then threw out into the street marked him as the saloon's swamper and indicated that he'd just finished mopping up the place. He had halfway turned around to go back inside the building when he saw Smoke and the others and stopped short. He stared pop-eyed at them for a heartbeat, then dropped the empty bucket with a clatter and dashed back through the batwings.

"Blast it," Cal burst out. "Those rustlers probably paid him to keep his eyes open and warn them if any strangers rode into town. They knew somebody might be coming after them!"

"That's right," Smoke snapped. "Come on!" He heeled his horse into a run and drew his Colt. He could already hear somebody, probably the swamper, yelling inside the saloon. The element of surprise he had hoped for was lost.

Before they could reach the end of the block, a window on the second floor of the Casa de Oro flew up and a man leaned out holding a rifle. The Winchester began cracking as he swept the street with lead as fast as he could work the repeater's lever.

CHAPTER 22

Smoke lifted the Colt and triggered it twice, sending a couple of slugs sizzling through the open window and into the rifleman's chest. The bullets' impact threw the man backward out of sight, but he dropped his rifle and it bounced and slid off the awning over the boardwalk, spinning into the street.

Even as the first of the rustlers crossed the divide, glass shattered and sprayed outward from several other windows as the men inside the rooms didn't take the time to open them. They just poked rifle and revolver barrels through the panes and opened fire on the men from the Sugarloaf.

Smoke veered his horse toward the boardwalk and left the saddle in a flying leap that carried him over the railing and onto the walk. His momentum made it impossible for him to stay upright when his feet hit the planks. He went down but rolled over and used the impetus of that to bring him back up on one knee.

A man wearing boots and long underwear slapped the batwings aside and rushed out of the saloon, carrying a shotgun. Before he could swing the scattergun's twin barrels in Smoke's direction, Smoke drilled him in the midsection. The shotgunner doubled over and his finger spasmed on both triggers, setting off the weapon with a thunderous roar. The double load of buckshot chewed a hole in the planks about a foot in front of him. He folded up on top of the cavity.

As Smoke leaped to his feet and charged toward the saloon entrance, he wished he had thought to ask old Toobin down at the general store just how many rustlers there were.

But they could count the bodies later, he supposed.

Cal and the rest of the men had followed his example and yanked their horses next to the boardwalk, so that the awning gave them some cover from the men firing from the second floor. Smoke glanced along the walk and saw that none of them were down, although he spotted bloodstains on a couple of shirts where their owners had been winged. With any luck, nothing too serious.

He dodged around the shotgunner's body, stopped next to the entrance, and thumbed fresh rounds into the Colt, filling the wheel. Then he reached over and gave the closest batwing a sharp poke. As it swung inward with a creaking of hinges, at least a couple of men inside the saloon opened up on it and blasted it full of holes. The swinging door flew back out wildly. Smoke went under it in a dive that had him sliding along the sawdust-sprinkled floor. As he came to a stop on his belly, he saw a man standing behind the bar with a rifle while another crouched at the foot of the stairs with a six-gun in each hand.

Smoke's Colt barked twice. The first shot ripped

into the man behind the bar and knocked him back against the shelves full of whiskey bottles behind him. The shelves—and the bottles—came down with a huge crash. Smoke's second shot roared so hard on the heels of the first one that it almost sounded like one report. That bullet shattered the right shoulder of the man next to the stairs and made him drop the gun in that hand, As he slewed halfway around, Smoke rolled to his left.

The rustler still held the gun in his left hand, and he put it to use, firing three rounds toward Smoke. The bullets plowed into the floor where Smoke had been an instant earlier and showered him with splinters. He fired while he was still on the move, and his uncanny skill allowed him to put a bullet through the rustler's brain. The man's head snapped back as the slug blew a large hole in his skull and painted the stair runner behind him with a gory mix of blood and gray matter. His knees buckled and he pitched forward.

Smoke got his left hand and his knees under him and surged up. Cal and several of the other men charged into the Casa de Oro just as four more gunmen appeared on the second-floor balcony and sent a hail of lead angling down into the main room.

"Scatter and hunt cover!" Smoke bellowed over the gun-thunder. He kicked a table over and crouched behind it. Bullets thudded into the wood and made it shiver, but none of them penetrated all the way through. Smoke snapped a couple of shots at the men on the balcony, but they ducked back as soon as they triggered their guns, so he didn't have a good angle on them.

Cal took cover behind an overturned table as well, and two of the ranch hands wound up underneath the roulette wheel. Shards of red- and black-painted wood flew in the air as bullets sought for them and found the gaudy wheel instead. The other men had made it underneath the balcony, but from there they couldn't see the rustlers any more than the rustlers could see them.

A fifth man appeared on the balcony holding a woman in front of him with his left arm clamped brutally around her neck so that her body shielded him. He thrust his right hand with a gun under her right arm and fired as he began forcing her down the stairs.

One of Smoke's men under the roulette wheel yelled and fell backward as he clutched a bullet-drilled shoulder.

The woman had a wild mass of tangled blond hair and wore only a thin shift that ended high on her thighs. She had to be one of the soiled doves who worked there, and she'd probably been asleep with the man when all hell broke loose.

"Cover me, Smoke!" Cal called as he leaped out from behind the table. Smoke put a pair of rounds over the rustler's head, close enough to make the man flinch and stop shooting for a second. That gave Cal enough time to charge up the stairs. He hit the rustler and the girl and knocked them apart. The dove screamed as she wound up tumbling down the rest of the way. Cal and the rustler wrestled on the stairs. The man shoved Cal against the banister, and it broke under his weight. He fell, landing on a table that collapsed underneath him and left him sprawled in its wreckage.

The rustler aimed over the edge of the stairs, poised to send a slug hammering down into Cal. But he didn't have his human shield anymore. Smoke fired, and the rustler slumped and dropped his gun as Smoke's bullet crashed into his head just above his left ear.

Unfortunately, another rustler had darted out onto the balcony and was aiming a rifle down at Cal. Smoke started to swing his Colt back in that direction, unsure whether or not he would be in time to save his friend's life.

He didn't have to. At that moment another gun roared, farther along the balcony, and the rifleman twisted around as a slug tore through him. He tried to catch himself against the railing but wound up going backward over it as blood welled from the hole in his side. He crashed facedown on the barroom floor not far from Cal, who was trying to shake the cobwebs out of his head.

"Yeee-hahhh!"

The shout came from Steve Markham, who moved along the balcony in a crouch as the gun in his fist geysered flame and smoke. He had shot the man about to kill Cal and led the charge as he and two more of the Sugarloaf hands who had been left behind at the cattle pens mopped up the rest of the rustlers. Taken by surprise by the attack from a different direction, the thieves didn't have much of a chance. After half a minute of deafening gunfire, everything fell silent in the Casa de Oro.

Then Steve Markham, grinning as usual, stepped up to the edge of the balcony with gray tendrils of smoke curling from the muzzle of his gun, and called, "You all right down there, Mr. Jensen?"

"Yeah," Smoke said as he got to his feet and started reloading again. "Just getting a mite too old for this."

CHAPTER 23

Four of the Sugarloaf hands were wounded, but none of the injuries were life-threatening. The worst one was the bullet-drilled shoulder of the cowboy who had taken cover under the roulette wheel. Cal took all four of the men down the street to the residence and office of Black Hawk's only remaining physician to get them patched up.

Smoke and the other men checked over the bodies of the rustlers to see if any of them were still alive. That proved not to be the case. Black Hawk's undertaker would be busy for the next two days nailing together pine coffins, and the local Boot Hill would see a surge in population.

At the same time, Smoke studied the faces of the dead men to see if he recognized any of them. He didn't. If Monte Carson had been there, he might have known some of them from wanted posters he had seen, but Monte was almost a hundred miles away in Big Rock, or so Smoke assumed, anyway. He wouldn't have left the town and set out to chase down the rustlers knowing that Smoke was already on the trail.

Steve Markham stood next to the foot of the stairs with his shoulder propped against an unbroken section of banister.

Smoke waved a hand toward the bodies and asked the new hand, "Ever seen any of those hombres before?"

"Why do you reckon I would have, Mr. Jensen?"

"I don't, necessarily. But they're rustlers, and somebody who's worked on as many spreads as you told Cal you have might have run into some of them."

The concern that had sprung up on Markham's face at Smoke's question disappeared. "Oh, That's a relief. I was worried you thought I might've rode with a bunch of no-goods like that. No, sir, I can tell you for certain-sure I never laid eyes on any of those varmints before."

"I'm glad to hear it." Smoke paused. "I told you and the others to stay down at the cattle pens and keep an eye on those cows."

"Yeah, I know." Markham toed the floor and smiled sheepishly. "But then all the shootin' started, and me and a couple of the other boys just couldn't resist comin' up here to lend a hand. I spotted some outside stairs at the back of the place, and we charged up those and busted down the door at the top. That put us in a good position to ventilate those rascals."

"And save Cal's life in the process," murmured Smoke. "I reckon I can't get too upset over you not doing what I told you, Steve. Just don't make a habit of it."

"No, sir, I sure won't," Markham promised. "And some of the fellas *did* stay down there at the pens like you said to do, so it ain't like all of us abandoned our duty."

"No, I suppose not."

The soiled dove who had been used as a hostage and human shield sat at one of the undamaged tables in the saloon with a blanket wrapped around her bare shoulders. She was shaking, and tears had streaked her face. The other girl who worked at the Casa de Oro sat next to her and tried to console her.

A man with a few strands of hair combed over a bald pate patted her on the shoulder and said, "There, there, Jill, it'll be all right. Just a little ruckus, that's all."

Smoke approached the man, who wore a hastily donned suit and a shirt with no collar or tie "You're the owner of this place, mister?"

"That's right. Garvey's the name."

Smoke nodded toward the bodies that still littered the floor. "You know you were renting rooms to a bunch of rustlers, don't you?"

"I know it now," said Garvey, "but I didn't when they rode in and paid me to stay here. I'm not in the business of asking a bunch of questions, my friend."

"I don't recall saying that we're friends," Smoke said. "They give you any names?"

"I don't ask for those, either." Garvey looked around the room and sighed. "I would like to know who's going to pay for all this damage, though. Just replacing all the broken windows is going to cost a fortune."

"I reckon you can go through their belongings and see if they have any cash left from selling those cows they stole from me. By rights that money should be mine, but"—Smoke shrugged—"from the looks of this town, you need it more than I do."

Garvey's surly attitude eased a little at that. "You claim they stole that herd they brought in?"

"I do more than claim it. I can prove it. My brand is still on those animals. I'm Smoke Jensen, from the Sugarloaf Ranch."

The saloonkeeper's eyes widened. Clearly, he had heard of Smoke. "I, ah, didn't realize who you were, Mr. Jensen. You're right about how any cash they have left ought to belong to you—"

"No, I said it was all right, and I meant it. I'm going to get more than half of the rustled stock back, and that's more than I really expected when we came after the varmints."

"Well, I appreciate your generosity." Garvey pulled out a handkerchief and mopped his mostly bald head. "There's no denying that all of us left in Black Hawk are struggling to make ends meet these days. I'm afraid that in another year or two this will be a ghost town." He brightened slightly as he put the handkerchief away. "But you never know. Things could change. One of the mines could strike a rich new vein, and that's all it would take to make Black Hawk a boomtown again. Say, speaking of the mines, if you don't want to drive those cows all the way back to your ranch, you ought to talk to Jack Buell at the Fountain Mine. He'll give you a decent price for them and save you all that trouble, to boot."

Smoke nodded and said, "I was already thinking about doing that."

By that afternoon, the bodies had been hauled away

and Garvey had men working to repair the damage at the Casa de Oro. They boarded up the broken windows. New glass would have to be brought from Denver. Smoke didn't know if the saloonkeeper would go to that much expense, given the town's declining state, or just leave the boarded-up windows like they were, but that was none of his business. He left Cal in charge of things in town and rode up to the Fountain Mine, following the directions that Garvey gave him.

Jack Buell turned out to be the sort of mine superintendent Smoke had met numerous times in the past, tough, smart, and hardheaded. He drove a hard bargain, too, but he and Smoke concluded a deal for the cattle.

"I'll leave them there in the pens and have them butchered as we need them," Buell explained. "There's no place up here to keep that many cows."

"Better be careful they don't get stolen again," Smoke warned.

"Folks in Black Hawk will keep an eye on them. The town's pretty dependent on this mine these days."

Again, those arrangements were none of Smoke's business. He shook hands with Buell, wished the man well, and headed back down the mountain to Black Hawk, arriving there late in the afternoon.

After Smoke told Cal about the deal he'd made with Buell, the foreman said, "Garvey at the saloon says we can stay there tonight since he doesn't have any other guests at the moment, and he claims the two of you reached an accommodation about the money those rustlers had. I figured you'd want to wait and get started back home first thing in the morning, since there's no real hurry now."

"That'll be fine," Smoke said with a nod. "Any time I'm away from home, though, I start getting the feeling that it'll be good to be back."

Cal laughed. "I feel the same way about the Sugarloaf."

It wasn't just the Sugarloaf, Smoke mused. He was eager to see his family again.

The man with the wounded shoulder was staying at the doctor's house since he was the most badly hurt of the ranch hands. The others had suffered only nicks from the bullets flying around. Smoke paid a visit to the wounded man, and the doctor told him it might be several days before he would be in good enough shape to make the long ride.

"I can get back all right, Smoke," the cowboy assured him. "I don't want the rest of you fellas havin' to wait around here because of me."

"Are you sure about that, Dave?" asked Smoke.

"Yeah. Wish I could get in the saddle sooner, but Doc Knight here says it ain't a good idea."

Smoke took a double eagle from his pocket and handed it to the sawbones. "That ought to take care of the bill."

"That will more than cover it," the man said, nodding. "I'm obliged to you, Mr. Jensen."

"Just take good care of Dave."

Satisfied that he'd done all he could for the wounded man, Smoke returned to the Casa de Oro as dusk settled down over the town. Inside the saloon, some of the men were drinking and playing cards.

Jill, the soiled dove who had been so upset after the gun battle, and the other girl who worked there approached a few of the cowboys. Jill appeared to have gotten over the close call, and her obviously pragmatic nature had risen to the forefront again.

Smoke wasn't going to say anything if any of the men wanted to take the doves upstairs. He hired ranch hands, not choirboys. He watched with some interest, though, as Jill sidled up to Steve Markham and said something to him. Markham smiled at her, but he shook his head, and Jill moved on to one of the other punchers.

Markham's reaction to Jill's proposition was none of his business, Smoke told himself yet again . . . but at the same time, he was sort of glad to see it, and he wasn't sure why.

CHAPTER 24

The Sugarloaf

"You gonna throw a saddle on him and try to ride him again?" Brad asked as he hung on the gate of Rocket's stall. With awe in his eyes, he looked over it at the black mustang.

Denny leaned on the gate beside the youngster and said, "Why would I do that? He's already proven that he can't be trusted. I don't really think he's a natural-born killer, like everybody says, but I'm not sure I want to risk riding him again."

Brad looked over at her. "Yeah, you do. I can tell. You don't want to turn your back on a challenge."

Denny snorted. "I'll bet you think you're pretty smart for a kid."

"You're not much more than a kid yourself."

"Yes, I am. I'm a grown woman. And I'm your aunt, so show some respect when you're talking to me."

"Yes, ma'am," Brad said, polite on the surface, but Denny thought she heard a trace of mockery in the boy's voice.

"Maybe I'll ride Rocket again one of these days . . . but I'll decide when the time comes."

Brad dropped from the gate to the ground and said, "I wish Smoke and Cal would get back. Haven't they been gone long enough to find those rustlers?"

"Yeah, it seems like it." Denny lifted her head as she heard the sound of hoofbeats outside the barn. She headed in that direction as she said, "Maybe that's them now." She couldn't keep a bit of excitement out of her voice.

As she walked toward the entrance, though, with Brad hurrying beside her and almost breaking into a run to keep up, she realized only one horse was approaching, not the bunch that would be coming in if her father and the men who'd gone after the rustlers were returning. She and Brad stepped out of the barn.

The brim of Denny's hat shaded her eyes, but Brad had to hold his hand up to his forehead so he could see. "That ain't Smoke or Cal."

"That *isn't* Smoke or Cal," Denny corrected him. She knew her mother would have done that if she'd been there, so Denny supposed she might as well, too.

"I don't reckon I know who that fella is."

"I do." Denny had recognized the rider on the powerful sorrel.

Brice Rogers reined in and lithely swung down from the saddle. He held the sorrel's reins as he nodded and said, "Howdy, Miss Denny."

"You don't usually call me miss," she told the young deputy U.S. marshal.

"Well, it's been a while since I've seen you. Seemed proper to be polite." He smiled at Brad. "Hello, son. You're Mrs. Buckner's boy, aren't you?"

"Yeah, but my ma is Mrs. Jensen now. She and Louis Jensen got hitched a few days ago."

Brice nodded. "I know. I would've come to the wedding, but I had to be somewhere else, working." He looked at Denny again. "I'm sorry I couldn't make it. I would have been here if I hadn't been off, well . . ."

"Chasing outlaws," Denny finished for him. "Don't worry. Sheriff Carson made your excuses for you."

Brad's eyes got bigger as he looked up at the newcomer. "Are you a lawman?"

"That's right. Deputy United States Marshal Brice Rogers."

"Where's your badge?" Brad wanted to know.

"I don't wear it pinned to my shirt. Got it in a little leather folder I carry, along with my other bona fides. When I'm working, I generally don't like to announce who I really am."

Denny said, "I suppose it went all right? The job that kept you from attending the wedding, I mean?"

"I'm here," Brice said, and Denny knew what he meant by that. The outlaw he had gone after was either behind bars . . . or dead.

Brice was a good lawman, smart and determined and good with a gun. Denny was well aware of that. They had met a year earlier and sparks had flown immediately between the two of them. Not necessarily the good kind, though. They had fought side by side against evil, but they had also quarreled as much as they had worked together.

Her father would probably say that was because they were too much alike, too strong-willed and always convinced that they were right. And maybe there was some truth to that, thought Denny. Just being in Brice Rogers's presence made her feel as if she were being challenged somehow . . . the way Brad had talked about Rocket being a challenge she didn't want to turn her back on.

At the same time, she couldn't help but remember how she had kissed him for luck when they were about to go into danger. *Supposedly* for luck. But she could have wished him that without kissing him . . .

He broke into those thoughts—and Denny was glad that he did—by saying, "Sheriff Carson told me you had trouble out here. Some cattle rustled and a couple of men killed?"

"That's right. Joe Bob Stanton and Harley Briggs. You may have met them."

Brice scowled. "I think I did. I'm mighty sorry to hear about what happened to them. Your father and some of the hands went after the men who did it?"

"They started on the trail." Denny shook her head. "I don't have any way of knowing if they caught up yet."

"Well, I hope they do, and I hope good luck is on their side when they do."

There he was, talking about luck and stirring up memories in her head again . . .

"At this point," he continued, "I don't reckon there's anything I can do to help."

"You couldn't anyway," she told him. "Those aren't federal crimes. You wouldn't have any jurisdiction."

"I haven't always let that stop me in the past."

"No, I don't suppose you have." Denny's chin

lifted. "Do you have some other reason for being out here, Brice, or is this a social call?"

"I just wanted to apologize for missing the wedding and maybe offer Louis and his new bride my congratulations—"

"They've gone east on a wedding trip. They'll be back in ten or twelve days."

Brice nodded. "I see." He smiled at Brad again. "Well, you can pass along my best wishes to your ma and your new pa, can't you, son?"

"Sure, Marshal," the boy said. "I'd be glad to."

Brice thumbed back his hat and then put a hand on the saddle horn. "Reckon I'd better be going, then—"

"Look!" Brad suddenly exclaimed. "Riders coming!"

Denny turned to look where he was pointing and saw the group of more than a dozen men on horseback riding at a deliberate pace toward the ranch headquarters. There was no mistaking the broad-shouldered figure in the lead.

Smoke Jensen was home again.

Even though she had more confidence in her father than in any man alive, Denny still felt a wave of relief go through her as she saw that he appeared to be just fine. Riding beside him was Calvin Woods, and he didn't seem to be hurt, either. Denny spotted a couple of cowboys sporting bandages and one had his arm in a sling, but those were the only injuries she saw.

Brad broke into a run to go and greet the men.

Brice smiled at Denny and said, "You probably want to do the same thing."

"Please. I'm more dignified than that." The comment might have been more effective if she didn't

still have horse patties on her boots from stepping in
some earlier, but she gave him a haughty look anyway.

Sally must have sensed that Smoke was nearby,
because she stepped out onto the front porch and
waved.

Brice said, "I'll go pay my respects to your mother
and then tie my horse over there by the house. I
wouldn't mind talking to Smoke and finding out
what happened."

"Fine." Denny followed Brad, although she didn't
run to greet the returning men like he had.

Smoke held a hand down to Brad, clasped wrists
with the boy, and lifted him onto the horse's back in
front of the saddle. Denny walked alongside as she
said, "Hello, Pa. I'm glad you're back."

"Any trouble while we were gone?" asked Smoke.

"Not a bit. Did you find those rustlers?"

"We found 'em," Smoke replied, his voice flat and
not giving anything away.

Denny had already guessed as much from the fact
that several of the men were wounded, but she wanted
to hear the details. She would have to wait until later
to do so, though. She knew Smoke wouldn't go into
any of that while Brad was around.

Another of the men moved his horse forward and
said, "Howdy, Miss Denny." Steve Markham's grin
and carefree voice were unmistakable.

"Well, it looks like you didn't get yourself shot up,"
she said to him.

"Nope. I'm fit as a fiddle and glad to be back."

Denny glanced at the ranch house and saw that
Brice Rogers had climbed onto the porch after tying
his sorrel at the hitch rail and was talking to her

mother. She realized that she was kind of glad Brice was there, after all, at the same time as Markham and the others were getting back.

Then she frowned slightly to herself. She wasn't certain *why* she felt that way . . . but she was pretty sure she didn't like it.

CHAPTER 25

"It's good to see you again, Brice," Sally Jensen said as the young lawman stepped up onto the porch and took the hand she held out to him. He held his hat in his other hand. He could tell she was clearly distracted by her husband's arrival back on the Sugarloaf, but that wasn't going to stop her from being gracious in greeting a guest. "You haven't been out here to visit us much in a long time."

"My job keeps me pretty busy, ma'am."

"I'm sure it does. Smoke and I appreciate all your efforts to bring law and order to this area."

Brice smiled. "I'd say that you and Mr. Jensen did more than just about anybody else to establish law and order in this valley, ma'am. With help from Sheriff Carson and Pearlie, of course."

Sally laughed softly. "And from some of those old mountain man friends Smoke always called on for help in those days." Her smile was a little wistful as she went on. "I'm afraid that's a vanished era now."

"Those days might be gone, ma'am, but I don't reckon they'll ever be forgotten."

"We can hope not. A lot of men and women worked hard and risked their lives to make something out of the West, and their efforts and sacrifices *shouldn't* be forgotten. And that's just about enough ma'am-ing me. Call me Sally."

"I don't know if I could—" He stopped short at the stern look she gave him and said, "Well, maybe Miss Sally."

"That'll do, I suppose. Now, if you'll excuse me . . . my husband is home." She hurried down the steps as Smoke dismounted.

He met her at the bottom of them, drew her into his arms, and gave her an enthusiastic and unabashed kiss that Sally appeared to return with equal enthusiasm. Denny stood nearby, smiling and holding the reins of Smoke's horse in one hand while her other hand rested on young Brad Buckner's shoulder.

Calvin Woods and the other members of the Sugarloaf crew who'd accompanied Smoke had peeled off to head for the bunkhouse, where Pearlie greeted them with handshakes and a round of backslapping.

Brice watched them from the porch and briefly envied their easy camaraderie. For the most part, his was a solitary job, although occasionally he was assigned to a case with other deputy marshals.

Smoke and Sally came up the steps arm in arm and paused long enough for Sally to say, "You'll stay and have supper with us, won't you, Brice?"

He hadn't been expecting such an invitation, but as he glanced at Denny, he realized it held a certain appeal. He nodded. "I sure will. I'm obliged to you for your hospitality, ma'am—I mean, Miss Sally."

She smiled and went on inside the house with Smoke.

Denny and Brad came up the steps and stopped on the porch, where Brad gazed up at Brice and asked, "Will you tell me about all the outlaws you've killed, Marshal?"

"Why, I don't make a habit of killing folks, Brad. I don't ever shoot anybody unless they just don't give me any choice in the matter."

"But you *have* shot some outlaws?"

"Well . . . yeah. It's nothing I'm all that proud of, though."

Brad couldn't seem to grasp that, so Brice was a little relieved when the youngster finally went on into the house. That left him alone on the porch with Denny. "I hope you don't mind that your ma asked me to stay for supper."

"That's not really up to me, is it?" she returned coolly.

"I reckon how you feel about it is."

She shrugged and shook her head. "I don't care one way or the other."

He wasn't sure which would be worse—if she was telling the truth about that, or if she wasn't.

Before either of them could say anything else, a new voice hailed Denny. Brice looked around to see one of the cowboys who had ridden in with Smoke walking toward the ranch house. Brice didn't recall ever seeing him before, but that wasn't unusual. As seldom as he got out to the Sugarloaf, he was sure there were plenty of men in Smoke's crew he didn't know.

This puncher was tall, rangy, and redheaded, wearing a grin that Brice instantly pegged as arrogant.

The cowboy rested his hands on the hitch rail as he said, "Ain't you glad to see that them rustlers didn't fill me full o' lead, Miss Denny?"

"Of course I am. I'm glad all of you made it back safely."

"All of us except for that fella name of Nelson. He got plugged in the shoulder, in the front and out the back. The sawbones in Black Hawk says he's gonna be all right, but he couldn't ride yet. He ought to be back in a week or so."

"Well, I'm sorry to hear that anybody was seriously injured."

The cowboy's grin widened. "We got off a whole heap luckier than them rustlers did. Every one of them no-good skunks has been planted in Black Hawk's Boot Hill by now." His gaze shifted to Brice, and his eyes narrowed. "Who's this hombre? Don't recollect seein' him around the ranch before."

"This is—"

"Brice Rogers," Brice cut in, stepping down the steps and sticking out his hand. "I'm just an old friend of the Jensen family." He didn't identify himself as a lawman and had spoken up to keep Denny from doing so.

He wasn't sure why he did that. His identity was no secret. If the puncher asked around in Big Rock or even brought up his name with other members of the Sugarloaf's crew, somebody was bound to tell him that Brice was a deputy U.S. marshal.

Instinct had warned Brice to keep that to himself for now, and he had learned to trust what his gut told him.

The redheaded cowboy hesitated, then clasped Brice's hand in a firm grip. "Steve Markham," he introduced himself.

"Have you been riding for the Sugarloaf long?"

"Not that long." The grin reappeared on his face as he glanced at Denny. "I signed on after I saved Miss Denny's life."

Brice couldn't stop himself from giving Denny a surprised look. "He saved your life?"

"I never said that—"

"She don't want to admit it," Markham broke in, "but there was this horse race, see, the day of her brother's wedding, and she snuck into it on this wild killer mustang called Rocket even though she wasn't s'posed to, and he run away with her and was about to go sailin' off into this gully and break both of their necks, when I come along and plucked her outta the saddle as neat as you please—"

"That's not the way it was at all!" Denny exclaimed, breaking into the flood of boasting words coming from Steve Markham's mouth.

"Oh?" the cowboy said challengingly. "And just what part of that little yarn I was spinnin' was wrong, Miss Denny? I ask you."

"I would have gotten Rocket under control and stopped him before he went into the gully."

"Didn't look like it to me."

Brice stood there looking back and forth between them, and he couldn't help but notice the intense way in which their eyes dueled. He recognized that attitude because Denny had looked exactly the same way at *him* during some of their arguments in the past, a mix of anger and . . . intrigue.

For some reason, the cocksure cowboy named Markham interested her.

And that made Brice's hackles rise. He didn't care for the feeling.

He turned to his horse and reached for the tied reins, saying, "Denny, I've just remembered that I need to check on something in Big Rock, so I can't stay for supper after all. Will you convey my regrets to your mother and tell her again that I appreciate the invitation?"

"So you're just going to ride off?" Denny asked, sounding annoyed. "Just like that?"

"Like I said, it's part of the job."

"And it won't wait until you'd get back to town this evening?"

"No, I'm afraid not."

Markham said, "Don't argue with the fella, Miss Denny. He's already done told you that he's got to go."

She drew in a breath deep enough to make her nostrils flare as Brice untied the sorrel's reins. "I suppose you're right, Steve. I'll tell my mother, Brice. She'll be sorry you weren't able to stay."

"Yeah, so am I." He swung up into the saddle, turned the sorrel away from the house, and heeled the horse into an easy lope. He wanted to look back over his shoulder and see if Denny and Steve Markham were still talking but kept his gaze fastened straight in front of him.

CHAPTER 26

Denny didn't see anything of Steve Markham for a couple of days after that and supposed that Cal was keeping him busy around the ranch.

She had seen the way Brice had looked at Markham and knew the deputy marshal wasn't fond of the cocky young cowboy. It seemed to be an instinctive reaction on Brice's part, and while Denny wasn't vain enough to think it was prompted entirely by jealousy, neither was it unreasonable to think that might be part of the reason.

Denny had always been a straightforward sort of girl. She didn't have any interest in toying with men's affections or playing them off against each other. She would be lying, though, if she claimed that having both of them interested in her didn't make a little thrill of pleasure go through her.

At supper one evening, Sally announced, "I'm taking the buckboard into Big Rock tomorrow to pick up some supplies and visit with friends. Does anyone want to go with me?"

"I do," Brad answered enthusiastically, without any hesitation at all.

"One of the hands could pick up the supplies," said Smoke.

"I know," Sally said, "but the Ladies' Aid Society is having a quick, informal meeting, too, to go over some last-minute plans for the next town social. It's coming up quickly, you know. This Saturday, in fact."

"Well, I don't reckon Cal or any other members of the crew would have any valuable advice about that," Smoke said with a grin, "so I guess you'd better handle it."

"And I'll come along to keep an eye on the kid," Denny volunteered with a nod toward Brad.

"Hey!" he objected. "I don't need anybody to keep an eye on me. Big Rock's not Tombstone or Deadwood, you know."

Smoke said, "Big Rock's seen its share of trouble in the past. So even though I suspect Denny really wants to go along just to get away from the ranch for a while, it's a good idea for the two of you to kind of keep an eye on each other."

It was Denny's turn to protest. "I don't need a chaperone. Especially a nine-year-old one."

"It's settled. You're both coming with me," Sally said.

"Can I ride a horse?" Brad asked.

"Well . . ."

Smoke said, "Rafael can find a horse that'll be safe enough for you to ride, Brad."

"How about Blaze?" asked Brad, referring to the horse Rafael had been working with recently.

Smoke shook his head. "I was just talking to Rafe

about him yesterday. He's not ready yet, but we've got some nice, gentle saddle mares."

"Oh." Brad looked a little disappointed, but he summoned up a smile and went on. "I guess that'll be all right." Then he turned to Denny and asked, "Are you gonna ride Rocket?"

"No," Denny, Smoke, and Sally all answered at once.

Denny knew she could have ridden on the buckboard with her mother, but when she emerged from the house the next morning, she was dressed in boots, hat, and range clothes. She wore a gun belt buckled around her trim hips, and a .38 caliber Colt Lightning revolver with an ivory bird's-head grip rested in the holster.

Denny had put in a lot of hours practicing with that gun and was fast and accurate with it. She didn't anticipate running into any trouble in Big Rock, but it never hurt to be prepared.

Her mother might have something to say about her packing an iron in the open like that, but Denny knew there would be a Winchester in the buckboard. Sally Jensen didn't believe in being taken by surprise, either. Jensen women didn't go around unarmed.

Denny went to the barn and found Brad already there with Rafael de Santos. Rafael was supervising while Brad saddled a gray mare that was easy to handle. He had to stand on a stool to place the saddle onto the horse's back, and he grunted from the effort required to lift it. Denny would have offered to help him, but she knew he would have refused. She would have done the same if their positions had been reversed.

"You want me to saddle a horse for you, Miss Denny?" asked Rafael.

"No, thanks. I can handle it," she told him.

From the look on his weathered face, he had known that *she* would refuse the offer, too. She and Brad had the same sort of independent streak.

When she got her saddle on a rangy lineback dun she liked to use as a saddle mount, she and Brad led their horses out of the stable. She saw one of the cowboys bringing the buckboard around from the shed in which it was kept and realized the puncher handling the team was Steve Markham.

One of the horses from the Sugarloaf's remuda was saddled and tied on at the back of the vehicle, as well. The sight of that made Denny frown a little as she thought about what it might mean.

Markham smoothly brought the buckboard to a stop in front of the ranch house, looped the reins around the brake lever, put a hand on the seat beside him, and vaulted lithely to the ground. He landed gracefully and looked up to grin at Denny and Brad as they walked toward him.

"Mornin'," he greeted them. "I hear y'all are goin' to town."

"That's right," Denny said.

"So 'm I," Markham announced.

That was what Denny had thought he might say, based on that saddle horse being tied on behind the buckboard.

He pulled a folded piece of paper out of his shirt

pocket and went on. "Cal—I mean, Mr. Woods—gave me this order for some fence posts and wire I'm supposed to give to Mr. Leo Goldstein at the store in Big Rock."

"I can do that." Denny held out her hand. "Let me have it. I'm sure you have better things to do here on the ranch."

Markham pulled the paper back and stuck it back in his pocket. "No, ma'am. The foreman done give me an order, and I intend to carry it out to the best of my ability."

"I think you're just trying to get out of actual work."

"It wasn't my idea," Markham insisted with a shake of his head. "You can go ask the boss about that if you want."

Denny wasn't going to waste her time standing around arguing with him. "Just tell me one thing . . . did Cal ask for volunteers for this little job?"

Markham's smiled widened. He admitted, "Well, he might have. And I might've been a little quicker to speak up than the other fellas."

"All right. You do whatever you want, as long as you stay out of our way. Isn't that right, Brad?"

The boy looked a little puzzled by the conversation, but he said, "Sure, I guess, Denny. But what are we gonna do?"

"As a matter of fact, I thought we might stop at Mr. Goldstein's store ourselves. He has a pretty good selection of candy, you know."

"I know! I look through that glass counter at it every time I'm in there. My ma lets me get a piece every now and then, but not every time because she says too much candy's not good for me." Hopefully, he added, "It's been a while."

"That's what I figured."

Markham said, "I wouldn't mind havin' a peppermint stick myself."

"You can pay for your own," Denny told him.

Sally came out of the house then, pulling on gloves for handling the buckboard's reins, so Denny's sparing with Markham came to an end. Sally looked at her daughter and said, "I'm not surprised to see that you're riding horseback, Denny. Are you and Brad ready to go?"

"I sure am," Brad said.

Markham moved quickly around the buckboard, saying, "Let me give you a hand, ma'am."

"That's not necessary, Mr. Markham," Sally told him. "I've been climbing onto and off of wagons by myself for a long time." She demonstrated that by stepping up onto the buckboard before Markham could reach her. As she settled herself onto the seat, he untied the saddle horse from the back of the vehicle, prompting her to ask, "Are you coming into town with us?"

"Yes, ma'am. Mr. Woods gave me a job to do there."

"We'll enjoy your company then," Sally said with a smile.

Denny wasn't sure about that, but there didn't seem to be any way of *avoiding* it, that was for sure. She swung up into the saddle, aware of Markham watching her movements with admiration in his eyes.

Sally slapped the reins against the backs of the two horses hitched to the buckboard. They started off smoothly and the buckboard rolled away from the house. Denny nudged her dun ahead, and Brad fell in beside her. The two of them led the way along the trail that after half a mile passed under the arched entrance with the Sugarloaf's name on it and joined the main road to Big Rock. Steve Markham brought up the rear. Denny didn't look back at him, although she thought at times she could feel his eyes watching her.

Maybe she was just imagining that, though. She wasn't sure if she hoped that was true or not.

CHAPTER 27

Big Rock

Leo Goldstein was a handsome young man who had taken over the general store a few years earlier when his father, who had founded the business, retired. He took the paper that Steve Markham handed him, looked at the list Cal had written on it, and said, "Of course, this won't be a problem. I don't have this much wire on hand, but I'll get it sent out from Denver right away. Tell Cal it should be here in, oh, three days."

"I sure will," said Markham with a nod. "Obliged to you."

Denny watched that exchange from the corner of her eye. She and Brad stood in front of the glass-fronted counter where the candy was displayed. There were a number of different kinds, and it made for a colorful, appetizing assortment. Brad was bent over, face close to the glass and hands resting on his knees as he studied the selection with wide eyes and occasionally licked his lips. He looked like he could happily stand there all day.

Denny wasn't going to rush him. She stepped back a little to let the youngster gaze to his heart's content, heard a footstep beside her, and glanced over to see that Markham had joined them.

"Well, I got Cal's little chore done," he said.

"I suppose that means you can head on back out to the ranch."

"Naw, Cal said it was all right for me to just stay and ride back with you and your ma and the boy."

"Did Cal come up with that, or did you *ask* him if that would be all right?"

A sheepish grin appeared on the cowboy's raw-boned face, and he chuckled. "You know me too well, Miss Denny, and that's a plumb fact. But he didn't argue, and, well, he's the foreman, ain't he? If he says it, it's all right."

"Fine," Denny muttered.

"You know, I can't quite figure out why you act like you don't like havin' me around," he said quietly. They weren't the only customers in the store, but other than Brad no one else was close by, and the tall shelves of merchandise partially shielded them from view. "I know for a fact that ain't true."

"What do you mean by that?"

"I mean, you like havin' me around. I know you do. And I like bein' around you." He lifted his left hand and lightly touched her right arm, about halfway between her elbow and shoulder. At first his fingertips just grazed her through the shirt sleeve.

"What are you doing?" Denny asked tightly.

His touch shifted and tightened a little. He wasn't really holding her arm, but his hand closed loosely around it. In a hoarse whisper, he said, "I knew the first second I laid eyes on you, Denny, that you and me were meant to get together. It's as plain as day that you like me and I like you. I like you a hell of a lot, in fact."

Denny cut her eyes toward Brad, who had his back to them. He didn't seem to be paying the least bit of attention to them with all that candy on the other side of the glass to keep him enthralled, but it was always difficult to say just how much kids were aware of what went on around them. They could be surprisingly observant.

"Stop it," she told Markham. "This isn't the time or place—"

"I know it, but it's been durned near impossible to get you by yourself. This is as close as I've been able to come."

"Well, it's too close," Denny snapped. "Get your hand off my arm."

"If you're sure . . ."

"I'm sure."

Markham let go of her arm. But he looked around quickly, as if checking to see if anyone was watching, and then put his hands on her shoulders and turned her to face him and leaned down to press his lips to hers. The kiss took Denny completely by surprise, and her first impulse was to jerk back, ball her hand into a fist, and punch him in the face.

For some reason, though, she didn't do that. She stood there and allowed him to continue kissing her for what seemed like a minute or more but was probably only a few seconds. She thought her heart had beaten only a handful of times when he stepped away and let his hands fall from her shoulders.

"If that gets me fired, I pure-dee don't give a damn." The familiar grin stretched across his face. "It was worth it!"

Denny's pulse hammered in her head. In a way, she still felt like hitting him, but she knew she wasn't going to do that. She also knew, whether she wanted to admit it or not, that she wouldn't mind if he were to kiss her again . . .

To put that thought out of her head, she said sharply, "You shouldn't be as worried about being fired as you are about what my father might do!"

"The famous Smoke Jensen's gonna shoot it out with me 'cause I stole a kiss from his daughter? That don't seem very likely."

"What about thrashing you within an inch of your life? Hell, *I* might do that."

That finally made Brad notice something was going on. He turned his head to look back at them and said, "Denny, you said a bad word. I've gotten in trouble with my ma for sayin' things like that."

"Well, I'm a grown-up, so I can say whatever I want," Denny responded. "But your mother's right to tell you to watch your language. How you speak has a lot to do with what people think of you."

"I reckon." With the shifting attention span of childhood, he changed the subject and asked, "How many pieces of candy did you say I can have?"

"I didn't say . . . but I suppose two wouldn't hurt." She didn't think Melanie would mind that, assuming that she ever found out about it.

"Then I want a piece of licorice and a peppermint stick."

Markham laughed. "Those sound like mighty good choices to me, too. Reckon I'll have the same thing."

"Do you have money to pay for it?" Denny asked him.

"I do. I wasn't dead broke when I showed up in Big Rock, you know. Just durned near."

Denny motioned Leo Goldstein over as soon as the proprietor wasn't busy with another customer, and Brad made his selections. Denny paid for them, and the two of them strolled out of the store while Markham remained to make his transaction.

Sally had already given the list of supplies she wanted to Goldstein, and a couple of clerks were packing up the order. They would load it onto the buckboard when it was ready. Sally had gone to the town hall to have her meeting with the Ladies' Aid Society. For the moment, the buckboard sat empty in front of the store's high porch, which also served as a loading dock.

Brad bit a piece off the short length of licorice Denny had bought for him and stood there chewing it while the two of them looked around town. Big Rock was a fairly busy place on the summer morning, with a wide variety of people on the boardwalks and plenty of horses and wagons moving in the street. Brad's eyes eagerly took in all the activity.

Boots clomped on the porch behind them as Markham emerged from the store and joined them. Instead of going for the licorice first thing, he was licking the peppermint stick he had bought.

"What's this town social your ma was talkin' about?" he asked Denny.

"What do you think it is? You've gone to socials before, haven't you?"

"You mean with dancin' and little cakes and sweet punch that the local boys slip a little tanglefoot into? And when the boys and girls get tired of dancin', they slip outside under the trees for a little sparkin'?"

"That's right. Big Rock has one of those every few months, and the next one is this Saturday. It's a shame Louis and Melanie have to miss it, but I'm sure they're having fun by themselves, wherever they are."

"Oh, I reckon so," said Markham, with just enough of a leer in his tone to make Denny frown briefly at him in disapproval. He went on. "Is everybody in the valley invited to these here socials?"

"Of course. People come from miles around."

"Like they did to your brother's weddin'."

Denny smiled. "Yes, that's right."

"And I suppose the fellas ask the girls they like to go with them."

"That's right." Denny paused. "Except for one time each year when turnabout is fair play and the girls ask the fellows instead."

Markham's eyebrows jumped up. "Does this happen to be one of them special times?"

Denny hesitated. She didn't want to tell him the truth, but at the same time, he could find out from just about anybody in town. After a moment, she said, "Yes, it is."

"Which means you can ask any fella you want to be your beau for that night." A look of realization came over him. "That is . . . unless you already asked somebody . . ."

Denny glanced at Brad, who was enjoying his

licorice and completely ignoring any talk about town socials and what went on at them. For a second, she considered telling Markham that she had already asked Brad, but she had tried to use that excuse at the dance following Louis and Melanie's wedding and that hadn't really worked out. She couldn't think of anything else, so she told the truth. "No, I haven't."

"Well, then . . ." Markham preened, wiggled his eyebrows, and grinned expectantly.

Denny stood there, well aware that he was going to keep on pestering her until she made up her mind. She tried to shove the thought of that kiss out of her head, but without much success. The seconds ticked past, and finally, out of exasperation as much as anything else, Denny said, "Oh, all right. Steve Markham, will you go to the town social with me?"

The words were barely out of her mouth when she glanced past him and saw Brice Rogers coming up the steps at the end of the porch, well within earshot of the question she had just posed.

CHAPTER 28

Brice had been climbing the steps briskly, but he slowed and then stopped as he reached the porch. The puzzled, angry frown that appeared on his face told Denny that he had heard what she said to Markham. She had hoped that he hadn't, although it wouldn't have really mattered, she realized. Markham would have crowed about it anyway.

Which is exactly what he did, his grin widening as he said, "Will I go with you to the town social, Miss Denny? Why, I sure will! I'll be pleased as that punch the boys are gonna be spikin'. It'll be a pure honor to escort you to that fandango." His voice was loud enough that everybody in the vicinity of the general store must have heard him, not just Brice Rogers.

Brice was aware of what was going on, that was for sure. He came closer.

Markham noticed him and said, "Why, howdy there, Rogers."

Brice ignored the greeting and looked intently at Denny. He pinched the brim of his brown hat and nodded as he said, "Morning, Miss Jensen." His voice was coldly formal.

"Hello, Brice." She gestured vaguely toward Markham. "You know Steve Markham . . ."

"Yeah, we met at the ranch the other day." Brice's tone was even chillier as he added, "Hello, Markham."

"You hear the news?" Markham said. "Miss Denny just asked me to go to that town social with her. Ain't that somethin'?"

"Yeah, it sure is." Brice looked at Denny again. "Hope you enjoy yourself, Miss Jensen."

Before Denny could respond, the sound of a train's whistle shrilled through the air. In a minute or so, the westbound would be pulling up to the platform of the big redbrick station at the end of the street.

Brad caught hold of Denny's hand, tugging on it. "Let's go watch the train come in! I like trains."

Denny saw an opportunity and seized it. "Steve, why don't you walk down to the depot with Brad and watch the train come in?"

"You and I were talkin'—" Markham began.

"We've finished our conversation for now."

Brice had turned away and started toward the door of the general store.

"I thought of something else I need to ask Mr. Goldstein."

Brad let go of her hand and tugged on Markham's sleeve. "Come on, Steve," he urged. "I want to be there when the train lets the steam off. It makes these big clouds!"

"All right," Markham said with some reluctance. He added to Denny, "We'll talk more later."

"I'm sure we will," she agreed. As Brad and Markham started down the steps to the street, she hurried into the store where Brice Rogers had just gone.

She caught up to him before he reached the counter in the rear of the store. "Brice, I want to talk to you."

He stopped, turned, and regarded her coolly as he said, "I'm not sure what we have to talk about."

"Oh, don't be like that, blast it," she said as her exasperation overcame her desire to smooth things over. "I'd planned to ask *you* to that social, but I've barely seen you for weeks."

"My job keeps me pretty—"

"Busy, I know. There's no guarantee that you'll even be in town on Saturday night, is there? You may be off somewhere chasing a bunch of owlhoots."

"There are no guarantees in a lawman's life," said Brice.

"That's right. So don't act offended that I asked Steve Markham instead. I know he'll be available."

"You don't hardly know the fella. He hasn't even been around here a month."

"But in the time he's been here, he's helped me out,"—Denny was still a little reluctant to admit that about the horse race, but it was true—"fought rustlers side by side with my father, and probably saved Cal's life. I'd say he's made a pretty good impression."

"He must have, for you to ask him to go with you to that social."

Denny threw her hands in the air. "It's just one dance, Brice!"

"Seemed like it was more than that to Markham, the way he was so excited about it. I hope you have a good time, Denny. Now, if you'll excuse me . . . Got to stock up on ammunition. Never can tell when I'll have to go off chasing owlhoots again."

He gave her a polite nod—his natural chivalry wouldn't allow him to do any less than that, she knew—and turned to walk toward the counter again.

Denny let him go. If he wanted to be like that, she thought, then that was just fine. She wasn't going to worry about his delicate little feelings, she told herself with a mental snort of dismissal.

Still, she wished things hadn't turned out quite that way, and the feeling nagged at her as she walked toward Big Rock's railroad station.

The westbound train had arrived by the time she got there, of course, and in fact was just about ready to roll out again after passengers had disembarked and others had boarded. All the freight bound for Big Rock had been unloaded. Men were taking crates from a stack on the platform and placing them on wagons pulled up at one end of the building.

Denny spotted Steve Markham and Brad standing on the platform not far from the big Baldwin locomotive. Brad was talking animatedly and pointing.

As Denny came up to them, Markham said, "Ol' Brad here knows a whole heap about trains, lemme tell you. He's been explainin' to me what all the parts of this locomotive are."

"I wouldn't mind being an engineer someday," Brad said. "If I'm not a cowboy, that is. Or a famous explorer."

"I've got a feeling you can do whatever you set your mind to," Denny told the youngster.

"Did you get your, ah, business finished with that Rogers fella?" Markham asked.

Denny was about to tell him that that was none of

his business, but she reined in the impulse. Instead she said, "Don't worry about Brice Rogers."

"He's a lawman, you know," Brad piped up.

Markham looked down at the boy and frowned. "He is?"

"Yep. A deputy United States marshal, he told me. I guess he was telling the truth. He didn't show me his badge or anything."

Markham glanced at Denny. "You didn't tell me my competition was a deputy marshal."

"The two of you aren't competing for anything," she said.

"I ain't so sure about that."

"Well, I am," Denny said.

She might have said more, but at that moment someone behind her called, "Miss Jensen?"

She turned to see a redhaired, freckle-faced boy about sixteen hurrying toward her. He wore black trousers and vest, a white shirt and a string tie, and had a green eyeshade on his head. Denny knew his name and that he worked at the Western Union office as a messenger and part-time telegrapher. He clutched a little envelope in one hand, the sort of envelope in which telegrams were delivered.

"Hello, Lester," she said. "What can I do for you? Is that telegram for me?"

"No, ma'am," said Lester, "but it is for your pa. I was gonna ride out to the Sugarloaf and deliver it later this afternoon, but I saw you walking through the depot lobby and figured if I could catch up to you and let you take it, Mr. Jensen would get it sooner. If you're heading back out to the ranch before too much longer, that is."

"We won't be starting back until my mother is ready to go," Denny explained, "but that shouldn't be too much longer." She took the envelope from the young man. "Thank you, Lester. I'll be glad to give it to my father."

"Thank *you*, Miss Jensen." Lester ducked his head, scuffed his foot against the platform, and turned to hurry off.

Markham laughed. "Did you see how that young fella was blushin'? I guess just talkin' to you got him all hot and bothered, Denny."

Brad said, "Why would he be hot and bothered? Was he scared of you, Denny?"

"Maybe a little, Brad," she said as she gave Markham another quick frown.

He laughed again and gestured toward the envelope. "Don't you wonder who that wire's from?"

"It's none of my business. It's addressed to my father."

"Yeah, but I'll bet you're curious, anyway."

Denny shrugged. "Doesn't matter. I'm not going to open it and read it, if that's what you're implying."

"Don't you ever break the rules? Oh, wait a minute. You snuck that Rocket mustang into the race at your brother's weddin', didn't you?"

"I've broken plenty of rules," Denny snapped, then immediately regretted it because she supposed she shouldn't have been saying such a thing in front of Brad. She was a grown-up, after all, and ought to be setting a good example for him.

The train's conductor walked along beside the cars and let out the traditional leather-lunged bellow of *"Boooaaarrrdd! All aboard!"* Up in the locomotive's cab, the engineer pulled the whistle cord again, and the shriek was loud enough to prevent any further conversation on the platform. With a hiss of steam and rattle and clank of drivers on the steel rails, the train began to move.

As it pulled out of the station, Denny put a hand on Brad's shoulder and turned him toward the depot lobby. "Come on. Let's go see if my mother's ready to head back to the ranch yet."

CHAPTER 29

The Sugarloaf

"It's from a rancher up in Montana named Bob Coburn," Smoke said as he held the yellow telegraph flimsy. He had just read the message printed on it in block capitals. "His Circle C spread is one of the best in that part of the country. I met him a while back while I was on a trip to Kansas City. He talked about buying some horses from me." Smoke tapped a fingertip against the telegram. "Seems he's ready to make the deal." He sat behind the desk in his office and study.

Denny had just brought the telegram in to him after she, Sally, Brad, and Markham returned from Big Rock.

"I didn't know you were looking to sell any horses," Denny commented. The possibility that she might be running the day-to-day operations on the Sugarloaf at some point in the future had occurred to her, so she tried to keep up with everything that was going on and learn from it.

Smoke dropped the telegram on the desk and

nodded. "Rafael's been working hard, and we have more good saddle mounts than we really need. Those horses have to have steady work to stay in top form, and we can't give it to them." He smiled. "Besides, Bob will pay top price for them."

Denny nodded. She knew her father didn't really need the money. Many years ago, when he was a young man, he and the old mountain man, Preacher, had found a gold deposit and worked it with the help of Smoke's adopted brother Matt. That had given Smoke a good stake, and the success of the Sugarloaf as a working ranch had increased his wealth. Despite that, Smoke still believed in getting a good price whenever he sold horses or cattle. He thought the livestock ought to fetch what it was worth, and Denny certainly couldn't disagree with that.

She said, "I'd be happy to help round them up and drive them to Big Rock so they can be shipped up to Montana."

Smoke's smile widened as he leaned back in his chair. "That's another part of the deal that appeals to me. The railroad doesn't run that close to Bob's ranch. It occurs to me that we could ship that horse herd part of the way by rail, then drive it the remainder of the distance to the Circle C the old-fashioned way. It's about eighty miles or so, as I recall. I haven't been on a real trail drive in quite a while. These days it's just not necessary." He shrugged. "This would be horses instead of cattle, but still, it might be fun."

Denny thought the same thing. "All right." She then declared emphatically, "I'm coming along."

Smoke cocked his head to the side. "That's not really necessary. I can handle the drive just fine.

Besides, I'm not sure how your mother would feel about you traipsing off to Montana like that."

Denny leaned forward and rested her hands on top of the desk. "I've never *been* on a trail drive. I've heard you and Cal and Pearlie talk about them plenty of times, though. I think it's something I ought to experience for myself, before it's too late."

"It's a lot of hot, dusty work," Smoke said. "Inexperienced hands ride drag. You'd eat a lot of dust."

"You just said it would be fun."

Smoke grinned. "Riding point will be . . . and that's where I'll be."

"When will you take the herd up there?"

"Not for a while yet. I'll have to trade some more wires with Bob and finalize the deal, and anyway, I'm not going to miss the town social this Saturday after your mother and the other ladies have put so much work into planning it. So I figure it'll be a week or ten days before we start for Montana."

"Then this conversation isn't over," Denny said. "There's still time to convince you I'm right and ought to go along." She paused. "Speaking of the social, there's been a development on that front."

"Not a problem, I hope. Like I said, your mother's put a lot of work into it."

"No, nothing like that. Nothing to do with the social itself. But you remember, this is the one where the ladies can ask the men?"

Smoke nodded. "Sure."

"Well, today while we were in town, I asked someone to go with me."

"Ran into Brice Rogers, did you?" Smoke knew

that she and Brice had been attracted to each other in the past.

Denny was well aware that her father was too observant not to have noticed that. Normally, she didn't discuss such things with him, but since this involved one of his ranch hands . . . "I did see Brice, but I didn't ask him. I asked Steve Markham to go with me."

"Markham," Smoke repeated with a frown.

"I don't need your permission to ask somebody to a dance—"

He held up a hand, palm outward, to stop her. "Hold on. Take it easy, Denny. I didn't say you needed my permission. But I thought you and Markham didn't even get along that well. You're always, well, barking at him whenever he's around."

"Sometimes he deserves being barked at," said Denny. "But he was a good man to have on your side when you caught up with those rustlers down in Black Hawk, wasn't he?"

Smoke nodded and said, "That's true. He came in mighty handy."

"And I know you don't look down on him because he's just a forty-a-month-and-found cowpuncher."

"Not at all," Smoke agreed. "Men like that are the backbone of the cattle business. But from what he's told us, he's never had any interest in being anything else, and men like that don't settle down very often."

"It's just one social! Nobody said anything about settling down."

Smoke nodded. "That's true. I'm just saying it might not be a good idea to go too fast or get too serious about a man like Steve Markham."

"Don't worry. I'm not going to sneak off into the trees and surrender my virtue to him."

Smoke cleared his throat and looked uncomfortable. "Why did you even bring up this subject, Denny?"

"I just didn't want you to see me with him at the social and be surprised, that's all." She wondered briefly if that really *was* all, though. She wouldn't allow her father's disapproval to stop her from doing anything she really wanted to do, but on the other hand, it was always nice to have his approval.

"All right," he said. "You don't need my blessing for something like this—"

"Damn right I don't."

"But Markham seems like a decent enough young fella, if a little shiftless," Smoke went on. "The two of you enjoy yourselves at that dance."

"I intend to."

"One thing I'm a mite curious about, though . . . You said you saw Brice Rogers in town. Does *he* know that you're going to the social with Markham?"

"It's none of his business," Denny said, then shrugged and continued. "But as a matter of fact, he does. I don't think he was very happy about it, either. But if he was around here more often and not gallivanting all over the countryside, things might not have happened this way."

"Being a deputy marshal keeps him on the move a lot."

"That's not my fault."

"No, I reckon not," Smoke admitted. "You have anything else you need to tell me?"

"No, that's all. Except for the fact that we're going

to continue that discussion about me going along on the trip to Montana."

"I'm sure we will," Smoke said.

After Denny left the office, Smoke began drafting a reply to Bob Coburn's telegram, but he kept pausing as other thoughts intruded on his mind, and after a few minutes he set the pen aside and sat back with a slight frown creasing his forehead.

Denny *had* surprised him with the interest she'd expressed in Steve Markham. Plenty of cowboys had a certain cockiness to them, but Markham's self-confidence bordered on arrogance. Smoke figured a lot of that was due to Markham's youth and that, sooner or later, life would take him down a notch or two and give him the necessary humbling that maturity required. For now, though, Smoke would have said that Denny found him more annoying than appealing.

But he had never been an expert at recognizing what women were thinking or feeling, he reminded himself. He knew Sally better than any other woman on earth, and she still contained plenty of mysteries that were beyond his grasp.

Preacher had warned him that it would always be that way.

Anyway, as Denny had pointed out so vociferously, it was just one town social. She would dance with Markham, among others, and maybe drink some punch with him, and that would be it.

However, as Smoke sat there he recalled what Pearlie had said about Markham reminding him of someone. As far as Smoke knew, his old friend had never figured out why he felt that way, but it didn't have to mean anything. Pearlie had known hundreds of hombres, good and bad, over the years. The fact that Steve Markham maybe resembled one of them was no reason to worry.

Smoke tried to convince himself of that, but he wasn't entirely successful.

CHAPTER 30

Denny wore a light blue dress with white lace at the neckline and hem. When Brad saw her before they left the Sugarloaf, he said with a surprised expression, "You're not wearin' a six-gun."

"Well, that would look kind of silly, wouldn't it, to have a gun belt strapped around a dress like this?"

"I suppose so. I'm just not used to seein' you without a gun somewhere close by."

Denny just smiled. She couldn't very well pull up her dress and show the boy the two-shot, over-under, .32 caliber derringer in a holster fastened to her thigh. She had positioned the holster so that it shouldn't interfere with her dancing that evening.

Sally, wearing a darker blue gown with long sleeves, looked beautiful, too, and Smoke had donned a brown Western-cut suit for the occasion. Denny tried not to be sentimental, but when she saw them coming arm in arm out of the ranch house onto the porch, she was touched by how wonderful they looked together. *That* was the sort of marriage she wanted to wind up in . . . when she met the right man and the time was right. That man wasn't going to be Steve Markham, she was confident of that.

It didn't occur to her until they were on their way into town that the same thought regarding Brice Rogers hadn't crossed her mind.

The Sugarloaf had a two-seat buggy for special occasions. Smoke handled the reins with Sally beside him on the front seat. Denny and Brad rode in the back. Brad pulled at his shirt collar just as much as he had at the wedding.

"You'd better quit messing with that," Denny told him as the buggy rolled toward town.

"Aw, I just hate havin' anything around my neck. It makes me feel like I'm bein' choked."

"You can stand it just for this evening."

"I don't know why I have to go in the first place," Brad muttered. "I'm not gonna dance with any ol' girl. I could've stayed at the ranch with Pearlie."

"There'll be punch," Denny reminded him. "And the kids usually play some games outside."

His mood brightened a little as he shrugged. "Well, maybe it won't be *too* bad."

"Besides, Pearlie's going to the social, too. I heard Cal say that Pearlie planned to get slicked up and dance with all the widows."

Brad made a face. "Why would anybody want to do *that*?"

"You'll figure it out one of these days," Denny told him.

"I reckon I'd just as soon not," Brad declared emphatically.

Up front, Sally laughed, looked back over her

shoulder at them, and said, "Don't worry, Bradley, you have plenty of time to figure out that and everything else."

When they reached Big Rock, Smoke parked the buggy in front of Longmont's. They would have to walk farther but wouldn't have to deal as much with the crowd already gathering along the street. Smoke got out first and helped Sally down, then Denny and Brad climbed out of the buggy on opposite sides.

"I told Steve Markham I'd meet him here, and then we'd walk to the town hall together," Denny said.

Sally began, "I'm still not sure—"

But Smoke interrupted her and said, "Brad, you come with Sally and me. We'll go get some of that punch I keep hearing about." He looked at Denny and added, "See you down there."

"In a little while, I imagine," she said with a nod.

Her mother gave her a skeptical look, then linked arms with Smoke and took Brad's hand.

"I could wait and come with Denny and Steve," the boy suggested.

"You don't want to hang around with those two all evening," said Smoke. "You'll have more fun if you come along with us."

"Yeah, you're probably right." Brad rolled his eyes. "They'll just act all moony around each other!"

Smoke broke out in a laugh at that. "I've known Denny a lot longer than you, son. One thing I've never seen her do is act moony over some fella!"

"Thanks for that, anyway," Denny muttered.

The other three headed down the boardwalk toward the town hall four blocks away. Denny waited in front of Longmont's, knowing the group of ranch hands from the Sugarloaf wouldn't be long in arriving. As she stood there, she could feel the excitement and anticipation growing in Big Rock. This gathering would be one of the highlights of the summer, along with the big Fourth of July celebration the next month.

"Ah, Denise, the very sight of you is balm to a man's weary eyes!"

She turned and saw that Louis Longmont had emerged from the doors of his restaurant and saloon. He was elegantly dressed, as always, and would have looked equally at home on the streets of New York, Boston, or San Francisco. He smiled at her and went on. "Smoke and Sally have already gone on to the social?"

"That's right. I'm waiting for someone I told to meet me here."

"Deputy Marshal Rogers? He was by here earlier . . ."

So Brice was in town this evening after all. Denny told herself that didn't matter and shook her head. "No, I'm going to the social with Steve Markham, one of the men from the Sugarloaf."

Louis arched one eyebrow for a second, then said, "I hope you have a very pleasant evening."

"I intend to," Denny said firmly.

He smiled again and moved on, clearly heading for the town hall himself. Denny watched him go, then turned as she heard the sound of horses approaching.

About two dozen members of the Sugarloaf's crew had ridden into Big Rock for the social. They were all dressed in their best clothes, which in most cases

meant their cleanest, least-patched range garb, often
ornamented with brightly colored bandannas around
their throats.

Cal and Pearlie were in the lead, and as foreman
and retired foreman, they owned actual suits. They,
along with the rest of the cowboys, were bathed and
barbered and shaved, and Denny could almost smell
the waves of bay rum coming off them from where
she was on the boardwalk.

Steve Markham was close behind Cal and Pearlie.
He had on boots and jeans, of course, but he had dug
a white shirt and a black vest and a string tie out of
his gear. His hat was brushed free of dirt and dust,
and the brim was curled just right. A big grin spread
across his face when he spotted Denny watching him
ride closer.

Markham moved his horse forward and said to
Cal, "I'll see you boys later. The little lady I'm goin' to
the social with is waitin' for me right here."

Cal reined to a stop in the street in front of Longmont's and leaned his hands on the saddle horn as
he asked, "Miss Denny, is this big ape telling the
truth? You're really going to the social with him?"

"No, he's going with me," Denny replied with a
smile. "This is the one where the ladies do the asking,
remember?"

"Well, I suppose if you say so." Cal turned to give
Markham a hard look. "You're going to be on your
best behavior tonight, aren't you?"

"Don't reckon I'd dare be otherwise, when everybody around the whole ranch is hell on wheels, in-
cludin' the lady her own self."

"And don't you forget it," Pearlie added.

Denny laughed. "Pearlie, you look positively dashing tonight."

Pearlie swept his hat off his head and bowed low in the saddle. "Thank you, Miss Denny. You're mighty easy on the eyes, too."

With that, the Sugarloaf hands rode on up the street toward the town hall while Markham dismounted and tied his horse at the hitch rack in front of Longmont's.

"Good evenin'," he said as he stepped up onto the boardwalk and took off his hat. "I don't figure on lettin' that old codger outdo me on the compliments. You look plumb beautiful, Denny."

"And you're surprisingly respectable."

"Thanks. I put some effort into it." He clapped his hat back on his head and extended his arm. "Ready to go?"

Denny linked her arm with his, and they started walking toward the town hall.

After a moment, Markham went on. "I reckon I know why you wanted to meet down here and walk the rest of the way."

"Oh? Why is that?"

"You wanted to be sure everybody got a good look at the handsome fella you're with. And that's all right. I don't mind you showin' me off. I reckon I understand."

Denny laughed. "So that's it. I'm glad you explained it to me."

Even though his attitude amused her, she wondered if there was any truth to what he said. Did she really want people to see the two of them walking to the social together?

Or . . . one person in particular?

The front and back doors and all the windows in the Big Rock town hall were open to allow the evening breeze to flow through. That let plenty of light spill out around the building to guide the steps of the people flocking toward it in the twilight. It was Saturday night, and people had come from all over the valley to attend the town social.

A number of them greeted Denny as she and Markham approached the town hall. In the year since she and her brother had returned permanently to the Sugarloaf, she had met quite a few people in the valley and was friendly with most of them, although she hadn't made any close friends, due to her own reserved nature. She didn't get close to people easily, but when she did, she was deeply devoted to them.

Several girls she was acquainted with giggled and wanted to know who her beau was. Denny smiled and introduced him, and Markham responded gallantly, taking his hat off and bowing and stopping just short of kissing the backs of some hands. Denny was familiar with that sort of behavior, having seen it from aristocrats all over Europe while she and Louis were living in England.

The thought of how some of those so-called aristocrats and noblemen acted made an angry frown cross her face for a moment, but she put those memories firmly out of her mind.

Arriving at the large, whitewashed town hall, they went up the steps to the entrance, which was crowded with people at the moment. A loud buzz of conversation and laughter came from inside. The music and dancing hadn't gotten underway yet, but they would probably start before too much longer.

Denny spoke to several more people while she and Markham waited to go in, and then the logjam in the doorway cleared and they strolled into the building. Denny looked around the packed room for her parents and Brad.

An opening suddenly formed around them as people stepped back, and although the noise continued in the room in general, in their particular vicinity the voices suddenly trailed off in startled silence. With Markham beside her, Denny stopped short, not sure what was going on but heeding the instincts that told her something wasn't quite right.

The next moment, she understood why she had sensed that. A man stepped out of the crowd, and if she and Markham hadn't stopped already, he would have forced them to, the way he planted himself resolutely right in their path.

That same grim resolution was on Brice Rogers's face as he said, "Denny, I want to talk to you."

CHAPTER 31

Brice wore a brown suit and a cravat with a turquoise stud holding it in place. He was freshly shaved, too, and in that moment of intense confrontation, Denny noticed a couple of tiny spots of dried blood on his throat where he had nicked himself. His light brown, slightly wavy hair was carefully combed and brushed. He was handsome enough that when he came into the town hall, he had probably drawn the attention of every young, unmarried lady there . . . and more than likely some of the not-so-young, married ones, as well.

He wasn't wearing a gun, since coming to a town social armed was frowned upon, except for Sheriff Monte Carson. But even without a Colt on his hip, an air of taut menace surrounded him. An open challenge lurked in his eyes as he stared at Denny and Markham.

"Howdy, Rogers," the cowboy said in a flat, noncommittal tone, as if he were willing to be friendly but was going to wait and see what Brice had to say next.

"I wasn't talking to you."

That curt response made Markham's jaw tighten.

Denny saw a little muscle jerk in it, and since her arm was still linked with his, she tightened it a little to rein in whatever he might do next.

She didn't want trouble, especially there, so she said quickly, "What do you want, Brice?"

"I told you, to talk to you."

"Well, here I am."

Brice glanced at Markham and said, "I need to talk to you alone."

"Take a look around." Denny used her free hand to gesture toward the crowd. "That's going to be pretty hard to do tonight, don't you think? Whatever you have to say, you might as well go ahead and say it."

Brice jerked his chin toward Markham and snapped, "Not in front of this no-account saddle tramp."

"Listen, fella, you're actin' a mite too proddy there," Markham said. "You got no call to be talkin' to the lady like that . . . or sayin' such things about me."

"Just telling it the way I see it," Brice replied coldly.

Denny felt Markham starting to move forward and tightened her grip on his arm again. "Let me handle this," she murmured to him.

"I ain't scared of this fella, marshal or no marshal."

"My job doesn't have anything to do with this," said Brice. "This is purely personal."

Too many people were watching. Denny didn't mind being the center of attention, but not like that. She slid her arm out of Markham's and stepped forward. "All right, Brice, I'll talk to you. We can go back outside."

"Now hold on," Markham objected. "You don't

have to do that, Denny. Whatever this fella's problem is, he can just take it somewheres else."

"She's talking to me, not you," Brice shot back. "Stay out of it, Markham."

"For God's sake," Denny muttered. She took hold of Brice's arm and pulled him toward the door. "Let's just get this over with. Steve, I'll be back in a minute."

For a second, Markham looked like he was going to follow them, but then he jerked his head in a nod. "If you ain't," he said in a warning tone, "I'll be comin' out there to look for you."

The crowd that had closed in a circle around them opened up again to let Denny and Brice through. They had to wait for a moment until there was a gap in the steady stream of people coming into the town hall, then they stepped out into the warm, pleasant evening. Only a faint line of light remained in the west to mark the sunset. Full night would soon be upon the valley.

Denny led Brice off to the side, out of the way, and said, "All right. What's so important that you had to make a scene like that?"

"I thought we had an understanding—"

"Why the devil would you think that?" Denny demanded. "Because of a kiss now and then? We've never talked about anything beyond that, Brice, and you know it."

"We've fought outlaws and gunmen side by side," he insisted. "When you do things like that, there are some things you ought to just know."

"Well, that might be true if you're talking about another lawman or something like that, but in case you haven't noticed, I'm not a *man* of any sort."

Brice drew a deep breath, blew it out in apparent exasperation. "I've noticed. Believe me, I've noticed. But I figured things between us would sort of just grow on their own . . ."

"You figured wrong."

"Are you saying you don't have any feelings for me?"

"You never told me you have any feelings for *me.*"

"Blast it, I thought you knew—" Brice stopped short and said, "We're just going around and around in circles, aren't we?"

"Seems like it."

"Even if what's between us isn't exactly what I thought it was, you shouldn't have come to the social with that cowboy. He's not near good enough for you."

"That's not a decision for you to make," Denny told him. "Sure, Steve's a little rough around the edges, I guess, but I haven't seen anything to indicate that he's not a good man. And before you start talking about him being just a cowboy who'll never amount to anything, at least he's not risking his life all the time by going out and chasing outlaws. A woman wouldn't have to wonder every time he rode away if he'd ever come back again."

Brice stared at her in the light that came from inside the town hall. "You sound like you're talking about . . . about marrying him and settling down—"

"Don't be ridiculous," Denny interrupted. "I'm not planning on marrying anybody anytime soon. Good grief, Brice, it's just one social! I don't know what's going to happen in the future, any more than you do."

He grimaced and rubbed his chin. "I still don't like it—"

"I don't care if you do or not. Who I see doesn't have anything to do with you."

Through gritted teeth, he said, "If that's the way you want it—"

"That's the way it's going to be . . . unless something happens to change it."

"What's that going to be?"

She shook her head. "You'll have to figure that out for yourself. Now, I'm going back in there, and I expect you to leave me and Steve alone for the rest of the evening."

"You're going to dance all your dances with him?"

Denny smiled. "Probably not. I expect there'll be some other fellas who'll ask me. And I might make Brad dance with me, just to start getting him used to the idea that all girls aren't terrible. Are you hinting that you're going to ask me to dance?"

"I might," Brice said stubbornly.

"And I might say yes . . . or not. I reckon we'll have to wait and see." With that, she turned and started toward the door.

He didn't try to stop her.

Markham was watching for her and hurried toward her when she got back inside. As he came up to her, he looked past her and asked, "Where's the lawman?"

"Outside, I suppose. His whereabouts aren't any of my concern."

Markham frowned. "He behaved himself out

there, didn't he? If he didn't act proper-like, I'll find him and—"

"He didn't do a thing except talk to me," said Denny. "That's all, Steve."

Markham nodded, appearing to be somewhat mollified, anyway. "What'd he want? Just to run me down some more?"

"Actually, he didn't." Of course, that was because she hadn't allowed him to, thought Denny, but Markham didn't need to know that. "He just wanted to get a few things straight about where things stand between us."

"And where do they?"

"Right now . . . they don't. I admire him as a lawman, but that's all."

"Well . . . all right." A smile spread across Markham's face as the musicians at the front of the room began tuning their guitars and fiddles and basses.

The same group of cowboy musicians that had played at the dance after Louis and Melanie's wedding would be providing the tunes tonight, along with a few others who were joining in.

"Sounds like they're gettin' ready to start."

A few minutes later, the mayor of Big Rock climbed onto the little platform at the front of the room and called for everyone's attention. When the clamor settled down, the mayor welcomed everyone to the town social and reminded them to be on their best behavior. "Don't forget, our sheriff is here," the mayor said as he waved a hand toward Monte Carson, who stood at the side of the room with Smoke, Sally, and Brad.

"That's right," Monte responded with a smile, "and I intend to spend the evening enjoying myself instead of hauling troublemakers off to the hoosegow!"

That brought laughter and applause.

The mayor joined in, then said, "All right, everyone, have a good time!" He signaled the musicians, who struck up a lively tune, and folks immediately began pairing off to dance.

CHAPTER 32

Denny had danced with Markham at the wedding, so she knew he was surprisingly graceful and light on his feet. She enjoyed herself as they circled and swung around in intricate steps, along with many other people attending the social.

They danced through three songs before Denny, slightly breathless, suggested that they sit the next one out.

"All right," Markham said. "Want some punch?"

Denny laughed. "If I want any, I'd better have it now before all the cowboys here manage to spike it. Pearlie has told me that by the end of some of these gatherings, what was in the punch bowl was mostly whiskey."

"Don't the sheriff try to stop 'em from doin' that?"

"He does, but you know how tricky cowboys can be."

"Reckon I do," Markham said with a chuckle.

"And by now, it's kind of a tradition, I think. So maybe Sheriff Carson doesn't try *really* hard to stop them, after the evening reaches a certain point."

"Sounds like a smart man. I'll fetch the punch. Where'll you be?"

"I'm going to look for my parents and Brad and see how they're doing."

"I'll find you," promised Markham. He began making his way through the crowd toward the side of the room where the long tables with the punch bowls were set up.

Denny soon lost sight of him and headed for the front of the room. She knew Smoke and Sally might have danced a little, but mostly at the socials they spent their time greeting and talking to friends. No one in the valley had more friends than Smoke and Sally Jensen.

Denny found them where she expected to. Her mother was sitting on one of the chairs next to the wall, with Smoke standing beside her. Pearlie and Brad were with them. Denny smiled at Pearlie and said, "I thought you intended to dance with all the widow women."

"I've made a start on it," he replied with a grin, "but I ain't as young as I used to be, you know. A feller's got to catch his breath now and then."

"And I thought you were going to play with the other kids outside," she said to Brad.

"I'm goin' to," he said. "I kind of like the music, though, even if I don't want to dance." He lifted the cup of punch he held. "And I wanted to get some punch, too."

"I figured it was still early enough to be safe," Smoke said, dropping a knowing wink.

"Safe from what?" Brad wanted to know.

"Never mind about that," Sally told him. "When you finish, you can go find your friends. Just don't wander off away from the town hall."

"I won't," the youngster promised.

Smoke said to Denny, "How are things going with Markham?"

"Fine. He's a good dancer."

"Earlier, before things really got started, I saw a little commotion over by the door. What was that about?"

Denny wasn't surprised that her keen-eyed father had spotted the confrontation with Brice. Smoke didn't miss much of anything that was going on around him. She said, "It didn't amount to anything. Brice just wanted to talk to me for a minute."

"He didn't try to cause any trouble? A lawman's got feelings like anybody else, you know."

"It's fine," Denny insisted. "We just needed to clear the air."

Smoke nodded without probing any further.

Brad gulped down the rest of his punch and then hurried out to join the other children. He passed Markham, who was approaching holding two cups. "Hey, Steve," Brad greeted the cowboy as he rushed past.

"Howdy," Markham called after him, then, grinning, he held out one of the cups to Denny. "Here you go."

She took it and said, "Thank you." When she sipped the bright red liquid, she nodded. "Not extra potent . . . yet."

"I might have some more once it is, too." He nodded to Smoke and Sally. "Howdy, Mr. Jensen, Miss Sally. I don't mean to say that I plan on gettin' drunk or nothin'—"

"I know what you meant, Steve," Smoke told him. "It's fine, as long as you take good care of my daughter."

"Oh, I intend to, sir. You got my word on that."

Sally asked, "Are you enjoying yourself, Mr. Markham?"

"Oh, yes, ma'am, I sure am. Where I come from, folks didn't really get together like this. They was always too busy tryin' to scrape out a livin', I reckon. There wasn't much time for enjoyin' life. They just tried to survive it."

"That sounds terrible," Sally told him with a shake of her head.

"It wasn't really that bad, I reckon. Just a matter of what you're used to."

Smoke said, "Where are you from, if you don't mind me asking?"

"No, sir. I grew up down in south Texas, not far from the border. It was pretty rough country in those days."

"From what I hear, it still hasn't settled down all that much."

"No, and I don't reckon it ever will. They grow folks prickly down there, just like the chaparral."

Smoke laughed. "I've been there a few times. You're right!"

Denny was glad to see her father and Markham getting along. Smoke had warned her not to get too serious about this cowboy, and she didn't intend to, but as long as he was around, there was no reason they couldn't have a pleasant friendship.

And when the day came that he decided to ride away, Denny told herself she could accept that, too.

They stood there chatting and sipping punch through two songs, then Markham said, "I'm about ready to get back out there and start traipsin' around the floor again. How about you, Denny?"

Denny drank the little bit of punch left in her cup and nodded. "That sounds good to me."

"Give me your cups," Smoke said. "I'll take them back over to the table."

They did so, and then Markham took Denny's hand as the musicians finished one song and got ready to start another. The guitar player who was the leader of the group talked to the other members while the dancers stood and talked as they waited. From the looks of it, there was some minor disagreement among the musicians about what the next tune should be.

During that pause, Brice Rogers suddenly appeared at Denny's elbow. She had seen him a few times while she and Markham were dancing earlier. Brice hadn't found himself another partner and gone out on the floor. Instead he had been standing against the wall with some of the other men who weren't dancing. He'd had a scowl on his face, and Denny figured he was still brooding over the whole situation.

"You told me you'd give me a dance," he said to her.

Markham started to say something, but Denny put a hand on his arm to stop him. Things were less likely to escalate into a real problem if she handled it and Markham just stepped back.

"That's not exactly what I said," Denny responded

to Brice. "I told you you could ask, but I didn't say how I'd answer."

"Well, are you gonna, or not?"

Something was off about him, Denny realized. At first she wondered if he might be drunk. Even though she hadn't seen any evidence of it, she was sure that flasks were being passed around among some of the men as they snuck nips of whiskey.

She decided that wasn't the case with Brice. His eyes were clear, and she didn't smell any liquor on him. He was just upset, she thought, and that was because she had come to the social with Steve Markham and not him.

"I'm sure there are plenty of girls here who would be happy to dance with you, Brice," she said. "More than happy. You're a handsome man, and everyone respects you."

The compliment didn't work. He just snapped, "Not everybody."

Markham couldn't restrain himself any longer, despite Denny urging him to do so. He said, "That's right, mister. Some of us just wish you'd go away and leave us the hell alone." Then he did possibly the worst thing he could have done. He slung an arm around Denny's shoulders, smirked at Brice, and said, "Ain't that right, honey?"

Denny saw the rage flare to life in the deputy marshal's eyes and said hastily, "Brice, don't—"

The plea came too late and probably wouldn't have done any good anyway. With a snarled curse, Brice lunged forward and swung a punch with blinding speed at Markham's jaw.

Markham was taller and heavier than the lawman,

but Brice packed a lot of power in his compact frame. The blow landed cleanly and knocked Markham away from Denny. He backpedaled a quick couple of steps and lost his balance, falling to the floor as several people waiting for the dancing to start again scrambled out of the way.

Markham landed hard but bounced right back up. Denny let out a despairing groan as the cowboy pushed himself to his feet, growled something incoherent, and charged at Brice with fists clenched and ready to lash out.

CHAPTER 33

Markham looked like a maddened bull as he stomped forward. Denny was going to try to get in his way and stop this fight before it went any further, but before she could do more than take a single step, somebody caught hold of her arms from behind and held her back.

"Better stay out of his way," said her father. "As loco as he is right now, he'll run right over you."

Denny didn't really believe that, but she couldn't break loose from Smoke's firm grip. All she could do was stand there and watch.

Brice didn't wait for Markham to come to him. He lunged forward again to meet the cowboy's attack. Markham swung his right fist in a looping round-house punch that Brice ducked underneath. Markham's rush brought him within reach of Brice's fists, and the lawman hammered a fast left-right-left combination into Markham's ribs.

The blows jarred Markham to a stop, but he didn't give any ground. He chopped a punch at Brice's head and connected, although it was only a grazing hit above Brice's left ear. That was enough to make

Brice stumble a little, though, and it gave Markham the chance to hook a left into Brice's belly. Brice doubled over and moved back a step.

That put him in perfect position for the right that Markham sent whistling toward his jaw. A few feet away, Denny saw what was happening and her heart leaped in alarm. She knew that if Markham's punch landed, it would not only end the fight but might also break Brice's jaw.

Brice looked sick from the hard punch to his gut, but his instincts worked. He dived under the blow Markham aimed at him and tackled the cowboy around the thighs. Both of them went down, crashing hard to the floor.

The townspeople attending the social had all drawn back to form a circle and give the combatants plenty of room. Some men yelled encouragement to either Brice or Markham; it was difficult to say which. Some of them were just yelling in excitement.

Monte Carson appeared at Smoke's side, saying, "I'd better put a stop to this."

"Wait," Smoke said. "Let them battle it out if you can, Monte. Might be better to let them settle things between them."

"All right," Monte said reluctantly. "As long as they're not doing any damage to anything besides each other."

Denny was about to object, but she realized her father was right. As long as Brice's resentment continued to fester, the potential for trouble would always be there. She didn't know if this fight would get rid of that, but there was a chance it might.

Cal and Pearlie came up on Denny's other side.

Cal said, "That blasted Markham—"

"Brice threw the first punch," Denny told him. "He's to blame for this."

Cal looked at her with raised eyebrows. "Really?"

"That's right." Denny turned her head toward Smoke. "You can let go of me now, Pa. I'm not going to try to interfere with what those two idiots are doing."

"Got your word on that?" Smoke asked with a faint twinkle of amusement in his eyes.

"Yeah. Maybe they can knock some sense into each other . . . but I kind of doubt it."

Smoke nodded, released Denny's arms, and moved alongside her to watch the fight as it continued.

While the talk was going on, Brice and Markham had been rolling around on the floor, alternately wrestling and throwing punches. Using his superior weight, Markham managed to plant a knee in Brice's belly and pin him down. Markham loomed over the smaller man and began pounding him in the face, punishing him mercilessly.

Brice wasn't out of the fight, though. He kicked his right leg high and managed to hook his calf in front of Markham's throat. When he straightened his leg, the move levered Markham off of him and made the cowboy sprawl onto his back.

With blood smeared on his face from his mouth and nose and the cuts Markham's fists had opened around his eyes, Brice dived after his opponent. He landed with *both* knees in Markham's belly. Clubbing his hands together, he swung them from left to right and smashed a powerful blow to Markham's jaw. The impact twisted Markham's head far to the side. It would have been enough to knock most men unconscious.

Markham was far from out cold. He roared in anger, got hold of the front of Brice's shirt, and flung him away. With blood dripping from his mouth, Markham clambered up and went after Brice, who had come to a stop on his belly after rolling several feet.

Markham lifted a booted foot and tried to bring it down hard on Brice's back, which might well have broken a rib or two, but Brice was quick enough to roll onto his side. He grabbed Markham's boot, and heaved. Markham went over backward again.

Brice was slow getting up, but Markham was slower. When both men reached their feet, they stood glaring at each other while their chests heaved from exertion. Brice's face was bloodier, but a big multicolored bruise was already forming on Markham's jaw and he had other swollen, battered places on his face. Clearly, both of them had been through the wringer.

But they weren't finished yet.

Panting a curse, Markham stumbled forward with his fists clenched. Brice stayed where he was, but he raised his hands and closed them into fists, too, in anticipation of the cowboy's attack. Markham threw a right, but he was slower now, and Brice had been quick enough even at the start of the fight. He weaved to the side and the fist went harmlessly past his right ear. Brice snapped a right jab to Markham's nose. Blood spurted.

Markham hauled up a left uppercut that Brice evidently wasn't expecting. It caught Brice under the chin and rocked his head back. Markham chopped at his exposed throat. Brice got his chin down just in time to block the blow's force and keep it from crushing his windpipe. He threw a couple of wild, close-range punches. Markham didn't do anything to avoid them, but Brice missed anyway. He was too tired; his blows lacked the crispness they'd had.

Markham didn't even try punching again. He just bulled forward and spread his arms, grabbing Brice around the torso and lifting him off the floor. Markham squeezed hard in a bone-crushing bear hug.

Eyes wide in desperation, Brice cupped both hands and slapped them against Markham's ears as hard as he could. The move worked. Markham yelled in pain as the air compressed against his eardrums, and he lost his grip on Brice. The lawman dropped the few inches to the floor and almost fell, but caught his balance in time to smash another punch to Markham's already bleeding nose. Markham stumbled back, managed to catch himself, and swung a wild right at the same time as Brice did likewise.

Both men missed. Didn't even come close, in fact. The momentum of the punches turned them around. Their knees buckled, and both fell. Unable to rise again, they lay there, breathing hard.

"All right. That's blasted well enough," Monte Carson said.

Smoke's tone was dry as he said, "I think they agree with you."

After a few seconds, Steve Markham groaned and tried to push himself up. A few feet away, Brice Rogers stirred as well, muttering something to himself. Clearly, both men wanted to try to continue the fight even though they were in no shape to do so.

Before Monte Carson could step forward, Denny did so, coming to a halt between them. "You two just stop it," she said sharply. "You've pounded each other almost into raw meat, all over nothing."

Markham lifted his head. With air wheezing through his swollen and bleeding nose, he said, "You ain't . . . ain't nothin' . . . Denny. Not . . . hardly."

Brice pushed himself up and gasped, "Damn . . . saddle . . . tramp."

"That's enough." She bent and reached down . . .

And took hold of Markham's arm.

She couldn't really say why she did that. She supposed it was because he was the one who had come with her to the social, and Brice *had* pressed the issue and thrown the first punch. If she was going to help either of them, it just seemed fair that it should be Steve Markham.

While Brice watched, looking shocked and disappointed, almost devastated, Denny helped Markham to his feet. Telling him, "Lean on me," she led him toward the chairs along the wall so he could sit down. The crowd, which had fallen silent, formed an aisle through which they made their way.

Brice had pushed himself to his knees.

Smoke stepped forward, took hold of the deputy marshal's arm, and effortlessly lifted him to his feet. "Come on. You could use some cleaning up, and probably a drink."

Brice looked at Monte Carson and asked, "Are you gonna . . . arrest me?"

"I reckon not," Monte replied. "From the looks of your face right now, you've been punished enough."

Brice gazed across the room to where Markham had sat down and Denny hovered over him. Using a lacy handkerchief she had produced from somewhere, she dabbed at the blood on his face.

"Yeah, I'd say you're right, Sheriff," Brice said bitterly. "And I can sure use that drink you mentioned, Mr. Jensen."

CHAPTER 34

Smoke sat easy in the saddle and looked over the herd of horses grazing in the pasture not far from the ranch headquarters. A couple of hands were posted nearby, also on horseback, to make sure none of the animals strayed, but actually, that was pretty unlikely. The Sugarloaf's saddle horses had been well trained to stay where they were put unless commanded otherwise.

Cal rode up beside Smoke and reined in. "There they are. Seventy-five head of fine stock, Smoke. If you ask me, Bob Coburn's getting the best end of this deal."

"I think it's a fair bargain for all concerned," said Smoke. "And it'll be good to see Bob again."

"Isn't he the fella who's got that boy who's always spinning yarns?"

Smoke grinned. "Yeah, that little shaver's a born storyteller, I'd say. He can come up with a tall tale at the drop of a hat." Smoke grew more serious as he went on. "We'll drive them to the station in Big Rock tomorrow and load them on the train bound for Cheyenne."

Cal thumbed back his hat and shook his head as he said, "It's a shame we have to follow such a round-about way to get them to Montana. Up to Cheyenne and then all the way east to Chicago before heading west again on the Northern Pacific. It would be a straight shot and a shorter trip if we just drove them the whole way to the Circle C."

"Shorter in distance but not in time," Smoke pointed out. "By using the railroad we can get them to Stirrup in three days and then on to Bob's ranch in another couple of days. It would take a couple of weeks, at least, to drive them the whole way."

"Yeah, I know," Cal said. "Reckon I'm just missing the old days."

Smoke laughed "You're still too young to be doing that. Leave the reminiscing about the old days to fellas like me and Pearlie."

"Yeah, like the two of you are decrepit or something." Cal paused, then asked, "You have any thoughts about which of the hands should go along, Smoke?"

Smoke shook his head. "I leave decisions like that to you, Cal. You know that."

"It's just that I was wondering about Steve Markham."

In the three days since the battle with Brice Rogers at the town social, Markham had been hobbling around the ranch like a stove-up old-timer, although he seemed to be recovering somewhat from his nicks and bruises.

"You think he's up to a trip like this?" asked Smoke.

"I imagine so. It would still be a while before he has to sit a saddle all day. I reckon he can ride in a railroad car without any trouble."

"He's proven himself to be a decent hand when it

comes to handling stock." Smoke shrugged. "Take him along if you want."

"It's just that I didn't know . . ."

When his old friend and foreman hesitated, Smoke said, "Spit it out, Cal."

"All right. You're planning on going along, aren't you?"

"You bet I am."

"Well, I didn't know if you'd want Markham left here on the ranch with Denny when you weren't around."

That blunt statement didn't surprise Smoke. He had already had a hunch that was where Cal was headed with the question. "I don't think we have to worry too much about Denny. She's pretty good about taking care of herself. Plus her mother will be here, as well as Pearlie and some of the other hands. Markham would have to be pretty damn reckless to try anything he shouldn't. So don't let that affect your decision either way."

Cal nodded and said, "I reckon that makes sense. Putting all that aside, Markham *asked* me if he could come along on the drive, so I don't think he's got any worrisome plans."

"He did, did he? He happen to say why?"

"Said he's never been to Montana and wants to see it."

Smoke laughed again. "I understand the feeling. When I was young, anywhere I hadn't been, I wanted to go, too. All right. I suppose it's settled. Markham can come with us, as long as he's recovered enough from that ruckus."

"I'll have everybody ready to go in the morning," Cal promised.

Smoke lifted a hand in farewell for the moment and turned his horse back toward the ranch head-quarters. Sally had looked a little peaked during lunch, he had thought, and he wanted to make sure she was feeling better.

As he approached the house, he saw Brad sitting on the front steps, whittling on a piece of wood with a clasp knife. He was still there by the time Smoke had put his horse away and was walking toward the house. The boy was concentrating intently on what he was doing. He frowned, and the tip of his tongue stuck out one corner of his mouth.

"What are you whittling?" Smoke asked.

"I don't know," Brad replied without looking up. "I don't have it uncovered yet."

Smoke knew from his reading that master sculptors sometimes took that attitude toward their work. He didn't see why it couldn't apply to whittlers, too.

"Miss Sally inside?"

"Yeah, she's the one who sent me out here, Smoke. Said she had a headache and I didn't need to be gettin' underfoot."

It was Smoke's turn to frown. That didn't sound like Sally. Maybe something actually *was* wrong. He wanted to go inside and check on her, but as he started up the steps beside where Brad was sitting, he paused long enough to say, "You know, you can call me Grandpa if you want."

"I know. It's just that everybody calls you Smoke. Denny even calls you Smoke sometimes, instead of Pa. I reckon that's because you're so famous."

"Fame's a fleeting thing, son. Most folks will forget about me as soon as I'm gone, if not before. But as long as the people who really matter remember you . . . the people you love and who love *you* . . . you've done all right for yourself."

"I reckon so . . . Grandpa. Does that sound all right?"

Smoke squeezed the boy's shoulder. "It sure does." Then he hurried on into the house, taking off his hat as he entered the foyer. He hung it on a hook and called, "Sally?"

"What is it?" she asked from the parlor. He turned in that direction and spotted her sitting in an armchair, doing some needlework.

"I just wanted to see if you were all right," he told her as he came into the room. "I thought at lunch you looked like you didn't feel very good."

"Nonsense." She set the needlework aside on a small table and stood up. "It's true that I have a bit of a headache and haven't really felt like myself for the past couple of days, but I'm sure I'll be . . . be fine . . ."

She had taken a couple of steps toward Smoke while she was talking, but she stopped short and put a hand to her forehead, pressing the fingertips just above her right eye.

"Sally?" Smoke said as alarm sprang to life inside him. She was as pale as a bucket of milk, he noticed.

"Oh, my . . . goodness," she said as he reached for her.

Before he could touch her, her eyes rolled up in their sockets and her knees buckled. She would have fallen if Smoke hadn't sprung forward to catch her.

Her face rested against his chest as he held her up.

Even through his shirt he could feel how hot her skin was. With his heart pounding, he lowered her into the armchair where she'd been sitting and cupped her cheek in his hand. He could tell she was running a high fever.

"Denny!" he shouted, not knowing if their daughter was in the house or not. "Inez!"

Brad actually reached the parlor first, letting the screen door slam behind him as he skidded to a stop in the arched entrance between the foyer and the parlor. He exclaimed, "Gosh, Smoke, what's wrong?"

"You stay there, Brad," said Smoke. He didn't know what was making Sally run such a fever, but there was a good chance it was contagious.

Inez appeared, stepping around Brad and wiping her hands on a towel. "Señor Smoke! What—*dios mio!* Señora Sally! What has happened?"

"She passed out just now," Smoke replied grimly. "She has a very high fever."

"We must get her up to bed. Brad, run to the kitchen, fill a basin with water from the pump, and get a handful of rags from the bin under the sink. Hurry, child!"

Brad's footsteps slapped against the floor as he rushed to follow the housekeeper's orders. At the same time, Denny appeared in the parlor entrance and said, "Pa, what in the world—Oh, Lord." A frightened hush came into her voice. "What's wrong with her?"

"I don't know," Smoke said as he looked at his wife. Then he glanced at Denny and saw that she was in range clothes. "Ride to Big Rock and get Doc Steward out here as fast as you can!"

"All right. Pa . . . don't let anything happen to her."

Smoke didn't say anything. He didn't know what to say. Sally had been through health crises before, falling ill so suddenly and seriously that he had been afraid he was going to lose her. But she was a strong woman and each time she had pulled through.

As he had before, he wondered if the odds had finally caught up to the woman he loved. Had caught up to them both, because he wasn't sure if he could live without her.

The one thing he was certain of was that he wouldn't be going to Montana tomorrow after all.

CHAPTER 35

Thin, sandy-haired Dr. Enoch Steward came out of the bedroom carrying his black medical bag. He found Smoke, Denny, Brad, Cal, Pearlie, and Inez waiting for him. The group just about filled up the second-floor hallway.

"Mrs. Jensen is resting easily now," Steward reported.

"What's wrong with her?" Smoke asked. "Is she going to be all right?"

Steward placed the bag on a small table next to the wall and took a handkerchief from his pocket. He removed his glasses and began polishing the lenses with the cloth. "At this point, I can't answer either of those questions definitively. There are any number of conditions that can cause a high temperature. She doesn't seem to have any symptoms other than the fever, except that she roused enough to speak to me for a moment and said that all her muscles and joints ached badly. That leads me to believe it may be the grippe." The doctor shrugged. "That's unusual for this time of year, but not impossible by any means. Especially since she was around a great many people just a few days ago at the town social." He smiled slightly as he put the spectacles back on. "If it *is* the grippe, I'm likely to have a busy couple of weeks in front of me. It spreads quite easily and quickly, you know."

"What do we do?" Smoke wanted to know. "Is there some kind of medicine you can give her?"

"Actually, there is, and I administered a dose of it a few minutes ago. It's rather new, and the company that makes it calls it 'Aspirin'—"

"I know what that is," Denny said. "One of the doctors in Europe told Louis it might be good for his heart."

"That's one of the things the chemists claim," said Steward. "Is your brother taking it?"

Denny shook her head. "No, we came home not long after that, and he's been doing better here, so he never tried it."

"It's something to think about if his condition worsens again. However, there's a great deal more research to be done on the subject. For now, we know that it usually lowers a fever more effectively than cool compresses do." Steward looked at Inez. "Although the compresses you were applying when I got here certainly did no harm and may well have helped some. I would recommend that you continue with them."

Inez nodded and said, "Of course, Doctor."

"What else do we need to do?" asked Smoke.

"I'm afraid that's all that can be done, Mr. Jensen. I'll leave some of the Aspirin powders for later, and I'll come back out here tomorrow to check on Mrs. Jensen. Just let her rest, and if she wakes up, try to get her to drink. It's very important in cases like this that the patient drink as much as possible."

Smoke nodded. *The patient*, he thought. That wasn't just a patient in there. That was Sally, the love of his life.

"I won't sugarcoat things, Mr. Jensen," Steward went on. "If it *is* the grippe, it can become serious, even fatal."

"No!" Denny exclaimed.

"But the important thing to remember is that more patients survive than don't, and most of the ones who don't are either very young or in poor health to begin with. Mrs. Jensen was in good shape before she fell ill, wasn't she?"

"As far as I know," Smoke said, nodding.

"Then her chances for recovery are excellent. I know she'll receive good care here—"

"The best," Inez vowed.

"So try not to worry, all of you. I'll be back tomorrow."

"I'll walk with you out to your buggy, Doc," Pearlie offered. "Want me to carry that bag for you?"

"That's all right, Mr. Fontaine. It's not that heavy and I like to hang on to it."

As Steward and Pearlie went down the stairs, Brad asked, "Can I go in and see her?"

"No," Inez answered before Smoke or Denny could say anything. "I will tend to Señora Sally. The rest of you should stay away. You heard what the doctor said about how easily the sickness spreads. You should not be around her any more than you already have."

"You're going to keep *me* out of there?" Smoke said.

Inez fixed him with a hard, level gaze. "I do what is best for everyone, Señor Smoke."

"Yeah, I suppose so," he admitted grudgingly. "But if you need anything—"

"I will let you know."

Smoke nodded and turned to Cal. "Come on down to the office," he told the foreman. "We have things to talk about."

"I'm coming with you," Denny said. "What you and Cal are going to talk about concerns me, too."

"I don't see how," Smoke said, but he had a strong hunch that he actually did.

They went down to the first floor and into Smoke's office. Smoke sank wearily into the chair behind the desk, while Denny and Cal stood. The foreman held his hat in front of him.

"You want me to send a wire to Bob Coburn and tell him he'll have to wait a while longer for those horses?" Cal asked.

"Bob sounded like he was in need of them," Smoke said. "I hate to ask him to wait."

"But there's no way you can take that herd all the way to Montana now, with Miss Sally sick the way she is."

"No, it's going to be up to you to do that." Smoke looked squarely at his foreman. "Comes right down to it, I don't really need to go along anyway. You'll be in charge of the drive, Cal. I don't doubt for a second that you'll get those horses to the Circle C just fine."

"Well, I appreciate the vote of confidence, Smoke, but—"

"But there ought to be a Jensen along," Denny broke in. "Those are Sugarloaf horses, after all."

Smoke's gaze bored into her. "You'd go running off on an adventure while your mother is so sick she might die?"

A flush crept over Denny's face. Smoke couldn't tell if it was from anger or embarrassment or both.

"You heard Dr. Steward say there's a very good chance she'll recover just fine," Denny said.

"None of us *know* that," Smoke pointed out.

"Are you going to send *Louis* a wire and tell him to rush home from his wedding trip?"

"Louis isn't here," Smoke repeated. "That's the difference. You are."

"I wasn't around all those other times when Ma got sick or was kidnapped or shot by outlaws. She came a lot closer to dying when those things happened while Louis and I were off in Europe, didn't she?"

"This is different," Smoke insisted. "And even if it wasn't, there's no real need for you to go. Cal can handle things just fine."

Denny looked over at the foreman. "I know that. Don't think for a second that I don't believe that, Cal."

"This is between you and Smoke, Miss Denny," Cal said tightly. "It's family business. In fact, I don't rightly feel comfortable even being here for this conversation—"

Smoke said, "You've been around the Sugarloaf for so long you're pretty much family yourself, Cal. You and Pearlie both."

"I feel the same way," said Denny. She drew in a deep breath. With uncharacteristic humbleness, she went on. "You're right, Pa. I shouldn't have even considered going to Montana. I need to stay here to help any way I can."

She sounded sincere, and Smoke believed that she was. For a moment, Denny's impulsiveness and endless thirst for excitement had gotten the best of her common sense, but she saw where her true responsibilities lay.

"That's good," Smoke said, nodding.

"I think I'll go see where Brad is," she went on. "He's probably pretty shaken up by everything. I'll be around somewhere close by in case Inez needs anything." She left the office.

Once the door was closed and Denny's footsteps had receded down the hall outside, Cal said, "Don't worry about those horses, Smoke. I'll take care of everything."

Smoke frowned. "I know that. But I didn't promise Bob Coburn that we'd be leaving here on a particular day. We can hold off on driving them to the railroad for a day or two without having to notify him. I don't reckon he'll ever know the difference."

Cal looked puzzled. "But earlier you said—"

"I know. I think I might have been a little unfair to Denny, though. I've made it clear to her that if she wants to, one of these days she'll be running this ranch. But sometimes when she tries to stand up and take some responsibility, I slap her right back down."

"If I'm speaking plain here, I wouldn't go so far as to say you did that, Smoke. The situation being what it is, this *isn't* a good time for her to be leaving. And nobody would blame you for being worried about your daughter going all the way to Montana with a bunch of wild cowboys . . . including one who's been courting her."

"She's gone off on a lot more dangerous—and downright loco—jaunts than this one, like when she wound up joining that outlaw gang last year so she could get the goods on them. I trust her to be able to handle Steve Markham. She's not going to lose her head over him."

"You sound pretty sure about that."

"I am." Smoke sighed and shook his head. "But none of this can be decided now. It's going to have to wait until we see how Sally's doing. Maybe by tomorrow, things will be different."

The question, Smoke told himself, would be whether they were better . . . or, unthinkably, worse.

CHAPTER 36

Denny found Brad sitting on the front steps. He held his clasp knife in one hand and a piece of wood that had been carved on in the other, but he wasn't doing any actual whittling at the moment. He just stared straight ahead with a gloomy expression on his face.

He looked over, though, when Denny sat down beside him. "Is Sally going to die?"

"I don't think so." Denny thought about it and realized she wasn't just trying to be encouraging; she really *didn't* believe that the sickness would claim her mother. To think of her dying was just inconceivable. "She's really strong, and you heard the doctor say that was a good thing. She'll fight off whatever it is that's ailing her, I'm sure of that."

"I hope so. I haven't even known her that long." Brad was trying not to sniffle. "Do you think she'd mind . . . if I called her Grandma? Smoke said I could call him Grandpa."

Even under the circumstances, just the thought of calling Smoke and Sally Jensen Grandpa and

Grandma almost made Denny laugh. They were such vital people that they seemed much younger than their actual years. And yet it was true that Brad was their step-grandson, and it was entirely possible, even likely, that there would be grandchildren-by-blood in the Jensen family in the not so distant future. Melanie was young enough that she and Louis could have a whole passel of sons and daughters.

The likelihood of *her* presenting any grandbabies to her parents was a lot smaller, Denny mused.

In answer to Brad's question, she said, "You'll have to wait and ask her about that once she gets better, but I really don't think she'll mind."

"Okay. I'll do that."

She nudged his shoulder with an elbow. "Want to practice some with your lasso?"

"I'm getting pretty good at it." A faint smile curved Brad's lips. "Maybe better than you."

Denny laughed. "I don't think so! Come on."

As Brad got the rope he'd been using, built a loop, and started trying to drop it over a fence post, Denny reflected on the notion that had crossed her mind a few minutes earlier. It wasn't that she didn't *want* to ever have children, but doing so required somebody to be the father, and Denny didn't see anybody who fit that description on the horizon at the moment.

Her thoughts went back to the night of the social. While she had cleaned some of the blood off his face, Steve Markham sat there for a few minutes, breathing hard as he tried to recover from the battle with Brice Rogers. Then he had reached up, closed his hand around the wrist of the hand holding the cloth, and lifted his eyes to hers.

"*You don't have to do that, Denny,*" he said. "*I don't reckon I deserve to have a gal like you takin' care of me, after all the trouble I've caused.*"

"*You didn't start it,*" she pointed out. Then she shrugged a little and added, "*Well, maybe you did, with some of the things you said and the way you put your arm around my shoulders, but still, you didn't throw the first punch. Brice made the decision to do that.*"

"*Yeah, but he wasn't thinkin' straight.*" Markham chuckled. "*Bein' around you would keep just about any man from thinkin' straight.*"

"*That's enough flattery. That's some of how we got into this, remember?*" She moved his hand from her wrist and bent to the task again. "*Now sit still and let me clean some of these cuts and scrapes. What we really need is something to put on them.*"

"*How about some whiskey?*" he asked with a smile as he slipped a small silver flask out of an inside pocket in his vest. "*I know I ain't supposed to have this, but I figure I ain't the only cowboy who brung in a little who-hit-John tonight.*"

"*Not by a long shot,*" Denny muttered as she took the flask from him. Keeping her back to the rest of the room so it wouldn't be quite so obvious what she was doing, she got a corner of the handkerchief wet with the strong-smelling liquor and began wiping it on the injuries.

Markham caught his breath sharply and grimaced.

Denny told him, "*Stay still.*"

After a few more minutes of work, she had tended to his wounds the best she could and handed the flask back to him.

He took the bloody handkerchief from her as well. "I'll wash this for you."

"That's not necessary. Just throw it away."

"Not hardly! If nothin' else, at least it's a momento from a, uh, what do you call it, an auspicious evenin'."

"I don't know about auspicious. It's been eventful, though. Nobody can deny that."

"Walk outside with me? I could use some fresh air."

Denny hesitated. She looked around the room. Somebody had wiped up the drops of blood that had fallen on the floor, the musicians had started playing another tune, and folks were dancing again. She saw that she and Markham were still the objects of some people's attention, but for the most part those who had come to have a good time had gone back to that.

She didn't see Brice anywhere. Maybe he actually had left.

"All right," she told Markham. "I think I'd like that, too."

She was aware of eyes still on them as they made their way through the town hall to the doors. There was nothing unusual about couples stepping outside during the evening to stroll under the stars, but the two of them had a bit more notoriety than normal because of Markham's fight with Brice. Denny just did her best to ignore the attention. She didn't figure it was anybody else's business what she did.

The air still held a hint of the day's heat, but it was beginning to cool off and felt good on her face as she and Markham walked into the dappled shadows under the trees that grew near the building. They weren't the only ones out there. She heard the low murmur of male and female voices from not far away. The shadows provided a certain amount of privacy, but enough light came through the nearby windows that it wasn't like the strolling couples were completely unobserved. A suitor might try to steal a kiss, but that was about as far as such things ever went at one of those affairs.

"I reckon I lost my head in there," Markham said when they paused. "I sure am sorry about that."

"You don't need to apologize," Denny told him.

"Yeah, I do," he insisted. "Ain't no excuse for brawlin' at what should've been a friendly occasion for all concerned."

"Well . . . try to remember that next time." Even in the shadows, Denny could see the grin that spread across his face.

"I'm hopin' there won't be no next time. Maybe Rogers has finally got the idea that you ain't interested in him no more." When Denny didn't respond to that statement, Markham asked, "You ain't interested in him, right, Denny?"

"At this point, that's still none of your business, Steve."

"It ain't, huh?" Without warning, Markham took her in his arms and kissed her. It took her by surprise when his lips pressed hers, and her first impulse was to pull away, after which she would give him a good hard slap for being so bold.

She didn't do either of those things. She put her arms around his neck and kissed him back, and it felt good.

Long seconds ticked past while they embraced.

Finally, Markham lifted his head. "Still say it's none of my business?" he asked.

Denny had a little trouble finding her voice, but when she did, she told him, "Don't push me, Steve. I don't like that. You ought to have figured that out by now, even if we haven't really known each other all that long."

"Sure," he said easily. "You know I didn't mean no offense."

"I'm not offended," she said, and that wasn't a lie.

What she was . . . was confused.

* * *

Brad's triumphant whoop broke into her reverie. She looked over at him and saw him yank the loop tight where it rested around the fence post that had been his target.

"Just like Smoke—I mean, Grandpa—taught me."

"Good job," Denny said.

He went to the fence and loosened the rope, then, coiling the lasso, he walked over to Denny and held it out to her. "Want to try?"

"Sure." She welcomed the distraction. She took the rope, shook out the loop, twirled it a few times over her head, and then made her throw. The loop sailed out, opening perfectly, and settled over the post. With a flick of her wrist, she snapped it closed.

Brad let out a whistle of admiration. "That was pretty slick!"

"I've roped a lot of calves. A fence post isn't running and trying to get away."

"Can you teach me how to rope a calf?"

"We'll get around to that," Denny promised. She glanced toward the house. She had distracted Brad from worrying about Sally, and she was grateful she'd been able to do that. The concern for her mother still lurked in her own mind, though, crowded in there along with everything else she had to worry about.

CHAPTER 37

Smoke was in the kitchen the next morning, frowning as he drank some of the coffee he'd found Inez Sandoval brewing when he came in from the living room, where he had slept in a chair. Inez had reported that Sally had spent a restless night, but that an hour or so before dawn had fallen into a deep sleep. Inez had come downstairs to put the coffee on and get started on breakfast. Sally normally took care of that while Inez prepared breakfast for the crew, but the ranch hands would have to rustle up their own grub this morning while Inez took care of the Jensen family.

Smoke had tried to tell her that he wasn't hungry, but she'd insisted that he eat some flapjacks and bacon. Once he started, he discovered that he had more of an appetite than he thought. He had cleaned the plate and was nursing his second cup of coffee. Denny and Brad weren't up yet, and Inez had gone to check on Sally.

The way the cook/housekeeper hurried into the kitchen made Smoke fear the worst for a second. He sprang to his feet and was about to ask her what was wrong when he realized she had a big smile on her face.

"Señor Smoke, Señora Sally is awake. The fever has come down. She still feels warm to me, but not like before."

"I'm going up to see her," Smoke declared. His tone made it clear that this time, he wasn't going to be denied.

He practically charged up the stairs, much like he had gone up San Juan Hill with Teddy Roosevelt and the rest of the Rough Riders a few years earlier. The bedroom door was open, and as his broad shoulders filled it, he said, "Sally?"

"Smoke." The voice from the bed was weak, but he had never been happier to hear it. He rushed to her side and gazed down at her in love and relief.

Rather than being pale as she had been the day before, Sally's cheeks were a bit flushed, an indication that she was still running a little fever. Her thick, dark hair was damp with sweat. Smoke rested the back of his hand against her forehead for a few seconds. Definitely still warm, he thought, but not burning up the way she had been before.

"Wh-what happened?" she asked in a strained whisper. "I remember being in the parlor and . . . and not feeling well, and then you came in . . . Was Dr. Steward here? I seem to recall seeing him, but it's all fuzzy, like . . . like a dream . . ."

"He was here, all right," Smoke said. "You're sick, Sally. Mighty sick. But you're better now, and you're going to keep getting better until you're well."

"Oh, Smoke . . . I'm sorry . . ."

"Sorry?" he repeated. "What in the world are you sorry for? You haven't done anything wrong!"

"I'm sure you've all . . . been worried."

A damp rag lay next to the water basin on the bedside table. He picked it up and wiped it gently against her cheek. He could tell from the way she sighed that the coolness felt good.

"You're damn right we've been worried," he said, the gruffness of his voice trying but failing to conceal the depth of the emotions he felt. "You know good and well the Sugarloaf can't get along without you. But it's not your fault you got sick, honey. Not even close."

"Where are . . . Denise . . . and Louis?"

"Denny's here," Smoke said, "but Louis is off on his wedding trip with Melanie. Don't you remember?"

A new worry cropped up in his thoughts. What if the high fever had affected her brain? He had heard stories about people who got so hot from being sick that they were never the same afterward.

But then she said, "Oh . . . of course. How . . . silly of me. I just forgot . . . for a moment . . ."

"That's all right," he told her. "I'll fetch Denny in a minute. She'll be really happy that you're doing better. So will Brad."

Sally smiled and nodded weakly. She didn't ask who Brad was, and Smoke was glad of that.

He didn't have to fetch Denny. She appeared in the doorway, hair disheveled from sleep, clutching a robe around her. "Inez woke me up and told me Ma was better this morning."

"That's right," Smoke said, beckoning her over.

Denny hurried to the bedside. "You really had us worried—"

"None of that, now," Smoke broke in. "There's nothing to worry about." He hoped that was true, but a note of caution sounded in the back of his brain. Logically, it was really too soon to know if Sally was out of the woods. She was still sick, after all. Still running a fever even if it wasn't as high as it had been the day before.

For the moment, they had hope, and that wasn't to be discounted, either.

Dr. Enoch Steward's buggy pulled up in front of the house around the middle of the morning. Smoke greeted the physician and told him about Sally's improvement. Steward went directly upstairs to check on her, telling Smoke and Denny and Brad to wait in the parlor for him.

The smile on Steward's face when he came back down the stairs was enough to make all of them heave sighs of relief.

"I believe the crisis is over," the doctor announced. "Mrs. Jensen is still running a slight fever, and she'll feel bad for several more days, perhaps a week, but unless her temperature shoots up again—which I don't think it will—she should be out of danger."

Smoke was on his feet, as were Denny and Brad. Smoke grabbed Steward's hand, pumped it enthusiastically, and said, "We sure can't thank you enough for what you've done, Doctor. That medicine you gave Sally did the trick."

"The Aspirin powders helped a great deal, I'm sure, but her own constitution and determination probably did more to shake off the illness than anything else. Most people don't realize just how important their own attitude is to their health."

Denny said, "Nobody could ever complain about my mother's attitude. She's about as fierce and determined as anybody you'll ever find."

"That's why I had high hopes for her recovery," Steward replied with a nod. "Now, she'll need to continue to rest for at least a week, perhaps two. When she starts to feel better, she may want to go back to her normal routine right away. Don't let her do that. That might increase the chances of a relapse."

Smoke nodded. "Inez and I can see to that, Doctor."

"I'll come back to check on her every day for a few days, and then we should be able to cut back on the visits."

"We've all been in to see her this morning." Smoke's gesture took in himself, Denny, and Brad. "Hope that was all right."

"Well . . . it might have been better if you'd waited another day or so, but you'd all been exposed already, so now all you can do is hope that you haven't picked up the illness."

"What about you, Doctor?" asked Denny. "It seems to me that you must be around sickness all the time."

Steward smiled. "I certainly am, Miss Jensen. I've been lucky that I've never come down with anything serious. The odds may catch up with me one of these days, but that's just part of being a physician, I'm afraid." He put his hat on. "I need to get back to Big Rock. I've given Señora Sandoval detailed instructions on how to care for Mrs. Jensen. Don't hesitate to send for me if you need me."

He left the house, and a minute later they heard the rattle of buggy wheels as he drove off.

Brad said, "Let's go up and see her again."

"Hold on," Smoke said. "You heard what the doctor said. Sally needs to rest as much as she can. There'll be time to visit with her later. For now, let's just go on about our business." He looked at Denny. "You and I need to go back to the office and talk."

A slight frown appeared on her face. "I want to talk to you, too."

"What about me?" asked Brad.

Smoke put a hand on the boy's shoulder and said, "I've got an important job for you, Brad. I know that all the members of the crew have been worried about your grandma. I want you to go out and find Pearlie and tell him everything the doctor just said. He can spread the word among the rest of the hands. It'll be a real load off their minds. Can you do that?"

"Sure!" Brad turned and hurried out of the house.

Smoke and Denny didn't say anything else until they were in Smoke's office. Then Smoke perched a hip on a corner of the desk and said, "That was mighty good news, eh?"

Denny crossed her arms and her frown deepened as she looked at him. "You told Doc Steward that you and Inez would take good care of Ma. What about me? You think I won't pitch in and help out?"

"I know you would if you were here," Smoke said.

"But considering what the doctor told us, I've got a hunch that you won't be."

"You mean . . ."

Hoping that he wasn't making a mistake—he hadn't forgotten that Steve Markham would be helping deliver those horses to Bob Coburn on the Circle C—Smoke said, "You were right when you said that a Jensen ought to be going along on that trip to Montana, and under the circumstances . . . it looks like you're elected."

CHAPTER 38

Big Rock

Clouds of dust hung in the air along the siding where Sugarloaf cowboys were loading the horses into livestock cars. When the train bound for Cheyenne arrived later that morning, it would pick up those cars and start the horses on their long, roundabout trip to their new home in Montana.

Denny and Cal sat on horseback, watching the loading. The mounts Bob Coburn was buying were well-behaved, but if any of them got spooked and tried to break away, Denny and Cal were there to head them off.

The operation went smoothly, though, which came as no surprise to Denny. She knew that Cal hired top hands for the Sugarloaf crew.

That included Steve Markham, who was doing a good job getting horses up a ramp into one of the cars. Denny found herself keeping an eye on him more than she should. She knew she ought to be supervising the entire crew.

"Can I speak plainly, Miss Denny?"

"Of course you can, Cal. You're my pa's foreman, and besides, like Smoke said, you're practically a member of the family. One thing, though . . . You're going to have to stop calling me Miss Denny. Might be times out on the trail when you'll need to get my attention or tell me something in a hurry, and there's no point in wasting time with that 'miss' business."

He nodded and said, "All right, Denny. What I've got to say is about Steve Markham."

She felt her face growing a little warm. Cal must have noticed the way she was watching him. She vowed not to let herself get distracted like that in the future. This trip was for business, not pleasure.

Cal went on. "Once Miss Sally got better and Smoke decided you could go along with those horses to Montana, I expected him to tell me that Markham *wasn't* going. But he didn't say a thing about it."

"He didn't say anything to me, either, and I was a little surprised by that," Denny admitted. "But Steve's a good hand, and Pa knows it. It makes sense that he'd want good hands to deliver the horses."

"I reckon," Cal said with a shrug. "But that was up to him, and I'm not in the habit of second-guessing Smoke's decisions." His voice got a little harder and flatter. "I'm also not in the habit of being a chaperone. Whatever happens between you and Markham, I'm not getting mixed up in it. My job's to get those horses safely to the Circle C, and that's all I'm concerned about."

Denny gave him a curt nod. "Good. Like you said, that's your job. And mine, too, and Steve Markham's, and everybody else's who's going along on the trip. That's *all* that's going to happen, Cal."

He shrugged again. "Like I said, none of my business."

Denny could tell that both of them felt uncomfortable, but in a way, she was glad that Cal had brought up the subject. Now they had cleared the air, and they could put the whole thing behind them.

Gene Cunningham, the cowboy Cal had picked for the position of segundo on the journey, rode over to them and reported, "We've just about got 'em all loaded and should be ready to close up the cars in just a few minutes, Cal."

"Thanks, Gene. You boys have done a good job." Cal took his turnip watch from his pocket and opened it to check the time. "Still an hour or so until the train gets here. Pick a couple of men to keep an eye on these cars and tell the others they can get a beer. *One* beer. Anybody who comes back here pie-eyed not only won't go to Montana, he'll be out of a job, period. We'll go a little shorthanded if we have to."

"I don't reckon you have to worry about that. Everybody likes working for Smoke too much to risk it."

Cunningham turned his mount and loped back toward the railroad cars and the rest of the crew.

Cal thumbed back his hat and said to Denny, "I reckon I know what you'll be doing before we pull out."

"What's that?" she asked.

He nodded toward the main part of town. Denny turned her head to look in that direction and saw Smoke riding leisurely toward them.

Denny frowned. She had already said her good-byes

to her parents and Brad. She'd sat next to her mother's bed that morning and assured her that she wouldn't go to Montana if Sally thought it was a bad idea. Denny remembered the quick conversation.

Sally's cheeks were still a little pink from the temperature she was running, but her eyes were bright and alert and she had her appetite back. Earlier, she had eaten the breakfast Inez had brought up to her on a tray, and part of a cup of coffee sat on the night table that she picked up and sipped from now and then.

"Don't worry about me, I'm fine," she assured Denny. "However . . ."

"I sort of figured there might be a however," Denny said with a smile.

"I'm not sure how proper it is for a young girl to travel all that way, alone with a bunch of cowboys."

"I'm not that young," Denny insisted. "I'm a grown woman. And I lived with a gang of outlaws for a while last summer, remember."

"I certainly haven't forgotten. I probably never will."

"But I won't really be alone," Denny went on. "Cal is going along, and he'll look out for me, I'm sure."

"I trust Cal with my life. But I'm your mother, Denise. I'm going to worry."

Denny reached out and clasped one of Sally's hands in both of hers.

"It's going to be all right. And if it's Steve Markham you're concerned about, you don't need to be. As far as I'm concerned, while we're gone, he's just another of the hands."

* * *

That had been her intention, but she wasn't sure she could stick to it completely. And Cal, while he would protect her life with his own if it came to that, had just made it clear he wasn't going to interfere in her love life, no matter what Denny had told her mother.

All of that might be moot, she thought as she nudged her horse into motion and rode toward Smoke. She hoped that him showing up unexpectedly in town didn't mean that her mother had taken a turn for the worse.

"What's wrong, Pa?" she asked as she came up to him and reined in. "Is it Ma?"

Smoke shook his head. "No, she's fine, or as fine as she's going to be until she's completely over that sickness. She's doing so well, in fact, that she told me to come on into town to see you off. I reckon she knew I wanted to."

"Oh," Denny said, relieved. "Well, I'm glad to hear it."

"Brad insisted on coming along, too. He stopped at Goldstein's, but he'll be along in a minute." Smoke shrugged. "I gave him a couple of pennies for candy."

Denny grinned. "He made you feel guilty about not letting him go to Montana with me, didn't he?"

"He *really* wants to go." Smoke shook his head. "I told him his mother wouldn't allow it, though. If she and Louis got back and found out that he'd gone traipsing off to Montana, she wouldn't be happy, I'll bet."

"You're right." Brad had complained plenty to Denny during the past twenty-four hours about her being allowed to go when he wasn't. He resented that enough that the good-bye hug he'd given her that morning had been a grudging one. She leaned her head toward the siding and went on. "The horses are loaded. We're just waiting for the train. Cal let the men go get a beer before they leave."

"Where's Markham?"

Denny's shrug was casual. "Don't know. With the rest of the boys, I reckon."

Smoke nodded slowly. "You keep that attitude, this trip ought to work out fine."

"It *will* work out fine. Cal and I will see to that."

Brad rode up then on the blaze-faced horse. He said excitedly, "Look, Denny. Rafael said I could ride him today."

"He'll make a good saddle mount for you, Brad. The two of you will sort of grow up together."

"How about you and Rocket? Did you bring him along?"

Denny laughed and shook her head. "I'm not sure that loco horse will ever grow up. But maybe I'll work with him some more when I get back from Montana."

"I still wish I was goin' with you," the boy said with a sigh. "The next time you drive horses or cattle somewhere, I get to come along. I'm callin' that now."

That would be up to Melanie and Louis, thought Denny, but she didn't point that out to Brad. Nor did she mention that this might be the last time a crew from the Sugarloaf set off on an old-fashioned drive. The world was moving fast. Pretty soon the railroads would be everywhere, and Denny had heard that there were automobiles on the streets of Denver and Cheyenne.

She and Smoke and Brad chatted for a while longer,

then the shrill whistle of a locomotive sounded in the distance. The Sugarloaf hands began drifting back toward the railroad station on foot. They had already loaded their saddle mounts in one of the cars on the siding.

Denny needed to do the same with her horse. "Time to get busy. So long, Pa. Be good, Brad." She leaned over in the saddle to exchange hugs with both of them, then turned her mount toward the siding. As she rode up to the one car where the doors were still open and the loading ramp still in place, she saw Steve Markham standing nearby.

"You didn't go get a beer with the others?" she asked as she swung down from the saddle.

"Nope. I volunteered to stay here with Gene and keep an eye on things. I'll load that horse for you and unsaddle him."

"I can do that," Denny said sharply. "I carry my weight when it comes to work."

"Oh, I never doubted that," Markham replied with a smile.

"Cal's the boss, and as far as this trip is concerned, I'm just one of the hands."

Markham continued smiling, but he looked like he didn't really believe what Denny had just said.

She felt a brief surge of irritation. "Until we get back, the two of us are just cowboys, Steve. Understand?"

"Sure," he said, then added in a drawl, "pard."

Denny growled a curse under her breath and put the horse up the ramp. Steve Markham had better not get any fancy ideas during this trip, she told herself, or he would find himself with all kinds of trouble on his hands.

CHAPTER 39

Brice Rogers rested his hands on the little counter in front of the window in the Western Union office located inside the Big Rock railroad depot. That was the most convenient place for it since the singing wires followed the same route as the steel rails.

"You're sure there's nothing from the chief marshal in Denver?" Brice asked as he frowned.

On the other side of the opening, the telegrapher sat at the desk where his telegraph key rested. He wore a green visor, white shirt, dark vest, string tie, and sleeve garters. He shook his head in response to Brice's question and said, "Sorry, Marshal. Were you expecting a wire from Chief Marshal Long?"

Brice sighed. "No, not really. I just had a hunch he might have a new assignment for me."

"If I do get a message from him, I'll send a boy to find you."

Brice nodded, thanked the man, and turned away from the window. The depot lobby was practically deserted at the moment. A train had already come through today, and there wouldn't be another until the evening.

Brice walked out to the street, where he paused, took off his hat, and raked his fingers through his hair. He sighed. For the first time since he'd pinned on a badge, he almost hoped some trouble would crop up. Anything to take his mind off the fact that Denny Jensen had left Big Rock two days earlier, bound for Montana . . . with Steve Markham.

Of course, she wasn't *alone* with Markham, he reminded himself. Calvin Woods and a dozen other hands from the Sugarloaf had gone along on the trip to deliver those horses. Brice had heard all about it. Whatever the Jensens did was always news in Big Rock, since they were the leading family in the entire valley.

And it was none of his concern what Denny did. He had been trying very hard to convince himself of that. He'd been attracted to Denny from the very first time he'd met her, despite the fact that she could be mighty annoying a lot of the time. She was set in her ways, that was for damn sure, and had strong opinions on just about everything, including how she should act. She didn't like anybody telling her what to do.

Brice supposed he couldn't blame her for that, even though it went against the way most folks thought ladies should conduct themselves.

As Denny might say, she was no damn lady . . . except when it suited her to be one.

Brice clapped his hat back on his head and strode away from the depot. Standing there brooding wasn't accomplishing a blasted thing.

Denny would still be gone.

After a minute, he realized his steps were carrying him toward Monte Carson's office. He hadn't spoken to the sheriff in a while, so when he reached the large, square stone building that housed not only Monte's office but also Big Rock's jail, he stopped and opened the door.

Monte glanced up from the old, scarred desk that sat in front of a gun rack holding a number of rifles and shotguns. The lawman had papers scattered on the desk, a pencil in his hand, and an irritated look on his face. He put the pencil down and sighed. "Come on in, Brice. I'm glad to see you. No offense, but almost any visitor would be a welcome distraction right now."

"Paperwork, Sheriff?" Brice asked.

"That's right. The bane of any star packer's existence. Does the chief marshal make you fill out a paper for everything you do?"

Brice chuckled. "Not as bad as some I've heard about. When he was packing a deputy marshal's badge, he hated all that rigamarole as much as anybody, or so the stories go. Still, he's got to follow the rules, too."

Monte leaned back in his chair and reached for his pipe. As he began filling it with tobacco from a soft leather pouch, he asked, "What brings you here today?"

"Boredom. I was just over at the telegraph office, checking to see if I had any wires from Denver."

"Lester would have come looking for you if you did."

"Yeah, I know. I just hoped there might be something for me to do that would get me out on the trail for a while."

Monte scratched a match to life on the sole of his left boot, held the flame to the pipe, and puffed until he had it going. He blew out a little smoke and said, "Out on the trail away from Big Rock . . . and the Sugarloaf."

Brice felt his face growing warm. "Maybe," he admitted. "Anything wrong with that?"

"Oh, not as far as I'm concerned. I understand. I may be pretty far past the age when a gal can tie my guts up in knots, but I remember what that was like, I promise you."

"My guts are just fine," Brice insisted.

"Whatever you say." Monte sat there puffing tranquilly on the pipe.

After a moment of awkward silence, Brice asked, "Got any new wanted posters? There might be some outlaw wanted on federal charges I could try to track down."

Monte opened a desk drawer, pulled out a stack of papers, and placed them on the desk. "Help yourself. I didn't know you were supposed to take off after any fugitives without specific orders, though."

"Like I said, Marshal Long gives us some leeway." Brice picked up the stack of reward dodgers and carried them over to an old sofa against the side wall. He sat down and started looking through them while Monte picked up his pencil again, sighed, and started writing on one of the papers on the desk in front of him. The pencil's scratching was the only sound in the room for a few minutes.

When the door opened again both men looked up in relief.

Pearlie Fontaine, Smoke's old friend and retired foreman, ambled into the office. "Howdy, Monte."

He glanced over at Brice. "Marshal. Didn't expect to find you here."

"You're a sight for sore eyes, Pearlie," Monte greeted him. They were old friends as well, having been acquainted with each other even before they first met Smoke. Both men had hired out their guns in those days, not really owlhoots but not far from it, and although they had usually fought on the same side of whatever dispute involved them, that hadn't always been the case. Luckily for their friendship, they had never actually traded shots with each other.

"I don't know if you'll say that once you find out why I'm here," said Pearlie.

"That sounds like trouble brewing," Brice commented from the sofa. "Something wrong out at the Sugarloaf, Pearlie?" He frowned suddenly. "It's not Mrs. Jensen, is it? I heard that she's been sick and that Dr. Steward has been treating her."

Pearlie shook his head and waved off the question. "Nope, I'm happy to say that Miss Sally's steadily gettin' better. The doc said she wasn't hardly runnin' any temperature this mornin'. I got somethin' else on my mind."

"Well, then, spit it out." Monte grinned. "You don't want to strain that brain of yours."

"My thinkin' matter is just fine, thank you most to death," Pearlie snapped. "I want to look at your old ree-ward dodgers, Monte. You got a collection goin' back a long time, don't you?"

"Twenty years or more," Monte said, nodding. "And before you go accusing me of being a pack rat, I know I ought to go through them and weed out the ones on fellas who are dead or spending the rest of their lives in prison. I just haven't gotten around to it yet."

"Uh-huh. Where are they?"

Monte pointed to a cabinet in the corner. "Right in there. Help yourself."

Pearlie went to the cabinet and opened the doors. He let out a whistle when he saw the stacks and stacks of paper inside. "Are these in any kinda order?"

"Oldest on the bottom. You did say you wanted to look at old ones, right?"

"Yeah." Pearlie bent, took a stack off the bottom shelf, and carried them to the desk.

"Reminiscing?" asked Monte as Pearlie began flipping through the wanted posters. "We probably rode with some of those fellas, back in the bad ol' days."

"Not exactly. You remember a polecat called the Santa Rosa Kid?"

It was Monte's turn to whistle in surprise. "I don't see how I could forget anybody like that. The Santa Rosa Kid was about as bad an hombre as I ever ran across."

"You met him, personal-like?"

Monte shrugged. "We signed up for the same job. Rancher down along the Rio Grande in Texas wanted some Mexicans run off from land he'd decided was his. He didn't care if they were burned out or hung from the branch of a cottonwood tree. The whole business put a bad taste in my mouth, but the Kid loved it. Used to brag about the Mex farmers he strung up . . . but only after he made those fellas watch what he did to their wives and daughters." Monte's face hardened into stone as he went on. "I remember him talking about one time when he took a knife to some little señorita . . ." He shook his head. "I gave the rancher back his money and rode on. It was either that or gun the Kid down like the hydrophobia skunk he was. Looking back on it, that's what I should have done, and I'm sorry I didn't."

"Yeah, that was the Santa Rosa Kid, all right," Pearlie agreed. "Sorriest son of a gun I ever knew. And the most vicious." He turned over another of the wanted posters and drew in a sharp breath, then froze as he stared down at it. "Speak o' the devil."

"That didn't take long," said Monte. "Is he the one you were looking for?"

"Yeah. And I found him." Pearlie tapped the poster. "Take a gander."

Monte did so and immediately exclaimed, "I'll be danged."

Knowing that the normally soft-spoken sheriff had to be really shocked to react like that, Brice set aside the new wanted posters *he* had been looking through and stood up. He stepped over to the desk and stood beside Pearlie to look down at the reward dodger for the Santa Rosa Kid with its hand-drawn portrait of the murderous outlaw.

Brice felt as if a hard fist had just been sunk deep in his guts. Staring back up at him from the wanted poster was the spitting image of Steve Markham.

CHAPTER 40

The three men stared at the poster in stunned silence as a long moment dragged past.

Then Monte Carson burst out, "That's loco! The Santa Rosa Kid's been dead for fifteen years, at least. I don't remember exactly when the law caught up to him and stretched his neck, but I know that's what happened. I talked to people who were there at Yuma when he walked up the steps to the gallows!"

"Maybe so," Pearlie said, "but I know as soon as I laid eyes on that Markham jasper for the first time, I thought I recognized him. I was in the same crew as the Kid a time or two myself, and you don't forget an hombre like him."

Thoughts clamored through Brice's head. He tried to calm them and force his brain to function logically. That wasn't easy to do when an icy dagger of fear for Denny's safety was shoved in his belly. But after a few seconds, he was able to say, "Hold on a minute, both of you. Even if this Santa Rosa Kid was still alive somehow, he'd have to be in his forties, maybe even close to fifty years old. There's no way Steve Markham is that old."

"You sure about that?" asked Pearlie. "Some fellas don't look their age."

"Pretty damned sure. I've gotten several good close looks at him, remember, while we were whaling the tar out of each other."

"Brice is right," Monte said as he tapped a finger against the poster. "Yeah, Markham bears a mighty strong resemblance to the fella on this dodger, but they can't be the same person. It's just not possible."

Pearlie didn't look convinced, but he said, "Well, how do you explain it, then?"

Brice thought about it some more and then said, "Maybe Markham is the son of this Santa Rosa Kid. Do you know what the Kid's real name was?"

Monte and Pearlie looked at each other.

Monte shook his head. "I don't reckon I ever heard it."

"Me, neither," said Pearlie. "We just called him the Kid. He wasn't even really all that young, come to think of it. He must've been twenty-four, twenty-five, somewhere in there."

"All the more reason to think that he and Markham aren't the same person, even though they look so much alike," Brice said. "They could almost be twins, but the age difference rules that out, too. The only thing that makes sense is if they're father and son."

Monte said, "I ought to be able to find out what the Kid's real name was. I can send a wire to the warden at Yuma Prison, down in Arizona Territory. That's where he was locked up and finally hanged." The sheriff rubbed his chin and frowned in thought. "Although that might not actually prove anything. The

Kid could have been using some alias when he was locked up."

"And we don't have any proof that Steve Markham is the other fella's real name, either," Brice pointed out. "All we have to go on is what Markham told us. One or both of them could have lied."

Pearlie said, "Well, then, the only real evidence we have is that right there", his finger jabbed the picture on the wanted poster—"and it ain't lyin'. No two fellas ever looked that much alike without bein' related."

"And Denny's gone to Montana with him," Monte muttered.

The same thought loomed enormously in Brice's mind. He wasn't the sort of man given to panic. If he had been, he never would have been able to become a deputy U.S. marshal. But the idea that Denny was off somewhere far away, possibly alone with the son of a brutal killer, made his insides clench in tight knots.

"Cal's along on that trip, too," said Pearlie, "as well as Gene Cunningham and some of the other hands, and they're all good fellas. They'll look out for Denny, whether she wants 'em to or not."

"She won't," Brice said. "And she's mighty stubborn about getting her way."

"Something else we need to consider," Monte said. "Even if Markham is the Santa Rosa Kid's son—"

"He is," Pearlie broke in. "Ain't no doubt in my mind of that. That's why I felt like I knew him all along."

"Even if he is," Monte went on, "that doesn't mean he's the same sort of man his father was. A man can have an owlhoot for a pa and not be on the wrong side of the law himself."

Brice said, "That's true, but what are the chances?"

Monte shrugged. "That's just it. We don't know."

"We don't know a damned thing." Brice picked up the wanted poster and stared at it, seeing the features of Steve Markham in the lines printed on the page. He wanted to crumple the paper and throw it against the wall. "That's the problem. We don't know what Markham's up to, if anything. But it's too dangerous to let a man like that run free until we find out what he's planning."

"How do you figure on doing that?" Pearlie asked.

Brice shoved the fear aside in his mind. He needed to think quickly and clearly. A lot might be depending on it. "Those livestock cars with the horses in them have probably been changed over to a Northern Pacific train in Chicago by now and are heading west toward Montana," he said, thinking aloud. "What's the name of the town where they're going?"

"Stirrup," Pearlie supplied. "It's the closest stop to the Circle C Ranch, about eighty miles south of there."

"I don't think Markham would try anything while they're on the train," Brice mused. "Too many people around. If he's up to no good, he won't strike until they're driving that horse herd north."

"What could he do?" asked Monte. "Try to steal the horses?"

"More likely he'd try to kidnap Denny. Get her off alone somewhere, grab her and tie her on her horse, and take off."

Pearlie snorted. "He'd have his hands full doin' that, I'll damn well betcha."

"Yes, but if he's ruthless enough . . . and he takes her by surprise . . ." Brice's mouth twisted bitterly.

"She probably trusts him and would never expect anything like that."

"All right. Let's just take it easy," Monte said. "I'll send a wire to the local lawman in Stirrup and ask him to take Markham into custody when the train gets there. He can hold him until we get this straightened out."

Brice started to nod, then stopped and shook his head. "If it turns out that Markham actually is innocent, and Denny finds out we had him arrested, she'll be mad as she can be."

"Send the wire to Cal instead," Pearlie suggested. "That boy's plenty tough and levelheaded. If Markham's up to no good, Cal will put a stop to whatever it is. And if there ain't really anything to worry about, Cal will keep his mouth shut and Denny won't have no reason to be aggravated at any of us."

"We're all forgetting something very important," Monte said. "Smoke. We need to tell him what's going on. If he ever finds out we knew his little girl might be in trouble and we didn't tell him about it . . . Well, let's just say I don't ever want to have Smoke Jensen that mad at me."

Pearlie shook his head. "I know what you're sayin', Monte, and I ain't claimin' you're wrong, but the problem is that Miss Sally's just now startin' to get over whatever was ailin' her. If she finds out Miss Denny's in danger, it's liable to make her get sick all over again. I don't think we can risk that when we don't know for sure that Markham's up to no good."

Brice knew it in his gut, regardless of what either of the other men said, but how much were his instincts being influenced by jealousy and his dislike of Markham? Honestly, he couldn't answer that question.

"You don't reckon Smoke could keep it from Sally until we find out something for sure?" Monte asked.

"Smoke's never been able to keep secrets from Miss Sally," Pearlie replied. "She'd be able to tell that somethin' was wrong, and she'd get it out of him, mark my words on that." He sighed. "I don't like it, not one little bit, but I think we got to handle this one on our own, boys. Send that wire so it'll be waitin' at Stirrup for Cal, Monte. That's all we can do."

Brice was still holding the wanted poster with the Santa Rosa Kid's likeness on it. He dropped it on the desk and said, "That's not all. I'm going to Montana."

"Damn it, boy, they got too big a lead on you! You can't catch up to 'em."

"I'll be traveling faster on the train than they will once they start driving those horses north," Brice argued. "And then when I get to Stirrup, I can pick up some extra saddle mounts and switch off between them, so I can move twice as fast as they will with the herd. If I push hard, I'll have an outside chance of catching up to them before they reach the Circle C."

Monte's face and voice were grim as he said, "Maybe that's true, Brice, but if Markham's planning some sort of deviltry, odds are he will have made his move before then."

"You're right, Sheriff," Brice admitted, his own voice showing the strain he was under. "But I have to try. If I didn't, and if anything happened to Denny, I . . . I'd never be able to live with myself."

Monte looked at him for a long moment and then

nodded. "I reckon I understand, son. But what if the chief marshal tries to get in touch with you and give you a new assignment, and you're off in Montana chasing after Denny and Markham?"

"Then it'll probably mean I lose my badge, but I'll just have to take that chance."

CHAPTER 41

Montana

Denny stood on the platform at the rear of the car, watching the rolling, grassy hills as they swept past. Folks called it Big Sky Country, and she could see why. The arching blue vault of the heavens seemed enormous.

The slight rocking of the train as it traveled along the rails didn't bother her. Not only had she ridden on many trains before, she had also made a number of voyages by ship, crossing between Europe and America, and had never had any trouble getting her sea legs. Compared to Louis, who spent most of his time on board hanging over the railing, the trips had been downright pleasant for her.

She had her own car for that part of the journey, and that bothered her. When the train had reached Chicago, she'd found that her father had wired ahead and made arrangements for the private car. Smoke never flaunted his wealth, but he had a number of lucrative investments, including a considerable amount of stock in the railroad. The men who ran it were glad to do him a favor, and Denny hadn't seen a gracious way of refusing, even though it didn't seem fair.

Cal and the other hands from the Sugarloaf weren't traveling in luxury like that, but they were comfortable in a converted freight car with a dozen bunks and several tables in it. It was the next car back from Denny's car, and most of them were in there, playing poker, mending harness, darning socks, and swapping lies. In other words, the same sort of things they would be doing if they were in the bunkhouse back on the ranch.

Steve Markham emerged from that car onto its front platform, which was only a few steps from the rear platform of the private car where Denny stood. He rested his hands on the railing, grinned out at the passing landscape, and called across the gap to her, "Mighty pretty country, ain't it?"

"It is," Denny agreed, "but no prettier than Colorado."

"Oh, I reckon it's prettier right now."

"How do you figure that?" she asked.

"*You're* here."

Denny smiled and shook her head. She should have known he would say something like that, she told herself. He seemed to be a born flatterer. She told herself she didn't like it, but she wasn't so sure about that.

Markham had kept his distance for the most part, and she was glad of that. It made things simpler, less complicated. They had worked together taking care of the horses at times, but someone else had always been around. Cal hadn't had to go out of his way to chaperone them, which he'd said he wasn't going to do anyway.

They had also toiled side by side while they were moving the horses from one set of stock cars to another in Chicago. Markham had been all business, not even speaking to her unless it had to do with the job at hand.

She wouldn't have minded seeing some of the sights in Chicago if they hadn't had to leave almost right away on the other train. She and Louis had been to the Windy City a number of times, but they were always just changing trains and passing through. She hoped her brother had enjoyed visiting the city with Melanie before they went on farther east.

Without being invited, Markham stepped from one platform to the other, his long legs making it easy for him to cross the gap. Once he was on the rear platform of Denny's car, he stood at the railing beside her. "We'll be pullin' into Stirrup soon, I reckon. That's the name of the settlement where we get off the train, ain't it?"

"That's right. Then it'll take us three or four days to drive the horses the rest of the way to the Circle C."

"Three or four days of bein' out in the open air, in pretty country like this, with a beautiful gal like you for company . . . I'm sure lookin' forward to that."

Denny frowned slightly as she said, "Steve, you've been behaving so far—"

"I'm still behavin'," he protested. "I didn't grab you and plant a big ol' smooch on you, did I? And that's what I wanted to do when I seen you standin' there lookin' like that, with your hair blowin' in in the wind—"

"Getting cinders in it, you mean?" she interrupted, laughing.

"Well, that's part of travelin' by train, I reckon. I don't mind sayin', I'm happier on horseback."

"To tell the truth, so am I."

A companionable quiet settled over the platform, broken only by the clatter of the rails and the chuffing and rumbling of the locomotive up at the front of the train. Denny enjoyed just standing there with Markham at her side.

"I can imagine what this country was like when herds of buffalo covered these hills and the only folks around were the Injuns," he murmured after a while. "Lonely but beautiful."

"More than likely,"

Denny agreed. The train swept into a long, gentle curve, and from where they stood, they could see a wide, shallow valley opening up before them. She spotted some roofs in the distance, as well as a church steeple, and pointed them out to Markham. "That'll be Stirrup. We'll be there in just a little while."

"Are you excited to go on a drive like this?" he asked.

She nodded. "Honestly, I am. It's like the buffalo you mentioned. Times are changing and the old ways are vanishing, and it's nice to be able to experience them and bid them a proper farewell."

"Sounds like poetry. Did you learn how to talk like that in Europe?"

"Not hardly." She waved a hand at the landscape. "It's this country that brings it out. This big, big country . . ."

A short time later, the train rolled into Stirrup and pulled onto a siding. The locomotive slowed to a stop when the stock cars were in position to be cut loose and unloaded.

Denny had already gathered her gear. She didn't have much. She slung her war bag over her shoulder and swung down from the platform to join the other hands heading back along the rails to the waiting cars.

They unloaded their saddle mounts first and got them ready to ride. Then some of the men led the horses Bob Coburn was buying down the ramps and turned them over to mounted hands, Denny among them, who hazed them into what was normally a large cattle pen. It was too late in the day to start the drive to the Circle C, so the stock would remain there overnight and head north in the morning.

A rawboned cowboy with a drooping salt-and-pepper mustache rode up to the pen while that was going on and announced, "I'm lookin' for Calvin Woods."

Cal heard him, motioned Denny over, then reined his horse around. "I'm Woods. What can I do for you?"

"Haskell Sherman," the puncher introduced himself. He leaned over in the saddle to shake hands with Cal. "Call me Hack. I ride for the Circle C. The boss sent me in to wait for you fellas and ride along to the ranch with you. He figured you wouldn't have no trouble findin' the way, but he said I could be sort of a Justin Case."

"Glad to have you along, Hack." Cal introduced her as well. "This is Miss Denise Jensen."

Sherman pinched the brim of his dusty old black hat. "Pleasure to meet you, miss. Hope you know I don't mean no offense when I say it was a plumb disappointment to find out your pa couldn't make the trip. I was lookin' forward to shakin' hands with the famous Smoke Jensen."

She pulled the leather glove off her right hand and stuck it out. "I hope you're not too bothered by it, Hack. Call me Denny."

He grinned and shook with her. "No, I wouldn't say I'm a bit bothered," he drawled. "If you don't think I'm bein' too bold, you're a whole heap easier on the eyes than this bunch of hairy-legged cowboys. And speakin' of cowboys"—he turned back to Cal— "you know Mr. Coburn would've been happy to send a crew down here to pick up those hosses. You fellas didn't have to make the trip all the way out to the ranch. The boss said it was Mr. Jensen's idea, though, so he was willin' to play along with it."

"It'll be good for these boys," Cal said as he nodded toward the hands working with the horses. "Some of them have never driven stock more than a few miles to town. They don't know what it was like to set out across hundreds of miles of rugged country, pushing wild longhorns to the railhead." He chuckled. "To tell you the truth, I was born too late for that particular memory myself."

"I wasn't," said Hack Sherman. "I came up the trail from Texas more than once, mostly as a wrangler. I wasn't much more 'n a button then. Glad I had the experience, but I'd just as soon not eat dust for a couple o' months ever again!"

Cal and Sherman discussed getting the men from the Sugarloaf some rooms for the night in Stirrup's lone hotel. Mostly cattle buyers stayed there, and it wasn't a busy season for them, so Sherman didn't expect it to be a problem.

"Why don't you come along with us?" he suggested to Denny as he turned his horse. "If John Pearsol, the fella who runs the place, needs any convincing, I reckon having Smoke Jensen's daughter with us might make a difference."

"I was helping with the horses—" Denny began.

"The unloading is nearly done, and the boys can handle the rest of it without any trouble," said Cal.

Denny shrugged and nudged her horse into motion. She and Cal and Hack Sherman rode along Stirrup's main street toward the hotel, leaving the Sugarloaf hands to finish up the job behind them.

Steve Markham was sitting easy in the saddle with his hands resting on the horn, taking a momentary break from the work, when an irascible voice said from behind him, "I'm lookin' for Calvin Woods."

Markham turned his head and gazed over his shoulder. A bow-legged little man on the far side of middle age but not quite old yet was standing there with a telegraph envelope in his hand. He wore town clothes and was probably the local Western Union agent.

"You got a wire for Cal, mister?"

"That's right. Where'll I find him?"

Markham glanced along the street. Denny and Cal were just pulling up in front of the hotel, along with that fella from the Circle C. Another glance told him that none of the other Sugarloaf hands were close by, and they were all concentrating on the job of getting the horses in the pen, not paying attention to him. When he was sure of that, he gave in to the sudden impulse that had sprung to life inside him and reached a hand down to the little telegrapher.

"I'm Calvin Woods," he said.

"Why the hell didn't you say so to start with?"

"I don't have to explain myself to you, mister. Now, I'll take that wire."

Grumbling, the telegrapher handed it over, turned, and stumped away on his bowed legs. Markham let him get a little distance, then tore open the envelope and slid out the yellow telegraph flimsy inside.

The look that appeared on his face as he read the words printed on the paper in block capitals was only there for a second, but anyone who caught a glimpse of it probably would feel a twinge of unease.

Because at that moment, Steve Markham looked like he wanted to kill somebody.

CHAPTER 42

Denny got a hotel room to herself, of course. Everybody else bunked two to a room. Still not fair, she thought, but better than the cowboys' accommodations on the train.

"You're in with me, Markham," Cal told the red-headed puncher that evening.

Except for a couple of hands who'd been left to watch the horses, they all gathered in the hotel dining room for supper. Someone would relieve them later.

Denny knew Cal wasn't really expecting trouble, just being cautious, as was his habit. She would have volunteered to take a turn guarding the horses, but it wouldn't do any good. He'd just say that was all taken care of already.

"All right, boss," Markham responded. "You don't snore over-much, do you?"

"Just worry about the racket *you're* making," advised Cal.

One of the other men said, "I noticed a saloon down the street, Cal. Think we could pay a visit to it?"

Cal frowned. "We've come this far. I'm not sure it

would be a good idea to cut loose your wolf when we're this close to where we're going."

"You let us have a drink in Big Rock before we started," another man pointed out.

Hack Sherman was eating supper with the Sugarloaf crew. Cal looked at him and asked, "Is that saloon the sort of place where a man finds it easy to get in trouble?"

Sherman cocked a bushy eyebrow and said, "A feller can get in trouble just about anywhere if he's bound and determined to do it. But no, the Red Top is a square joint. The poker and faro games are honest, the drinks ain't watered and won't give a man the blind staggers, and Ben Hubbell, who owns the place, don't allow no sportin' ladies on the premises. For that, you got to go on down the street to Mamie's." A flush suddenly came over the cowboy's weathered face. "Beggin' your pardon, Miss Jensen. I didn't mean to talk quite so plain. I just plumb forgot there was a lady amongst us."

"That's all right, Hack," Denny assured him. "I know what goes on in saloons. And I'm flattered that you'd think of me as just one of the hands."

"Hard to do if anybody catches more than a glimpse of you, I reckon," Sherman muttered.

"What about the saloon, Cal?" the cowboy who had brought it up pressed.

Cal thought about it for a moment longer and then nodded. "All right. But if anybody gets the urge to break loose, you'd better hold it in, just like I told you back in Big Rock. Anybody who shows up hungover enough for me to notice it in the morning won't be working for the Sugarloaf anymore."

The men nodded their agreement and continued shoveling in food.

When the meal was over, most of the hands stood up and headed for the saloon. A few who didn't drink went up to their rooms to make an early night of it, since morning would come quickly and the day would feature a lot of long hours in the saddle. Two of the men went to relieve the pair of guards at the horse herd.

Steve Markham lingered in his chair, sipping from a cup of coffee.

Denny leaned back in her chair and asked him, "Aren't you going to the saloon with your friends?"

"Maybe. But I wanted to ask you first if you'd like to go for a walk. It's a nice evenin' outside."

Denny glanced at the other end of the table, where Cal was deep in conversation with Hack Sherman. Quietly, she said, "I'm not sure that would be a good idea."

"I'll conduct myself like a plumb gentleman," Markham promised.

"If you didn't, I'd punch you in the belly. Or use a knee on you somewhere else."

Markham grinned at her over his coffee cup and tut-tutted. "Such scandalous language, Miss Jensen."

"I believe in plain speaking, too."

"Then how about that walk?"

Denny thought about it and shook her head. "Not tonight. This has been a good trip so far, without any melodrama. I'd just as soon keep it that way."

"Suit yourself," he told her. "In that case, I reckon maybe I will go have a beer after all. Might sit in on a poker game for a few hands."

"Just don't get mixed up in any trouble."

"Don't worry about that. Any time I see trouble on the horizon, I turn around and gallop the other way!"

A florid-faced bartender with muttonchop whiskers set a foaming mug of beer on the hardwood in front of Markham. Markham slid a dime across the bar and picked up the mug. As he sipped the sudsy brew, he turned and let his eyes play across the main room of the Red Top Saloon. His fellow punchers from the Sugarloaf were lined up at the bar, except for a couple who had headed straight for the faro layout in the back of the room.

Markham's attention was focused more on the poker game going on at one of the tables. Four men were playing, all of them dressed in range clothes. One man, the oldest of the quartet, sported somewhat more expensive duds than the other three. Curly dark hair, lightly touched with gray, spilled out from under his pushed-back black hat. A prominent nose overhung a thick dark mustache.

One of the other players threw down his cards disgustedly and announced in a voice that carried to Markham's ears, "That's enough for me, damn it. I can't buck this bad luck that's got hold of me tonight."

"Sometimes you've just got to walk away from it, all right," said the older man. The other two players had folded as well, and he raked in the small pot.

The one who had complained scraped back his chair and stood up. He snorted, shook his head, and turned to stalk out of the saloon.

The older man caught Markham's gaze, cocked an

eyebrow, and gestured at the empty chair. Still holding his mug, Markham sauntered over to the table.

"Care to join us?" the older man asked. "I never did cotton to playing three-handed poker."

"Don't mind if I do," said Markham. "As long as the stakes ain't too high."

"They're only as high as you want them to be, friend."

Markham nodded, said, "Fair enough," and sat down to nurse the beer and play cards.

"Name's Bert Rome," the older man said. "That's Harry Castle and Joe Foster."

The other two men grunted and nodded in turn as Rome introduced them.

"Steve Markham."

"Glad to meet you, Markham. I noticed you came in with those other punchers."

"Yeah, we're all from a spread called the Sugarloaf, down in Colorado. Delivering a herd of horses to the Circle C, north of here."

Rome had been shuffling the deck while they were talking. He slid it over to Markham to cut, then commenced dealing.

For the next half-hour, the four men played poker in a desultory fashion. None of the hands got too long and drawn out, and none of the pots were huge. Markham broke even, within a dollar or two. If any of the others could be said to be the big winner, it was Bert Rome, and he was only up about twenty dollars.

None of them had much to say, and Markham himself was unusually subdued. No one in the Red Top paid any attention to what was going on at the table.

Finally, Markham folded rather than pursue another small pot. "I reckon that'll do it for me, boys. Got to be up early in the mornin'."

"Headed for the Circle C, was it?" Rome asked.

"That's right."

"Well, good luck, Markham." Rome placed the deck in the center of the table. "I think I'll call it a night, too."

Foster and Castle just grunted again. They really weren't talkative sorts.

Markham stood up and carried his empty mug back to the bar. He paused long enough to chat idly with some of the other Sugarloaf cowboys for a few minutes. When he looked around, Rome, Castle, and Foster were gone. He said his good nights and left the saloon as well.

He had walked two blocks when a dark shape stepped out of an alley mouth in front of him. Markham slowed his pace as his hand drifted toward the gun holstered on his right hip, but then he relaxed as a familiar voice said, "Back here."

The man retreated into the darkness, and Markham stepped into the alley. The shadows were so thick he had to rely on sound more than sight to follow. After a moment, the other man stopped. Markham heard a match rasp, and the sudden flare of light revealed the rugged face of Bert Rome as the man held the flame to the tip of a thin black cheroot.

"About time you got here," Rome said quietly. "But where the hell is Smoke Jensen?"

CHAPTER 43

While the match in Rome's thick but deft fingers still burned, Markham glanced around and saw that they were in a small alcove set in the side of the building. Some empty crates were stacked next to a door. No one could see them from the street, which was why Rome had felt safe in lighting the match.

"Jensen's not here," Markham replied, keeping his voice low, too.

"I know that, you damned fool," said Rome, his voice edged with steel. He dropped the dying match at his feet. "His daughter came along instead. I've heard the gossip around town since the train pulled in this afternoon. And it's hard to miss a girl who looks like that, even when she's dressed like a ranch hand."

Markham stiffened a little at the mention of Denny. He didn't like the hint of a leer he'd heard in Rome's voice. He liked even less the way Rome was talking to him.

Rome puffed on the cheroot and went on. "You were supposed to keep us informed. Why the hell didn't you let us know Jensen wasn't coming?"

"The whole thing came up at the last minute, the day before we were supposed to leave the Sugarloaf." Markham was irritated at having to explain himself, but he knew Rome wouldn't settle for anything less. "Jensen's wife got sick all of a sudden, too sick for him to leave. I figured he'd just trust his foreman to deliver those horses, but then . . . the girl . . . ups and decides that a Jensen ought to come along on the trip, and she's the only one who can do it. She talked Smoke into agreeing."

He hoped Rome hadn't noticed his slight hesitation when he was speaking of Denny. He had almost referred to her by her name, and some instinct told him such familiarity might not be a good idea. He didn't want Rome to think that anything was distracting him from the job at hand.

"And you didn't have any chance to let us know?"

"No, I didn't," Markham replied bluntly. "Hell, there was never supposed to be any close contact between us in the first place, you know that. If Jensen or his men ever caught me sneaking around and passing word to a bunch of owlhoots, that would've ruined the whole plan, wouldn't it?"

"What about somewhere along the way? You could've sent a wire—"

"I watched for an opportunity to do that. There just wasn't one."

There was some truth to what Markham said, but it wasn't the whole story. There hadn't been much of a chance to get to a telegraph office, but actually he hadn't tried that hard to get in touch with Rome because he wasn't sure what he would tell the man. Sally

Jensen's illness had been an unwanted, unexpected complication, and Markham hadn't known how the plan would change because of it.

Rome puffed harder on the cheroot, making the tip glow red in the darkness. Markham's eyes were adjusted to the gloom by now, and even that faint illumination was enough for him to make out Rome's features. The red cast made Rome look vaguely satanic.

"All right," he finally said. "I need to warn Brant if I can, but it may be too late for that. I'll send a wire to him in Big Rock first thing in the morning. He and the rest of the boys down there may have already left town and headed for the high country to lie low until it's time for them to make their move."

"Even if they have, that don't mean things won't work out all right," said Markham. "Brant's got fifteen good men with him, and there are only a handful of punchers left on the Sugarloaf right now. They should be able to handle the job."

"Smoke Jensen counts for more than one man," Rome said. "A hell of a lot more, if all the stories are true."

Markham winced in the darkness. "From what I've seen of him, they might be."

Rome dropped the cigar butt and ground it out as he said, "Louis Jensen is still supposed to be back in three days, right? That hasn't changed?"

Quickly, Markham counted the days in his head. He had been careful about finding out when Louis and Melanie were expected back at the ranch without being too obvious about it. Having checked the dates again, he said, "Yeah. He should be there."

"Well, I suppose we can kill Smoke Jensen down there as well as we could have up here," Rome grumbled. "It's just that *we* were expecting him, and Brant won't be. Either way, he'll be dead, Louis Jensen will be our prisoner, and his mother will pay us all the money she has and can raise to get him back alive. One thing, though . . . we have to wipe out that bunch of hands with the horses. If any of them survive, they might get word back to the Sugarloaf. Then Jensen would be ready for trouble."

"No survivors, huh?" Markham heard the hollow note he couldn't keep out of his voice.

"That's right. They all die." Rome paused. "But not the girl. She's worth ransom money, too. You all right with that, Markham?" A mocking quality came into his voice as he added, "Just how much do you take after your old man? The Santa Rosa Kid would never let a woman, even one as pretty as this girl, get in the way of what he wanted."

Markham had to force the words out, but he said, "Don't worry about me. I'll do whatever it takes."

"I'm glad to hear that. Because if I think for a second that you're fixing to double-cross us, Markham . . . or you just hesitate at the wrong moment . . . I'll put a bullet through your brain myself."

Markham's fingers trembled with the urge to grab his gun and blast Bert Rome right there. He didn't do it, though. He reminded himself of how much money he stood to make if all their plans worked out. "Are we through here?" he asked coldly.

"Yeah." Rome sounded a little amused. "Just don't

forget, Markham. Day after tomorrow, early afternoon. That's when we'll hit that horse herd."

"I'll be ready."

"See that you are."

When they left the alcove, they turned in opposite
directions, Markham toward the street and Rome
deeper into the shadows. Markham paused just
inside the alley mouth and leaned forward to check
the street. He didn't want to step out right in front
of a Sugarloaf hand and have the man get curious
about what he was doing hanging around in alleys.

The street was empty of movement. Markham
didn't waste any time heading back to the hotel. He
hoped Cal had already turned in. He didn't want
the foreman asking him how the evening had gone.
He would lie about that, of course, if he had to, the
same way he had been lying about so many other
things in recent weeks.

He hoped even more that he wouldn't encounter
Denny. He had to figure out what he was going to do,
and the sight of her would just make that more difficult. Everything had been so simple starting out,
when his father's old partners Bert Rome and Sam
Brant had approached him with the scheme. Find a
way to get a man working on the Sugarloaf, learn
from him the best time to ambush Smoke Jensen and
get him out of the way, then kidnap Louis Jensen
and collect a fortune in ransom from the young
man's mother.

Each step of the way had gone perfectly, too, lucky
break after lucky break, starting with that horse race,
which had given him the chance to rescue Jensen's

daughter and put the man in debt to him. Then the business with selling the horses to the Circle C had come up, which should have put Smoke Jensen a long way from the ranch so that it would be easy to dispose of him as a threat. Everything was going the gang's way, and it looked like Markham's first job, his first real chance to live up to the legacy of the Santa Rosa Kid, was going to be a smashing success.

And then, damn it, he'd had to go and fall in love with Denny Jensen!

CHAPTER 44

It was still dark outside when Cal pounded a fist on the door of Denny's hotel room. She didn't have to drag herself out of bed, though. She was already awake and dressed, eager to get started on the trail drive to the Circle C.

Cal cocked an eyebrow in surprise when Denny swung the door open. "You look like you're ready to go," he commented.

"I am," she said as she buckled the gun belt and holstered the Colt Lightning around her hips.

"Well, I'm rousting the boys out now. You can come on down to breakfast in a few minutes."

Denny nodded. She didn't intend to wait that long. As soon as Cal had moved on to awaken the rest of the hands, she picked up her war bag and Winchester and went downstairs to the dining room. Might as well get a head start on a cup of coffee, she thought.

She wasn't the only one who'd had that idea, She entered the room and saw Steve Markham already at the long table, sipping from a cup with tendrils of steam rising from it.

"Mornin'," he said with a smile. "Sleep well?"

"As a matter of fact, I did." She set the war bag in a corner and leaned the Winchester against the wall beside it. "How about you?"

"Slept the same way I always do. Like a baby." Markham sipped the coffee again and then grinned. "Yep, fretted and cried all night."

Denny tried not to smile at the feeble joke, but she couldn't quite manage it. She sat down beside him, and a yawning waitress brought her a cup of coffee, too.

Over the next quarter of an hour, the other cowboys from the Sugarloaf drifted into the dining room, most of them yawning as well, and sat down to help themselves from the platters of flapjacks, steaks, bacon, biscuits, and eggs that the sleepy waitress carried from the kitchen and placed on the table. Syrup and gravy boats were passed around, and the girl was kept busy making sure their cups stayed full. The clatter of silverware on china punctuated the chorus of chomping and slurping. It wasn't an elegant meal, like many of the ones Denny had had on the Continent, but it was more important that the hands put away enough grub to fuel them through the long day ahead.

Denny ate with the same enthusiasm as the rest of them. Markham didn't bother flirting while there was food to be shoveled into his mouth, and Denny was glad of that, while at the same time sort of missing the easy banter that often took place between them.

When they were finished, Cal gave them a few minutes to finish up any final preparations for departure and told them to assemble in a quarter-hour at the pen where the horses were being held. Denny picked up her gear and headed that way.

"I can carry that for you," Markham offered as he joined her in walking toward the pen at the edge of the settlement.

"You know better than that," Denny told him.

"Yeah, I reckon I do, but I didn't think it'd hurt anything to offer." He grew more serious. "You sure you want to go through with this, Denny? You could wait right here in Stirrup until the rest of us get back from the Circle C."

She paused to frown at him in amazement. "What are you talking about? You think I came all this way to sit and wait in a hotel in a backwater burg like this? Of course I'm going along on the drive!"

"It's just that I got to thinkin'—"

"Well, there's your problem, right there."

"It's just that I got to thinkin'," Markham plowed ahead stubbornly, "that you've likely never spent all day in the saddle before. I know you're a fine rider, but doin' it for a little while ain't hardly the same as stayin' on a cayuse's back for twelve, fourteen hours straight."

"I'll be fine," Denny said a little stiffly. "I've done a lot of riding since Louis and I came back to the Sugarloaf last year. Maybe not for *that* long at a time, but enough that I know it's not going to bother me."

"I just don't want you sufferin'—"

"Don't worry about me," she insisted. "Just worry about yourself."

He sighed and said, "Believe me, I am." For once, he didn't sound as if he were joking.

It took Denny a minute or so to wonder what in blazes he meant by *that*.

The horses didn't give any trouble about leaving the pen, and they stayed together nicely as the cowboys pointed them north. Cal told Denny she could ride point with him and Hack Sherman, but she shook her head.

"I'm the most inexperienced hand," she said. "I'll ride drag, just like I'm supposed to."

Markham was close enough to hear what she said. He laughed. "You're probably the first person to ever volunteer to ride drag and eat all that dust."

"I'm just trying to do the right thing," Denny protested.

"That's fine," Cal told her. "Somebody's got to ride drag. I suppose it might as well be you."

"And I'll be back there with you," Markham said.

Denny frowned. "It's Cal's job to decide where everybody's going to ride."

"Yeah, but if a man wants to volunteer for that job, I'm not going to stop him," the foreman said. "Go ahead, Markham. You and Denny fall back behind the herd."

Markham grinned and ticked a finger against his hat brim. As he turned his horse, he said, "Come on, Denny. We got dust to eat."

Denny glanced at Cal, who shrugged. He had warned her that he wasn't going to interfere, for or against, where she and Steve Markham were concerned. She had wanted him to treat her like any of the other hands, and that was exactly what he was doing.

With a nod to him, she pulled her horse around and followed Markham toward the rear of the herd.

She found that in those grassy hills, the horses didn't really raise that much dust, so riding drag there wasn't as unpleasant a chore as it would have been if they'd been pushing several thousand head of longhorns across Indian Territory toward the railhead in Kansas. Denny had heard old cowboys talk about those drives some thirty to thirty-five years earlier. The old-timers always had fondness in their voices, but she was willing to bet that they hadn't enjoyed it much at the time.

She didn't mind jogging along at an easy pace with Markham beside her and the huge blue vault of the Montana sky overhead. The horses they were driving were well-behaved; occasionally one or two of the animals dropped back too far or even stopped to crop at a particularly appealing patch of grass. When that happened Denny and Markham would prod them ahead and make them rejoin the herd. The most stubborn was a big bay that tried to veer off to the side every now and then.

"I know this isn't anything like the old days," Denny commented later in the morning, "but I'm glad I got to experience it anyway."

Markham took off his hat and sleeved sweat from his forehead. The sun was high enough in the sky that heat was starting to build. As he settled the hat on his red thatch again, he said, "Nothin's really like it was in the old days, I reckon. The West is tame now. It won't ever be the same."

Remembering her experiences with outlaws and killers the summer before, as well as the previous Christmas, Denny said, "I don't think it's completely tamed. There'll be some new sort of troublemaker crop up sooner or later, I'll bet. There'll always be owlhoots, my pa says. We'll just call them something else." She laughed. "Like politicians, maybe."

"Yeah, I guess." Markham paused, then asked, "Denny, you plan on runnin' that ranch one of these days, don't you?"

"That's right," she answered without hesitation. "Although not anytime soon, I don't expect. Smoke's still a long way from stepping aside and taking up a rocking chair on the front porch."

"Smoke Jensen in a rockin' chair," mused Markham. "Yeah, that *is* sort of hard to imagine, ain't it? But what I was gettin' at, since you're gonna be in charge sooner or later, maybe you ought to stop actin' like a common puncher and be the boss, instead. Ride on ahead of the herd and get to the Circle C first so you can finish up the deal with Coburn. He'll have a bill of sale drawn up, I expect, and he'll still have to pay you. I'll bet if you pushed on ahead this afternoon, you could make good enough time that you'd get there tomorrow instead of the next day."

Denny shook her head. "There's no rush. There'll be plenty of time for all that once we get there. Besides, I want to enjoy every bit of this trip." She grunted. "Anyway, Cal wouldn't like it if I rode on ahead by myself."

"Well, I didn't really figure on you headin' off like that by yourself . . ."

"Oh, so that's it," Denny said as understanding

dawned on her. "This whole idea was just an excuse for you to get me off somewhere by myself so you could woo me."

A sheepish grin appeared on Markham's face. "Well, you can't hardly blame a fella for tryin', can you?"

"I suppose not. And riding along with your main view being dozens of horses' rear ends isn't the most romantic activity in the world, is it?"

"That's the honest truth! So what do you say? Cal can get somebody else to ride drag."

"Of course he can, but that's not the point. This is our job, and we're going to do it."

"Whatever you say," Markham replied. He was still smiling, but his voice was a little cooler. His jaw tightened slightly, as if he were under some sort of strain.

Denny wondered for a second if something more was going on than was apparent.

But then Markham started cracking jokes about horses' rear ends, and Denny couldn't help but laugh as she rode on, completely forgetting about that fleeing moment of misgiving.

CHAPTER 45

Evening shadows had started to gather when Brice Rogers swung down from the train that had just stopped in Stirrup. He had a rifle in one hand and hefted his saddle with the other. He was traveling light. Everything he needed was in his saddlebags.

The platform was small and so was the station building, just large enough for a postage-stamp waiting room and a combined ticket and telegraph office. Mostly, trains stopped in Stirrup to pick up cattle. There wasn't much passenger traffic.

Brice set his saddle down by the wall and went into the waiting room. A few steps took him to the ticket office window. He looked through and saw a crotchety-looking man in late middle age flipping through some paperwork. He didn't glance in Brice's direction until the deputy marshal cleared his throat.

"Yeah?" the man asked.

"I'm looking for the telegrapher."

"That's me. Name's Robeson. I manage this place for the railroad, too. And sweep it out. What do you want?"

The man's cold, impatient attitude annoyed Brice.

He had never been one to flash his badge, but he drew the leather folder from his pocket and opened it, holding it up so the man couldn't miss the symbol of authority it contained.

"Deputy United States Marshal Rogers," Brice introduced himself. "I need to ask you some questions, Mr. Robeson."

The station agent sounded a little less surly as he said, "Sure, Marshal. What do you want to know? We ain't had any trouble around here lately, as far as I recall."

"Did you get a telegram yesterday addressed to a man named Calvin Woods?"

"I'm not supposed to talk about what's in any of the wires that come through here—"

"You don't have to tell me what was in it," Brice broke in. "I *know* what it said. I just want to know if it came and was delivered all right."

"Oh." Robeson leaned back in his chair and nodded. "Yeah, I remember it. Woods was one of those cowboys who brought in the horse herd to take up to the Circle C."

"That's right." Brice felt his impatience growing and wished he could hurry up the old-timer.

"To tell you the truth, I wouldn't have minded going with them. I used to be a top hand myself, you know, until I got too stove up to sit a saddle anymore. Now I ride this chair instead and wrangle a telegraph key."

"Did Woods get the message or not?"

"No need to get snippy with me, even if you *are* a lawman." Robeson sniffed. "Yeah, he got the message. Handed it to him myself."

A wave of relief went through Brice. He closed his eyes for a second and blew out a breath. "Do you have any law here? Was one of the cowboys arrested and locked up?"

"What?" Robeson frowned. "Not that I know of. I didn't see it with my own eyes, but I heard they all pulled out with those horses this mornin'. If there had been any trouble, somebody would've told me. And to answer your question, the county sheriff's got a deputy who has an office here, but he ain't in town right now. He's off servin' some legal papers, I think. He's gone more of the time than he's here."

Brice was relieved that Cal had gotten the warning about Steve Markham's possible connection to the Santa Rosa Kid, but at the same time he was puzzled about the foreman's evident failure to do anything about Markham. Maybe Cal had decided to keep the information under his hat for the moment and just watch Markham like a hawk. That struck Brice as a risky strategy, but he couldn't guarantee that Cal hadn't gone that route.

"You say they left with the herd this morning?"

"That's right."

Brice had gotten very lucky on changing trains in Chicago. The schedule had worked out so that he'd barely had time to get off one train before he was boarding another one. That had allowed him to reach Stirrup only about twelve hours behind the horse herd.

"I need to rent a saddle mount. Maybe a couple of them."

Robeson nodded. "Fulger's Livery Stable, other

side of the street in the next block. He'll rent a horse to you, and a rig, too."

"I've got my own saddle."

Brice started to turn away, but Robeson stopped him by asking, "Is this here official deputy marshal business you're on?"

Brice didn't have any idea if that was true, but he said, "Yeah, that's right."

"I wouldn't tell that to ol' Fulger. He hates the gov'ment and will charge you the highest price he thinks he can get away with."

Brice didn't care about that. He just wanted a good horse with speed and sand, and the sooner it allowed him to catch up with Denny and the rest of the Sugarloaf crew, the better.

They made about thirty miles with the horses that first day, moving at a decent pace without pushing either man or beast too hard. Late in the afternoon, they came in sight of snowcapped mountains to the north and west. Denny had seen the Rockies farther south in Colorado, of course, and the Alps and the Pyrenees in Europe, but those Montana mountains still struck her as beautiful.

They also reached a creek with small but sturdy cottonwood, aspen, and willow trees lining the banks. The stream flowed swiftly and was cold from snowmelt.

Cal said, "We'll make camp here tonight. If we cover as much ground tomorrow as we did today, we'll get to the Circle C early afternoon the day after that."

There was no way to corral the horses, but after a day of traveling they were tired and likely would stay

where they had good graze and water. Just to make
sure of that and prevent any stampedes, some of the
cowboys would take turns riding nighthawk. The sky
was clear, so bad weather wasn't expected, but one
never could tell when a wolf or even a bear might
come along and spook the livestock.

After supper, which Cal took charge of himself
since he had more experience than anyone in the
group at cooking on the trail, the hands spread their
bedrolls along the creek bank. For propriety's sake,
Denny made sure that hers was a decent distance
away from the others. Even so, she thought about
what some of the older ladies back in Big Rock must
be saying about her, an unmarried young woman
traveling with a bunch of men out in the middle of
nowhere. She was sure most of them thought it was
terribly scandalous . . . which meant it was a good
thing she didn't really care what they thought of her,
she told herself with a smile.

Steve Markham came over to her and asked, "Are
you gonna be all right?"

"What do you think?" she shot right back at him.

"I think that if you hear some ol' lobo start howlin'
durin' the night and it scares you, you know where I'll
be." He pointed to one of the bedrolls about twenty
yards away. "You just gimme a holler, and I'll come
a-runnin'."

"There's not going to be any hollering," Denny
told him. "No wolf is going to bother a bunch this
big, and if one does, I'll just shoot it." She paused.
"The same goes for any bothersome varmint, four-
legged or two."

Markham chuckled. "I'll be sure to remember that." He ambled off toward his bedroll.

The night passed quietly, no wolves, bears, or other "bothersome varmints." None of the horses strayed.

All the hands were up early the next morning, well before dawn, and were ready to start pushing the herd north again once it was light enough to see where they were going.

Since Denny and Markham had ridden drag the day before, Cal put them out on the left flank. Denny was grateful for that. The previous day hadn't been unpleasant, but the view would be better on the flanks.

Markham noticed her shifting around a little more than before in the saddle and said with a grin, "All those hours on horseback yesterday sorta took a toll after all, didn't they?"

"I'm fine," she insisted. "Maybe I *am* a little sore, and it didn't help that a rock was poking me through my bedroll last night and I couldn't seem to find it. So I'm a mite sleepy, too."

"I'd 've been happy to help you look for that pesky rock."

"Oh, I'll just bet you would have."

"Just tryin' to be helpful," drawled Markham. "You know me."

"Yeah, I do." Denny thought about the way he had looked for a moment the day before and added, "Although sometimes, I'm not completely sure that I do."

"What do you mean by that?" he asked, his forehead creasing.

Denny shook her head. "Never mind. We'd better keep an eye on that bay that gave us trouble yesterday.

He seems even friskier today, like he wouldn't mind a chance to gallop off and run for a while."

"Maybe there are mustangs up in those hills over to the west. Wild fillies can be a powerful temptation."

"I'll bet," Denny said dryly. "Just watch him."

Once again, Cal set a brisk but not punishing pace.

By the middle of the day, the mountains to the west had extended much closer to their route. Denny could see rugged foothills cut through with canyons stretching to within a mile or so of where they stopped to rest the horses and make a meal of jerky and biscuits left over from the night before.

After eating, Denny sat down with her back against a little hummock of ground and closed her eyes, figuring she would bask in the sun for a few minutes and enjoy its heat.

She had barely gotten settled when a dark shadow fell over her, blocking the sun. She cracked her eyes open and glared up at the man standing so that he loomed over her, looking enormous. "What do you want?"

Markham hunkered on his heels in front of her. "It's that dang bay horse you were talkin' about earlier. He ain't with the herd no more."

Denny sat up sharply. "What? We need to tell Cal—"

Markham's lifted hand made her pause. "Hold on. I think I saw that troublesome nag wanderin' over toward those foothills. We should go take a look once the herd starts movin' again. We'll be on that side, so it won't take no time at all to ride over there, have ourselves a gander up the canyon where I might've seen that hoss, and then get back to the herd. Ol' Cal will never know we're gone."

"But how could the bay have gotten away from the other horses without anybody noticing?"

Markham shrugged. "All the fellas are a mite drowsy, just like you were. I ain't sure who was supposed to be watchin' the herd, but whoever it was, I wouldn't want to get 'em in trouble just because some hardheaded critter wandered off."

"Damn it," Denny muttered under her breath. "You're right about that." She narrowed her eyes at him. "You're sure you saw the bay heading for those foothills?"

"Now that I think about it, I'm plumb certain."

"This isn't just some trick so you can get me off by myself and steal a kiss?"

"Denny!" He placed a hand over his heart. "You wound me, girl."

"I'll do worse than that if you try anything funny. But I guess we can take a look up that canyon when we go by. If we don't find the bay pretty quickly, though, we'll have to tell Cal so he can stop the herd and find it. My pa wouldn't want to lose even a single head of stock."

"Neither do I," said Markham. "But I got a hunch we'll find what we're lookin' for."

CHAPTER 46

Brice Rogers felt the horse wearying underneath him and reined to a halt. He swung down and immediately started unsaddling the sorrel so he could switch the rig to the rangy gray. He had rented both mounts from Fulger's Livery Stable back in Stirrup, which, based on the two citizens Brice had met, seemed to be inhabited entirely by cantankerous gents about to slide over from middle-aged to old-timer status.

Brice finished tightening the cinches and stepped back from the gray. He took off his hat, switched it to the hand that also held the reins, and scrubbed his right hand over his face. Like his horses, he was weary, too, right down to his bones. He hadn't slept much on either of the trains, just dozed a little sitting up, and the previous night, after leaving Stirrup, he had ridden until well after midnight before finally stopping to grab a couple of hours of sleep.

He would have kept going even then, only the moon had lowered enough that he could no longer make out the trail left by the horse herd. Earlier, he'd been able to follow it with a fair degree of confidence.

By switching back and forth between mounts, he hoped to catch up to the herd today. Since he had two horses, he could push them harder than he would have dared with only a single mount.

That meant pushing himself hard, too, but he was willing to do that. Denny's safety . . . her very life . . . might depend on it.

A moment more to catch his breath and he was on his way again, following the unmistakable tracks left by the dozens of horses he was following.

He rode on through the morning, stopping from time to time to check the manure left by the herd. He could tell the droppings were fresher, which meant he was getting closer.

By midday he was able to make out a faint dust haze hanging in the air ahead of him. It was difficult to judge the distance, but he thought it originated no more than a mile away. It was stationary, too, which meant the animals that had kicked it up had stopped moving for the moment.

Knowing he was that close made him urge even more speed from the sorrel. The gray trailed behind on a lead rope, but it hadn't been all that long since he had changed mounts. As he rode on, Brice wondered if he should let the gray go and come back to retrieve the horse later. That way he could push the sorrel even harder.

He bit back a groan as he realized the dust cloud was moving again. He'd hoped to catch up while the herd was stopped for its noon rest. He was still moving faster than they were, so it was only a matter of time until he caught up, but it would take longer now that the herd was moving again.

Fifteen minutes later, he came in sight of a dark mass moving over the gentle hills in front of him. That was the horse herd, he thought. He was almost there.

The terrain had changed somewhat, with snow-capped mountains drawing in from the west. The lower slopes were heavily forested, while higher rose sheer, massive slabs of rock climbing to those white peaks. Under different circumstances, Brice would have appreciated the beauty of the scenery, but he barely saw it. His attention was focused on what was directly in front of him.

He reined in at the top of a rise when he saw that the herd had entered a broad basin stretching for several miles. It was the first chance he had gotten to take a good look, so he reached into his saddlebags and brought out a pair of field glasses. He lifted them to his eyes and peered through them.

His quarry seemed to jump a lot closer. He could see the individual horses through the glasses, as well as the riders coming along behind them and travel-ing out to the sides. He swung the glasses slowly from right to left, searching for Denny. If she had her blond hair tucked up under her hat, he might not have been able to spot her. She would look like one of the other slender, athletic young cowboys.

No, wait!

Far out on the left flank—farther out than they should have been—two riders had veered away from the herd and appeared to be headed toward the mouth of a rugged-looking canyon in the nearby foothills. Brice saw the flash of sunlight on hair that tumbled around one rider's shoulders. He thought the other rider had red hair . . .

Denny. And Steve Markham, he thought. *Leaving the herd together and headed for God knows where.*

Brice's breath hissed angrily between his teeth as he jammed the field glasses back into the saddlebags. He untied the gray's lead rope from the saddle and let it drop to the ground.

Then he jammed his heels into the sorrel's flanks and sent the tired but willing horse leaping forward into a gallop that carried him toward the foothills where Denny and Markham were disappearing from sight in that canyon.

"This is a mistake," Denny said. "We should have stayed with the herd."

"But what about that pesky bay?" asked Markham. "You said yourself, your pa wouldn't like losin' even one head of stock on a drive like this."

"I know, I know. But we should've told Cal. Actually, we should have taken a better look around the herd before we rode off over here. Maybe the bay's still with the others, and we just didn't notice it."

"We both looked." Markham sounded a little impatient. "The damn horse ain't there."

"Well, I don't see him in this canyon, either." Denny jerked a hand at their surroundings. "Do you?"

The canyon was about fifty yards wide, brushy in places, open in others, with walls too steep for a horse to climb. Here and there a boulder had rolled down from above in ages past. A bend with rocky ridges on both sides lay several hundred yards ahead of them.

"Let's just ride on up around that bend and take a look," Markham suggested. "If we don't see the bay by then, maybe I'll admit that I was wrong."

"And then we'll tell Cal and stop the drive until we find the bay."

"And then we tell Cal," Markham agreed.

Side by side, they rode up the canyon toward the bend.

Along the way, Denny watched the brush to make sure the bay wasn't hiding somewhere in the thick growth. She didn't see the horse, and although she admittedly wasn't much of a tracker, she didn't spot any hoofprints where they were riding, either. "I think we're on a wild goose chase. The bay was never here."

"Well, we've had a nice ride, if nothin' else," he replied. "I'll never complain about spendin' time with you, Denny. In fact, I'd be plumb pleased to spend a whole heap more time with you, for a long time to come—"

"Wait just a minute," she snapped as she reined in. "This whole thing really was just an excuse to get me off by myself, wasn't it? Now you're going to start flattering me and making calf eyes at me—"

"Good Lord, woman!" he burst out, finally unable to contain his frustration. He brought his mount to a halt as well. "Don't you ever take that burr out from under your saddle? Every time a fella starts to talk plain about how he feels, you've got to cut the legs right out from under him! You ever stop to think about how intimidatin' you are, Denny Jensen? Why, you're rich and beautiful, and you got a pa who's ten feet tall that no other man could ever live up to. A fella unlucky enough to fall in love with you might as well have a mountain as big as those up yonder to climb over!"

Breathing a little hard, Denny waited for the words to stop spilling out from Markham's mouth. When they finally did, she asked, "Are you trying to say you're in love with me?"

"Well, why the hell else would I have done all the things I did? I knew from the first second I laid eyes on you—"

The swift rataplan of hoofbeats from somewhere behind them cut into whatever he was about to say. Both of them turned in their saddles and saw a rider just entering the canyon, heading toward them at a fast clip. Whoever it was, he was too far away for Denny to recognize him immediately, but at the rate he was moving, that wouldn't last long.

"Cal must have seen us leaving and sent one of the hands after us," she said. "Now we're going to be in trouble."

Even more unexpected and alarming was the faint popping that suddenly came to their ears. Denny had heard that sound before and stiffened in the saddle as she realized what it was.

"Shooting!" she exclaimed. "Something's wrong at the herd!"

The rider following them must have heard the gunfire over the pounding of his horse's hooves, too, because he reined in sharply and half turned the mount, as if he couldn't decide whether to turn back or gallop on toward Denny and Markham.

Denny was going to save him the trouble of deciding. She lifted the reins and said, "We have to get back—"

"No, Denny." Markham's voice was flat and hard, and the menacing tone in it made a chill shoot down her spine. "We're not goin' anywhere."

She turned her head and saw the gun in his hand, its barrel aimed directly at her.

CHAPTER 47

Steve Markham tried to swallow the sick feeling that welled up his throat. Pointing a gun at Denny Jensen was the last thing on earth he wanted to do, but she wasn't giving him any choice. Didn't she know that he was just trying to save her life?

Well, probably not. There was no way for her to know that, he realized. She didn't know that Bert Rome and the other men with him were attacking the Sugarloaf cowboys. Rome hadn't told Markham exactly when the ambush would take place, only that it would occur near the middle of the day, so he had gotten Denny away from the herd as soon as he could after they'd stopped at noon.

And just in time, too, because Rome would have carried out the attack even if Denny was still there. Rome had made it clear that he didn't want anything to happen to her—if they took her prisoner, they could demand a big ransom for her, too—but when bullets started to fly, anything could happen.

She stared at him, speechless for a few seconds, then demanded, "Steve, what the hell are you doing?"

"Keepin' you from gettin' hurt, Denny," he told

her. "You're gonna come with me now. We'll ride on up this canyon, around that bend where we'll be safe, and then we'll wait until all this trouble is over. You'll see that I'm just thinkin' about you—"

"No!" she cried. "You're thinking about *you*! If you think that kidnapping me will make me love you, you're crazy!"

No, not crazy. Instead of turning her over to Bert Rome, Markham had realized that the two of them could just keep riding, far away from there. It would mean giving up whatever his share of the profits from the scheme would have been, but the certainty was growing inside him that Denny Jensen was worth it. All he had to do was make her understand how he really felt . . . "You've just got to give me a chance—"

A shot fired somewhere nearby made Markham interrupt his plea and jerk his head around. The rider who had followed them into the canyon was galloping toward them again, and as Markham turned his horse that way, he saw the man fire a second shot into the air.

Too late, Markham realized the man was trying to distract him, and it had worked. Denny jabbed her boot heels into her mount's flanks and sent the horse lunging forward wildly. Her horse's shoulder rammed into Markham's horse and the collision staggered both animals. They almost lost their footing and went down. As Markham hauled on the reins with his left hand and tried to regain control, Denny left her saddle in a flying leap and tackled him.

He outweighed her by a lot, and she never would have been able to knock him out of the saddle if he'd been expecting it. But he was taken by surprise and felt himself slipping. He dropped the reins and grabbed for the horn, but that just allowed his already spooked horse to start capering around even worse. Markham toppled off with barely enough time to kick his feet out of the stirrups.

He hit the ground hard with Denny on top of him. That was enough to jolt the air out of his lungs. Gasping, he shoved her away. The fall seemed to have stunned her, so she didn't put up a fight. He rolled onto his belly and got his knees underneath him.

As he pushed up, he saw the rider pounding closer and recognized that damned deputy marshal, Brice Rogers. A part of Markham's brain was stunned by that recognition. What was Rogers doing all the way up there in Montana?

Markham's instincts still worked, he still had the Colt in his hand, and he lifted it.

Denny hit him again before he could pull the trigger. Either she had recovered quickly or hadn't been as stunned as he'd thought. She grabbed his wrist and forced the gun back down as she threw her shoulder into him and tried to knock him to the ground again. He saw that the holster on her hip was empty. The Lightning must have fallen out when they took that spill from the horse.

He started to backhand her and knock her away from him, but he realized that was the wrong move and grabbed her instead, looping his left arm around her neck. She writhed in his grasp, but he was too strong for her. She couldn't get loose. Twisting so that her back was to him, he dragged her squirming body against him and shoved his gun hand under her right arm so the weapon pointed toward Rogers, who was reining up hurriedly about twenty feet away.

"Let her go!" the lawman called as he leaped out of the saddle. He couldn't risk a shot as long as Markham had Denny in front of him like that.

"Go to hell, law dog!" Markham yelled back at him. He tightened his arm around Denny's neck.

She stopped struggling, evidently realizing that it wouldn't take much effort for him to choke her into unconsciousness or even snap her neck.

Markham was about to open fire on Rogers—there was no reason to stand around and flap his jaws about this—when the deputy marshal ducked behind one of the boulders littering the canyon floor. Markham still had a shot at him, but not a very good one.

He had Denny, though, and she was the winning card in any hand.

"Throw your gun out, Rogers! I got no interest in killin' you, as long as you don't try to stop me and Denny from leavin' here."

"I'll never go . . . anywhere with you!" Denny forced out past the forearm clamped like a bar of iron across her throat.

"You'll figure out I love you, if you'll just gimme a chance," he told her.

"Let her go," Rogers said again. "If you hurt her, I swear I'll kill you, Markham!"

"I'd never hurt Denny!"

"You're . . . hurting me now," she grated.

"I'm sorry about that, I truly am, but I don't have any choice." Markham gestured curtly with the gun. "What's it gonna be, Rogers? All you have to do is throw that iron down and not try to stop Denny and me from ridin' away from here. If you do that, I promise I won't shoot you."

Rogers laughed coldly. "You think I'd ever believe the son of a vicious killer like the Santa Rosa Kid?"

Denny's mind whirled dizzily. First she'd been stunned by the fact that Steve Markham would pull a gun on her, then she had been every bit as surprised as Markham by Brice Rogers showing up. The herd was under attack by unknown ambushers, too, and Denny wanted to get back and help Cal and the others fight off the assailants.

But even with all that spinning around in her thoughts, she was aware of the way Markham stiffened suddenly at the mention of the Santa Rosa Kid, a name she had never heard before.

"Shut up!" Markham said. "You got no right to talk about him. It was lawmen like you who hounded him to death!"

"And you're following in his footsteps, is that it?" asked Brice from behind the boulder. "A thief and a murderer and who knows what else? You think Denny's going to fall in love with you after you've kidnapped her and helped butcher her friends?"

"I'm gettin' sick and tired of you, Rogers. I reckon maybe I *will* kill you after all. You can't stop me, not without shootin' this gal—"

Denny stomped down hard on the top of his foot. She wasn't going to do any real damage that way, but the blow hurt enough to make Markham yelp in pain and bend forward a little. At the same time, Denny jerked her head back and it hit him squarely on the nose with enough force to make blood spurt from his nostrils. Markham's grip on her slipped just enough for her to get both hands under the arm around her neck, force it down a little more, and twist away from him.

He bellowed a curse and triggered the Colt. Shots boomed out from it, but he wasn't aiming at her. The slugs whined off the rock where Brice had taken cover. As Markham blazed away at the deputy marshal, Denny's frantic gaze fell on the Colt Lightning that had fallen from her holster. She dived toward it, scooped it up, rolled over, and came up on one knee.

Flame geysered from the muzzle of the .38 caliber double-action as she pulled the trigger three times as fast as she could. The slugs pounded into Markham's chest and rocked him back a couple of steps. He didn't drop his gun, but his arm sagged and that gave Brice the chance to return his fire. Two shots crashed from Brice's .45. Those bullets ripped into Markham's body and slewed him halfway around.

He fell to his knees and dropped the gun as he put his hands out to catch himself. For a long moment he stayed there like that on all fours, and Denny felt sick as she saw blood running from the holes in his body and pooling on the ground underneath him. With a groan, he fell over onto his left side and seemed like he was trying to curl up around the agony that filled him.

She got to her feet as Brice rose from behind the boulder. With their guns still pointed toward Markham, they advanced slowly toward him. Denny's eyes flicked toward Brice as she asked, "Are you all right?"

"Yeah." His voice showed the strain he was under. "How about you?"

"My throat's going to be a little bruised where he choked me, but I'm fine. What the hell's going on here, Brice?"

"He's an outlaw," Brice said. "And that's probably his gang trying to steal the horse herd right now."

In fact, the gunfire still continued out in the basin where Cal and the rest of the crew had been driving the horses. Denny wanted to go to them and help them, but something compelled her to holster her gun, kneel beside Markham, and ease him over onto his back.

"Careful, Denny," said Brice as he continued pointing his gun at Markham.

"He's shot to pieces, Brice. I don't think he's a danger to anybody anymore." She paused. "Not even himself."

Markham's breath rasped in his throat. His eyes were closed. At the touch of Denny's hands and the sound of her voice so close to him, he forced them open and blinked up at her. Struggling to talk, he said, "I . . . I'm not . . ."

"Not what?" she asked. She tried not to look at the bloody ruin that was his chest, a lot of the damage inflicted by her own Colt Lightning.

"Not . . . an outlaw. Not . . . really. My pa was . . . an owlhoot . . . the Santa Rosa Kid . . . just like . . . the lawdog said. But I never . . . never did anything . . . all that bad . . . rustled a few cattle . . . here and there . . . stuck up a store . . . or two . . . but then Bert Rome . . . and Sam Brant . . . came to me . . . They used to ride . . . with my pa . . . said they had a plan . . . make us all rich . . . said if *your* pa was dead . . . your ma would pay a fortune . . . to get your brother back . . . alive . . . but they needed an inside man . . . workin' on the Sugarloaf . . ."

Denny's eyes widened in horror at the enormity of the plan spilling from Markham's blood-frothed lips. In the back of her mind was the knowledge that she had actually started to care for this man and she ought to be sad that he was dying right in front of her eyes, but what he was saying forced out any other thoughts.

"Denny . . . I'm . . . sorry," Markham managed to get out. "I never wanted . . . to hurt you . . . Never figured on . . . fallin' in—" The words choked off as his eyes went glassy. A final shudder went through his body as his head tipped slowly to the side.

Denny knelt there in silence for a long moment before Brice said quietly, "He's gone, Denny."

"I know." She took a deep breath and stood up. Opening the Lightning's loading gate, she shook out the empty brass from the rounds she had fired and started replacing them with fresh cartridges from the loops on her shell belt. "But his no-good friends are still out there trying to kill *my* friends, and I intend to go put a stop to that right now."

CHAPTER 48

Brice could tell that Denny was making a valiant effort to hold herself together and keep her emotions under control as they rode hard toward the canyon mouth. Steve Markham's body lay behind them where it had fallen. There was nothing they could do about it now. Denny had seen the outlaw's true colors, but she had considered him a friend and maybe more, and his death had some effect on her.

She was as coolheaded in times of danger as anyone Brice had ever met, though, man or woman, so he knew, whatever those feelings were, she would put them aside . . . until the fight ahead of them was over, one way or another.

Side by side, they burst out of the canyon and galloped toward the herd, which was close to a mile farther north. As they rode, Denny pulled her Winchester from its saddle sheath, and Brice did likewise.

They could hear the shooting over the pounding hoofbeats. It sounded like a small war was going on. That came as no surprise to Brice. Calvin Woods and the other cowboys from the Sugarloaf weren't the sort of men who rolled over and died. They would battle to the last breath and fight with every bit of heart, soul, and guts they possessed, no matter how much they were surprised or how badly outnumbered.

Brice saw riderless, unsaddled horses running around ahead of them. The herd must have scattered when the shooting started, he thought. Originally, while he was traveling to Montana as quickly as he could, he had believed the outlaws were after the horses, although that really wouldn't have been much of a payoff for a plan elaborate enough to require an inside man.

Judging from what Markham had blurted out while he was dying, he'd been involved in a much more ambitious scheme than that, one that involved kidnapping Louis Jensen. Possibly Denny, too, although Brice was fuzzy on the details.

Maybe they would find out if they were able to capture one or more of the men attacking the Sugarloaf crew.

Before they got any closer and blundered right into some of the enemy, Brice reined in and signaled for Denny to stop.

She slowed her mount and then brought it to a halt, but she didn't look happy about it. "We've got to go help Cal!" she protested.

"Getting ourselves killed won't do him any good. Listen. You saw the horses from the herd running wild. That means Cal and the other hands turned them loose. They must have gone to ground somewhere to put up a fight against Markham's gang."

"It wasn't *his* gang," said Denny. "You heard him. Two of his father's old partners dragged him into it.

What did you say his father was called? The Santa Rosa Kid?"

The two outlaws—Rome and Brant, Brice recalled—probably hadn't had to do too much convincing to get Markham involved, but that didn't matter. None of it did. "I can explain all that later. Do you happen to know this country?"

Denny shook her head. "Not one bit. I've never been here until today."

"Neither have I. None of my assignments ever brought me this far." He turned his horse a little and gestured with the rifle he held. "We'd better circle around and get the lay of the land."

"Brice, there's no time—"

"We can't just rush in blind." Brice knew it would rile her, but he went on. "I'm the one with the badge, Denny, so I'm in charge here."

Anger flared in her eyes, as he expected it would. "Maybe one of these days, *I'll* have a badge, too," she shot back at him.

"Maybe so," he said, although he didn't see how that could ever happen when her goal was to run the Sugarloaf. "But for now, come on. We're going this way."

He heeled his horse into motion and headed west, back toward the foothills that bulged into the basin. He didn't look back to see if she was following him, but after a moment he heard the swift clatter of her horse's hooves and then she drew alongside him.

"You're not always going to be able to boss me around this way, you know," she called over to him.

"I don't recollect *ever* bossing you around before."

"And you're not now! I just happened to decide you were right for a change, that's all."

Brice managed not to grin at her deeply ingrained stubbornness. He nodded and said, "Let's find out just what sort of trouble Cal and the rest of the hands are in."

It didn't take them long to discover how the battle had shaped up. They stopped just below the crest of a long ridge and dismounted, then took their hats off and on foot eased up high enough to peer over it. About two hundred yards away lay an old buffalo wallow, a wide depression about five feet deep with fairly steep walls. Cal and the other Sugarloaf cowboys had taken cover in it and were shooting up at the higher ground surrounding it. Puffs of powder smoke came from those lopsided knolls as the ambushers returned the fire.

It was a standoff, but it wouldn't continue indefinitely. The advantage definitely belonged to the attackers. The Sugarloaf hands had dismounted and sent their horses galloping out of danger, so they had no way to escape. They had limited supplies of ammunition and probably didn't have any water down there, so as the afternoon heat continued to build, they would start to bake and thirst would torment them.

Before the day was over, the defenders wouldn't be able to put up a fight anymore, and the outlaws would roll over the buffalo wallow and wipe them out. Brice saw that immediately, and judging by the grim expression on Denny's face, so did she.

"Look at that powder smoke," she said quietly. "There must be fifteen or twenty of them."

"More than likely," agreed Brice. "Too many for a couple of us to make much difference."

Denny bristled. "We can't just go off and abandon Cal and the boys!"

"I never said we were going to. But if we just gallop up and start shooting, we won't last thirty seconds."

She wasn't able to argue with that. She nodded and asked, "What did you have in mind, then?"

"We'll have to whittle down the odds a few at a time." He looked intently at her. "That's going to mean some close work. Are you up to that, Denny?"

"What the hell do you think?"

Brice motioned her back down the slope. When they were out of sight of any of the attackers, he put his hat back on and said, "I think we'll work around there a little farther to the north and then start closing in from behind them."

Denny had done her share of gunfighting since returning to the West to live. More than her share, considering that she was a young woman and young women didn't do such things to start with. But she had smelled powder smoke and felt it sting her eyes. She had experienced the deafening roar of gunfire and the jolt of a revolver bucking in her hand as she squeezed the trigger. She had heard bullets singing their deadly song close beside her ears.

Most important, she had killed. She had seen men crumple and die before her gun, had known the terrible gravity of what it was to end a human life. Remorse hadn't haunted her dreams—all the men she'd killed had had it coming to them, to be honest—but it wasn't something she took lightly.

With her friends' lives in danger, she was more than willing to shoulder that responsibility again.

She and Brice left their horses where they were and moved ahead on foot, staying low and using every bit of cover they could find. Few trees grew in the basin, although the slopes not far away were heavily timbered. There were clumps of brush and clusters of boulders, though, and the two of them took advantage of that.

The shooting from the outlaws continued. Shots still blasted from the defenders in the buffalo wallow, too, but it seemed to Denny that the return fire was more sporadic than before.

"They must be running low on ammunition," she said in a half-whisper to Brice. "Sounds like they're trying to make it last as long as possible."

"Yeah. Let's just hope it lasts 'em a little while longer, until we're in a position to do some damage and maybe change the odds."

A few minutes later they bellied down and crawled through brush until they reached a spot where they could peer out through gaps in the growth. Ten yards away, two outlaws knelt behind a slab of rock and fired rifles down at Cal and the other men from the Sugarloaf.

Denny glanced over at Brice and saw him grimace. "You let me handle this, Denny," he told her in a whisper. "You don't need to do what's got to be done here."

"Shoot them in the back, you mean? You're a lawman, Brice. That's got to rub you the wrong way."

"But you're a—"

"A woman?" She shook her head. "Right now, I'm

just a Sugarloaf hand like Cal and those other boys down there. That means I ride for the brand. The Jensen brand. And I'll be damned if you or anybody else stops me from helping my trail partners."

Brice sighed but nodded. "All right." He settled his rifle against his shoulder and peered over its barrel. Both of them had already levered rounds into the Winchesters' firing chambers when they began their deadly stalk. "We'll try to time it so we fire when they do. The rest of the bunch will be less likely to notice that way."

"I understand," Denny breathed. She had the butt of her rifle snugged up against her shoulder. She lay her cheek against the smooth wood of the stock and lined her sights on one of the outlaws. "I've got the one on the right."

"I'll take the one on the left, then. They've been raising up and shooting together. As soon as they do it again . . ."

Denny was ready. As the two owlhoots lifted themselves above the boulder and raised their rifles, she slipped her finger inside the Winchester's trigger guard. The finger curled around the trigger . . .

A second later, as the outlaws' rifles roared, Denny squeezed.

CHAPTER 49

By the time another quarter of an hour had passed, the gunfire from the defenders in the buffalo wallow had dwindled almost to nothing, just an occasional shot to keep the ambushers honest. Denny had a feeling Cal had ordered the others to stop shooting in order to save some of the bullets for the inevitable last-ditch fight.

But in that quarter of an hour, Denny and Brice had stalked and killed four more outlaws, planting Winchester rounds squarely in their backs. What they were doing was cold-blooded murder, Denny knew . . . but she also knew that under the circumstances, her father would have done the same thing. So would her uncles, Luke and Matt, and her cousins, Ace and Chance. Jensens were, by nature, honorable men, but that didn't stop them from being practical, especially when some devil was trying to hurt them or their friends.

"You reckon they're starting to notice that no more shots are coming from this side?" she quietly asked Brice. With so many guns going off, by timing their own shots to blend in the way they had, they'd hoped their efforts would go undetected for a while.

"I don't know," Brice replied. "If they have, they're liable to try to sneak up on *us*."

The same thought had occurred to Denny. For that reason, she had been casting frequent glances over her shoulder. So far she hadn't detected any threats, but she wasn't going to let down her guard.

They moved on in search of more outlaws to deal with. The gun blasts made it easy to track them by sound. They crawled up into a scattering of smaller boulders and found themselves with clear lines of fire at three rough-looking men.

Propped on her elbows, Denny took a breath to settle her strained nerves and then started to draw a bead on one of the outlaws. Since there were three of them instead of two this time, even if she and Brice shot perfectly, one of the outlaws ought to have time to whirl around and get a shot off at them. That was a risk they had to take.

Before either of them could squeeze the trigger, a rock clattered somewhere behind them. It was only a small sound, but as taut as Denny's nerves were, it sounded like an avalanche. Brice heard it, too, and lunged up off the ground. He flung himself to the side, and Denny realized just before he landed on her that he was throwing himself into the line of fire, shielding her body with his own.

Shots roared. Brice grunted, and at the same time, a slug whined wickedly off one of the rocks only inches from the two of them. Denny squirmed halfway out from under him and twisted toward the gunfire. A bullet sizzled through the air next to her cheek. Part of her brain clamored with alarm, but she remained cool enough to realize the Winchester was too awkward for close work. She dropped the rifle and palmed out the Lightning instead as a pair of outlaws rushed toward them, firing revolvers.

The Lightning barked, drilling a .38 slug into the forehead of one man. He continued running, but aimlessly now since it was only momentum that kept him moving. He was already dead on his feet. His legs tangled up after a couple of steps and he tumbled to the ground.

Brice's Colt blasted close enough to Denny's ear that she flinched. The sound was like a giant fist hammering her. She saw the bullet punch into the second man's guts and double him over. He went down, too.

They weren't out of trouble yet. More shots slammed through the air and ricocheted from the rocks around them. Denny rolled over as bullets struck the ground near her head and sprayed dirt in her eyes. She gasped and blinked, and through watery vision she saw the three outlaws she and Brice had been aiming at a few moments earlier. Hearing the shots behind them, the men had whirled around and opened fire.

Denny came to a stop behind a rock that was less than a foot tall, so it didn't provide much cover. Even so, she tried not to hurry her shot as she thrust the Lightning over the rock and fired. She was aiming for an outlaw's chest, but the bullet went a few inches high and tore into his throat—even more effective. The man dropped his gun and clapped both hands to his throat, but he couldn't stop the crimson fountain spurting from it. Denny knew her bullet had ripped through an artery. The man stumbled a couple of steps and then pitched forward onto his face.

Two men were still doing their damnedest to kill Denny and Brice.

The lawman's .45 boomed and one of the outlaws reeled to the side clutching at a shattered shoulder. That brought him into the line of fire just as the third owlhoot triggered his rifle. The close-range shot caught the wounded man in the back of the head and sent half his skull flying into the air, accompanied by a gruesome spray of blood and brain matter.

Just one man left, and he staggered back as Denny and Brice fired at the same time and their bullets hammered into his chest. He flopped onto his butt and then went over onto his back with his arms spread out. He gave a couple of spasmodic kicks and was motionless after that.

Without holstering the Lightning, Denny scrambled over to Brice, who lay among the rocks on his side, propped on his left elbow. "Are you all right? I know you got hit!"

He pushed himself into a sitting position and nodded down at his left thigh. A bloody circle about the size of a fist stained his jeans. "Just barely nicked me. It kind of stings, that's all."

The taut chin strap of Denny's Stetson had kept the hat on her head the whole time. She yanked it off and swatted him with it, making him flinch in surprise. "You damned fool!" she raged at him. "What the hell were you thinking, jumping on top of me like that? You could have gotten yourself killed trying to protect me!"

"It would have been worth it," he said simply.

Denny just stared at him for a moment, seeing the sincerity on his face. There was no way to argue with a sentiment like that. In fact, she felt a little ashamed of herself . . . and even a bit awed that someone would feel that way about her.

The attack on the Sugarloaf crew continued, leaving no time for such things. Even worse from their perspective, angry shouts sounded as more men approached their position.

"Those bushwhackers finally realized they're under attack, too," said Brice. "And some of them are charging around here to see what all the commotion's about."

"We'll be outnumbered," said Denny, "even with the ones we've already killed." An idea occurred to her. "It's time to call in our reinforcements."

"What reinfor—" Brice began, but before he could go on, Denny leaped to her feet and charged forward, so the men who had taken cover in the buffalo wallow could see her.

With her hat still in her hand, she whooped and waved it over her head in sweeping motions as if she were signaling someone behind her. "Come on, Sugarloaf!" she shouted. "Come on, Smoke! Come on, Pearlie! We'll wipe 'em out!"

Her words and actions made it appear that she was leading a formidable force into battle. Bullets began to hum around her as outlaws raced toward her and opened fire. Behind them, the rest of the ambushers swung away from the buffalo wallow to meet the new threat.

That gave Cal and the men who were trapped down there the opening they needed to launch a counterattack of their own. They swarmed over the top of the earthen barrier around the wallow and charged up the slope, firing as they went. Their bullets slashed into the outlaws from the flank.

Brice, limping heavily on his bullet-creased leg, caught up to Denny, grabbed her around the waist, and bore her to the ground. "Get down, blast it!" he cried as slugs whipped through the air above them. "You're gonna get yourself killed!"

"Reload!" Denny told him. "We've got to make those owlhoots think there's an army out here!"

They lay among the rocks and thumbed fresh rounds into their revolvers, then fired as swiftly and accurately as they could so that lead scythed into the outlaws from two directions at once. It wasn't exactly a crossfire, but it would do until the real thing came along.

The end result was that most of the would-be murderers and kidnappers fell, drilled by Sugarloaf lead in a frenzy of back-and-forth firing that lasted maybe a minute but seemed to stretch out longer. The three who were left unscathed threw down their guns and shoved their hands in the air, shouting, "Hold your fire! Don't shoot! We give up!"

The Sugarloaf hands surrounded them, grabbed them, and wrestled them to their knees. The outlaws were lucky they didn't just shoot and be done with it.

Denny and Brice stood up.

Denny waved and called, "Cal!"

The foreman went over to them, also limping a little and with a streak of blood on his cheek from a bullet scrape. "Denny!" he exclaimed. "You're all right?"

She nodded. "I'm fine. Brice got nicked, but it's not too bad."

"Where's Steve Markham? The last we saw, he was with you, not long before that bunch jumped us."

Denny's face turned grim. "Steve's dead," she told Cal. "He was . . . one of them. He tried to get me away before the ambush, but he didn't succeed."

Cal grunted then looked at Brice. "I reckon you showing up out of the blue had something to do with that, Marshal. I was wondering why you're here in Montana."

"It's a long story, as they say," replied Brice. "How bad is it with your bunch, Mr. Woods?"

"Two men dead, four more wounded but not too bad, I hope. Our saddle mounts are gone, and the horse herd's scattered hell-west and crosswise!"

"Your saddle horses probably didn't go far," Denny said. "Brice and I left our horses not far from here. I'll go get them, and one of the boys can use Brice's horse to help me round up your mounts. Then you can go after the herd and round *them* up."

"I can ride my own horse," Brice protested.

"Your leg's wounded," Denny told him. "And I don't give a damn if you've got a badge, you're not giving me orders anymore."

Brice looked like he wanted to argue, but then he shrugged. "All right. The most important thing is get this handled as quickly as possible."

"That's right," Denny said. "Because hell's going to break loose down on the Sugarloaf, and somebody's got to warn Smoke about it!"

CHAPTER 50

By the time Denny and the Sugarloaf hand who'd borrowed Brice's mount got back to the buffalo wallow, driving the crew's saddle horses in front of them, someone had tied a makeshift bandage around Brice's wounded thigh and the other injuries had been tended to, as well.

Cal greeted Denny by saying, "The marshal's been telling me what Markham said. I talked to those men we took prisoner, too, and they confirmed what the rest of the bunch is planning to do back home."

"I'm a little surprised they admitted it," said Denny.

A grim smile touched Cal's lips. "A fella gets talkative when you put a gun to his head and he can tell you wouldn't mind pulling the trigger." He paused for a second, then went on. "You were right, Denny, somebody needs to warn Smoke. I don't see any way of doing that, though, short of heading back to Stirrup. That's where the nearest telegraph office is."

She nodded. "I know. I'm giving myself that job. I know my pa would want those horses delivered to the

Circle C despite what's happened, so you and the rest of the men take care of that."

"Figured that's what you'd say," Cal replied with a nod of his own. "We'll take those prisoners with us, too. They can be turned over to the law once the job's done and we're back at Stirrup. And . . . before we go, we'll find Markham's body and give him a decent burial."

"Thank you, Cal," Denny said, her voice a little hushed with emotion.

Brice had been standing by quietly, favoring his wounded leg. "I'm coming with you, Denny."

"You're hurt."

"Nothing that'll keep me from sitting a saddle. Cal, while you were questioning those owlhoots, did they say anything about *when* the raid on the Sugarloaf is supposed to take place?"

"They all claimed they didn't know for sure," Cal said with a note of disgust in his voice. "They were scared enough that I believe them, too. They're just common hardcases, not the sort who the leaders of the gang would let in on the planning for a job." The foreman shook his head. "It may be too late already."

"I'm not going to allow myself to believe that," Denny declared. "There's always something that can be done. And I'm going to do it."

"I won't slow you down," said Brice, "but I'm coming with you, whether you like it or not."

"You'd better be ready to ride, then," Denny snapped. "As soon as I switch my saddle to a fresh horse, I'm heading for Stirrup."

"I'll be ready, all right. Just watch what happens if anybody tries to stop me."

Unfortunately, even switching back and forth between horses so the animals stayed fairly fresh, it would take the rest of the day and most of the next to reach Stirrup and send a telegram to Big Rock. Denny intended to ride all night in order to cut that time down as much as possible, but late in the afternoon, when she glanced over at Brice, she saw how pale and drawn his face was.

"Better hold up for a minute," she said as she drew back on the reins.

"No, it hasn't been long enough since we rested the horses last time."

"I'm not talking about resting the horses. You look like you're about played out. You must have lost more blood than you let on."

They had slowed the horses but not stopped. Brice kept his gaze fixed stonily ahead of them and said, "I'm fine. We're not stopping on my account. Bad enough we've slowed down."

"Blast it, Brice, you don't have to be so stubborn—"

"I'm being practical, not stubborn. If something happens to a member of your family, or even some of the crew at the Sugarloaf because we don't make it to Stirrup in time, you'd never forgive me, Denny."

"That's crazy! None of this is your fault, Brice." She hesitated. "You tried to warn me about Steve Markham . . ."

"Well . . . not really. I didn't have any idea he was

an outlaw, or the son of an outlaw." Brice shook his head. "No, I was just crazy jealous, that's all."

"Jealous because . . . ?"

"Are you fishing for it, Denny? Trying to make me say it?" He finally looked over at her. "I like you. One hell of a lot, in fact. Might as well come out with it. I love you."

Denny swallowed hard. She'd had a pretty good idea of how Brice felt about her, of course. She would have had to be blind to miss it, whenever they had been together over the past months. The way he had reacted to the attention Steve Markham paid her was another sure-fire indicator.

But hearing it put into words was different. Men had declared their love for Denny before, in England and on the Continent, as well. Some of them she had wanted to believe. Deep down, though, a part of her had always remained skeptical, and she had been right to feel that way. She had never truly accepted that those expressions of love were sincere.

Until now. She knew in her heart that Brice Rogers meant every word of it.

What she *didn't* know was how she felt in return, or what she should say back to him.

She didn't have to figure it out yet, though. He swayed in the saddle and grabbed the horn with his free hand to keep from toppling off. Denny yanked her horse to a stop with one hand and used the other to grasp Brice's arm and steady him. His horse stopped, too.

"Blast it! I knew you were pushing yourself too hard, Brice. You nearly passed out just then, didn't you?"

"I'm all right," he insisted, but the thinness of his voice suggested otherwise.

"The hell you are. We're stopping, right here and now." Denny looked around and saw a clump of brush not far away that would provide some firewood, so she wouldn't have to hunt for buffalo chips. "This isn't a bad place."

"Denny . . ."

"Just hush. Unless you want to start talking about your badge again."

Brice just sighed and shook his head, as if he knew that arguing wasn't going to do any good. Denny threw a leg over the saddle and slid to the ground, managing to hang on to his arm at the same time. She helped him down from the horse.

"I feel like a damn fool," he muttered. "Or a helpless little baby."

"You're neither of those things," she told him. "Now sit down. I'll get a fire started and put some coffee on to boil. Then I'll unsaddle the horses. Honestly, all of us could use a chance to rest a little more. It's been a long day."

As Brice sat down on the ground, Denny noticed a spot of red on the bandage around his thigh. She nodded toward it and added, "We'll tend to that, too."

She hobbled the four horses they had taken from the trail drive's remuda, leaving with Cal the mounts Brice had brought from Stirrup. Once she had the coffee going, she knelt beside Brice to untie the bandage.

She unwound it from his leg, then used the clasp knife she carried in her pocket to cut away more of his trouser leg. "Did anybody clean this with anything?" she asked as she studied the gash in his thigh.

"Whiskey."

"Well, that's good," she said with a shrug. "It bled some more, but it looks like it's stopped now. We'll just put a fresh bandage on it, and you can have a doctor look at it when we get to Stirrup tomorrow."

She pulled her shirt out of her jeans, revealing a little of the smooth flesh of her belly. She saw Brice looking at it while she used the knife to cut a strip off the bottom of the shirt. The fact that he was so interested in the revealed skin made a warm flush creep over her face. She didn't acknowledge either reaction, his or hers.

"Lift your leg a little," she told him. She worked the cloth around the injury and bound it in place. Her fingers couldn't help but touch his leg, and even though she was trying to be coldly clinical about it, the unavoidable intimacy deepened the flush in her features.

If Brice noticed, he didn't say anything about it. Denny was grateful for that.

"There," she said when she was finished. "The coffee will be ready in a few minutes. I'll fry up some bacon for us, too. After a while, we can push on toward Stirrup, if you feel up to it."

"I'll feel up to it," Brice promised with determination in his voice. "Thank you, Denny. And about what I said earlier—"

"Right now, I'm not thinking about anything except doing what we can to stop those varmints from attacking the Sugarloaf."

Brice didn't press the issue. "If Louis is their target,

he and Melanie must be scheduled to be back from their trip."

"Yeah, I've lost track exactly of when they were expected," Denny admitted, "but it ought to be any day now. They may have even gotten back to the Sugarloaf today."

"If that's the case, they're in danger, too, along with everyone else on the ranch."

"Yeah, but don't forget . . . Smoke's there, and they may not be expecting him."

"And that will make the difference?"

"All the difference in the world," Denny said.

Denny was good at steering by the stars, so after they had eaten and Brice had rested, even dozing off for a while, they started south again. Long after midnight, Denny called another halt and they rested again. She was exhausted enough that she stretched out and used her saddle for a pillow for a couple of hours.

By the time the sun rose, they were on the trail again, and able to move even faster. They could see the tracks left by the horse herd and didn't have to determine their route solely by celestial navigation.

Neither of them brought up the things that had been said the day before, which was fine with Denny. Dealing with outlaws was one thing, but sorting through complicated emotions was something else entirely.

It was early afternoon when they reached Stirrup. Denny knew they had made good time, especially considering Brice's injury. When she brought her horse to a stop in front of a small, neat house with a sign on the fence that read DR. BENJAMIN HARMON, M.D., he said, "You should go on to the telegraph office, Denny. We can deal with this later."

"The doctor's office is on the way. Come on, don't waste time arguing with me."

"Yeah, it never does any good."

"What?"

"I said, give me a hand here. My leg's stiffened up quite a bit."

It took only a few minutes for her to get him into the house, where the white-haired doctor helped them into an examination room and Brice climbed onto the table.

"Go on," he told Denny as he made shooing motions. "Get that telegram sent to Smoke."

"All right." She turned to the physician. "Take good care of him, Doc."

"I try to take good care of *all* my patients," Harmon said.

"Yeah, I know, but this one . . ." Denny took a deep breath. "Ah, hell." She leaned over and kissed Brice on the mouth then hurried out of there while both men were giving her surprised looks.

Ten minutes later, she had printed out a message and stood at the window of the telegraph office while Robeson, the operator, sent it to Big Rock. She had done all she could do, Denny told herself as she left the depot and headed back to the doctor's office to see how Brice was doing.

It was all up to luck . . . and Smoke Jensen.

CHAPTER 51

Big Rock

The young man named Lester was dozing in the telegraph office inside Big Rock's railroad station. It was the middle of the day, and the chief telegrapher had gone to lunch, leaving Lester in charge. He was normally a diligent young man and wouldn't have been caught dead sleeping on the job, but he'd been up most of the night before with his pa, helping one of the family's cows give birth to a balky calf, so he was unusually tired.

The sudden chattering of the key made him jump. Instantly, he was wide awake, his instincts making him snatch up a pencil and pull a pad of paper to him. He had spent hundreds of hours practicing until the fast-paced dots and dashes were just as plain as day to him, as if someone were standing there speaking to him. His fingers worked smoothly, printing the letters, but his brain really didn't pay that much attention to the words they were spelling until the dots and dashes for the word OUT came over the wire and the message ended.

Then he stared at what he had written on the paper, his eyes widening until it seemed like they were about to pop out of his head.

Lester shot up out of his chair. Any drowsiness he'd felt a few moments earlier was completely gone. He looked around wildly as he tried to figure out what to do next. He'd been left in charge of the office, so he wasn't supposed to leave, but it was important that this message be delivered as soon as possible. Mighty important.

He looked through the wicket into the station lobby and saw one of the porters passing by. "Clarence!" he called. "Clarence, come over here!"

"Yeah? What you want, Lester?"

"You're gonna watch the telegraph office," said Lester as he tore the sheet with the message printed on it off the pad.

The porter stared, too. "I can't do that. I can't work one o' them blasted telegraph doodads. And all that clickin' is just noise to me!"

Lester yanked the door into the lobby open. "You don't have to send or receive any telegrams. If anybody wants to send a wire, tell them they'll have to wait a few minutes until I get back. And if one comes in, the operator on the other end will send it again when I don't acknowledge."

Clarence was still protesting when Lester ran out of the station. As soon as the young man was on the street, he looked back and forth, hoping to see Sheriff Monte Carson. The sheriff was nowhere in sight, though. Lester was going to have to find him. He broke into a run toward Carson's office, ignoring the startled looks that people on the street gave him.

As Lester ran, it occurred to him that he could have stayed in the office and asked Clarence or somebody else to go look for the sheriff. He had been so excited once he realized what the message said, he had never even thought about doing that.

Dodging around pedestrians, he was almost at the sheriff's office when the door swung open and Monte Carson stepped out onto the boardwalk. "Whoa there, Lester," Carson said as he held up a hand. "You're gonna run over somebody. What's the big rush?"

Lester skidded to a halt and thrust out the paper in his hand. Panting, he said, "This . . . this wire just came in, Sheriff! It's from Miss Jensen!"

Carson scanned the words, then exclaimed, "Good Lord! I've got to tell Smoke!" He jammed the paper into his pocket, practically leaped to the hitch rack in front of the office, and yanked loose his horse's reins.

That was a stroke of luck. He didn't normally keep a saddle mount tied in front of the office. But he had just gotten back into town from a trip out to one of the nearby ranches and had stopped at the office before going on to the livery stable to put up his horse.

Lester didn't know that, of course. He just watched openmouthed as Carson hauled his horse around, then called, "Thanks, Lester!" before urging the animal into a gallop that carried him toward the edge of town.

Lester closed his mouth, but only to gulp as he heard a train whistle in the distance.

Louis Jensen noticed that his wife was peering pensively out the window at the beautiful Colorado scenery through which the train was rolling. "Aren't you glad to almost be home, Melanie?"

"What?" She turned her head to look at him. A smile flashed across her pretty face. "Oh! Of course I'm glad. I can't wait to see Bradley, and everyone else on the Sugarloaf, of course. It's just . . . this was such a wonderful trip. More wonderful than I ever could have hoped or dreamed. Even with the delays the past few days, it's been an experience I'll never forget."

Those delays had just been their luck averaging out, thought Louis. Up until then, the trip had been everything that Melanie was gushing about. He was happier than he had ever been. With his poor health growing up, he had often thought that he wouldn't even live to be this age, let alone be married to such a beautiful woman. But his condition was improved, Melanie was his wife, and he even had a son. He was eager to see Brad again, too. Some missing bags that had ultimately been found and a broken carriage axle that had caused them to miss a train and take a later one couldn't even begin to compare to all the good fortune that had come to him. Nothing was going to ruin his fine mood.

"I suppose I was just thinking about the future," Melanie went on. "And if anything, I'm a little worried for you."

"For me?" said Louis. "Why would you be worried about me? I'm the luckiest man in the world. Don't you know that?"

"You're going to have to tell your mother that we're leaving again in just a couple of months, so you can start your classes at Harvard."

Maybe something *could* dampen his mood a little

after all. He and Melanie had been ready to rush back when they'd gotten the telegram from his father saying that his mother had fallen ill, but it was soon followed by another wire letting them know that the crisis was over. Sally was improving, and she insisted they continue with their trip.

"I'm not sure I should break the news to her so soon after she's been sick," Louis said. "It might cause her to have a relapse."

"Well, you should wait and see for sure how she's doing, "but you can't delay too long, Louis. You don't want to tell her one day and have to leave the next."

He sighed. "No, I suppose not. Perhaps she'll take it better than I expect. After all, it's not as if we're leaving forever. In fact, once I'm practicing law in Big Rock, we won't ever have to leave again."

"I'm looking forward to that. The day when you have your profession, and we have our own home, and . . . perhaps . . . some little brothers and sisters for Bradley . . ."

Louis smiled and slipped his arm around her shoulders. "What you're describing sounds perfect. And we're not going to let anything ruin that beautiful life."

The Sugarloaf

Smoke and Pearlie had just ridden in from checking some of the summer range in the hills at the edge of the valley. The errand hadn't really been a crucial one, but the two old friends had seized on it as an excuse for a leisurely ride on a pretty day.

As Pearlie had put it, "A fella's got only so many

pretty days in his life, so it'd be a plumb shame to waste one of 'em."

Smoke couldn't argue with that, and since Sally was almost back to normal, he had agreed with his former foreman's suggestion.

Pearlie was complaining at the moment, though. "Bet we're gettin' back too late for lunch," he said as he and Smoke rode into the ranch yard. "Took a mite longer to get up there and back than I expected. And that ain't right, Smoke. I know ever' foot of this ranch, like you do, and I shouldn't ought to make mistakes like that. My brain's gettin' plumb ossified, I reckon."

"Your brain's fine," Smoke told him. "And we're not *that* late. I've got a hunch Inez will have saved something for us and kept it warm."

"I hope so. That woman sure can cook, as well as bein' mighty handsome."

Smoke grinned over at his friend. "When are you going to make an honest woman of her, Pearlie?"

"What? An honest—Dadgum it, Smoke, nobody said nothin' about such a thing! Why, I'm too old and set in my ways to ever settle down. It just wouldn't be fair to a woman to saddle her with an ol' mossback like me!"

"If Cal was here, I suspect he'd agree with you," Smoke said, "but I think the only one whose opinion really matters is Inez."

"Well . . . we ain't talked about it . . . exactly . . . but I, uh, she's given me to understand that, uh . . . she wouldn't exactly *object* to such an arrangement—" With a note of relief in his voice, Pearlie changed the subject. "Look there, Smoke. Miss Sally's sittin' out on the porch, takin' the air. All the boys sure are happy that she's doin' better."

"So am I." Smoke and Pearlie rode up to the porch and reined in. Grinning at Sally as she sat in a rocking chair, he said, "Good afternoon to you, Mrs. Jensen."

"And to you, Mr. Jensen," she said, returning his smile. "Did you boys enjoy your ride?"

"We did. Pearlie's a little worried about his stomach, though. He seems to think that Inez is going to let him do without his lunch, so he'll starve."

Sally laughed. "I don't think there's any chance of that happening. The two of you go on inside. There's food in the oven for you."

"That's mighty good news," said Pearlie as he started to swing down from the saddle.

He hadn't made it when a rifle cracked somewhere in the distance, a bullet ripped through the air, and with a curse Pearlie fell from his horse.

CHAPTER 52

Smoke kicked his feet free of the stirrups and threw himself out of the saddle. He landed at the foot of the porch steps and took them in two leaping strides as another bullet chewed splinters from the railing. He didn't know how bad Pearlie was hit, but the first thing he had to do was get Sally inside where she would be safe.

She was already on her feet, saying, "Smoke—!"

He wrapped both arms around her and lifted her off her feet to cradle her against his chest. With his heavily muscled arms and shoulders, he was able to carry her as if she weighed no more than a child.

He didn't have to slow down to open the screen door. Inez heard the shots from inside the house and threw the door open. As Smoke went past her, carrying Sally, she looked out into the yard and cried, "Pearlie!"

The door slammed behind her as she rushed out. Smoke set Sally on the floor in the foyer and swung back around. He pulled the Colt from its holster on his hip and slapped the screen door aside as he charged back out onto the porch.

Inez had reached Pearlie's side and helped him to his feet. Smoke didn't see any blood on the former foreman's clothes, and Pearlie confirmed that by yelling, "I ain't hit, blast it! Just twisted my knee when I fell!"

Inez had an arm around Pearlie's waist to support him as they hurried toward the porch steps in a crouching run. Smoke met them halfway up the steps and grabbed Pearlie's arm with his free hand. As he helped his old friend to the porch, he felt as much as heard the wind-rip of a slug as it passed close by his head. He wasn't sure where the rifle shots were coming from, and a handgun wouldn't be much use against them, anyway.

Then a swift rataplan of hoofbeats made Smoke turn his head toward the sound. He saw at least a dozen men on horseback charging the house, blazing away with the guns in their hands.

"Inside!" he barked at Pearlie and Inez as he gave Pearlie a shove to hurry them along. Bullets smacked and thudded against the wall as he swung around, dropped to a knee behind the porch railing, and returned the fire. One of the attackers flung up his arms and pitched out of the saddle, but that didn't blunt the attack. The other riders continued pounding toward the house.

"Smoke, get in here!" Pearlie shouted from the doorway as he leaned against the jamb because of his gimpy leg. He had a Winchester in his hands and was steady enough to lift the rifle to his shoulder and start cranking off rounds as fast as he could work the weapon's lever. Another attacker fell, and a third man's horse suddenly collapsed and sent its howling rider flying through the air.

With Pearlie providing covering fire, Smoke scuttled backward as he emptied the Colt. He ducked through the door and Pearlie retreated as well, still triggering the Winchester until Inez slammed the inner door, which was built of solid oak thick enough to stop anything short of a cannonball.

All the doors in the ranch house were like that, as were the shutters that could be closed over the windows. The house was designed and built to be defended, because the Sugarloaf had been raided before. It had been a number of years since such a shocking outbreak of violence, but Smoke would never stop being prepared for trouble.

"Are you sure you're all right?" he asked Pearlie.

"Yeah, I'm just a durned fool, that's all. That first shot came so close to my ear that it spooked me and I lost my grip while I was dismountin'. That's all. Bunged up my knee a mite when I hit the ground, but it's nothin' to worry about."

Sally hurried up to Smoke and thrust a Winchester into his hands. "Fifteen in the magazine and one in the chamber. I knew you'd want it full." Her demeanor was cool and calm, yet angry. This was her home, and she wasn't going to stand for anyone attacking it.

A fresh wave of gunfire made Smoke leap to the parlor window, which had, so far, escaped being shattered by flying lead. He saw powder smoke spurting from the barn doors, which had been pulled closed except for a small gap through which defenders could fire. One of the hands knelt in the small opening above the doors, which was used to load hay into the loft, and raked the attackers with rifle fire.

One of the raiders twisted in the saddle and snapped a shot at the man in the hayloft door. The bullet punched into the cowboy's midsection and doubled him over. He dropped the rifle and tumbled forward through the opening, turned over once in the air, and crashed down on his back in the limp sprawl of death.

Smoke's spirits had taken a leap when he saw the counterattack coming from the barn, but anger filled him at the sight of one of his men being killed. He shoved the window up and knelt to put the Winchester to work. It cracked twice more in swift succession, and two more raiders fell from their horses.

He and Pearlie and the men in the barn had done some significant damage to the attackers, dropping nearly half their number, and the men who were still on horseback peeled away and retreated rather than continue the assault. Smoke had no idea who they were or why they were attacking, but he was convinced of one thing—they wouldn't just abandon whatever cause had brought them there. The fight wasn't over.

As if to tell him he was right, a fresh burst of gunfire came from somewhere behind the house.

Pearlie had taken his rifle to the other window in the parlor. Sally and Inez stood in the foyer, just outside the arched entrance to the front room.

Smoke turned his head to look at his wife and asked, "Where's Brad?"

Sally's hand went to her mouth as she gasped. "The last time I saw him, he said he was going out to the barn to watch Hank Sinclair mend a saddle. Oh, Smoke, he must still be out there!"

Smoke felt the same fear that he heard in his wife's voice and saw on her face. But he didn't give in to it and his words had a flinty edge as he said, "Hank and any of the other boys who are in the barn will look out for him. Don't worry, Sally, he'll be fine." He switched his attention to Pearlie and went on. "Stay here in case that first bunch doubles back to hit us again. I'll see what's going on in the back."

He jerked open a desk drawer and reached inside to grab a handful of Winchester cartridges from a box of shells kept there. He thumbed several of them through the rifle's loading gate to replace the ones he'd fired and then shoved the extras into his pocket, knowing he might well need them soon enough.

He reached the big kitchen and stepped onto the enclosed porch on the back of the house. Shots came from his right. The smokehouse and springhouse lay in that direction. Smoke spotted a couple of his men using the small structures for cover as they fired toward a grove of trees about fifty yards away.

The men in the trees spotted Smoke. He had barely emerged from the house when bullets began to rip through the screening around the porch. He dropped below the solid wood half-wall and returned the fire, triggering three fast shots before he paused and called to the Sugarloaf hands, "You boys get up here! I'll cover you!"

Smoke started firing again as the two men dashed for the house. They made it to the porch safely and dropped behind the half-wall.

"Either of you hit?" Smoke asked as he paused

again in his shooting. He knew even a wounded man could be pretty spry when his life was at stake.

"No, we were lucky," one of them answered. His name was Jerry Walker, Smoke recalled. The other man was Ed Magruder. Both were experienced ranch hands in their mid-twenties who had been riding for the Sugarloaf for a couple of years.

"What were you doing around here?" asked Smoke.

Magruder said, "As soon as the shooting started, Hank told us to grab some rifles from the tack room and go out the back of the barn, then circle around here to make sure nobody tried to attack the house from the rear."

"That was mighty smart of him," added Walker. "We hadn't hardly got around on this side of the house when we spotted some of the varmints in the trees back there. They opened up on us and we opened up on them. It was pretty hot and heavy there for a minute, until Ed and me made it to some cover."

"What's goin' on, Smoke?" Magruder asked. "Who are they?"

"I don't know," Smoke answered honestly. "We haven't had any trouble lately except with those rustlers, and we took care of that bunch down in Black Hawk."

He wasn't surprised that Hank Sinclair had acted quickly and decisively in sending these men around to the other side of the house at the first sign of trouble. Hank was a veteran hand who had been through more than one range war.

"Who else is out there in the barn besides Hank?" Smoke asked. During the middle of the day, most of the men who had stayed behind on the Sugarloaf would be out riding the range. Only a handful would be at the ranch headquarters.

"Jack Floren's there," Walker said. "I think I heard Hank tell him to take a rifle and climb up in the hayloft."

Smoke grimaced. That meant Floren was the man who had been shot and most likely killed.

"And Fred Judson the wrangler," put in Magruder. "They're the only ones. Well, except for the boy, of course."

"The boy," Smoke repeated hollowly, knowing perfectly well who Magruder meant.

"Yeah, Brad. The little shaver who's Louis's stepson now. He was watchin' Hank mend a saddle and pesterin' him with a bunch of questions."

That sounded just like Brad, all right, thought Smoke. For the time being, he would have to rely on Hank Sinclair and Fred Judson to keep the youngster safe.

Smoke was going to be busy . . .

A large force on horseback suddenly charged out of the trees toward the house, and renewed firing came from the front.

The Sugarloaf was under attack from two directions, and the defenders were badly outnumbered.

CHAPTER 53

Sam Brant lowered the field glasses from his eyes and grated a bitter curse. He had been watching the attack from a hilltop about a quarter of a mile from the Sugarloaf ranch house, and so far he didn't like what he had seen.

"That's Smoke Jensen down there!" Brant exclaimed. "He's supposed to be dead—or at least in Montana!"

Two members of the gang were with him, but he had thrown the rest of his force against the ranch, splitting them into two equal groups. Jensen and the other man who had ridden up to the house with him had taken a considerable toll on the bunch that had attacked from the front. Brant wasn't sure how it was going in the back, but a lot of gunfire was coming from that direction, so his men hadn't waltzed in and taken over as he had hoped. As *would have happened* if everything had gone according to plan.

Brant was a tall, gaunt, hawk-faced man with gray hair under his steeple-crowned hat. He and his partner Bert Rome had served in the army together, twenty-five years earlier, before they had decided that it would be more profitable selling guns to the Indians instead of fighting the savages.

That enterprise had led to other criminal activities, and eventually a third partner had joined them, a man named Eli Markham, better known as the Santa Rosa Kid. The Kid was a former hired gun who had drifted all the way across the line into full-blown outlawry, and he was as useful a tool as Brant and Rome had ever picked up.

Even though the Kid got an equal share, the other two men did all the thinking for the trio. What the Kid was good for was killing. Point him at anybody they wanted dead, and the Kid would take care of it, usually grinning and laughing while he did it.

What no one knew except Brant and Rome was that when they'd decided the Kid had outlived his usefulness, they were the ones who tipped off the law where to find him. They figured the Kid would never let himself be taken alive. He had been, but that hadn't helped him. He'd been tried and convicted and hanged, all in pretty short order.

Fortunately, Steve Markham was just as dense as his old man had been. They had been able to recruit him for the gang and convince him to be their inside man on the Jensen ranch without any trouble. Somewhere along the way, they would have betrayed him, too . . . but only after they'd gotten their hands on the fortune in ransom money they intended to demand from Sally Jensen.

But Smoke Jensen wasn't dead after all. Brant had worried about that when he hadn't heard from Rome, who was in charge of the Montana part of the operation, or from Steve Markham. He'd told himself that Rome just hadn't had time to get to a telegraph office yet, but he hadn't been able to fully believe that. For some reason, misgivings had gnawed at Brant's guts, which never happened when they were pulling a job.

His worries had been justified, and for a fleeting moment, Brant wondered if he ought to just cut his losses and ride away. Maybe some plans just weren't meant to work.

"What're we gonna do, Sam?" Sherm Winslow asked.

Winslow was short and fair and balding, with a pot gut and a permanently sunburned face. He didn't look all that threatening, but he was the best man with a shotgun Brant had ever seen.

And the *last* thing anybody saw who was unlucky enough to find themselves looking down the barrels of Winslow's Greener.

Brant's other companion was a mountain of a man named Reese Butler. More than one hombre had made the mistake of thinking that Butler was just a slow-moving tub of lard. They generally got their ribs crushed or their necks snapped for making that mistake.

In answer to Winslow's question, Brant said, "We're going down there." He shoved the field glasses back in his saddlebags. "I haven't seen any sign of Louis Jensen. Maybe he and his wife didn't get back when they were supposed to."

"Ain't he a sickly sort, though?" asked Butler. "Maybe he just stays in the house and don't never come outside."

Brant ignored that and went on. "There might

be something almost as good in the barn, though. Remember that kid we saw going in there?"

"Yeah, I think so," said Winslow.

"Well, he didn't come back out, so he's still in there. And he's Louis Jensen's stepson, according to what Steve Markham told us. That means he's Smoke Jensen's step*grand*son. He ought to be worth a hell of a lot of ransom, too."

Winslow frowned "I dunno, Sam. He ain't a blood relative. Anyway, you said Smoke Jensen wouldn't pay any ransom, that he'd be more likely to track us down and kill us if we took his kid. That's why you decided to wait until he was gone before we hit the ranch and grabbed Louis. And then killin' him up in Montana would really open the door for us to collect from his widow."

Brant forced down the irritation he felt welling up inside him. "You're not doing anything except telling me things I already know, Sherm. A man's got to be able to adapt when things don't work out like he's planned. Jensen's not dead, and he's not gone. He's here, and we've got to deal with him. And I don't believe he'd be as likely to risk a kid's life by being stubborn."

In reality, that was just a hope on Brant's part. He didn't *know* how Smoke Jensen would react to the kidnapping of his new grandson. But the way things had worked out, short of abandoning the whole plan that was all Brant and his men could do.

Brant hitched his horse into motion and started down the hill. Winslow and Butler fell in on either side of him.

"We'll go in the back of the barn," Brant said.

"Whatever you do, don't kill the kid. Anybody else who's in there, though . . . blow 'em to hell."

Brad cowered inside an empty stall as he listened to the thunderous roar of guns that filled the barn. Whenever it got too loud, he clapped his hands over his ears. He just wanted it to end.

At the same time, he felt a strong sense of shame eating away at his insides. He knew there was at least one more rifle on the rack inside the tack room. He ought to go in there and get it, he told himself, so he could fight back against the evil men who had invaded the Sugarloaf.

But he was afraid. He was a kid, after all. He couldn't fight grown men, especially ones who didn't hesitate to gun down their enemies. He had seen Jack Floren lying out there where he had fallen from the hayloft, not moving, with a dark puddle forming under and around him. That was blood, Brad knew, and Floren was dead.

Besides, Hank Sinclair had told him to go back there and hide. "Crawl under the straw if you have to," he had said. "It'll stink like hell, but you don't want those varmints to find you."

No, he didn't want that, thought Brad. He sure didn't.

It seemed like the shooting had been going on forever, but it had only been a few minutes. Brad wished his mother was there, but as soon as that thought went through his head, he was glad she *wasn't*. Wherever she and Louis were, they were safe.

The person Brad *really* wished was in the barn with

him was Smoke. That would make all the difference in the world. Smoke would never let anything bad happen to him.

Brad's head jerked up as he heard a sound from the back of the barn. Fred Judson, the wrangler, had barred the door there so nobody could get in, then Fred had joined Hank Sinclair at the front of the barn so they could shoot at the attackers. But it sounded like somebody was trying to get in back there, and although the bar had looked secure to Brad, the thought still scared him . . .

He ought to go and tell Hank and Fred, he thought. They would know what to do.

He scrambled to his feet and had just stepped out of the stall into the center aisle when a loud crash sounded and the barn's back door flew open, the brackets that held the bar having been torn from the wall by the impact. The huge man who had just broken down the door stumbled through the opening and weaved to the side so two more men could charge in right behind him. One held a rifle, the other a shotgun.

Hank Sinclair and Fred Judson had heard the crash. Both men raced into the aisle carrying their rifles. The intruder with the shotgun fired first, bracing the terrible weapon's stock against his hip. The double charge of buckshot smashed into Judson's chest and shredded it to bloody ribbons. He flew backward as if a giant had just yanked a string attached to his back.

The third attacker had his rifle at his shoulder. From just outside the stall where he'd been hidden, Brad watched in horror as flame lanced from the

Winchester's muzzle and split the gloom inside the barn with orange flashes. The rifle cracked three times, and with each shot, Hank Sinclair jerked and twisted. Finally, he collapsed onto his knees and then folded to the ground.

The huge man who had broken down the door spotted Brad and rumbled, "There's the kid!" He made a grab for Brad's arm and moved with such surprising speed that Brad didn't have a chance to dart away. The man gathered him in, lifting him and holding him wrapped up in arms like tree trunks.

The rifleman who had just killed Hank Sinclair stepped up and gave Brad an ugly grin. "You're coming with us, Brad, and there's not a damned thing you can do about it."

The fact that the man knew his name didn't make Brad feel one bit better. In fact, he was so scared that he was numb all over and was convinced that he was about to die.

CHAPTER 54

Smoke, Jerry Walker, and Ed Magruder laid down a withering fire from the back porch as the mounted attackers charged the house. Bullets smacked into the walls around them in seemingly endless fashion. It would take a long time to patch all those gouges and holes, Smoke thought wryly as he peered over the Winchester's sights and squeezed off another round.

Despite being outnumbered, he and his two companions had the advantage of good cover. The raiders were out in the open. They suffered heavy losses, dead and dying men and horses spilling on the ground, and after an eternity that actually didn't last much more than a minute, the survivors wheeled their mounts and pounded away. Smoke, Walker, and Magruder hurried them along with a few more well-placed shots.

As the gunfire died away to be replaced with a ringing silence, Smoke said to the two cowboys, "You fellas hold the fort back here. I need to see what's going on up front."

"Don't worry about us, Smoke," said Magruder. "If those skunks come back, we'll durned well fumigate 'em."

Staying low in case any of the raiders who had fled were thinking about trying a long-range shot, Smoke slid back into the house and then hurried toward the parlor. He didn't hear any shots coming from there and hoped Sally, Pearlie, and Inez were all right.

Sally was in the foyer, holding a revolver. Smoke recognized Pearlie's Colt and knew he must have given it to her in case any of the attackers managed to break in the front door. Pearlie still knelt at one of the parlor windows. Inez had taken Smoke's place at the other front window and held a rifle. A tendril of smoke still curled from its barrel, testifying to its recent use.

Smoke put a hand on Sally's shoulder and asked her, "Are you all right?"

"I'm fine, Smoke," she assured him. "I didn't have to do anything. Inez and Pearlie are the ones who fought off those men."

"Yeah, but you've been sick—"

"I'm *fine*," she said again. "Maybe still a little weak from the illness, but I haven't had any fever for a couple of days."

"I know." He nodded and turned to Pearlie. "Those varmints light a shuck?"

"Yeah," Pearlie said, "after leavin' a few more carcasses out there. And it happened sudden enough that it was almost like they got some sort of signal tellin' 'em to break off the attack."

"Maybe they did."

"Smoke . . ." Pearlie's rugged face was set in grim

lines as he paused. "There toward the end of the ruckus, I didn't hear any shootin' from out in the barn."

"My God," Sally said. "Brad." She reached for the front door.

Smoke stopped her, gently moving her back away from the entrance. "I'll go see about him. Some of those men could still be lurking around out there. They might be trying to trick us into thinking they're gone."

Smoke's instincts told him that wasn't the case, that the raiders who had lived through the fight were gone, but the other possibility couldn't be ruled out and he wasn't going to let Sally risk her life on that. "Cover me from the window," he told Pearlie as he closed his free hand around the doorknob and stepped out onto the front porch with the Winchester held at the ready.

No shots rang out. Smoke's head was on a swivel, moving constantly as he searched for danger. Seeing none, his long strides carried him quickly across the ranch yard toward the barn. He paid particular attention to the sprawled bodies of the raiders, in case any of them were only pretending to be dead. None of them moved, though. Flies were already starting to congregate around some of them.

When he reached the open doors, he hooked one with a booted foot and jerked it wider, then went through the gap in a rush. His eyes needed a second to adjust to the gloom after being in the afternoon sunlight outside.

He cursed bitterly as soon as he spotted the two huddled shapes lying on the hard-packed dirt of the barn's center aisle. He hurried to the side of each man in turn but didn't stop to examine the bodies. A glance was enough to tell him that Hank Sinclair and Fred Judson were dead, gunned down brutally by intruders who must have gotten into the barn from the rear.

A second later Smoke saw the busted-down door and wondered what sort of battering ram they had used to do that. Not that it mattered. The bastards had forced their way in, and that was all that was important. That, and . . .

"Brad!" Smoke called. "Brad, where are you?"

There were a lot of hiding places in a cavernous barn and stable, he told himself. Brad could have crawled into one of them and stayed there safely, not budging even when Hank and Fred were killed. He could emerge from whatever hidey-hole he had found and come running to Smoke . . .

"Brad!"

The name echoed hollowly, mockingly, from the rafters.

Smoke bit back another curse and started searching. He looked in every stall on both sides of the aisle, then in the others at the rear. That crazy mustang Rocket tossed his head and whinnied, but that didn't tell Smoke anything. He called Brad's name several more times but still didn't get a response.

"Smoke!" That was Pearlie's voice, coming from the front of the barn.

Smoke swung around and hurried in that direction, thinking that maybe Pearlie had found Brad somewhere.

The former foreman was alone, though, standing just inside the entrance holding his rifle. "Smoke, did you find the younker?"

Smoke shook his head, unable to put into words the unavoidable answer to Brad's whereabouts.

"Miss Sally's about to go loco from worryin'," Pearlie went on. "It's all Inez can do to keep her calm. I sure wish we could take Brad in there to see her."

"So do I," Smoke said, "but the only ones here are Hank Sinclair and Fred Judson."

Pearlie nodded grimly. "I seen 'em. They was good boys, Smoke. The men who done this—"

"They'll pay for it—the ones who got away," vowed Smoke. "And they'll pay for taking Brad, too. If anything happens to that boy . . ." He couldn't bring himself to finish. After a couple of seconds, he drew in a deep breath and said, "I'd better go tell Sally."

"I'll come with you." Pearlie glanced over his shoulder. "Then I'll get some of the fellas and we'll do what we can for Hank and Fred."

The two of them started across the ranch yard, weaving around the carnage of dead raiders and horses, only to stop abruptly when they heard hoofbeats rapidly approaching. They swung their rifles up as a horseman appeared, riding hell-for-leather toward the ranch house.

"Hold your fire," Smoke said a second later. "That's Monte Carson."

The sheriff slowed his horse as he came closer. Monte's eyes widened as he looked around at the bodies littering the open area in front of the house. Relief was in his gaze as he turned it toward Smoke and Pearlie and reined in. "I'm glad to see you fellas are still alive, but Lord, it looks like you fought a war here!"

"That's the way it seemed for a while, Monte," said Smoke.

"You're all right, Smoke? Pearlie?"

"Yeah," Pearlie said, "no permanent damage done to us, but Hank Sinclair and Fred Judson weren't so lucky. They're in the barn, dead, and Jack Floren is layin' over there where he fell from the hayloft after they gunned him."

"Damn it! They were good men. What about Sally?"

"She's all right," Smoke said. "She's in the house with Inez Sandoval. What are you doing here, Monte?"

The lawman scowled. "I came to warn you about something like this happening, Smoke. I'm mighty damned sorry that I was too late."

Smoke's eyebrows rose in surprise. "Warn us? How'd you know about it?"

Monte dismounted and pulled a crumpled piece of paper from his pocket. "This message came for you at the telegraph office. Lester was so shaken up by it that he didn't even print it out proper-like, just brought me what he wrote down on his pad."

Smoke took the paper and read it.

OUTLAWS TO ATTACK SUGARLOAF STOP
KIDNAP LOUIS STOP STEVE MARKHAM
PART OF GANG STOP HIS BUNCH HERE
TRIED TO STEAL HORSES STOP TWO
MEN DEAD BUT HERD SAFE STOP CAL
DELIVERING TO COBURN STOP HEADED
BACK WITH BRICE ROGERS STOP
DENNY STOP
STIRRUP MONTANA OUT

Smoke's jaw was tight with fury as he lifted his eyes from the message. "Markham was an outlaw? And what in blazes is Brice Rogers doing all the way up there in Montana?"

Monte and Pearlie exchanged a guilty glance.

Monte said, "He found out Markham might be up to no good—"

"Hold on," said Pearlie. "I ought to be the one tellin' this, since I figured out Markham was most likely the son of the Santa Rosa Kid."

Smoke's frown deepened. "You two *knew* about this?"

Monte gestured toward the message still in Smoke's hand. "We didn't have any idea what that bunch was planning. We didn't even know for sure there *was* a gang, or if Markham was mixed up with them. All we were certain of was that he was a dead ringer for an owlhoot called the Santa Rosa Kid. Pearlie and I both remembered him, from the days when he was a hired gun and hadn't gone all bad yet."

"He was pretty damn close to it even then," muttered Pearlie.

"Yeah," Monte agreed. "Anyway, Brice chased off after Denny to let her know that Markham *might* be up to no good. But I swear, Smoke, that's all we knew. We didn't have any idea his gang was going to try to kidnap Louis. Where *is* Louis? He and Melanie aren't back yet, are they?"

"They're on their way back, but they got delayed," Smoke explained. "They might be here today."

"Well, I guess that's one stroke of luck, anyway—"

"The gang took Brad."

Monte looked stricken at Smoke's words. "Brad?" he repeated. "The boy?"

"Yeah. They've got him . . . and we can only guess what they intend to do with him." Smoke's hands tightened on the rifle he held. "But no matter what, I'm going to track them down and kill them, every last one of them."

CHAPTER 55

Sally was too strong to fall apart in times of trouble, even when the stress was as terrible as it was. After Smoke told her that Brad was gone, apparently kidnapped, she cried for a minute or so as he held her, then stopped, pulled herself together, and looked up at him as she said, "Go get them. Kill them and bring him back."

"That's just what I figure on doing," he told her. "I've sent Ed Magruder and Jerry Walker to round up the rest of the men who are out on the range today, and when they get back, they'll be starting after us. Pearlie, Monte, and I are going to pick up the trail right now."

Inez said, "Not until I pack some supplies for you, Señor Smoke. It won't take long."

"That's all right," he replied with a grim smile. "I've got to gather up some ammunition, anyway."

Within half an hour, the three men were ready to ride. Smoke said his good-byes to Sally in front of the house as he put his hands on her shoulders and kissed her.

"Bring him back, Smoke," she murmured as she

tightly hugged his neck. "He's too young. It's too soon for him to die. He has his whole life still in front of him."

"I know," he told her. "Try not to worry."

"You know better than that."

"Yeah, I reckon. But have I ever let you down before?"

"No," she admitted. "No, you haven't. But I've never had a grandson before, either."

She was right about that, thought Smoke. He was about to brush a final kiss across her forehead when he heard something that made him look around.

Horses.

"Dadgum!" Pearlie exclaimed from nearby where he and Monte stood holding the saddle mounts the three men would use. "Look who's in that buggy."

Smoke recognized his son and daughter-in-law on the front seat of the approaching buggy. Louis was handling the reins, and fairly skillfully, too. Smoke could see the bags piled behind the seat.

"The train was coming in just as I rode out of town," said Monte. "They must have been on it."

"Oh, dear," Sally said. "What terrible news they're coming home to. I hoped . . . I hoped Brad would be back here safe and sound by the time they got here . . ."

"So did I," Smoke said. "It's not going to be easy breaking the news to them."

It wasn't. Louis and Melanie were all smiles when they climbed down from the buggy, glad to be home and eager to see everyone, especially Brad. That happiness vanished in an instant as Smoke explained what had happened. Melanie almost collapsed as she looked like she had just been punched.

Louis caught hold of her and drew her against him as he tried to comfort her. "Don't worry, We're going to get him back. He'll be fine."

"Pearlie and Monte and I are about to start out after them right now," Smoke said. "And more of the men will be coming along after us."

Louis looked over Melanie's shoulder as he held her. "I'm coming with you," he said to his father.

"No!" That exclamation came from Melanie and Sally in unison. Melanie drew back in Louis's embrace and stared up at him. "You can't do that, Louis."

"I can't stay here and wait. Brad is my son now. If it was me who had been taken . . . the way those outlaws first planned . . . you would have gone after me, wouldn't you, Father?"

"That's different," Smoke said gruffly.

"Why? Because Brad is my stepson and not my son by blood? Uncle Matt's not your brother by blood, but does that mean he's less important to you than Uncle Luke?"

"You know better than that, blast it. That's not what I meant—"

"No, what you meant is that I'm too sickly to come with you." There was no mistaking the bitterness in Louis's voice. "The same way I've been too sickly to do so many other things in my life. Well, I'm tired of it, do you understand? I can't live with myself if I don't do everything in my power to save Brad, no matter what happens to me!"

Melanie whispered, "I can't lose you both."

"You won't," he said, turning to her again. "You won't lose either of us. You'll see. We're going to get him back, and I'll be fine."

Smoke couldn't help but be proud of his son as he heard the determination and courage in Louis's voice and saw those qualities on his face. He understood why Louis felt that way, too. Despite his health problems, the blood of the Jensens flowed in Louis's veins. And it wasn't just a matter of blood, either, as Louis had pointed out about Matt. Matt had the fighting heart of a Jensen, and evidently, so did Louis.

"All right," Smoke said. "You're coming with us, son. Better put on some good clothes for riding and get a rifle and handgun while we saddle a horse for you."

"Smoke . . ." Sally began.

"Sometimes a man doesn't have any choice," he told her. "The trail's right there in front of him, and he has to follow it."

"Thanks, Pa," Louis said. "I'll be ready to ride in a few minutes."

Melanie lifted a hand toward him as if she were about to take hold of his sleeve, but then she stopped the gesture. She swallowed hard and said, "Be careful, Louis . . . but bring back my son. *Our* son."

"Count on it," he said with a nod.

Smoke's father Emmett had taught him some about how to follow a trail, and then the years he'd spent with the old mountain man Preacher had made him an even better tracker. Pearlie and Monte had considerable experience at such things, too, so it wasn't difficult for them to pick up the trail of the men who had taken Brad. It led toward the high, rugged country west of the valley where the Sugarloaf was located, just as Smoke expected. There were plenty of places up there where even a good-sized group of men could hide.

As the four men rode, Louis asked, "Are we absolutely certain these men we're following took Brad?"

"We searched all around the ranch headquarters," Smoke said. "He wasn't anywhere to be found. There's no other explanation for his disappearance. Besides, we know they were planning to kidnap *you*, and since you weren't there I reckon they decided to hold Brad for ransom instead."

"They can't be too smart," said Monte, "if they figured you'd pay ransom for anybody, Smoke. That's just not your way."

"I've been thinking about that. I've got a hunch they weren't expecting me to be here. Since Markham was working with them, he could have passed word to the gang that I was taking that horse herd to Montana. Then, when Sally got sick at the last minute and Denny went in my place, Markham never had a chance to tip off his partners."

Pearlie nodded. "That makes a heap of sense. From what Miss Denny said in her wire, they went after the horse herd, too. Most likely figured on killin' you when they stole those horses, Smoke. That way Miss Sally would be left on her own, and they believed she'd be soft and easy to buffalo into handin' over a pile of money." He laughed. "They don't know Miss Sally! I reckon she'd have strapped on a gun, climbed on a horse, and gone after the no-good varmints her own self."

"More than likely," Smoke said with a smile.

He had been studying the tracks as they rode, and he estimated that they were following between a dozen and two dozen men. Those weren't very good odds, or at least they wouldn't have been under normal circumstances. Pearlie and Monte Carson were seasoned fighting men, though, worth three or four hardcases apiece, in Smoke's estimation. He had no false modesty about his own abilities, either. He knew he could kill plenty of the bastards before they brought him down . . . if they got lucky enough to even do that.

The weak link . . . no, that wasn't fair, Smoke told himself . . . the unknown quantity was Louis, and not just his health, either. He had very little experience in dealing with trouble. Would he panic at the wrong moment and endanger not only his own life but that of his son and everyone else?

There was only one way to find out.

The tracks led them to the slopes and started up. They had been able to move fairly quickly, since the kidnappers apparently had made no effort to cover up their trail. Once they began climbing, though, they couldn't push the horses as hard. They hadn't brought extra mounts with them, since Smoke didn't expect it to be a long chase. The kidnappers didn't want to elude pursuit; they couldn't collect any ransom if they did that. They just wanted to have everything happen on their terms.

Because of that, Smoke wasn't surprised when he and his companions reached the top of a long rise, came out onto a narrow bench, and found a man on horseback waiting for them.

CHAPTER 56

The Wolf's Fang

At first glance, the man didn't appear to be much of a threat. He was short, pudgy, and red-faced. But the way he held a coach gun with its stock braced against his thigh and the barrels angled up indicated an easy familiarity with the deadly weapon. As Smoke rode closer, he saw that the man's pale blue eyes were as cold and hard as chips of ice.

"That's far enough," the man called when Smoke and his companions were about twenty feet away.

They reined in, and Smoke said, "Mister, you know we can fill you full of lead before you have time to lower that scattergun, don't you?"

"Well, hell, I'm not an idiot. You're Smoke Jensen. I don't know who those two older gents are, but they look like they've still got plenty of bark on 'em, too." He looked at Louis. "That would make the young tenderfoot Louis Jensen, I'm guessing. Just got back from your wedding trip today, did you, Louis?"

"Where's my son?" Louis snapped as he tightened

his reins. His horse was a little nervous, maybe picking that up from Louis himself.

"He's safe. Don't you worry about that. The fella in charge has made sure everybody understands that no harm's to come to that kid . . . unless and until he gives the order." The man smiled. "Anyway, I'm not worried about you boys gunning me down, because if you were stupid enough to do that, you wouldn't find out what we want you to know. And that would mean you'd never get the kid back alive."

"Whatever you've got to say, just go ahead and spit it out," Smoke rasped.

"Sure. Can't blame me for wanting to take my time with this, though. It's not every day a man gets to talk face-to-face with the most famous gunfighter ever to come down the pike." The man held up a hand to forestall any protest. "All right, You want it straight, here it is. You pay us two hundred and fifty thousand dollars, or you get the boy back in pieces."

"You—" Louis choked out as he started to move his horse forward.

Monte Carson reached over and put a hand on his arm to stop him.

"Name-calling won't do you any good," the man went on. "Nothing will do you any good except doing exactly what I tell you to do. Turn around, go back to your house, go to the bank in Big Rock, do whatever you have to do, but get that two hundred and fifty grand in cash and bring it back up here two days from now." He lifted his right hand and jerked the thumb over his shoulder. "See that ridge up there behind me?"

Smoke nodded. The ridge rose a hundred and fifty

feet in a sheer cliff of red sandstone seamed with cracks. "It'd be hard to miss."

"That's right, and from up there a fella can see everything that's going on down here and for miles around. There'll be plenty of riflemen posted along the rim, and more important, that's where my boss will be with the boy. If he spots any tricky business at all, anything that puts a burr under his saddle, well, he'll just throw the kid over the edge and we'll all ride away, poorer but wiser. Oh, and before you start thinking you'll distract us by having somebody pretend to deliver the money down here while more of you sneak up on that ridge . . . the only way up there is through a narrow cut that'll be guarded well enough a horse-fly couldn't get through. So any fancy thoughts going through your head, Mr. Smoke Jensen, you can just forget about 'em."

"Seems like your boss has thought of everything, mister," Smoke said. "Well, let me tell you—"

"All right." After his first angry reaction, Louis had sat scowling down at his saddle horn while the kid-napper talked. Seemingly in control of his emotions again, he'd raised his head and interrupted Smoke.

Smoke frowned and turned his head to look at his son.

The stocky outlaw seemed a little surprised, too. He asked, "All right what?"

"All right. You have a deal," Louis said.

"Now, wait a minute," Smoke said.

Louis heeled his mount forward so that it pulled even with Smoke's horse and even pushed a step ahead. Glaring defiantly, Louis said, "Brad is my stepson, and since his mother isn't here, any decisions are mine to make. And I'm agreeing to pay the ransom, just like this man demands."

"You don't have a quarter of a million dollars."

"I have money of my own, and I have a trust fund from Mother's family. And I'm sure I can find banks willing to loan me a considerable amount on the part of the Sugarloaf I'll eventually own."

That brash statement made both Pearlie and Sheriff Carson stare at him. This cool, defiant young man wasn't the same Louis Jensen they had gotten to know. But Louis's stepson had never been in mortal danger before, either.

"You're putting an awful lot of trust in this . . . this"—Smoke jerked a hand at the man in a curt gesture—"damned owlhoot!"

"Jensen, we don't *want* the kid," the outlaw said wearily. "We want the money. There's no reason for us to hurt him once we've got what we want." He laughed harshly. "Hell, we're not idiots. Double-crossing you and killing the kid once we've been paid off would be the best way in the world of getting you on our trail from now on. None of us want *that*. We'd always be looking over our shoulders for you."

"You're right," Smoke grated. "And you'd never see me until it was too late. I'd kill you all. Nothing would ever stop me." He rolled his shoulders. "It just rubs me the wrong way to pay a bunch of no-good bastards like you for invading my ranch, killing my men, and stealing my grandson."

"We don't have any choice, Pa," Louis said, quieter but still determined.

Smoke sighed and nodded. "No, I reckon we don't." He pointed a finger at the stocky outlaw. "You warned us about not trying any tricks. Now *I'm* warning *you*. You'd better live up to your end of the bargain."

"We will. Now, here's how it'll go. One man brings the money, in twenty-dollar bills split up in five bags. There'll be a horse picketed here. Tie the bags to the saddle and turn the horse loose. Then get back on your horse, turn around, and ride away. You can stop at the bottom of the slope and wait. When we have the money, we'll put the kid on a horse and send him down. From what I've seen, he's a pretty good rider, so he shouldn't have any trouble."

"He is a good rider." Smoke's throat was tight as he remembered watching Brad get used to the saddle and start turning into a fine young horseman.

"I assume you'll handle the payoff, Jensen—"

"No," Louis said. "I'll do it."

"That's loco!" Smoke burst out. "It was you they planned on kidnapping in the first place, blast it! And now you're talking about putting yourself right in their hands—"

"No, I like it," the outlaw said, grinning. "It seems . . . appropriate. I've got a hunch my boss will go along with it, too. Anyway, that quarter of a million is enough for us, no matter whose life it's paying for." He lifted his reins. "Nobody else comes up that hill. We see anybody but young Jensen here, the kid goes over the edge." He turned his horse and started riding leisurely toward the ridge.

Evidently a trail led up there that wasn't easily seen.

"I never believed in shootin' fellas in the back unless there wasn't no other way and it had to be done," said Pearlie, "but right now it'd feel plumb good to plant a slug between that old boy's shoulder blades."

"I feel the same way, Pearlie," said Monte, "and I pack a badge and shouldn't even think such a thing."

In a hard voice, Smoke said, "Let's go. There's nothing else to say or do here. Not now, anyway."

They turned their horses and started back down the slope behind them. The going was rough enough that they didn't talk, just concentrated on letting the horses pick their way back down to more level ground.

When they reached a flat area and stopped underneath some towering pine trees, Louis said, "I know you're upset with me, Pa—"

"What else could you do? They hold all the aces, looks like." Smoke grimaced and shook his head. "I just hate letting them win. Nothing's more important than Brad's life, though."

Before leaving the Sugarloaf, Louis had donned range clothes, but they were clean, neatly pressed duds that didn't look like they had ever been worn for actual work. His expensive, pearl-gray Stetson didn't have any dust or sweat stains on it. He thumbed it back anyway and said, "They're not going to win."

"You agreed to pay the ransom they asked for," Smoke pointed out.

"Maybe," Louis said, "but we're going to get Brad back safe and sound, and the only payoff those bastards are going to get will be in bullets."

CHAPTER 57

"Did you see what was behind that ridge the man kept talking about?" Louis asked as the four men rode back toward the Sugarloaf.

"Just a big ol' mountain," said Pearlie.

Louis nodded. "When I was at a sanitarium in Switzerland, I met a fellow patient named Horst von Wolffstricker. He was a German who was there because his lungs had been damaged by the thin air at great altitudes. He was a mountain climber, you see. He ascended the Matterhorn, the Zugspitze, and plenty of other peaks in Europe, but it wrecked his health. Still, he talked about mountaineering all the time. I remembered that back there, and it made me think that if we could climb that mountain from the other side and then descend the face behind those men—"

"You're not going to be doing any of that," Smoke said. "Your heart wouldn't be up to it."

Louis nodded and said, "I know. Plus those outlaws will be expecting me to deliver the ransom money. But they'll be watching *me*, not the mountain. That would give whoever makes the climb down the chance to take them by surprise."

"That could be dangerous for Brad," Smoke pointed out.

"I know. The safest thing would be to just pay the ransom and trust them to keep their word." Louis paused. "I can't bring myself to do either of those two things."

"It's a big risk all the way around." Smoke looked at Pearlie and Monte Carson. "What do you fellas think?"

"This is a family matter, Smoke," said Monte. "We'll back you and Louis in whatever you decide."

"I hate to say it," Pearlie put in, "but I ain't sure either Monte or me is up to clamberin' around over them mountains, though. We got a few too many miles on us for somethin' like that."

Smoke shook his head. "I know. I'll have to ask for volunteers among the hands who are still on the ranch." He smiled. "I wish some of those old-timers Preacher and I used to call on for help were still around. Those old fur trappers were as sure-footed as mountain goats. They've all passed on, though, the ones who weren't killed in some scrape or another years ago."

A short time later, they encountered Magruder, Walker, and the members of the Sugarloaf crew who had started out from the ranch behind them. The men sat and listened as Smoke explained the situation, muttering angrily when he came to the threats against Brad's life. Their interest grew when he went over the rudimentary plan to foil the kidnappers' scheme.

"Count me in, Smoke," Ed Magruder volunteered without hesitation. "I was born and raised in Arkansas, and I was scramblin' up and down those Ozarks almost before I could walk."

"I'm from the Missouri Ozarks, myself," said Smoke, "so I know what you mean."

Several other men spoke up, claiming that they also had experience at mountain climbing, from the Appalachians and the Great Smoky Mountains to the Tetons and the Sierra Nevadas. Smoke promised to consider all of them, although he didn't plan to decide on the final group until they were back at the Sugarloaf.

"The good thing," said Louis, "is that they've given us two days to deliver the ransom. It's going to take time to figure out the details of the plan, decide on the route, and make the actual climb. You'll need to be at the peak by tomorrow evening, so you can make the descent the next morning, before I ride up there with the ransom money at midday. Or what they *believe* is the ransom money, at any rate."

"You ain't takin' the loot for real?" asked Pearlie.

Louis looked at Smoke, who waited for him to make the decision. After a moment, Louis said, "No. The bags I take up there will be stuffed with blank paper instead of twenty-dollar bills. I will *not* pay those animals for stealing my son and killing my friends."

Smoke grunted. "That's the way I feel about it, too. Let's get back to the ranch and figure out the rest of this."

* * *

Melanie wasn't comforted much by the news the men had to tell her when they returned to the Sugarloaf late that afternoon, but Sally had had a calming influence on her. Her face was still pale and drawn from worry and strain as Louis explained the plan to her. When he finished, she said, "Two days?"

He nodded. "I'm afraid so. Those were the terms they gave us, and we had to agree, or at least pretend to. I suppose they thought it would take that long to get together a quarter of a million dollars in cash."

"It would," Smoke said, "if we were actually giving them that money."

"But you're going to trick them instead, hit them from behind, and rescue Brad," said Sally.

"That's right."

"You're playing games with my son's life," Melanie said.

"Believe me, nobody's playing games," Smoke told her. "This is actually the best chance we have of getting Brad back safe and sound."

"But if you pay them, they'll let him go!"

Louis said, "I've been thinking about it, and I don't believe that's the case. By now Brad has seen their faces and probably heard some of their names. He can identify them. They won't want to leave him behind and run the risk of him doing that." He nodded toward Smoke. "They're afraid of my father, but they'll be afraid of the law, as well. It's a risk for them either way."

Monte Carson said to Melanie, "For what it's worth, ma'am, I've dealt with a lot of lawbreakers over the years, and I agree with Smoke and Louis. Brad's a danger to them whether he lives or dies, so why not go ahead and do the simpler thing?"

"By killing him," Melanie said.

"Well . . . yeah."

She drew in a deep, shuddery breath and looked around at the group gathered in the parlor of the Sugarloaf ranch house. "It sounds like you have to go ahead with this plan, then. But please . . . please do everything in your power to bring Bradley back safely to me."

Louis was sitting beside her. He took her right hand in both of his and said, "Of course we will, darling."

"I just wish he didn't have to remain a prisoner of those terrible men for two more days!"

"If I know that boy," Smoke said, "he's doing his best to make an adventure of it."

The thought that Smoke wouldn't come to rescue him never entered Brad's mind. It was just a matter of time before he showed up with a blazing Colt in each hand, spewing death to the evil men who had taken him away from the ranch. It would be just like the scenes in the yellow-backed dime novels Brad had read, some of which had actually been *about* Smoke, although he had told Brad that they were all made up by drunken scribblers who didn't have any idea what they were talking about.

Maybe some of the so-called facts were made up, but Brad knew that didn't matter. Smoke was still a hero, and he would save the day.

The main thing Smoke would want him to do was

to stay calm. Brad made a real effort to do that. He wasn't a baby anymore. He couldn't curl up in a ball and cry. He had seen bad men before, had been in danger. He and his mother had survived that disastrous stagecoach trip through the Sierra Nevada Mountains the previous Christmas. As long as a man didn't panic and kept his wits about him, he had a chance.

"Here ya go, kid." The massive man called Butler dropped a tin plate with some bacon and beans on it in front of Brad, who sat with his back propped against a tree trunk at the edge of the firelight. One of the outlaws stood nearby with a rifle, guarding him.

"How am I supposed to eat it?" Brad asked. "My hands are tied behind me."

Butler scratched his jaw, which stuck out like a slab of rock. Then he grinned and said, "Bend over and eat it like a dog."

"I can't do that, either. I'm tried to the tree, remember?"

"Oh, yeah. Well, I'll untie your hands for now, but I'm gonna leave the rope around your chest that's holdin' you to the tree. Don't try nothin', or you'll get paddled like the little brat you are."

"I'm not afraid of a paddling."

"You better be," Butler said with a threatening scowl.

A swat from one of the outlaw's huge hands could break bone, thought Brad, so he really didn't want a paddling. But he wasn't going to give any of these men the satisfaction of knowing that he was scared.

Butler's thick, sausagelike fingers struggled to untie the ropes around Brad's wrists. He finally got the other outlaw to do it. Brad was able to pick up the plate. He had to eat with his fingers, but he managed and then licked the plate clean. When he was finished, Butler gave him a drink of water from a canteen.

"You're too young for coffee or whiskey," Butler jeered. "Maybe if you're lucky, you'll live long enough to try both. But I wouldn't count on it."

"I'll live long enough," Brad said.

"You sound mighty sure of that."

"Smoke Jensen will see to it. He'll ride in here and kill—" The words slipped out of Brad's mouth before he could rein them in.

One of the outlaws who was close enough to hear laughed. Brad had heard some of the others call him Sam. He was an older man who seemed to be the leader of the gang.

Sam came over to stand in front of Brad and sneer down at him. "You've got a lot of faith in Smoke Jensen, don't you, kid? Well, you might be interested to know that we've already talked to Jensen, and he's going to give us everything we want."

Brad shook his head stubbornly. "I don't believe that."

"It's true. He's going to pay the ransom. It was your stepfather's idea, but Jensen went along with it."

Brad's eyes widened. "My stepfather? Louis is back?" That was the first he had heard of that. He knew that his mother and Louis were supposed to have returned to the Sugarloaf the day before but had been delayed for some reason. If Louis was there, too, and was going to help Smoke rescue him . . .

Of course, that might be too much for Louis because of his health, Brad reminded himself. Still, just knowing that Louis was around made him feel a little better. Even though he wasn't much of a fighter, Louis was really smart. If there was a way to turn the tables on the outlaws, Smoke and Louis would figure it out.

Brad was about to say that when he realized that such bravado might not be a good idea. Sam and all the others seemed to believe that they had already won, that the ransom money was as good as theirs and all they had to do was wait for it to be delivered. Well, let them go on thinking that, Brad told himself. They would be more surprised when their evil scheme blew up in their faces.

Brad's lower lip trembled. He blinked his eyes rapidly until tears began to flow in them. His face scrunched up as he started to cry.

"That's right, kid, your pa's back, but you know he's not going to be able to help you. That's why you're scared, isn't it?"

"P-Please," Brad stammered. "Don't hurt me."

"Just do as you're told. Maybe you'll make it through this alive . . . but don't count on it."

The boss outlaw called Sam turned and walked away. Brad continued to sob as he slumped against the tree.

But even as he did, his eyes flicked up in a hooded glance at the man's back. *Just you wait, mister,* Brad told himself. *We'll see who makes it through this alive . . . and who doesn't.*

CHAPTER 58

The time that passed after Smoke, Louis, Pearlie, and Monte returned to the Sugarloaf with the grim news from Brad's captors went by like a whirlwind. There were a lot of preparations to be made.

Smoke's range ended before the mountain that loomed behind the bench where the "payoff" would be made, but he had been up there in the past, hunting. Not to the summit itself, but almost that high. And once Smoke Jensen had been over a stretch of ground, he never forgot it.

"We won't have to go all the way to the top," he told the ranch hands who would be accompanying him. "There's a high pass up there. I've seen it, although I haven't been through it. We'll climb the west face until we can get across that way. We need to be there by tomorrow evening, and it'll take a while to ride in a big enough circle that we can come in from that direction without the kidnappers spotting us."

He turned to Louis, who was sitting in on the meeting along with Pearlie. Monte Carson had returned to Big Rock, since he had responsibilities there. He'd been reluctant to leave, but Smoke had insisted.

He handed a piece of paper with a map sketched on it to Louis. "I had to draw this from memory, but I think it's pretty accurate. When that varmint with the shotgun mentioned the only way to get up on that ridge was through a well-guarded cut, I thought I remembered the place he was talking about. There's a switchback trail up to it at the northern end of that bench." He stood next to Louis and pointed at some of the markings on the paper.

"What they don't seem to know is that there's another, smaller trail about half a mile farther on, which comes out at the same point as the larger one, that gash in the rocks that leads up to the ridge crest. It's a hard ride, but horses can make it. We're going to have men waiting where that smaller trail starts, and when you've delivered that so-called ransom and ridden back down the slope to where they can't see you anymore, you light a shuck for that spot and join up with the others. When you hear the shooting start, head up that trail as fast as you can. By the time you get to the top, most of the guards at the cut will have fallen back to reinforce the main bunch. You'll have to shoot your way through any who are left."

"Don't worry about that," said Louis. "They won't stand in our way for very long."

Smoke nodded. "We'll be hitting them from behind, and if that's not enough, you'll come in from the flank and mop up any of the varmints who are left. The thing we all have to remember is to watch out for Brad. No wild shooting. Make sure you know where your bullets are going."

All the men around the circle nodded and muttered agreement. They wanted revenge for their fallen friends . . . but not at the cost of Brad's life.

Inez would prepare food and supplies for the group that would be spending the night on the mountain. Smoke told the men to get a good night's sleep, then failed to follow that advice himself. He lay awake most of the night going over every detail of the plan in his mind—the ones he could foresee, anyway.

Sally sensed his restlessness and reached out for him in the bed. "Are you worried, Smoke? That's not like you. You've always been the most confident man I've ever known."

"I'm confident we can do this," he answered. "I've faced long odds and come out on top too many times not to believe in myself, and my friends, too, for that matter. But it was never the life of my own grandson at stake before."

She snuggled against him and rested her head on his shoulder. "It's odd, isn't it, how quickly they come to be so important to us. We never even knew Brad for the first eight years of his life, and now he's a member of our family, as precious to us as any of the others. The same is true of Melanie. We can't even imagine living without them now."

"We won't have to," Smoke said gruffly. "The boy's going to be fine. Those outlaws don't have any reason to hurt him . . . yet. In fact, they've got good reason to keep him alive, just in case they need to use him for leverage if anything goes wrong with their plan."

Sally brushed her lips against the strong line of his jaw, and he tightened his arm around her. Finally, long after midnight, he dozed off.

Louis didn't sleep much, either, and he knew another restless night lay in front of him before he would play his part in rescuing his son. He didn't really think of Brad as his stepson anymore. He loved the boy as much as if Brad were his own flesh and blood, and that was the way it ought to be.

The next morning, he and Smoke went over the plan one last time.

"We'll start the climb down as soon as it's light enough to see," said Smoke. "We'll be using all the cover we can find, but there'll be places where they *might* spot us if somebody happened to look up at the wrong time. I believe all their attention is going to be pointed ahead of them, though, not behind. With that mountain at their backs, they'll believe they're safe in that direction."

"It'll be a dangerous descent," Louis said. "I'm no mountaineer, but I could tell that much just from looking at the peak."

Smoke smiled. "The Wolf's Fang. That's what the Indians called it, according to some of the old-timers around here. Men who trapped in this area long before your mother and I ever came here from Idaho. It looks kind of like a fang, I reckon."

"I just hope it doesn't bite any of us," murmured Louis.

Later in the morning, Smoke kissed and hugged Sally before leaving, hugged Melanie, shook hands with Louis, and then embraced his son roughly, clapping a hand on his back. "If everybody does their part, we'll have that boy home, safe in his mother's arms, by tomorrow night," he promised.

Louis stood with his arm around his wife's shoulders

as they watched Smoke, Magruder, and eight other men set out on horseback for the long, roundabout ride that would take them to the far side of the Wolf's Fang.

"I wish I was going with them," Louis said quietly.

"What you're going to do is important, too," Melanie said. "And after you've pretended to deliver the ransom, you're going to be with Pearlie and Sheriff Carson and the other men who attack the outlaws from the other direction."

Sally, who stood nearby, said, "I'm still not sure it's a good idea for you to go with them, Louis."

"Pa didn't argue with me when I said I was riding with that bunch," Louis pointed out with a smile. "He probably knew it wouldn't do any good."

"I know, but as your mother, I'm going to worry. There's no avoiding that." A grim smile touched Sally's lips, too. "But as a Jensen, I have to say I understand, Louis."

"I do, too," said Melanie. "We may be Jensens by marriage, but that counts, too, doesn't it, Sally?"

"You're darned right it does."

Once Smoke was gone, Louis talked to Pearlie, who was going to be in charge of the second force riding to Brad's rescue, and went over those details. The most important thing would be for the men to stay out of sight of the kidnappers as they made their way to the steep trail they would be using. The killers on the ridge couldn't be allowed to see anyone in the vicinity except Louis. He also put together the five bags of paper cut to resemble bundles of money.

With that taken care of, there was nothing left to do except wait—and that wasn't an easy thing. Supper was awkward and strained that night, and Louis tossed and turned, unable to stop worrying about Brad and hoping that the youngster was still all right.

The next morning was better. Louis was up early, glad to be leaving the torture chamber of his thoughts. There were things to do, things to keep his mind and hands occupied. He ate the hearty breakfast that Inez prepared, drank several cups of hot, strong coffee, and then checked over the guns he was taking along.

A Colt .45 had always seemed a little heavy and unwieldy to him. In the past, he had fired Denny's .38 caliber Lightning for target practice before deciding he could handle something a bit more powerful. The Colt Thunderer had proven to fit the bill, very similar in feel to the Lightning although it fired the slightly bigger .41 caliber round.

For a rifle, he picked a Winchester Model 1894 from his father's large collection of firearms racked in Smoke's study. It was chambered for .30-30 rounds, and Louis had shot it enough to be reasonably comfortable with it, although he knew he was far from an expert marksman. He wished that he had put in many more hours of practice, as Denny had. He'd never had any reason to think that someday his son's life might depend on his skill with a gun, though.

He had just finished with that when Melanie hurried into the room and said, "One of the men just came to the door and said that riders are coming, fast."

What now? Louis thought. Another attack? More bad news?

He took hold of Melanie's arms and said, "Stay inside. I'll go see what it's about."

"Louis, be careful. Like I told you before, I . . . I don't think I could go on if I lost you, too."

"You're not going to lose anyone," he told her. Taking the Winchester '94 with him, he strode to the front of the house and stepped out onto the porch.

Pearlie was walking quickly toward the house from the bunkhouse. The former foreman carried a Winchester, too, but his was an old Model '73 in .44-40, a long-barreled, heavy repeater. Two holstered revolvers hung from crossed belts buckled around his lean hips.

"You expectin' company?" Pearlie asked as Louis joined him in the ranch yard.

"No, but I'm ready for it if it's trouble." Louis hefted the .30-30.

Pearlie grinned for a second. "You're Smoke's boy, all right."

"Maybe, but I hope it's not like this all the time. This is exhausting!"

That brought a chuckle from the older man.

They stood side by side and waited, but not for long. Within moments, two riders came into view on the trail that led from the main road that ran between Big Rock and Red Cliff. The horsebackers were moving fast, pushing their mounts.

Louis exclaimed in surprise as he spotted long, blond, curly hair tumbling from under one rider's hat. "Good Lord! It's Denny!"

CHAPTER 59

Denny felt like she hadn't slept in days. To be honest, she *hadn't* slept much during the whirlwind journey she and Brice had made from Montana back to Colorado and the Sugarloaf.

They had pushed their mounts as hard as they could on the ride to Stirrup, then caught the first train, fortunately not having to wait long to do so. They had sat up in one of the passenger cars, then changed trains in Chicago and continued sitting up. All the Pullman cars were booked, and there was no way in hell Denny was going to wait to get back home just so she could be more comfortable during the trip.

She knew there was a good chance that whatever the rest of the outlaws were going to do, they had already done it. She and Brice might be too late to help, but on the off chance that they could still get in on the action, Denny wanted to return to the Sugarloaf as quickly as possible.

The first thing she saw as she and Brice galloped toward the ranch house was the pair of men in range clothes waiting to meet them. A shock of recognition went through her as she realized one of them was her brother.

"That's Louis!" she exclaimed. "And he's wearing a gun and carrying a rifle!"

"I reckon something must have happened here, all right," Brice said. "That's Pearlie with him, and it looks like they're ready for trouble."

Denny had seen Louis practicing with guns before, but something was different about him, some sense that he was the real thing.

They reined in and Denny was out of the saddle and off her horse almost before the animal stopped moving. She threw her arms around her brother, Winchester and all, and hugged him.

"Louis, you're all right? I didn't know if you'd be here or not. Those outlaws, they didn't kidnap you?"

"I'm fine," he assured her. "Physically, anyway. Melanie and I got back not long after that gang raided the ranch."

Denny stepped back. "Then they *were* here?"

"Yes." Louis nodded grimly. "And they took Brad."

Denny felt her eyes growing wider with shock. "Brad?" she repeated. "They . . . they kidnapped Brad?"

"Yes. I'm about to go pay them the ransom for him."

Denny struggled to grasp what her brother had just told her, and as she did, the hatred she felt for Steve Markham, even though he was dead, grew even stronger. He had been in on the plan from the beginning, which meant he was partially responsible for anything that happened to Brad.

She wished she could shoot him again, even though that wouldn't do any good.

She was about to demand more details from Louis,

but at that moment her mother and Melanie appeared on the ranch house porch.

"Denise!" Sally called. "Thank God you're all right."

Leaving Brice with Louis and Pearlie, Denny hurried up the steps to the porch and hugged her mother and sister-in-law. She said to Sally, "You're still recovering from that fever, Ma?"

Sally nodded. "I'm all right, just a little weak. That's all. But there's been so much else going on, so many terrible things . . ."

"I know. Louis just told us about Brad." Denny looked at Melanie. "He said he was going to pay some ransom money . . . ?"

"That's what they think," Louis said from the bottom of the steps. He had walked over there with Brice and Pearlie. "They're going to get a surprise, and they won't like it."

Denny's hand fell instinctively to the butt of the Lightning holstered on her hip as she turned toward her brother. "I like the sound of that. Tell me more."

They all went into the parlor, where Louis, with some help from Sally and Pearlie, quickly summarized the events of the past few days. Denny's anger grew as she heard about how Brad had been carried off and three Sugarloaf hands had been killed during the attack. She nodded her head in agreement as Louis explained about the plan to rescue Brad and deliver justice to the outlaws.

"Count me in on that," she declared when Louis was finished. She looked over at Pearlie. "I'm coming with you."

"So am I," Brice put in.

"Glad to have you along, Marshal," Pearlie said.

"I ain't sure about you comin' with us, though, Miss Denny."

"You're forgetting that I've had run-ins with owl-hoots before," she snapped. "Most recently that bunch up in Montana."

Louis said, "I don't think anybody's forgetting that. You've amply demonstrated that you can take care of yourself, Denny. I don't mind you coming along."

She was a little surprised by his attitude. Louis seemed to have changed. "Thanks, Louis." She looked at Sally. "I suppose you're going to argue with me, though."

"No, I wish I could pick up a gun and come with you."

"So do I," Melanie added.

Louis shook his head. "There's no need for either of those things. The two of you should stay here, so you'll be ready to greet Brad when he comes home." He picked up his rifle from the corner where he'd leaned it when he came in and went on. "As for the rest of us, we need to be riding. Denny, Brice, grab some fresh horses. We'll have a hard climb up to that cut, according to what Smoke said."

Yeah, thought Denny as she listened to Louis giving orders, her brother really *had* changed.

She just hoped his heart could keep up with it.

It was a grim-faced group of men who climbed to the high pass not far below the summit of the Wolf's Fang that afternoon. Even in summer, the air was cold at that height, and Smoke was glad he had brought along his sheepskin jacket. They made camp in the pass—a cold camp, since they couldn't risk a fire being seen.

The horses had been left below. The terrain up there was far too rugged for them. Once Brad was safe and the outlaws had been dealt with, some of the men from Pearlie's group could ride around the mountain and retrieve the saddle mounts for Smoke and the others.

With the sun setting behind the mountain, Smoke knew he wouldn't be seen from below if he walked out to the head of the pass on the eastern slope. Ed Magruder joined him, and as they peered down at the steep slopes and sheer drop-offs below them, Smoke pointed out a possible route down to the cowboy from the Ozarks.

"Looks passable, all right," Magruder agreed. "Can you see that ridge from here? The one where they are holed up?"

"Down there," said Smoke, pointing again. "They've built a fire out in the open, because it never occurred to them that someone could be up here to see it."

"Yeah, I spot it now. That's where the kid is, I reckon."

"I'm sure it is," Smoke said. "They'll keep him close until this is all over. It's just not going to end the way they think it is."

Magruder chuckled, then said quickly, "I'm sorry, Smoke. There ain't nothin' funny about any of this, and I know it. All the boys do. But we got to talkin' earlier . . . We've all heard so many stories about you and all the hell-raisin' that took place in this valley fifteen, twenty years ago, and it seemed like things have really tamed down since the turn of the century.

Us younger fellas, we sort of felt like we'd missed out on all the excitement of ridin' for Smoke Jensen. But now it's different, more like the old days. I just wish it hadn't taken some good men gettin' killed and poor little Brad bein' carried off the way he was, to bring those days back to life for a spell."

"Trouble, in one form or another, is always lurking just over the horizon, Ed. That's one thing life has taught me. But it keeps things interesting, I suppose." Smoke smiled. "A fella out in San Francisco once taught me a Chinese curse. 'May you live in interesting times.' I reckon there's a lot of truth to that." He clapped a hand on the cowboy's shoulder. "Let's try to get some sleep. We've got a long climb down in the morning."

CHAPTER 60

The ridge that served as the outlaws' stronghold dropped off sheer on its eastern side. Its western side, the one that backed up to the Wolf's Fang, had a more gradual slope to it, falling to a narrow valley between the ridge and the mountain itself. That valley was a hundred yards wide, with a lot of brush growing there but not many trees. Boulders that had rolled down from the heights clustered in places. All that provided enough cover for their approach, Smoke decided as he looked down from a ledge no more than twenty feet from the ground.

It was late the next morning. Smoke and the other men had started their descent early, before dawn when the sky was just gray enough for them to see what they were doing. Some of the drops were sheer enough that they'd had to lower each other with ropes, the last man leaving it in place. It was a good thing they had brought plenty of lassos along. Smoke had thought they might be needed, and so they were.

It was a nerve-wracking journey, not just because of the perilous descent itself but also the chance that one of the outlaws might start studying the mountain's face at the wrong time and spot the small figures moving lower. That didn't seem to have happened— at least no one had opened fire on them—but the possibility would exist until they were all safely on the ground again and ready to start their attack.

Using hand signals now that they were close, Smoke indicated that Magruder should tie a rope around an outcropping of rock. The cowboy did so, leaning on the strands to test their strength once he was done. Satisfied, he gave Smoke a curt nod. Smoke took hold of the rope in gloved hands and maneuvered himself over the edge. He braced the soles of his boots against the rock and walked down the stone face until he was close enough to let go and drop the last couple of feet to the ground.

He looked up at the ledge and motioned for Magruder to follow him. Then he took the Winchester that had been hanging from a leather sling on his back and catfooted into the nearby brush to scout. The outlaws could have posted a sentry back there, although Smoke thought it was unlikely.

One by one the other men descended until all ten members of the party were on the ground.

So far, so good, thought Smoke as he led them across the valley. When they reached the other side, they would have about seventy-five yards of slope to charge up in order to reach the top of the ridge. If they moved fast enough, they ought to be able to cover most of the distance before they were discovered.

Once that happened, it would be an all-out fight.

As he hunkered behind a boulder near the base of that slope, Smoke took out his pocket watch and flipped it open. Five minutes until noon.

Louis was supposed to ride out onto that bench at straight-up twelve o'clock.

Louis took a deep breath, snapped the gold watch closed, and slid it back into his pocket. The time had come. He heeled his horse into motion, rode the last few yards to the top of the trail, and came out onto the bench. The ridge loomed redly, ominously, on the other side of the level stretch. He glanced up at the rugged rimrock and imagined he could see the brutal outlaws crouched there with their rifles trained on him, even though he actually couldn't. As far as he could tell, no one was up there.

But a saddled and picketed horse was waiting for him, just as the stocky, shotgun-wielding kidnapper had said there would be.

Brad was up there, thought Louis. He couldn't see the boy, but he knew he was there. In his bones and his gut, he could feel Brad's presence.

Louis rode up to the other horse, dismounted, and began transferring the canvas money bags from one saddle to the other. What he was doing *looked* real enough, he thought. When he was finished, he slapped a hand on the saddle for a second and looked up at the ridge as if to say *There. I've done what you wanted*.

Helpless for the moment to do anything else, he untied the horse's lead rope from the picket pin, as he'd been instructed to do. Then he went back to his mount, swung up, and turned the horse to ride back down off the bench.

As soon as he was out of sight, he dug his heels harder into his mount's flanks and started moving faster. There was no time to lose.

* * *

Denny's nervousness communicated itself to her horse. The animal capered skittishly as she tried to hold it under control. Pearlie, sitting his horse at the front of the group with Sheriff Monte Carson, turned his head to look at her.

"Sorry," Denny muttered. "I reckon he's ready to go, just like I am."

"Smoke said for us to wait until the shootin' starts. That'll give the guards at that cut time enough to pull back and help the rest of that bunch of no-good skunks. Besides, Louis ain't here yet."

"Sounds like that might be him coming, though," Brice commented from where he sat his horse beside Denny's.

Denny heard the rapid hoofbeats, too.

A moment later Louis came in sight, riding hard. He reined in and asked, "Nothing yet?"

"Nothing," replied Denny. She saw something wild in her brother's eyes, something she had never seen there before. It was a mixture of anger, fear, and excitement. Anger at the outlaws, certainly, fear for Brad's life, the excitement of knowing that he would be going into battle very soon. It was all new to Louis, if not to Denny, and even though she had experienced such things before, she suspected the same look was in her eyes.

A sudden burst of gunfire from somewhere up above made all of them stiffen in their saddles.

"Let's go," Pearlie barked, and he put his horse into the steep trail that led up through the pines.

* * *

Smoke waved his men forward. Rifles held at the ready, they raced up the slope, darting from brush to rock and out into the open when they had to. As they neared the ridge crest, Smoke heard laughter and shouting and knew the outlaws were celebrating because they believed Louis had just left a fortune in ransom money down below for them.

It wouldn't be long until they found out how wrong they were.

Smoke and the others were only a few yards away when a man suddenly appeared at the top of the slope. Smoke didn't know what errand he was on, but the outlaw stopped short, gaped at them for a split second, and then opened his mouth to yell a warning as he clawed at his holstered gun.

Smoke fired from the hip. The rifle round bored into the outlaw's chest and flung him backward. He never got to raise that shout of alarm, but the sharp crack of Smoke's rifle was more than enough to alert the gang to the fact that something was wrong. *Bad* wrong.

Smoke bounded over the edge and saw the ridge spreading out in front of him. The gang's horses were to his right, penned up in a makeshift rope corral. One man was over there with the animals, while all the others were ranged along the rimrock, about fifty yards from the top of the slope. They whirled around and opened fire.

Smoke's force scattered, spreading out. They were at a disadvantage not only numerically but also because they didn't know where Brad was and had to look for him before they squeezed their triggers. Smoke's keen eyes searched among the kidnappers but didn't see the boy. A bullet whipped past in front of his nose and he pivoted to the right to drill the man who had fired the shot, the outlaw who'd been watching the horses. The man flew back against the rope corral, and the nervous horses inside the enclosure surged against it and knocked him forward again. He fell limply to the ground.

From the corner of his eye, Smoke saw riders galloping in from the left, the end of the ridge where the trail—both trails—came out. Those would be the guards, he thought, and with all hell breaking loose, they had abandoned their posts just as he'd figured they would. He whirled in that direction and with a pair of swift shots blew two outlaws out of their saddles.

The others had barely gotten their guns into action when they were hit from behind, as the group led by Pearlie and Monte Carson boiled through the cut and started blasting them. Smoke's breath caught in his throat as he spotted a familiar figure among the reinforcements, leaning forward in the saddle as the Colt Lightning in her hand cracked wickedly.

Denny had arrived home in time to get herself right in the thick of battle, and Smoke wasn't a bit surprised by that.

"Smo-o-o-o-ke!"

The frightened cry made him spin again. He spotted a small, frantically struggling figure clasped in the arms of a huge owlhoot. With him were the shotgunner from a couple of days earlier and a tall, gaunt man with gray hair and a hawk-like face. The big man held Brad in front of him like a human shield as the trio advanced toward Smoke.

"Call them off!" the gray-haired outlaw yelled. "Call them off or the boy dies!"

That was exactly the situation Smoke hadn't wanted. He'd hoped they could locate Brad and get him to safety as soon as possible after the shooting started. With the boy as a hostage, Smoke had no choice except to shout over the roar of guns, "Hold your fire! Hold your fire!"

Louis heard that order and wanted to cry, "*No!*" He knew his father was right, though. Brad looked tiny and fragile, held up against that behemoth. If those massive arms squeezed, surely they would crush every bone in the youngster's body.

"You're a damned fool, Jensen," the gray-haired outlaw went on. "Did you really think you could get away with double-crossing us?"

"Appears that we came pretty close to it," Smoke replied coolly.

"Not close enough. Was that ransom money real, or was that a trick, too?"

Smoke squared his shoulders. "None of us are going to *pay* you for what you've done, mister. But turn the boy loose and throw down your guns, and you can come down off this ridge alive, anyway."

The outlaw laughed. "Until they march us up the steps to the gallows, you mean. No, nobody's surrendering here unless it's you, Jensen. Let us ride out of here . . . *with* the boy . . . and then we'll be in touch later and try this again. And you'd better pay us the next time."

Brice leaned over in his saddle and whispered to

Denny, but loudly enough for Louis to hear, too, "The way we're bunched together, I reckon I can slip down off my horse without them noticing."

"What good's that going to do?" Denny whispered back.

"Looked like there were enough handholds just below that rimrock so I could work my way along it without any of that bunch seeing me. If I can get behind those three who've got Brad, I can take them by surprise."

"And get him killed," rasped Louis.

"No, not if I move fast enough. I'll grab him away from that big galoot, get him out of the line of fire, and then the rest of you can take it from there."

"It might work," Denny said, "or you might fall to your death, too."

"I'm willing to risk it."

Louis wanted to say that he should be the one to go, to attempt the daring move, but he was practical enough to know that he couldn't pull it off. Brice Rogers stood a chance, though. Despite his youth, he was an experienced lawman and had been in plenty of tight spots before. "All right. Thank you, Brice. Give me a minute to get their attention even more."

He walked his horse forward, causing outlaw guns to swing toward him. More important, all eyes did, too, including those of Smoke, who frowned at him, clearly uncertain what Louis was trying to do.

He dismounted and walked along the ridge until he was standing next to Smoke. Facing the outlaws, Louis said, "I wanted to make a deal with you all along. It was my father here who wouldn't agree and insisted that we try to trick you." He put a sneer on his face. "The high and mighty Smoke Jensen, unable to ever admit that someone got the better of him."

Pearlie gasped and exclaimed, "Boy, what the hell are you sayin'? You can't talk about your pa like that!"

Smoke asked, "Is that really the way you feel, Louis?"

Turning his head just slightly, Louis drooped his right eyelid just enough that he hoped Smoke would notice it. He said coldly, "You're damned right it is. Bradley is my stepson, and I won't have you risking his life any longer." He looked at the trio of outlaws right in front of them and went on. "Whatever arrangement you want to make, I'll agree to it. You can ride out of here, all of you, and I'll pay you whatever you want, as long as you don't harm that boy."

An ugly grin stretched across the gray-haired outlaw's face. "Well, I'm glad to see that one of you Jensens has got some sense."

"How do you want to handle this?" asked Louis. He didn't know where Brice was, how close the lawman might be to making his move. He needed to keep the kidnappers talking a little longer, anyway.

Suddenly the man with the shotgun said, "I don't trust the little pissant, Sam. He's trying to run some sort of windy on us. I say we kill the kid and shoot our way out of here!"

"No!" Louis said. "No, don't hurt him. I swear, I'm not trying to trick you."

Smoke said, "I wash my hands of all this, Louis. You can't make deals with animals like this." His voice took on an even harsher note. "But I should have known you'd take the coward's way out. You've always been like that, you sickly little pipsqueak!"

That was enough to tell Louis that Smoke had

figured out exactly what was going on. He never would have said such a thing if he hadn't been stalling for time just like Louis was. Smoke didn't know what Brice Rogers was attempting to do, but he knew something was in the works.

"And you've always been ashamed of me because I wasn't some notorious gunfighter like you," Louis shot back at his father. "I'm surprised you didn't just drown me like a kitten when I was born! You probably would have if you'd known how I was going to turn out."

"Maybe I should have," Smoke returned through clenched teeth.

The gray-haired outlaw called Sam made a slashing motion with his hand. "Damn it, there's no time for this! All of you drop your guns and back off right now, or I'll tell my friend here to crush that kid like a bug!"

"If we drop our guns, you'll just kill us all," Smoke protested.

"Well . . . I reckon you're just gonna have to take that chance . . ."

Brice Rogers came over the rimrock, scrambling and moving fast, and lunged forward to slam the gun in his hand into the back of the big man's head. It wasn't enough to budge the massive outlaw, but it made his grip on Brad slip for just a second.

Brad squirmed loose and dropped to the ground. Brice reached around the big man, avoiding the sweeping backhand the outlaw swung at him, and grabbed Brad's arm. Hauling Brad with him, Brice rolled toward the edge of the ridge.

"Now!" Smoke shouted.

Louis's hand dived toward the Thunderer on his hip. He was no fast gun, never would be, but as gunthunder welled up and seemed to fill the entire world, he drew with all the speed he could muster and lifted the gun. He saw flame spurt from the muzzle of the gray-haired outlaw's revolver and felt something whip past his ear. Louis had heard enough to know that this man was the architect of the plan that had put his son in such danger, and he felt a fierce satisfaction as he aimed the Thunderer and pulled the trigger.

The gun bucked against his palm and he saw the outlaw reel back a step. The man's gun blasted again. The bullet kicked up dirt and rocks at Louis's feet, but Louis didn't budge. He squeezed the trigger again and blood flew from the outlaw's side. He stumbled back, tried to catch himself, and screamed terribly as he failed and went over the edge of the cliff.

Smoke slammed a couple of slugs into the shotgunner's midsection. The man doubled over and jerked both triggers, but the twin loads of buckshot didn't do anything except tear up the ground right in front of him. He collapsed on top of the scattergun as he dropped it. Fred Judson's death was avenged.

That left the huge man who'd had hold of Brad. He didn't reach for his gun but charged forward with his arms outstretched, bellowing like a bull. Smoke and Louis fired at the same time, followed an instant later by Denny, Pearlie, and Monte Carson. All five slugs pounded into the man's chest and slowed him but didn't stop him. He managed to take several more steps before death caught up with his nerves and muscles. He sagged slowly toward the ground, going down like a slow-motion avalanche until he was finally sprawled on his face, unmoving.

Louis looked wildly for Brad and Brice Rogers. He didn't see them anywhere and remembered that Brice had been rolling toward the brink with Brad. Had they gone over accidentally . . . ?

No! There they were, rising from behind a rock at the very edge of the ridge. Brad broke loose and dashed toward Louis, practically leaping into the arms Louis stretched out to him. Louis held the boy tightly against his chest as Brad sobbed in relief and reaction to all the terror he had gone through.

The emotions going through Louis shook him so much that it was several moments before he realized all the shooting had died away. He blinked through some tears of his own as he glanced around and saw that the combined forces of the Sugarloaf had wiped out the rest of the outlaws.

A few feet away, Denny had dismounted and threw her arms around Brice. "I . . . I was scared you'd fall off and break your neck!"

He grinned. "I've always been good at climbing rocks. It didn't amount to much . . . as long as I didn't look down."

Smoke pouched the still-smoking iron he held and put one hand on his son's shoulder, the other on his daughter's. "Let's go home."

Turn the page for an exciting preview!

WILLIAM W. JOHNSTONE
and J. A. JOHNSTONE

DARK IS THE NIGHT
A DEATH & TEXAS WESTERN

**YOU ARE NOW ENTERING TEXAS.
SAY YOUR PRAYERS.**
*Bestselling authors William and J. A. Johnstone bring
the "wild" back to the Wild Wild West with their boldest
hero yet. Meet Cullen McCabe, a Lone Star sheriff
who has nothing to lose—and time to kill . . .*

DEATH ISN'T PRETTY
There are a million ways to die in the great state of
Texas. And on the lawless streets of New Hope, the odds
are even worse. Once the home of Comanche, the region
has been up for grabs since the Red River War drove off
the natives. Now it's a magnet for settlers looking for
cheap land, merchants looking to exploit its resources—
and outlaws looking for a place to hide in between
robbing and killing. With shoot-outs and showdowns
nightly occurrences, it's one of the deadliest places
on earth. And the governor ain't happy about it.
He wants to clean up the town. He wants to wipe away
the scum. And he knows just the man to do it . . .

Enter Cullen McCabe. A small-town sheriff turned
special agent, McCabe doesn't care what he has to do—
or who he has to kill—to rid this hellhole of every
rustler, robber, and ruthless cuss in sight. Especially
the notorious Viper Gang . . .

Look for *Dark Is the Night*, on sale now.

C

McCabe received a wire
Michael O'Brien in Aus
what the meetings w
strong was so c
the govern
had deal
ton

Leon Armstrong tur_____ _____ he heard the door open to discover the now-familiar image of Cullen McCabe in the doorway. Armstrong hurried to the telegraph window to fetch a telegram from the drawer. "Mornin', Mr. McCabe," he greeted him.

"Mornin'," Cullen returned. "Mr. Thornton, over at the store, said you have a telegram for me."

"That's right, I do," Armstrong said. "It came in day before yesterday. I told Ronald to let you know if you came into the store, in case I didn't see you." He handed an envelope to Cullen and stood waiting, hoping Cullen might comment on the message. When he failed to do so, Armstrong commented, "We like to deliver telegrams as soon as we can, but with you not living in town, nothing we can do but hold it till we see you."

"No problem," Cullen said as he folded the telegram and stuck it in his pocket.

Armstrong was itching inside with curiosity about the quiet man whom no one in the little town of Two Forks knew anything about, except him. And the only thing he knew was that, from time to time, Cullen

asking him to report to
_____n. The telegrams never said
_____ere about, and the reason Arm-
_____rious was the fact that O'Brien was
_____'s aide. Of course, Ronald Thornton
_____ngs with McCabe, but according to Thorn-
_____hey always consisted of a minimum of words to
place an order for supplies. The only noticeable difference in the size of his orders was whenever they
came after he had received one of these telegrams
from the governor's office. And as Thornton had
predicted, when Cullen returned to his store, after
picking up his telegram, he placed a larger order for
supplies than he normally did. Being the speculator
that Thornton was, he guessed that the quiet man of
few words had gotten another notice to travel.

When Cullen had completed his order, Thornton
thanked him for the business, then commented,
"From the size of that order, I'd figure you were fixin'
to take a little trip."

"Is that so?" Cullen replied, and gathered up his
purchases without further comment.

"I can give you a hand with those," Thornton offered.

"Thanks just the same," McCabe said, "but it's no
bother. I'll just make a couple of trips. That way, you
won't have to stand out there holdin' 'em while I
pack 'em in the sacks on my packhorse." As he said,
he left half of the supplies on the counter while he rearranged his packs, then returned to get the rest as
Clara Thornton came into the store. "Ma'am," he
said politely as he passed her on his way out.

When McCabe was out the door and in no danger

of hearing him, Thornton greeted his wife. "He's on the road again," he said.

"Did he tell you that?" Clara asked, every bit as curious about the man as was her husband.

"He didn't have to," Thornton insisted. "I could tell by the order he placed. I knew when Leon said he had another one of those telegrams from the governor that McCabe would be gettin' ready to travel."

"Huh," Clara snorted. "Maybe he just ain't plannin' to come into town for a while," she offered sarcastically. "I declare, you and Leon Armstrong will have everybody in town thinkin' Cullen McCabe is some kinda mystery man, just because he doesn't talk much."

"Is that so?" Thornton replied, standing at the front window now. "Then how come he's headin' straight to the blacksmith?"

"Maybe he needs something from Graham Price," Clara suggested, again sarcastically. "Why does anybody go to the blacksmith?" She walked back to the front window to stand beside her husband to watch Cullen approach Graham Price's forge. "You and Leon oughta take a lesson from him, so you wouldn't gossip so much."

"You're just as curious as I am," Thornton replied. "Don't try to make out like you ain't."

The object of Thornton's curiosity led his horses up the street and tied them at the rail in front of the blacksmith shop. Graham Price looked up from a wagon rim he was hammering out on his anvil. When he saw Cullen, he paused for a moment to say, "Howdy. Give me a minute and I'll be right with you." Cullen nodded, and Price continued to hammer out a section in the rim before dunking it in a barrel of water beside his anvil. "Yes, sir," he said then. "Your name's McCabe, ain't it? What can I do for you?"

"I'm thinkin' Jake here needs some new shoes," Cullen said. "Can you take care of him this mornin'? I'm gonna have to take a little trip sooner than I expected. If you can't, I'll . . ."

That was as far as he got before Price interrupted. "No problem a-tall," he said. "I can get right on it, if you wanna wait. It'll take me a little while. Have you got someplace else you've gotta go while you're in town?"

"I have," Cullen answered. He didn't expound on it, but he had planned to have himself a big breakfast at the dining room next to the hotel on this trip to town. It was something he had never treated himself to in Two Forks, and he figured he'd see if they had a decent cook. "I'll leave both horses here, but I think I'll take most of that load off my packhorse. No sense in makin' him stand around with all that on his back."

"You can just put it over in the shade of that tree," Price said, nodding toward a large oak at the back of his shop. "I'll get started on your horse right away."

"Much obliged," Cullen said, and led the horse to the back, where he relieved it of most of the heavier sacks. That done, he walked up the street to the hotel and the Two Forks Kitchen beside it.

"Mornin'," Porter Johnson greeted him when he walked in the door.

"Am I too late to get some breakfast?" Cullen asked.

"Almost," Johnson replied, "but Gracie ain't throwed out everything yet. She's still got a little pancake batter left and we've got plenty of eggs and bacon. Set yourself down and I'll go tell her to rustle you up something." He started for the kitchen, then paused. "Pancakes, bacon, and eggs all right with you?" When Cullen said that would suit him fine if the eggs were scrambled, Johnson continued to the kitchen. When he returned, he was carrying two cups of coffee. "Mind if I sit down with you?"

"Don't mind at all," Cullen said. "I was afraid I'd gotten here too late to catch breakfast." He had a feeling that the owner of the Kitchen was curious to find out more about him.

Johnson placed one of the cups before Cullen and sat down at the table. He didn't take long to confirm Cullen's suspicions. "Your name's McCabe, ain't it?" Cullen nodded. "I've seen you come into town a time or two," Johnson said, "but I believe this is the first time you've come in here to eat."

"That's a fact," Cullen answered simply, and tried a sip of the hot coffee.

"Ronald Thornton says you've got a place somewhere down the river," Johnson went on, determined to get some information on the solemn man. "You got a family? We're always glad to welcome new families to Two Forks."

"Nope, no family," was Cullen's short reply. He could sense Johnson's impatience, but he was not inclined to make small talk as a rule, and specifically not in Two Forks. The less people knew about him here, the better. His rough little cabin downriver from the town was not in an easy spot to find, and it served his purposes when he needed some peace and quiet between jobs. After a while in the solitude he preferred, however, he was usually ready to take on the governor's next assignment for him. So he was gratified to discover there was a telegram waiting for him when he came into town today.

"You don't strike me as a farmer," Johnson commented. "You in the cattle business?"

"Nope," Cullen answered, then sat back to give Gracie room to set a plate on the table before him.

"You're lucky you came in when you did," the stocky gray-haired woman said. "Porter came in the kitchen just when I was fixin' to empty that batter into the hog's bucket. So them's the last of the pancakes. Big feller like you might want more. If you do, you'll have to settle for cold biscuits."

"I'm sure that stack is plenty," Cullen said. "I 'preciate you goin' to the trouble. They look mighty good."

Johnson waited for Gracie to back away before continuing his questioning. "You ain't farmin' and you ain't raisin' cattle. What is your line of business?"

"Just one thing and another, I reckon," Cullen replied.

"You don't talk much, do you?"

"I reckon I've already talked a lot more since I sat down here than I figure I need to," Cullen said. He was saved from further interrogation by Gracie O'Hara.

"Porter, why in the world don't you let the poor man eat his breakfast?" She stood, hands on hips, shaking her head. "How's that coffee, honey?" she asked Cullen. "You need some more?"

"No, ma'am, not just yet."

In spite of Gracie's reproach, Johnson was about to continue, but was interrupted when the door opened and another customer walked in. Glancing up at Porter's face, Cullen detected an obvious expression of irritation as he pushed his chair back and got to his feet. "Sonny, what are you doin' back in here? Sheriff Woods told you not to come back here anymore. You still ain't ever paid me the money to fix that table you busted up, and you was supposed to do that as soon as you got outta jail."

"I'll pay you the money when I get it," Sonny said. "Right now, I've only got enough to eat some breakfast. And that stack of flapjacks that feller's eatin' suits my taste this mornin'."

"You're too late for breakfast," Johnson said. "This feller here just made it before Gracie cleaned up the kitchen and started workin' on dinner."

"If you can feed him, you can feed me," Sonny replied. "You owe me more than the trouble it takes to cook some flapjacks. After you went cryin' to the sheriff about that little ruckus with them two cowboys, he locked me up for two nights." He aimed a sassy smile in Gracie's direction, standing near the kitchen door. "Get your sloppy old ass in there and cook me some flapjacks."

"I ain't got no more batter," Gracie replied calmly. "Them's the last of it."

"You lyin' old . . ." Sonny started, then stopped and eyed Cullen for a few moments, who seemed to be making an obvious attempt to ignore him. He grinned, thinking Cullen's attention to his breakfast was really an attempt not to cause him any reason to come after him. "Never mind, old woman," Sonny said, "I'll just have them that feller's fixin' to eat. Bring me a clean plate."

Cullen had hoped it wouldn't come to this, but evidently, he was getting an unwelcome introduction to the town bully. He put his knife and fork down and turned his attention to the smirking young man. "What's your name, friend?"

"None of your damn business," Sonny replied, still sneering defiantly, "and I sure as hell ain't your friend."

"His name's Sonny Tice," Gracie volunteered, "but it oughta be Sonny Trouble."

Cullen nodded in response, then turned back to him. "All right, Sonny, it appears to me that you ain't ever been taught how to talk to ladies. So, you owe this lady an apology for your rough language to her. And you also don't know it ain't polite to interfere with folks eatin' their breakfast. Just lookin' at you, I'd guess you went to the saloon before you decided to come here lookin' for breakfast. So the best thing for you is to go back to the saloon and tell them you're hungry. Most saloons can fix you up with something to eat, even at this time of day. It won't be as good as these pancakes I'm fixin' to eat, but maybe it'll do till you get sobered up some."

Sonny was struck dumb for a few moments, astonished to hear the calm scolding coming from the stranger. Finally, he found his voice again. "Why, you dumb son of a bitch," he blurted. "You're fixin' to get your ass whupped."

Still calm, Cullen shook his head impatiently. "There you go again. You haven't heard a word I've been tryin' to tell you. You're gonna have to get outta here now." He paused. "After you apologize to the lady."

"Like hell I will!" Sonny responded, and reached for the .44 on his hip. Anticipating his move, Cullen grabbed Porter Johnson's coffee cup and threw the contents into Sonny's face, coming up out of his chair at the same time. When Sonny reeled, Cullen drove his shoulder into him, driving him backward to land on the floor. Still trying to draw his pistol, even though flat on his back, Sonny looked up at the formidable man standing above him, his weapon in his hand.

"Is it worth dyin' over?" Cullen asked calmly when Sonny started to pull his .44. Sonny realized at once that he had no chance. Scowling at Cullen, he raised his hands in defeat.

"All right," Sonny said. "You got the jump on me this time. I'm goin'." He started to roll over and get up from the floor.

"Hold it!" Cullen ordered, and cocked his Colt .44. "Apologize to the lady first."

Straining to contain his anger and embarrassment, Sonny nevertheless said, "I'm sorry, Gracie." He glared back at Cullen. "Now can I get outta this dump?"

"Yep, and when you think about it some, maybe you'll change the way you treat people," Cullen said, and turned to go back to his chair.

"McCabe!" Gracie screamed. Cullen looked back to see Sonny standing in the doorway, his pistol aimed at him. There was no time to think. He fired at almost the same time Sonny pulled the trigger and felt the sting of the bullet that grazed his upper arm. About to fire a second shot, he hesitated when Sonny's gun fell from his hand and he dropped to his knees, already dead from the shot in his chest. With his eyes seeming to be staring into the next life, Sonny remained on his knees for a few moments before he collapsed onto his side. Cullen returned his

.44 to his holster and remarked calmly, "Sorry about that. There wasn't much else I could do."

Stunned, Porter Johnson could do nothing but stare until Gracie broke his trance. "You're shot!" she exclaimed to Cullen.

He looked down at his arm. "I reckon I am," he said, "but it ain't much, just a graze."

"You might need to see Doc Taylor. Better let me take a look at it," she said. When Cullen said it was nothing, she insisted. "Slip outta your jacket and take your shirt off." He could see there was no use in arguing with her, so he let her take a look at the wound. As he had said, it was a minor creasing of his skin, doing more damage to his shirt and jacket than it did to his arm. She led him into the kitchen and cleaned the wound with a wet cloth before tying a clean cloth around his arm.

He was still in the process of buttoning the shirt when Clyde Allen, the owner of the hotel, walked in with the sheriff. Seeing Johnson still standing there looking at the body of Sonny Tice in the doorway, the sheriff exclaimed, "What the hell, Porter? What happened here?"

"That ain't my doin'," Johnson replied. "He drew down on McCabe and McCabe done for him."

"McCabe?" Sheriff Woods asked, "Who's McCabe?"

"That would be me," Cullen said, coming from the kitchen when he heard them talking.

Not waiting for Cullen to offer any explanation, Gracie spoke up. "That foulmouthed bully finally ran up against somebody who wasn't afraid of him. He waited till McCabe turned his back and then he drew down on him. He got what he deserved."

Calvin Woods turned back to Johnson. "Is that what happened, Porter?" Johnson replied that it was, but he went into more detail, describing the incident as it actually happened with emphasis on the quick reactions demonstrated by Cullen. After listening to his accounting, the sheriff said, "I reckon it was bound to happen. Sooner or later, he was gonna pick on the wrong man." He looked at Cullen. "Well, looks like there ain't no doubt it was self-defense, McCabe. What's your first name?" When Cullen replied, Woods asked, "When I go back to my office, I don't reckon I'll find any paper on Cullen McCabe, will I?"

Cullen smiled. "Reckon not."

"I'll tell Walter Creech to pick up the body," Woods said. "Then I suppose I'll have to ride out to tell old man Jesse Tice his youngest son is dead. That ain't something I look forward to. He ain't gonna take it too well, so if I was you, I'd make myself scarce, and I mean like right now. Sonny's got two brothers and his death ain't likely to set too well with 'em. And I don't want another shoot-out in my town, so the best thing for you to do is to get outta town."

"I'll be glad to," Cullen said. "Just as soon as Graham Price shoes my horse, I'll be on my way. He ain't likely finished yet, and I've got some pancakes that are pretty cold by now, but I might as well eat 'em, since I've gotta wait, anyway."

Woods reacted with a look of disbelief. "Mister, I don't think you're catchin' my drift. I'm tryin' to save your life. Those Tice boys are gonna come lookin' for the man that killed their brother. That ain't a guess, and I ain't sure I'll be able to protect you. It'll make my job a helluva lot easier if you ain't here."

"I 'preciate what you're tellin' me, Sheriff, and like I said, soon as Price finishes with my horse, I'll be on my way. I don't want trouble any more than you do."

Woods shook his head, exasperated with Cullen's apparent lack of urgency. "I'll take my time ridin' out to Tice's place, but I damn sure have to tell the old man about it pretty soon. I'd rather not have him find out on his own and wanna shoot up the town over it. Gimme a hand, Porter, and we'll drag Sonny out the door, then I'll go get Walter to pick him up." Cullen sat back down at the table to finish his breakfast. Clyde Allen, mute to that point, said he would help. Cullen heard Woods mumbling to them as they carried the heavy carcass outside. "It's bad enough havin' gunfights in the saloon without us startin' to have 'em in the dinin' room."

Gracie came to stand beside Cullen. "Sorry 'bout your pancakes. I'm warmin' up some syrup on the stove. Maybe that'll help 'em a little bit."

"Much obliged," he said. "How far is Tice's place from here?"

"'Bout four miles or so," she said. "Calvin was tellin' you the truth about the Tice boys."

"I believed him," Cullen assured her, "but I can't go till the blacksmith's through with my horse. Maybe it'll take the sheriff a little while to go out to tell Tice. And it'll take Tice a little while to come back here lookin' for me. And I ain't had my breakfast yet, so I might as well eat."

She had to chuckle. Shaking her head, she said, "McCabe, you're one helluva strange man. I wonder if you care whether you live or die."

"I don't," he said softly. She chuckled again, with no way of knowing the truthfulness of his short reply, or that it was the primary reason he was the one man so qualified to do the job the governor hired him to do.

CHAPTER 2

It was a little before noon when Cullen picked up his horses at the blacksmith's shop. As he had promised Sheriff Woods, he rode straight out of town, taking the road north to Austin. It was a full day's ride to that city, so he planned to arrive there before noon the following day. Gracie had said it was four miles out to Jesse Tice's farm. That should give him enough time to put a good bit of distance between him and the Tice boys by the time they rode into town. Had he been a little more thorough when looking into the situation, he might have asked her in which direction the Tice farm lay. As he was to find, Jesse Tice's farm was north of Two Forks about four miles, just off the road to Austin. He got his first clue when he met Sheriff Woods on his way back to town.

"McCabe!" Woods blurted when he pulled up before him. "Where the hell are you goin'?"

"Austin," Cullen answered matter-of-factly.

"I thought you had a place south of town somewhere," Woods exclaimed. "Are you just lookin' for trouble?"

It took only a moment for Cullen to figure out why

the sheriff was upset with him. "You're fixin' to tell me the Tice place is north of town, right?" Woods didn't answer, but his expression of disbelief was sufficient to tell Cullen he had guessed correctly. "Right off this road, I expect," Cullen continued, and received a nod of confirmation. "Are they right behind you?"

"No," Woods said, "but they won't be long in comin'. They're about as riled up as you would expect. I told 'em there were two witnesses to the fight, and Sonny pulled his weapon first. But it didn't do much to settle the old man down. I warned 'em that I didn't want any trouble in Two Forks over this, and Jesse said he was comin' in to get his son. I told him there ain't no law against that." He paused to look behind him before continuing. "But, mister, you'd best get movin' now. You ain't even a mile from the trail that leads to the Tice farm. If you don't wanna meet Jesse and his two boys, you'd best let that bay feel your heels."

"Pleasure talkin' to ya, Sheriff," Cullen responded, then promptly took the sheriff's advice and nudged Jake into a brisk lope. He had no desire to thin the Tice family out any more than he had already, so he held Jake to that pace until he was past a trail leading off toward the river. He guessed that to be the trail to the Tice farm and he continued on for another couple of miles before he reined Jake back to a walk. He counted himself fortunate to have avoided a meeting with Jesse Tice and his two sons. He hoped that he hadn't caused trouble for Sheriff Woods and the folks in Two Forks. He had no regrets for the killing of Sonny Tice beyond the trouble it might cause them. Sonny had made his choice and he paid for it with his life. What Cullen did regret, however, was the sudden notoriety cast upon him in a town where he didn't exist, as far as most of the population had been concerned. Prior to this day, he had only an occasional business relationship with Ronald Thornton and Leon Armstrong, and that was the way he preferred to keep it. Now he was known by half a dozen people. *I wonder if I should have let Sonny have the damn pancakes,* he thought, but decided it would have only emboldened the young bully to challenge him further. *What's done is done,* he told himself. *The only thing for me to do is report to Michael O'Brien at the governor's office and get on with whatever he's called me in for.*

Sheriff Woods saw them ride into town, their horses laboring as they pulled them to a hard stop in front of Walter Creech's shop. He left his office and hurried over to intercept them. Seeing the sheriff, Jesse Tice demanded, "Where's my son?"

"Just like I told you, Mr. Tice," Woods replied. "I had Walter Creech take care of the body, so it wouldn't come to no harm. He'll turn him over to you. There ain't no charge or nothin'."

"Damn right there ain't," Jesse said. "Now, where's the son of a bitch that shot him?" he asked as Creech walked out of his shop, having heard the commotion.

"You're welcome to take your son, Mr. Tice," Creech said. "I took the liberty to clean away some of the blood. It was about all I could do for him."

"Go in there and see," Tice told one of his sons, and Samson, the eldest, immediately obeyed. Tice turned back to the sheriff and demanded again, "Where's the son of a bitch that shot him?"

"I can't say," Woods answered. "He left town right after the gunfight, so I don't know which way he went."

"He went out by the stable, Sheriff." Surprised, Woods turned to see Walter Creech's six-year-old son pointing toward the north road to Austin, the road that Tice had just ridden into town. All attention turned immediately to the boy, who stood there grinning, still pointing north, thinking he had been helpful.

Creech quickly turned him around and sent him back inside the shop. "Go back to the kitchen with your mama," he told him. "Go on, now," he prodded when the boy was reluctant to leave. A glance in Woods's direction told him the sheriff was not pleased with the boy's efforts to help.

"I just rode in on that road!" Jesse Tice bellowed. "How long has he been gone?"

"I don't know," Woods answered. "He lit out right after the gunfight," he lied.

Samson came back out the door at that moment, so Jesse waited to hear what he had to say. "Sonny's in there," Samson reported. "He's laid out on a table with a sheet over him."

"Where was he shot?" Jesse asked.

His son responded with a blank expression, then answered, "In the Two Forks Kitchen is what they said."

"No, you jackass," Jesse retorted. "Where was the bullet hole?"

"Oh." Samson paused. "Right square in the middle of his chest."

"Like the witnesses said," the sheriff was quick to

point out, "Sonny was facin' the man who shot him. It was a gunfight, fair and simple." He declined to mention the part when Sonny had attempted to shoot Cullen in the back, thinking that might not set too well with the grieving father. To give the old man a little bit of satisfaction, he said, "Sonny got off a shot, grazed the other fellow's arm."

Jesse considered that for a moment, then said, "You ain't never told me that feller's name. What does he call hisself, this hotshot gunslinger?"

"I don't know that that's important," Woods stammered. "The main thing is he's gone from here to who knows where."

"I got a right to know who killed my boy!" Jesse stated forcefully.

"Cullen McCabe," Woods blurted, when all three Tice men dropped their hands to rest on the handles of their guns. "But he's long gone now," he said, in an attempt to derail the old man's thoughts of vengeance. "Here comes Jim Tilly," he said, nodding toward the owner of the stable, walking toward them. "I had him keep Sonny's horse for you. I reckon you wanna put Sonny's body on his horse and take him home now."

"I reckon that can wait," Jesse replied. "I'll get Sonny and his horse as soon as we get back. A man shoots my son has to answer to me. Get mounted, boys." Samson and Joe were quick to climb into their saddles. Without another word, Jesse wheeled his horse and led his two sons out the north road to Austin.

Left to puzzle over their departure, the three men involved looked at one another helplessly. Walter Creech was the first to speak. "Well, I never . . . What am I supposed to do with the body? There ain't no tellin' when he'll be back for it."

Jim Tilly shook his head in wonder. "Well, I reckon I'll have to feed his horse." He smiled at Walter. "I don't reckon you'll have to do that with the body." He laughed at his joke, but the other two didn't join him.

"I hope McCabe ain't wastin' no time," Woods said. "I tried to hold Tice back as much as I could, but my jurisdiction ends at the city limits. Ain't nothin' I can do to help him outside of town."

Unaware that he had a three-man posse on his tail, Cullen was intent upon creating some distance between him and Two Forks, nonetheless. It always paid to be cautious, but he figured if Jesse Tice was looking for him, he would likely go downriver, hoping to find his cabin. If he was lucky, maybe Tice wouldn't find his cabin. He had left nothing in it that he couldn't afford to lose. He never did when he was going to be gone even for as long as a day. That was the reason he could decide to ride on to Austin when he got O'Brien's telegram, instead of having to return to his cabin.

It was only a full day's ride to Austin from Two Forks, but he had gotten a late start, so he would ride until dark and camp overnight, then arrive at the governor's office before noon tomorrow. He already had a spot in mind, a creek about twenty miles from Austin, where he had camped before. As he had estimated, the sun was settling down behind the trees guarding the creek when he approached it. A whinny from Jake told him that the bay was ready to take a rest. "I reckon we could both use a little rest," he told the horse as he turned him off the road and walked him upstream about forty yards to a small grassy opening. After relieving his horses of their burdens, he let them go to the water before he went about the business of a fire and supper.

He settled for beef jerky and coffee on this night. He had treated himself to a big breakfast late that morning, although his pancakes had been allowed to get cold. And he would most likely buy a meal in Austin tomorrow, so jerky and coffee should do for tonight. When he had finished his supper, he let his fire die down to no more than a warm glow. It was not a cold night and there was no use to build up a fire that would announce his presence to anyone passing in the night. Normally, if he knew someone was trying to track him, he would take precautions to keep from being jumped in his bedroll, maybe roll up a dummy blanket near the fire while he found a place to hide. He gave it some thought, still of the opinion that, if Tice and his sons went after him, they would more than likely head south of Two Forks, looking for his cabin, instead of heading north. In view of that, he figured the odds were against their catching up with him before he got to Austin in the morning. That would be the time to be extra careful. With that thought in mind, he poked the fire up a little, so it would be easier to start up again in the morning, then he turned in, planning to start early the next day.

Although they pushed their horses hard, Jesse and his sons were making a slow process of their pursuit of Cullen. It was too dark to follow any tracks on the well-traveled road to Austin. Determined to catch up with him, however, Jesse continued on into the night, stopping at every creek and stream to send his two sons to look for a camp, Joe upstream and Samson downstream. It was the only way he could be sure they didn't pass by McCabe's camp in the darkness, and he naturally assumed his son's killer would have to stop for the night. It was the third such search that produced results. Joe came back to the road to announce, "I found him, Papa! 'Bout thirty-five or forty yards up the creek. I woulda shot him, but he's kinda curled up against a tree, and I was afraid if I missed, he'da found some cover."

"You done right," Jesse said, having already decided that he should have the first shot at his son's killer. "Tie these horses here, and we'll all three slip up on him. Samson, you cross over to the other side. Me and Joe will come at him on this side. Don't nobody get too trigger-happy and shoot before we all get close enough. I wanna make sure there ain't no chance we'll miss, so watch for my signal. If I wave my hand at you, just stay where you are until you hear me shoot. Then you can cut loose." All three experienced hunters, they took to the banks of the creek and moved quietly upstream toward the sleeping man.

When they were within about fifteen yards of the camp, Jesse signaled a halt. He was now able to understand why Joe had not chanced a shot. Their target had spread his blanket up close around the base of a sizable tree, in effect, giving himself protection against anyone sneaking in to take a shot at his back. *Pretty slick*, Jesse thought, *but it don't protect him from the front.* "We need to cross over to the other side with Samson," he said to Joe. He waved his arm back and forth several times before Samson saw his signal and waved back to signal he was waiting.

Samson looked back when he heard them coming up behind him. "What's the matter?" he whispered.

"There ain't no clear shot comin' up on him on that side," his father answered. "But he's wide open from this side."

"Where's his horses?" Samson asked. "I don't see no horses."

"Most likely in that grass on the other side of the trees. Make sure you don't shoot that way," Jesse cautioned. "We can always use a couple of good horses. We'll wade across the creek before we start shootin'. Be careful and don't go splashin' across and wake him up before we're ready." Eager to begin the execution, they carefully entered the thigh-deep water and pushed silently across, their rifles ready. After advancing undetected to within ten yards of their sleeping victim, Jesse pulled the trigger of his Henry and set off a barrage of .44 slugs that ripped the unprotected target as well as the tree trunk to splinters. "That's enough!" Jesse shouted when the sudden silence signaled that all three magazines were empty. With a hoot and holler from Joe and Samson, the three Tice men hurried up the bank to witness the damage. Only seconds later, they were stopped cold to stare at the bundle of tree branches wrapped in an old blanket, now shot to pieces. "Watch out!" Jesse blurted, trying to look in every direction at once. "He's tricked us! Get back to the creek!"

Looking wildly from side to side, expecting bullets

to start flying, both sons ran back to the creek and the cover of the bank. Two steps ahead of them, their father hunkered down under the creek bank, desperately searching the darkness enveloping the creek. "Where the hell is he?" Joe asked frantically while hurrying to reload the magazine on his rifle, dropping several cartridges in his haste.

"This don't make no sense," Jesse mumbled, then ordered, "Get back to the horses! He's up to somethin'." He didn't have to repeat it. They ran back down the creek bank, recklessly crashing through berry bushes and laurel branches, not at all in the stealthy manner used in their advance upon the camp minutes before. "Keep your eyes peeled!" Jesse called out unnecessarily. When he arrived mere seconds behind his two sons, it was to find them standing dumbfounded in the little gap where they had left the horses. But there were no horses. "What the . . ." Jesse started, then looked around him frantically, thinking it wasn't the right place.

"He stole the horses!" Samson whined. He and his brother started searching the bushes in a wide circle. "This is where we left 'em." He turned to his father. "What are we gonna do?"

Already working on that, Jesse said, "We're gonna find us a good spot to protect ourselves 'cause he'll be comin' after us, sure as hell." They started combing the bank at once, looking for a spot they could defend from all directions, and hopefully, one that would not permit McCabe to get too close without being seen. Thinking they had very little time to find that place, they quickly settled for a deep gully close to the edge of the water. With little room to spare, they hunkered down in the gully to await the attack they were sure was coming. Their rifles reloaded, they sat facing in three different directions, their eyes searching the dark shadows under the trees. Still, there was no sign of attack. Hours passed with not a sound from the trees beyond that of a whisper of a breeze that tickled the leaves of the trees along the creek bank.

The first rays of the new day caused Samson, who was facing the east, to blink as the trees and bushes began to take shape and separate from the veil of darkness of the night just past. As he stared, bleary-eyed from the night of constant vigilance, he suddenly detected movement in a stand of berry bushes. Quick to react, he raised his rifle and fired, startling his father and his brother into action as well. "I got him! I got him!" Samson bellowed. "I saw him drop!"

"Be careful, damn it!" Jesse warned when both sons started to scramble out of the gully. "You mighta hit him and you mighta missed. He might be playin' possum."

"I can see him where he fell!" Samson exclaimed. "He's still layin' in the bushes. He ain't moved."

"You be careful," his father repeated. "He might be tryin' to pull a trick on us. Spread out," he ordered when they left the protection of the gully. "You see the first little wiggle, cut down on him."

They continued to advance, slowly and cautiously, halfway expecting McCabe to suddenly spring up and start blazing away. When within several yards of the bushes, it became apparent that Samson had been right when he claimed he'd shot him. Although still dark in the shadows of the trees, they could make out the motionless body, and it showed no signs of moving. On a signal from Jesse, they suddenly parted the bushes to thrust their rifles through, ready to fire a volley into the carcass of a young deer. "Damn!" Jesse cursed, and paused to look around him as if expecting to see someone laughing at their foolishness. He dropped to one knee in an effort not to present such an obvious target. Joe and Samson did the same, taking the cue from their father. "What are we gonna do, Papa?" Samson asked.

Jesse didn't have an answer for him, so he took a long moment to try to come up with one. He feared that he and his sons were caught in an ambush, but he couldn't understand why McCabe didn't spring it. He had killed Sonny—what was he waiting for now? "We need to find our horses," he finally decided. "We find them and we'll most likely find him. He musta got in behind us and took our horses back where his are tied." Looking into the faces of his two sons, he could see they were still uncertain, so he reminded them, "He still ain't but one man against three of us. We've just gotta find where he's hidin', and I'm bettin' that's back there on the other side of his camp where he had his horses."

Once again, they followed the creek back to the campsite. Approaching it cautiously, they found no one there, so they continued on past the line of trees to the prairie beyond where they had figured his horses were. There was no sign of him or the horses. It was now to the point where all three Tice men were not only confused, they were uncertain about what was happening to them. McCabe had to be playing games with them, but for what purpose? "That son of a bitch has found him a hole to hide in," Jesse finally announced.

"It must be a big hole," Joe commented, "if he's got all the horses in it with him."

"He couldn'ta got very far from here," Jesse said. "We've just got to find him." They started a search then, up one side of the creek and down the other, checking out every likely place to hide all the horses. The sun was high in the sky when it finally registered with them. "He stole our horses and took off." The reality of it struck with the force of a sledgehammer: while they were sneaking up on his camp to kill him, he had simply circled behind them, taken their horses, and ridden away in the darkness. Left on foot, twenty miles from the town of Austin, and more than that from home, they were helpless to do anything about it. Their only option was to walk back to their farm, which was about a twenty-five-mile hike. In any case, it made no sense to start out for Austin, even presuming that was where McCabe was heading. They would need money and horses for that, two items they were now short of.

Both sons stood gaping at their father while he was obviously trying to think until Samson asked, "What are we gonna do, Papa?"

Jesse cocked an eye in his direction, as if irritated by the question. "What the hell do you think? We're gonna start walkin'. He skunked us good and proper and there ain't nothin' else we can do."

"I'm hungry," Joe complained, "and that's a long walk without somethin' in my belly."

When Samson said he was hungry, too, Jesse said, "I reckon we'd best go back and butcher that deer you shot. We might as well have us a good breakfast before we start for home." Three dejected-looking avengers turned and walked back along the creek to the spot where the deer was killed. To a man of Jesse Tice's violent nature, it was just as painful to have been so obviously outfoxed as it would have been to have gotten shot by the man who killed his son. He vowed to store the name Cullen McCabe in his memory and hope for the opportunity to cross his path again one day.

Connect with

Visit us online at
KensingtonBooks.com

to read more from your favorite authors, see books
by series, view reading group guides, and more.

for sneak peeks, chances to win books and prize packs,
and to share your thoughts with other readers.

facebook.com/kensingtonpublishing
twitter.com/kensingtonbooks

Tell us what you think!

To share your thoughts, submit a review,
or sign up for our eNewsletters, please visit:
KensingtonBooks.com/TellUs.